*her* Reformed Rake

# SCARLETT SCOTT

**Her Reformed Rake**
Wicked Husbands Book Three

All rights reserved.
Copyright © 2018 by Scarlett Scott
ISBN 978-1986341912
Paperback Edition
Edited by Grace Bradley
Formatting by Dallas Hodge, Everything But The Book
Cover Design by Wicked Smart Designs

For more information, contact author Scarlett Scott.
www.scarsco.com

# dedication

For my wonderful readers, with endless gratitude for making my dream into a reality. None of this would be possible without you. Thank you for welcoming my words.

# contents

## chapter one

*London, February 1881*

*T*HE BRASH AMERICAN CHIT HAD NOTHING TO do with dynamite. Sebastian would wager his life upon it. He watched her from across the crush of the Beresford ball as she flirted with the Earl of Bolton. He was trained to take note of every detail, each subtle nuance of his quarry's body language.

Studying her wasn't an unpleasant task. She was beautiful. A blue silk ball gown clung to her petite frame, emphasizing the curve of her waist as it fell in soft waves around lush hips down to a box-pleat-trimmed train. Pink roses bedecked her low décolletage, drawing the eye to the voluptuous swells of her breasts. Her golden hair was braided and pinned at her crown, more roses peeking from its coils. Diamonds at her throat and ears caught the light, twinkling like a beacon for fortune hunters. She wore her father's obscene wealth as if it were an advertisement for Pears soap.

Everything about her, from the way she carried herself, to the way she dressed, to her reputation, bespoke a woman who was fast. Trouble, yes. But not the variety of trouble that required his intervention.

She tapped Bolton's arm with her fan and threw back her head in an unabashed show of amusement. Her chaperone—a New York aunt named Caroline—was absent from the elegant panorama of gleaming lords and ladies. Dear Aunt Caroline had a weakness for champagne and randy men, and provided with sufficient temptation, she disappeared with ease.

Sebastian wasn't the only one who was aware of the aunt's shortcomings, however. He'd been watching Miss Daisy Vanreid for weeks. Long enough to know that she didn't have a care for her reputation, that she'd kissed Lords Wilford and Prestley but not yet Bolton, that she only smiled when she had an audience, and that she waited for her aunt to get soused before playing the devoted coquette.

As he watched, Miss Vanreid excused herself from Bolton, hips swaying with undeniable suggestion as she sauntered in the direction of the lady's withdrawing room. Sebastian cut through the revelers, following her. Not because he needed to—tonight would be the last that he squandered on chasing a spoiled American jade—but because he knew the Earl of Bolton.

His damnable sense of honor wouldn't allow him to stand idly by as the foolish chit was ravished by such a boor. Wilford and Prestley were young bucks, scarcely any town bronze. Manageable. Bolton was another matter. Miss Vanreid was either as empty-headed as she pretended or her need for the thrill of danger had dramatically increased. Either way, he would do his duty and by the cold light of morning, she'd no longer be his responsibility.

He exited the ballroom just in time to see a blue train disappearing around a corner down the hall. Damn it, where the hell was the minx going? The lady's withdrawing room was in the opposite direction. His instincts told him to follow, so he did, straight into a small, private drawing room.

He stepped over the threshold and closed the door at his back, startled to find her alone rather than in Bolton's embrace. She stood in the center of the chamber, tapping her closed fan on the palm of her hand, her full lips compressed into a tight line of disapproval. Her chin tipped up in defiance. He detected not a hint of surprise in her expression.

"Your Grace." She curtseyed lower than necessary, giving him a perfect view of her ample bosom. When she rose with equal elegance, she pinned him with a forthright stare. "Perhaps you'd care to explain why you've been following me for the last month."

Not empty-headed, then. A keen wit sparkled in her lively green gaze. He regarded her with a new sense of appreciation. She'd noticed him. No matter. He relied upon his visibility as a cover. He flaunted his wealth, his lovers. He played the role of seasoned rake. Meanwhile, he observed.

And everything he'd observed thus far suggested that the vixen before him needed to be put in her place. She was too bold. Too lovely. Too blatantly sexual. Everything about her was designed to make men lust. Lust they did. She'd set the *ton* on its ear. Rumor had it that her cunning Papa was about to marry her off to the elderly Lord Breckly. She appeared to be doing her best to thwart him.

He fixed her with a haughty look. "I don't believe we've been introduced."

She gave a soft, throaty laugh that sent a streak of unwanted heat to his groin. "You mean to rely on your fine English manners now when you've been watching me all this time? How droll, but I already know who you are just as you must surely know who I am."

His gaze traveled over her, inspecting her in a way that was meant to discomfit. Perhaps he'd underestimated her, for in the privacy of the chamber, she seemed wilier than he'd credited. "I watch everyone."

Tap went her fan against her palm again, the only

outward sign of her vexation aside from her frown. "As do I, Your Grace. You aren't as subtle as you must suppose yourself. I must admit I found it rather odd that you'd want to spy upon my tête-à-tête with Viscount Wilford."

Miss Vanreid was thoroughly brazen, daring to refer to her ruinous behavior as though nothing untoward had occurred. It struck him that she'd known he watched her and had deliberately exchanged kisses with Prestley and Wilford, perhaps even for his benefit.

He crossed the chamber, his footfalls muted by thick carpeting. Lady Beresford's tastes had always run to the extravagant. He didn't stop until he nearly touched Miss Vanreid's skirts. Still she held firm, refusing to retreat. Some inner demon made him skim his forefinger across the fine protrusion of her collarbone. Just a ghost of a touch. Awareness sparked between them. Her eyes widened almost imperceptibly.

"Wilford and Prestley are green lads." He took care to keep his tone bland. "Bolton is a fox in the henhouse. You'd do best to stay away from him."

She swallowed and he became fascinated by her neck, the way her ostentatious diamonds moved, gleaming even in the dim light. "I'm disappointed you think me as frumpy and witless as a hen. Thank you for your unnecessary concern, Your Grace, but foxes don't frighten me. They never have."

Her bravado irritated him. Even her scent was bold, an exotic blend of bergamot, ambergris, and vanilla carrying to him and invading his senses. He should never have touched her, for now he couldn't stop, following her collarbone to the trim on her bodice, the pink roses so strategically placed. He didn't touch the roses. No. His finger skimmed along the fullness of her creamy breast. Her skin was soft, as lush as a petal.

"You do seem to possess an absurd predilection for your ruination, Miss Vanreid."

She startled him by stepping nearer to him, her skirts

billowing against his legs. "One could say the same for you. Why do you watch, Your Grace? Does it intrigue you? Perhaps you would like a turn."

Jesus. Lust slammed through him, hot and hard and demanding. He'd never, in all his years of covert operations, gotten a stiff cock during an investigation. Thanks to the golden vixen before him, he had one now. While he'd decided she was not involved in the plot, he was still on duty until he reported back to Carlisle in the morning. He wasn't meant to be attracted to Daisy Vanreid, who was not at all as she seemed.

Still, he found himself flattening his palm over her heart, absorbing its quick thump that told him she wasn't as calm as she pretended. The contact of her bare skin to his, more than the mere tip of a finger, jarred him.

"Are you offering me one?" he asked at last.

Her lashes lowered, her full, pink lips parting. "Yes."

And he knew right then that he'd been wrong about Daisy Vanreid. She bloody well *was* the dynamite.

Desperation.

Weakness.

Fear.

Those were the reasons why Daisy stood alone in a private chamber with the Duke of Trent in the midst of the crush of the Beresford Ball, daring him to kiss her. Also, perhaps just a touch of madness.

But it was a madness and a desperation both borne of necessity. A fear fashioned by violence. The weakness was a sin purely her own, and she loathed herself for it. Oh, how she wished she could be strong and defiant. That she could be brave, unafraid, the author of her own rescue.

But she couldn't.

Why not, then, the handsome duke who'd been discreetly following her for the last month? His reputation preceded him. He was a rake, a rogue who belonged to the fastest circle in London society. Whispers and rumors about him abounded, but she didn't care. He was a dangerous sort of man, though not in the way that made her mouth go dry and her body brace for an incoming blow.

So why not indeed? Ordinarily, she suffered a man's touch as a means to an end. Lord knew she'd been engaged in the pretense of flirtation with as many suitable gentlemen as she could find in the hopes of routing her father's plans for her. In the glow of London society, she had become a bon vivant, adept at hiding the flinch that had once marked her for a woman with an expectation of violence.

The man before her, the altogether beautiful Duke of Trent, had somehow swept past all the barriers she kept carefully girding her true self from everyone else. She hadn't needed to feign her attraction for him. Hadn't even fought the urge to wince, for no wince had been forthcoming.

Something about him spoke to her on a primitive level, in a way she'd never known existed. Yes, the Duke of Trent possessed an altogether different aura of danger. She hadn't been prepared for the contact of his large, warm hand on her bare skin, for the way it had seemed to send sparks of electricity charging through the air between them. No fear. No almost insuppressible anticipation of pain. Nothing but *him*, consuming her world.

At such proximity, he was even more handsome than she'd supposed. His eyes were the most unusual shade of blue she'd ever seen, bright and lighter than the sky on a faultless summer day. They studied her now, dipping to her mouth.

Had she just offered him a *turn*? She didn't recognize herself. Indeed, everything about this enchanted, worry-free moment, suggested she was dreaming. Soon, she would wake. Surely.

"I cannot decide," he drawled, his patrician manner effortless, "if you are reckless with yourself because you're a schemer or because you're foolish enough to think you won't get caught." At last he moved his hand, his touch gliding upward, back over her collarbone to curve as if at home around her shoulder. "But as tempting as your offer may be, Miss Vanreid, I'm afraid I must decline."

With that, he released her and took a step away. She felt the loss of his touch like an ache somewhere low in her belly. Of course she should have known he wouldn't be so easy a conquest. Why then, had he been dogging her these last few weeks if it wasn't her touted American fortune he was after?

Unless he hadn't been following her or watching her? Perhaps it had been her overzealous imagination, fueled by one too many gothic novels she secreted from her father's censorious eye. After all, she had run across any number of the same lords and ladies at the endless parade of society functions to which she'd dutifully marched at Aunt Caroline's side.

She had to admit it was possible he had merely been a guest at the same events, and that he had accidentally stumbled upon her embrace with Lord Wilford. The thought of Wilford was enough to sour her mood. He'd been inebriated, and he kissed as she imagined a fish would. Even his mouth had tasted of an unlikely combination of champagne and algae.

Still, Daisy would have chosen him as a husband over the Viscount Breckly, which was why it had been so disappointing when Wilford had mumbled an apology and disappeared after she'd stiffened upon catching sight of an interloper.

That interloper stood before her now, handsome as sin. Rangy and broad and far too tan of skin and muscled of form to blend in with his fellow aristocrats. She had seen a flash of him in the partially ajar door of the music room where she'd slipped away with Wilford. And she'd been watching for him ever since.

But it would seem that the enigmatic duke didn't want to play a game that wasn't of his own making, and time was running out for her. In just a week, her father would arrive from New York, and he'd made his intentions clear. He expected an engagement to be finalized between herself and the officious Lord Breckly, a man who was thirty years her senior and smelled of sweat and unlaundered linens. A man who had attempted to lift her skirts and force himself upon her in the drawing room not two days past. Who would have, had not Aunt Caroline returned from the library bearing the book she'd been seeking in her flimsy ploy to force Daisy into spending time alone with the villain.

Daisy knew a stab of disappointment at the realization that the duke would not be the answer to her problems any more than Wilford had. However, she kept her expression neutral, as if she couldn't be bothered to care if he remained or left. "If you must decline, then I'd appreciate it if you wouldn't linger. Lord Bolton should arrive at any minute and it would be dreadfully awkward if he found you here."

The duke flicked a grimly assessing glance over her person that left her with the impression he saw far more of her than she would have preferred. In truth, she hadn't said a word to Lord Bolton. She'd flirted with him, but he'd had eyes only for her bosom, and she'd delivered a sound tap of her fan to his arm for his insouciance.

"Lord Bolton has a reputation of which you are undoubtedly unaware," he said then. "Run along back to your chaperone and forget you ever knew his name."

Aunt Caroline was long in her cups by now, and at parties such as these, she made a mockery of the term "chaperone," much to Daisy's relief. It rendered her attempts to thwart her father's plans a bit more sustainable. But she only had a week of such freedom remaining, and the Duke of Trent was encroaching on the days she had left.

She raised a brow. "Thank you for the advice, Your Grace."

She needed to find someone to marry her in haste, and this man was not he. Gainsaying her father would only earn her the most vicious bruises imaginable, all strategically placed where no one's eye would ever chance to fall. He liked to hit her in the stomach. He knew how to pull hair without ripping it from the root while causing the maximum amount of pain. His booted foot could do the most damage, she'd discovered the last time she'd gone against his wishes.

That grim knowledge was the ultimate source of the desperation propelling her—the frantic need to escape both her father and the life he'd predestined for her. If she had a choice between marrying Lord Breckly and anyone else, she'd decided anyone would do. Anyone at all who could help her to avoid a detestable marriage to a brute or another raised fist.

"Perhaps your American customs are not the same, Miss Vanreid," the Duke of Trent said then, his tone patronizing. "Only one thing will come of you awaiting Lord Bolton in this chamber for an assignation, and it most assuredly will not benefit you. You'll be ruined."

Truly. For a man who wanted nothing to do with her, he was an odd sort. Unless…her mind grappled with their brief exchange, with the handful of times she'd caught him watching her.

Her pride had made her second-guess herself, but her common sense now reminded her that he had come to this chamber. He had intentionally sought her out. Their gazes had briefly clashed earlier, and she'd hoped he would follow in her wake after she exited the ballroom. And he had. Something about him was decidedly not as it seemed.

Either way, her patience was at an end. If he didn't wish to kiss her, she didn't have any further need of him. For she required to be ruined. Compromised. The sooner the better to avoid becoming Viscountess Breckly and escape her father's wrath.

She stalked forward, intending to quit the chamber. "Good evening, Your Grace. If you won't leave, then I shall. And if you don't mind, seek someone else to harass in the future. Ducal condescension isn't to my liking."

But when she would have slipped past him, he caught

her upper arm in a firm yet gentle grip, forcing her to face him. His scent hit her, a masculine blend of shaving soap and musk. She drank in the sight of him despite herself. Something about all that flawlessness made her long to disturb it. To muss up his hair, flick open a button.

He was perfect, handsome symmetry: hair the color of mahogany, high cheekbones, sculpted lips, cleft chin…even his philtrum seemed somehow too perfect, stubbled by the shadow of the day's dark whiskers in an invitation to sin.

For a breathless beat, she imagined pressing her mouth there, in the groove just above his. Those whiskers would be rough to her lips. And she would inevitably slide her lips lower, until their mouths fused. The Duke of Trent would not kiss like a fish or taste of algae. She could tell.

"Why do you seek to ruin yourself, Miss Vanreid?" he demanded, as though he had every right to her answer. "Is there someone in New York you wish to return to?"

She thought fleetingly of Padraig McGuire, the man who oversaw the operations of her father's factories in New York. She'd cared for him once. Not any longer. Both he and her father had seen to that.

But she allowed nothing of her thoughts to show as she faced the duke with defiance. He was a stranger to her, and he had no right to ask such an intimate question. No right to invade the chamber she'd escaped to, no right to touch her, no right to offer unsolicited advice.

No rights at all. "How dare you presume to ask me such a thing? In your words, Your Grace, *I don't believe we've been introduced.*"

He sneered, the perfect picture of arrogance. "If there is a young man in New York, you'd do best to forget him. Just as you'd do best to stay away from Bolton."

Daisy wrenched herself free of his grasp. "While we're dispensing advice, Duke, you'd do best to stay away from *me*. I neither need nor want your interference. If you fancy yourself a Galahad, go do it with someone else."

Without a backward glance, she quit the chamber. After tonight, she had only six days left. Cerberus was at her heels, and she meant to secure her liberty by whatever means possible. The supercilious Duke of Trent could go hang for all she cared.

## chapter two

"I'D WAGER EVERYTHING I HAVE THAT THE CHIT knows nothing about any Fenian plots," Sebastian announced to the Duke of Carlisle as they rendezvoused in a private room of their club the next morning. "She's smarter than she allows others to realize, but her most pressing concern appears to be ruining herself by any means possible."

And that means last evening had been first the Earl of Bolton and then himself. For a brief, unwanted instant, he recalled the soft feel of her creamy skin beneath his fingertips. The scent of bergamot would forever be tainted by thoughts of a golden-haired American vixen who'd dared him to kiss her.

*Blast.*

Carlisle took a sip of his steaming coffee and settled the cup back into its saucer before replying. He was a quiet man, brooding by nature, the sort who observed without ever seeming to participate in the world around him. Now his dark, assessing gaze pinned Sebastian to his seat with the cutthroat precision of a dagger. "Since when have you taken to wagering anything, Trent? I didn't know you to be a gambling man."

He fought the urge to shift into a more comfortable position. With images of Miss Daisy Vanreid flitting through the corruptible corner of his mind, his trousers had grown deuced tight. "Merely a figure of speech, Carlisle."

The duke continued his practice of inwardly dissecting the person he engaged in dialogue with. He'd developed a method of studying tone, body language, words, and mannerisms that had half their brothers in arms believing him a mind reader. Sebastian had never found himself on the receiving end of the treatment before, and he had to admit he damn well didn't like it.

"I dislike figures of speech," Carlisle said at last. "They have a way of rendering precisely what one intends to say so bloody *imprecise*. Tell me, what did you learn from her at the Beresford monstrosity?"

He took great care to remain still and keep his expression blank, for as much as he trusted Carlisle and had worked directly beneath him for the past five years, something about the bent of this interview sent misgiving down his spine like a chill. "Nothing of import."

"Nothing?" Carlisle raised an imperious brow. "I understand you followed her to a chamber during the ball. The two of you remained in the chamber together for eight minutes. Surely a great deal can be said during such a generous span of time."

The misgiving blossomed in his chest, tight and heavy. Jesus, was he suspect? He hadn't been compromised. There was no damn reason for Carlisle to have a man following him. "You had someone watching me last night?"

"You know our credo, Trent." Carlisle's tone was calm, offhand, as though he described something as inane as a recent visit to the opera. That too was his gift, never allowing anyone to see beneath the masks he presented to the world. "Eyes and ears everywhere."

Of course he knew the goddamn credo, but he'd

believed he was the ears and the eyes. He stiffened before he could check himself. "Ears and eyes on your own men? For what purpose?"

"Only a fool trusts blindly," Carlisle quipped. "Eight minutes, Trent. Did you spend them wisely?"

No, damn it, he had not. He had lost his footing for a moment—for the first moment in as long as he could recall—and he'd been struck by Miss Vanreid's undeniable beauty. Not to mention her boldness.

*Perhaps you would like a turn.*

He still couldn't believe the minx had uttered those provocative words to him. She'd shocked him. Worse, he had wanted to do as she invited. To kiss that full, pink mouth of hers, yank down her bodice completely to reveal the bounty of her breasts and discover whether or not her nipples matched.

His mouth was drier than an old, worn shoe. But he wouldn't show his weakness to Carlisle. Not today. Not after discovering he'd been followed. "I learned that Miss Vanreid is exactly as I've suspected over the month I've been observing her. She is beautiful, clever, and manipulative. She...seems to have little concern for her reputation. I inquired whether or not she had a beau at home in New York as you requested, but she refused to answer one way or the other."

Carlisle nodded as though none of the information came as a surprise to him. "I imagine she turned her wiles upon you, Trent."

Hellfire. It took all of his years of training to suppress the heat that wanted to rise to his cheekbones. "I requested this meeting so that I could be relieved of my duties in regards to Miss Vanreid. Nothing I have uncovered over the last month has led me to believe she has any knowledge of dynamite production, Fenianism, or any plans to otherwise aid in the setting of bombs throughout London, to say the least of what happened in Salford. I respectfully request reassignment, as I can think of innumerable ways to better utilize my time and talents than chasing after an American minx as she flirts her way through the *ton*."

Carlisle was silent for far too long, sipping his coffee as if he hadn't a care. The only sounds in the room were caused by his cup tinkling back into its saucer. At last, he deigned to speak again. "I beg to disagree. Have you forgotten just who the girl's father is?"

Of course he hadn't. James Vanreid was well-known to the League, his entanglement with Fenians in New York undeniable. Though his father had been Dutch, his mother had been an Irish immigrant, and Vanreid had not forsaken his roots. He was sinfully wealthy, having amassed a fortune as a shipping magnate, and presided over no fewer than a dozen thriving factories. One of those happened to be an armament factory. And an inordinate number of illegal Vanreid firearms had recently been circulating in London. Vanreid had strong ties to the most aggressive of the Fenians in America, he had ships, he had an endless well of funds from which to draw, all beneath the guise of his various business holdings, and he was, simply put, a grave danger to England.

Sebastian had known all of those facts the first time his eyes had lit on Daisy Vanreid amidst a ballroom crush. But like the many men who hovered about her, drawn by the blinding combination of her sultry beauty and her fortune, he hadn't cared. For the first time in his years with the League, his assignment had been to gather intelligence on a woman as harmless as a reticule. He'd been drawn to her first, irritated second, and confounded by his inconvenient attraction to her last.

All that aside, he had been watching Daisy Vanreid closely. And he was a damn good spy. He wasn't about to allow Carlisle to run roughshod over him. His instincts were rarely wrong. Coupled with the fact that his observation of her had produced the same results as he would've anticipated had he been monitoring any other debutante, Carlisle's insistence that Daisy Vanreid was some sort of secret menace was ludicrous.

"I know bloody well who her father is," he gritted. "I also know that she eats eggs, poached with hollandaise for breakfast, she can't abide by strawberries, she prefers chocolate over tea, she receives callers from one o'clock to three o'clock in the afternoon, she reads as if it's her occupation, and that she enjoys courting scandal. Her aunt is meant to chaperone her, but the old biddy gets soused instead, and Miss Vanreid leads her suitors on a merry dance while good old Aunt Caro is snoring into her bosom or having a go at a randy rake in a dark alcove."

He paused, attempting to rein in the anger that had begun to burn within him as he spoke before silencing his superior with a raised hand and continuing in his diatribe. "Jesus, do you hear how ridiculous this sounds, Carlisle? Do any of those insignificant details seem important, by God? Our nation's security is at risk, and I'm chasing a vixen about ballrooms and running intelligence through her bloody chambermaids so I know which *ball* to attend. I feel like a lad in leading strings playing at being a spy with his younger brother."

Carlisle raised an imperious brow. "Have you finished with your little tantrum, Trent?"

*Tantrum.* Bloody hell, Sebastian longed to smash his fist into the perfection of Carlisle's long, aquiline nose. "I'm not having a goddamn tantrum. I am informing you that this nonsensical assignment must come to an end. Daisy Vanreid is as dangerous as an elderly governess, and I'm tired of trailing her about like a bloody spaniel."

"She's incredibly valuable to our cause." Carlisle slammed his fist down. Coffee splashed over the rim of his cup, the delicate china clinking in protest. "She's the daughter of the man responsible for financing the Fenians in New York, a daughter who is undoubtedly privy to all manner of information that could prove useful for us to possess. Keeping close to her keeps us close to Vanreid. The more we know about Vanreid, the better we're prepared to dismantle his web and prevent him from harming anyone on our watch. We need to do everything—bloody well anything—we can to uncover the identities of the dynamitards hiding in our midst. If we do nothing, more will come, and we'll be bloody well inundated. They'll stop at nothing until they see England brought low."

"I understand the importance of the task at hand," Sebastian snapped. "I merely question the wisdom of wasting so much time and resources upon one bloody female."

"The Home Office believes she has strong ties to the Fenians herself."

"Ties to the Fenians?" He couldn't contain his cynicism. Daisy Vanreid, a luscious heiress whose greatest concern was which ball gown to wear and what gentleman she ought to kiss? Who flitted about society like an exotic butterfly that made every man in London want to catch her and make her his? It hardly seemed likely. Indeed, it seemed laughable. Unbelievable.

The information the Home Office had received from their American contacts was ballocks.

Carlisle gave a short nod, warming to his cause. "Miss Vanreid was betrothed to a Mr. Padraig McGuire in New York. The engagement didn't last long for reasons that remain unclear. However, what is clear is that Padraig McGuire is a vocal Fenian and a known member of the Emerald Club. He's also Vanreid's right hand. McGuire is believed to be the lead man for the Fenian skirmishing fund, which supports their bloody endeavors along with Vanreid's purse."

Sebastian had heard whispers about McGuire from his sources in America as well. Knowing she'd been engaged to the bastard certainly did make her a bit more intriguing, but hardly enough to justify his continued trailing of her. "You believe he's raising money to facilitate the manufacturing of dynamite?"

"I know it. Over the last few weeks, he's been engaged

in a public speaking tour to win financial support for his cause. Given the reports of cheering throngs greeting him, it seems only a matter of time before things escalate. The intelligence coming to us from America is quite dire. The Fenians and their sympathizers grow stronger, larger, and more determined by the day. You know as well as I that the consequences promise to be deadly, Trent. An innocent boy has died at the hands of these monsters."

All the heat that had been building within his body since his encounter with Daisy Vanreid the previous evening suddenly fled. He was left with the aching, cold chill of winter. The kind of cold a man felt in his bones.

Irish-American groups had been calling for Irish home rule by any means for years. But recently, their call had grown ever more vicious. Increasingly, they sought to achieve their goal by the use of violence, waging a campaign of fear, destruction, and death, with dynamite as its chief weapon.

Three months earlier, Salford had seen the first demonstration of the Fenians' deadly capabilities when a bomb exploded at the armory there. A lad who'd had the misfortune to be walking by at the time of detonation had been killed.

If Miss Vanreid had been betrothed to a man bearing leadership positions in a known Fenian organization, it was nearly impossible for her to be ignorant of the plans being put into motion. England's network of spies in America had made it clear that a bomb detonation within London was imminent.

Sebastian and his fellow operatives on the ground on their native soil were doing everything within their power to see that such an atrocity never became a reality. London was a great deal more populated and vulnerable to blows than Salford. The casualties would be far greater than one boy, though that lone boy had been one casualty too many.

He took a breath to digest the information his superior had just revealed. Of course, it was Carlisle's way to only give him a grain of fact in an ever-changing sea of truths. He'd been told Miss Vanreid had suspected knowledge of the dynamite campaign originating from the Fenians in America. And so he had watched her flirt and kiss her way through every ball, musical, and supper thrown for the last month, trailing after her like a man wearing a blindfold.

Could it be that she was even wilier than he'd imagined? And had everything between them last night been an act? An attempt to distract him from his course? An attempt to glean information from him?

What was it she had said to him in her bold, stubborn way? Ah, yes. *Foxes don't frighten me. They never have.* He was beginning to get a different picture of Miss Daisy Vanreid, and he didn't like it. Not one bloody bit. For it seemed that perhaps she was the fox after all, or at the least the mistress of one.

With grim determination, he clenched his jaw and faced Carlisle. "What would you have me do?"

Carlisle paused in the act of raising his cup for another fortifying sip of coffee. "I'm afraid the answer to that question isn't one you're prepared to hear."

The misgiving spreading through him turned into grim foreboding. In the name of Crown and country, he'd been stabbed, shot, and almost burned to death. What could possibly be worse?

"What is it, Carlisle?" he demanded. "It could hardly be more difficult than anything I've endured while under your command."

The duke settled his cup back into its saucer without taking a sip, and for the first time in Sebastian's acquaintance with him, revealed a tell. He grimaced.

"You must marry the girl," Carlisle announced.

And Sebastian realized that he'd been wrong to think nothing could be worse than the dangers he'd faced and the risks he'd taken thus far. For marrying Miss Daisy Vanreid was surely the worst fate he could imagine.

There was devotion to one's country, and then there was

sheer stupidity.

"No," he denied vehemently. "I won't do it."

"No," Daisy said. "I won't do it."

Aunt Caroline took longer than necessary to react to Daisy's outburst. No doubt, the delay had something to do with the four glasses of wine she'd consumed over the course of their host's elegant dinner. "But Daisy, if Lord Breckly requests it, you must dance with him. He's reached a tacit agreement with your father for your hand. It wouldn't do to rebuff your future husband in so public a manner."

The thought of any agreement involving her hand—let alone the rest of her—and Viscount Breckly was an abomination. It made an unpleasant, ill sensation wash through her stomach. The heated crush of the ballroom didn't help the situation. Her cheeks were flushed, her skin prickly. A roaring sound rushed to her ears.

Four days remained until her father's arrival.

She'd gone from desperate to frantic. And she'd decided that tonight at the Darlington ball, she'd have to find a replacement groom. Anyone would do. Dancing with Breckly most assuredly did not fit into her plans of thwarting her impending nuptials with the wretch.

Panicked. That was the proper word to describe her current condition.

Four days, drat it all.

"Aunt Caroline, he smells of hair grease and soiled linen. I won't be able to bear it in this heat," she said truthfully. "I feel ill just thinking of it now. There is also the matter of what occurred in the drawing room."

Her father's sister frowned at her, but the overall effect was somewhat diminished by a rather indiscreet hiccup. "Oh dear. I'm afraid fish always tends to affect me in such a monstrous way. But that is neither here nor there. It wouldn't be seemly for you to deny him, and that is that.

Your father has a high opinion of the viscount, and if you don't make this match, he'll have my hide. I'm sure his lordship was overcome by your beauty, as all men are. You play with them, Daisy, make them into beasts."

Of course Aunt Caroline would blame the incident on Daisy, Aunt Caroline being cut from the same bolt of cloth as Father. Her marriage into an old blood Knickerbocker family in New York, the years she'd spent abroad, and the fact that she agreed with him in all things had made her Father's clear choice in chaperone.

"Would it be seemly for me to lose my dinner all over Lord Breckly?" Daisy inquired with sham politeness.

A bejeweled matron swept past them, angling a look of ill-disguised disapproval in their direction. Daisy was accustomed to thinly veiled contempt. It wasn't easy being an American girl who didn't fit into the mold of fine English womanhood. Having a wealthy tradesman father who was half Irish and an aunt who liked to tipple didn't exactly lend to being the belle of any ball. If she hadn't her wits and her father's wealth, she wouldn't have dredged up any suitors at all.

"Hush," Aunt Caroline directed before issuing another hiccup. "You mustn't ever speak your mind, Daisy, and certainly not in a ballroom, of all places. Someone could overhear."

Daisy didn't particularly care if anyone did overhear. How better to advertise that she was available, ready for ruining? Her dowry was worth a small fortune. Surely some impoverished aristocrat would oblige her by rescuing her from the awful fate that awaited?

She fanned herself, wondering if her face was as shiny as it felt. Of course she had left her pearl powder at home tonight. "Aunt Caroline, do forgive me. It's merely that I'm overheated in this crush of people. I think I need to step outside for a breath of air."

"Outside?" Her aunt's eyes narrowed with a prescient doubt.

"Before I faint," Daisy added for good measure. She felt not a speck of guilt for leading Aunt Caroline down the garden path, for she was as determined as Daisy's father to see her sold off to Breckly. "I would hate to cause a scene. Would you mind holding my champagne?"

Aunt Caroline's slitted gaze fell upon the champagne flute. "Very well then, but don't linger. And do not venture far. No good comes of young ladies flitting about in the dark."

Daisy pressed her glass into her aunt's outstretched hand, completely aware that the glass would be empty upon her return. "I wouldn't dream of it, Aunt."

With that, she took her leave of Aunt Caroline who, if past actions were to be an indication of future, would likely indulge in her champagne and spend the next few hours forgetting she had a niece at all. Which was just as well, for Daisy had to find an unsuspecting bachelor as expediently as possible.

She took great care to make her way through the revelers and toward the exit as she'd said she would, lest her aunt watched. In just a few minutes, Aunt Caroline ought to be sufficiently distracted and Daisy could re-enter the ballroom to assess her prey.

As she went, her eyes surveyed the room. The time for flirting and kissing was at an end. She needed to snare herself a husband by any means possible. The only means she could imagine that would force her father to acquiesce to a match other than the one he'd chosen was to ruin herself.

Yes, tonight, she would need to create quite a scandal. A scandal that destroyed her reputation and left her with no recourse except marriage to someone other than Viscount Breckly.

As she studied the gentlemen in attendance, her eyes collided with a familiar gaze. The effect was so stunning that she stopped where she was. Awareness sparked between them in live electrical wire fashion. The breath seemed to freeze in her lungs, and unwanted heat sluiced through her from head to toe, bathing her in a warmth that had nothing to do with the sultriness of the air and everything to do with the man watching her.

The Duke of Trent.

How was it possible that he was even more handsome tonight than the last time she'd seen him? Inexplicably, she recalled the sensation of his large hand, hot and heavy, pressed over her heart, directly to her bare skin. Had he followed her again tonight? Why did he watch her now, unflinching, his expression intense and unreadable? Hadn't she told him to go play Galahad with someone else?

Yet somehow, here he was, separated from her by a scant few feet and some lords and ladies in between. Looking at her as though he could see inside her, straight to the heart of her. She never wanted to be gazed upon in any other way for the rest of her life. He made her feel as though her entire body was a string pulled taut, waiting for the loving caress of a bow.

Some wicked part of her thought that if she must entrap any man, surely there was no harm in selecting a man as beautiful as he to be her dupe. A man who could make wanton thoughts consume her before a crowded ballroom of people as she stood there in her silk and diamonds.

Yes, let it be him.

At last, she severed the contact, turning to continue her retreat from the ballroom and its noisy crush. She felt his stare on her back like a touch, stinging her shoulder blades. Daisy fanned herself as she stepped into the calming night. It was unseasonably warm for late February, and several others slowly promenaded about the main terrace.

She skirted the perimeter and stole away into the shadows, farther from the din of the ball and prying eyes, farther away from reason and sanity, and deeper into unfamiliar, dangerous territory. For if she intended to carry out her plan to the fullest, she would require privacy.

She stopped when she reached a statue that loomed over

her, tall and eerie in the silvery night. Zeus perhaps? In the darkness, she couldn't be sure. She was far enough that she could no longer hear the conversations of the guests on the terrace. Far enough for what she intended.

A pang of guilt struck her then, for entrapping any man into marriage, let alone the insufferable duke, was the last thing she wanted to do. But when her only other option was accepting the grim fate her father had selected for her, she knew what she needed to do.

Save herself.

"I confess, I'm quite curious to hear why you have such a peculiar fondness for disappearing at balls, Miss Vanreid."

The voice, low and clipped in perfect born-in-the-purple English, sent a fresh wave of longing through her. She knew without bothering to turn that it was *him*. How neatly he'd fallen into her trap.

She searched for the bravado that seemed to have suddenly fled her as she slowly spun about. He stood a scant few steps away, gorgeous even in the dim light. Daisy offered him a full, perfect curtsy, for she could behave whenever the need arose. It was simply that she didn't prefer to behave, having spent her life forced into doing it. "Your Grace. You seem to have a similar, peculiar fondness for following me at balls. Perhaps I too should inquire as to the reason?"

"Inquire all you like, darling."

There was something about the way he uttered the term of endearment that made the otherwise ordinary word "darling" into a caress that she felt all over her body. Especially in her belly and...lower.

She could play the role of flirt quite well by now, but he had a patent way of disarming her, throwing her off-kilter. Daisy took a step toward him, willing herself to keep her goal foremost in her mind. The urge to trade wits and verbally spar with him was strong. But clashing with the Duke of Trent would not compromise her, and so she needed to resort to different tactics.

"If I ask, will you answer?" She took another step until she was near enough that she could smell him, and his scent began a steady ache deep within her. A need for something she didn't understand.

He still hadn't moved, his large body illuminated by the moon's sheen. "That depends."

Another step. "Upon?"

"Upon whether or not I'm to expect one of your suitors."

She smiled despite herself, enjoying this game, and unable to resist baiting him after all. "Do you refer to the Earl of Bolton? Or perhaps to Wilford? Prestley? Tell me, Your Grace, do you keep a ledger of them all?"

"I doubt any ledger of mine would contain enough pages." His tone was grim.

She flinched at the insult, but forced herself to take another step. She'd earned her reputation after all, even if it was in the name of a good cause: her own rescue. Little space separated them at all now, and in spite of his singular lack of charm, she was still determined to win her escape from Lord Breckly's officious clutches.

"One must wonder, Your Grace, why you followed me at all if your opinion of me is so poor," she said then, careful to keep her tone flippant and unaffected.

At long last, he moved, and with a lightning quickness that took her by surprise as he brought their bodies flush together. His hands settled on her waist when she would've lost her footing, anchoring her to him. Her breasts pressed to his chest. His breath coasted over her lips.

"I never said my opinion of you was poor, Miss Vanreid," he said slowly. "Quite the opposite, in fact."

"Forgive me if I doubt that." The breathlessness of her own voice alarmed her.

Indecision threatened her suddenly, making her feel skittish. In the darkness, the duke was a force of nature, tall and large and potent. She couldn't shake the odd notion that beneath his polished exterior lay a feral beast, waiting to

25

lunge. To claim.

There was more, far more, to the Duke of Trent than she had ever supposed. But she could sense it now, in the heat and strength of him, in the barely leashed savagery of the way he'd so neatly caught her in his trap.

And all this time, she'd been fancying she'd trapped him. It suddenly seemed quite the opposite. But she wasn't frightened. Rather, he intrigued her.

"I've decided I want my turn," he said.

She blinked, wishing she could better see his expression through the darkness. Wishing she could read him, but the man had her at a complete loss. "I'm sorry, Your Grace?"

"You asked me before if I wanted a turn." His hand traveled from her waist to cup her jaw with a tenderness that belied the strength radiating from him. The unexpected gentleness shook her. His thumb brushed over her lower lip, sending a rush of sensation through her frenzied body.

Ah yes, so she had, foolishly upon their last meeting. But she had meant to taunt him, to wring from him the truth of why he had seemed to dog her every move through society. It could have all been coincidence, of course. Anyone else— anyone whose mind didn't operate the way Daisy's did— would have likely never taken note. Would have never wondered. Would never have been suspicious. Dear Lord, not of a peer of the realm, and a duke at that.

But Daisy wasn't anyone else. She was herself, and she knew herself well enough to know that she was something of an oddity. She didn't seem to fit in with anyone anywhere, though her father had done an admirable job of attempting to force her into any number of roles that suited him. Thus far, she had dodged them all, and she didn't intend for that to change four days from now.

Which brought her back to her plan. Her *necessity*.

She needed the Duke of Trent to compromise her. Tonight.

She took a deep, steadying breath and exhaled over the thumb that continued its slow exploration of her lip. "So take your turn then, Your Grace. Take it now."

He made a deep sound in his throat, and she couldn't tell if it was a growl or a hum of satisfaction. "I believe I will."

In the next breath, his mouth was on hers, hard and demanding as she had imagined it would be. Daisy had been kissed many times before, but never the way the duke kissed her. His lips angled over hers, fitting perfectly, with a voracious hunger. This kiss claimed. It sent a flurry of something foreign washing over her, something that was part languor, part need.

She caught his broad shoulders, clutching him to her as he ravaged her mouth, feeling the powerful muscles hidden beneath his evening finery. His tongue swept the seam of her lips, seeking entry, and she opened without hesitation. Nothing about the way the Duke of Trent affected her was feigned or forced. There was something indefinable— something primitive and raw—within him that called to her. That told her she was where she belonged.

In his arms.

Yes, if she had to marry any man, please Lord let it be a man who kissed the way the duke did. Who smelled the way the duke did. Who looked and felt as he did. Let it simply be him.

Only him.

His mouth left hers to trail a path of fire down her throat, lingering over the sensitive hollow beneath her ear. Who had known such a place would not only long to be kissed but that his lips grazing her there would send a pulsing ache of pleasure to her core? And then he licked her, his tongue darting out to tease her flesh, to taste her. To drive her mad.

A mewling sound tore from her. She wanted more, even though she didn't know what *more* was. He caught her earlobe in his teeth and tugged, tongued the whorl of her ear. His breath was hot and decadent upon her as he moved his mouth lower still, to her collarbone, and from there downward to her décolletage.

He kissed over the swell of her breast, and she knew a poignant longing. How she wished for him to be unrestrained by her gown and corset, to be free to move his lovely mouth over every inch of her body. Especially to the aching tips of her breasts that had begun tingling in a most alarming fashion.

She wondered fuzzily why no man before him had ever taken such a liberty, and then she was instantly glad they had not. For she couldn't imagine enjoying this wickedness with anyone save him. She felt that she was made for him.

And then, he snagged the delicate tulle of her sleeve and tugged. The sound of fabric rending split the night, sending a rush of cold air over her. She stiffened in his arms, training so ingrained in her that despite seeking her complete compromise tonight, she nearly pushed him away. A torn bodice was the ultimate hallmark of sin. What could he be thinking? Daisy could not face her aunt or return to the ballroom with a ball gown that had been damaged.

Perhaps he had lost his head, for he seemed undeterred by the spoiling he'd just done, continuing to kiss his way across the bare expanse of her bosom. An odd calm settled over her then, a calm she hadn't felt in as long as she could recall.

She was ruined.

And it felt, in a word, *divine*.

Overcome by the urge, she ran her fingers through his thick, soft hair and then pressed an impulsive kiss to his crown. Even his hair smelled good. He stilled in his exploration, his lips still pressed to her skin.

Had she gone too far? Had he realized how far he, in turn, had gone? She'd never know, for he gave a quick, strong yank, and everything—her bodice, corset, and chemise—went down with it. Her breasts were bared, on full display in the moonlight.

Daisy, wicked girl that she was, forgot that she had only meant to allow things to reach a certain point before demurely demanding he return her to her aunt along with a marriage proposal. She forgot that they stood not far removed from a ballroom full of people. Forgot that she had no business guiding the duke's kisses lower, to the place she wanted them the most.

Because in the next instant, he took her into his mouth.

And in the next instant, she heard the shocked exclamation of none other than Aunt Caroline, who stood in the moonlight, gawping at them with a stranger by her side.

## chapter three

"DAISY?" HISSED THE AUNT, SOUNDING FAINT.

"Trent, is that you?" asked Carlisle, doing a fair impression of indignation for a man who had intentionally led the aunt into the darkness in search of her errant niece, knowing what they would find. "Good God, this is an outrage. You'll have to marry Miss Vanreid at once."

*Marry.*

The word turned the lust raging through his body into ice. Hastily, he hauled Miss Vanreid's bodice back into place. But not before being treated to one more glimpse of the luscious ripeness of her breasts in the moon's glow. There was no doubt about it—Miss Daisy Vanreid was pure, unadulterated temptation. And he had succumbed.

Despite his extreme distrust of her, despite knowing she was a manipulative flirt who had likely led half a dozen other suitors down the same path in the darkness, despite his deep resentment of being forced to compromise her and enter into a marriage that he most certainly did not want all in the name of the Crown…despite everything, he'd *enjoyed* kissing her.

He'd enjoyed how responsive she was, how her lips moved beneath his, how she'd tasted. He'd even enjoyed ripping her sleeve to further his cause and yanking down her bodice to take the sweet, hard bud of her nipple into his mouth. He hadn't been meant to disrobe her. Hadn't been meant to allow their embrace to escalate that far. Some kisses and a torn sleeve were all that was required.

But Sebastian had wanted more.

He still did, his cock a rigid reminder of just how much, a reminder that not even the cooling of his ardor could tame.

"Forgive me," he said wryly at last. "I seem to have lost my head."

Truer words had never been spoken.

Miss Vanreid remained oddly silent for a woman he knew to be quite forthright. The aunt sputtered, in fine dudgeon, demanding the situation be rectified. Carlisle did his part, offering grim comfort.

"There, there, Mrs. Stanley," the duke said. "I'm sure the duke will make amends as swiftly as possible. Is that not so, Your Grace?"

Sebastian gave a stiff nod. "Please accept my sincere apologies for the insult I've paid your niece this night, Mrs. Stanley. Rest assured that I will call first thing in the morning to make a formal offer for Miss Vanreid's hand."

That appeared to take the wind right out of the aunt's sails. "A formal offer?"

"Naturally," he bit out. "My admiration for your niece is great. I would be honored to make her my wife. In the meantime, to blunt further scandal, you'll need to take Miss Vanreid home."

There. He'd said it. He done what he'd sworn he wouldn't do, what he'd been uncertain he would allow on the carriage ride over. As sacrifices went, this was one of the ultimate, regardless of whether he was granted an annulment at the conclusion of the assignment as Carlisle promised. Marrying Daisy Vanreid was more than he'd wanted to give, but he had sworn an oath to protect his country. If he was willing to forfeit his life for the safety of his homeland, then he could damn well align himself with any woman in the world. Even if she was as lovely as she was deceptive. Even if he had reason to suspect she potentially possessed both the cunning and the deadliness of an asp.

By God, he would keep his distance. Tonight's aberration aside, of course. This stunt had been necessary to ensure that Miss Vanreid's father would agree to the marriage. There was something afoot between Vanreid and Lord Breckly, whose own mother hailed from Ireland. Some reason Vanreid was determined to wed his daughter off to an aging reprobate. Vanreid was aware he was under suspicion, and the League couldn't be certain Vanreid would've accepted Sebastian's suit, despite his being a duke.

But a ruining witnessed by the lady's aunt would justify nothing less or risk bringing undue attention upon Vanreid and his murky dealings with the Fenians.

And so he had done all but raise Miss Vanreid's skirts and take what he wanted: all of her.

What his body wanted, that was. For there was no denying the effect she had upon him. His mind, however, was different. He could govern his mind, and his mind could, in turn, rule his baser instincts. He would not touch Daisy Vanreid again. Not even if Carlisle told him that the safety of the Queen depended on Sebastian bedding the vixen.

Miss Vanreid finally broke her silence, interrupting the whirling tumult of his thoughts. "Aunt Caroline, I'm afraid my gown is…in disrepair."

"Merciful saints." The aunt actually gave a hiccup then, and he wondered just how far into her cups she'd already fallen this evening. "How will we manage to remove you without notice? Your father will be livid. You're meant to marry Lord Breckly."

Carlisle spoke up, ever the manipulator. "My dear Mrs. Stanley, fortunately, I am familiar with the grounds, having been a guest here on many occasions. I do believe there is a gate at the rear of the garden through which you and your niece may discreetly pass, with none of the other guests being aware."

The aunt was so vehement in her appreciation that she nearly vibrated with gratitude. And another hiccup. "Your Grace, I am much indebted to you for your kindness this evening. Do I trust we can have your—*hicc*—complete discretion in this matter?"

"Naturally, Mrs. Stanley. As long as Trent is willing to make amends by marrying your niece as soon as possible, I will consider this entire event expunged from my memory forever," Carlisle assured her.

Sebastian's jaw tightened. His senior in command was being a tad too dramatic for his liking. He'd never felt more like a villain than he did then, filled with a combined shame for his intentional compromising of Miss Vanreid and his loss of control both. As a covert operative who'd spent the last twelve of his thirty years in service to the Crown's most elite secret espionage branch the Special League, he had only needed to use women as pawns a handful of times, and he had disliked each time immensely. But he had never married any of them.

Nor had he ever wanted any of them the way he longed to slide home inside Miss Vanreid.

Sebastian shoved the unwelcome insight from his mind. "I will be more than happy to make Miss Vanreid my wife as quickly as can be arranged," he forced himself to say. "But for the nonce, I recommend Mrs. Stanley and Miss Vanreid take their leave before we draw any further attention to the matter. In a crush of this magnitude, no one will be the wiser."

"I do expect you tomorrow, young man," said the tipsy aunt, capable of giving him a dressing down despite the champagne and wine she'd consumed that evening. "You have much to answer for."

He wasn't accustomed to being taken to task or to being called "young man" rather than "Your Grace." "Of course, madam." He took care to keep his tone contrite. It wouldn't do to rile the aunt, who seemed to be holding herself together with remarkable aplomb thus far but who could lose her calm at any juncture thanks to her inebriated condition.

The aunt creating a scene was the last thing that any of them needed.

A wider audience would cause scandal and ruin to swirl about Miss Vanreid, but it also would impede his efforts as a spy in the process. The fewer who knew of their scandal, the better. The haste of their nuptials would be fodder enough.

But that was a matter for another day.

Tonight's work had gone well, even if the doing had left him feeling oddly aroused and hollowed at the same time, as though his conscience were at war with his prick. He'd become adept at burying guilt and banishing emotion from his every action. No man could successfully keep secrets from everyone around him, lie to others, and kill for his country, without removing weak sentiment from his life like an infected limb.

Yet despite all that, despite a dozen years and missions that he'd imagined had hardened him as surely as a lump of coal being formed in the earth, he felt like a complete blighter as he faced Miss Vanreid again in the moonlight. She had remained unusually quiet but for her lone revelation of the state of her gown. He had done the tearing that ripped her sleeve, had done irreparable damage to her. To them both.

For a good cause.

But damn it if he still didn't feel something dislodge inside his chest when he caught Miss Vanreid's gloved hand in his and raised it to his lips for a kiss. He bowed to her with drawing room formality. There was ample reason to distrust her, and nothing about the minx suggested innocence, but there was a small chance that she was not a part of her father's diabolical schemes. That she had nothing to do with dynamite, Fenian plots, or anything more malevolent than being a horrid flirt.

Of course, there was also the chance that she was everything Carlisle suspected her of and worse. That she was colluding with McGuire. That she was using her wiles against him to garner information for the enemy. That she sought to cause injury—perhaps even death—to the innocents of London, and indeed, all of England.

Somehow, the latter was difficult for him to reconcile with the soft, perfectly curved, altogether beautiful woman he'd kissed and held in his arms. He took a breath, careful to keep his tone devoid of all emotion before he spoke. "Miss Vanreid, I am so sorry. Pray accept my sincere apology for any insult I paid you this evening."

She leaned close to him, the first real move she'd made since they'd been unceremoniously interrupted. "Apology accepted, Your Grace, of course." And then she surprised him by moving nearer still, all but thrusting her bosom into his face. Her lips grazed his ear as she whispered for him alone. "But you should know that I'm not sorry."

Bloody hell. One thing was certain: Daisy Vanreid was trouble. The sooner he could move to a new assignment and be granted an annulment, the better. His first act as her husband would be to order her an entire wardrobe of high-necked dresses that buttoned all the way up to her throat.

*chapter four*

$\mathcal{A}$ SINGULAR EMOTION OVERCAME DAISY when she awoke the next morning: relief.

It stayed with her, unfurling in her belly like a summer blossom, as she dressed and went about her toilette with the assistance of her lady's maid. She took extra care in choosing a morning gown of deep purple silk that set off her complexion and blonde hair to advantage. It hugged her curves and had an elaborately flounced skirt and lace trimming on the bodice that drew the eye to her bosom.

She'd noticed that the Duke of Trent's eyes had a tendency to linger there. And last night, his mouth had been upon her. The recollection made heat suffuse her, coloring her cheeks.

"Miss Daisy, you're a vision in that dress," said Abigail as they both surveyed her efforts in the glass.

"Not precisely a vision," Daisy denied. "But this will do, I think."

"It will more than do, miss." Her lady's maid was quick to refute her in that effusive way she had. Abigail had been with her for as long as Daisy could recall, and her generous smiles and flattery sometimes seemed unnatural. "Not many ladies can carry off *aubergine* well, but you can claim that distinction."

"Thank you, Abigail. We both know I couldn't carry off anything at all if it weren't for your help. You're such a dab hand with hairstyles." She made a face at her reflection, dispelling the serene picture she'd presented.

If there was anything she'd learned in her twenty years of life, it was that she should never take herself or anyone else too seriously. Once, she had, and she'd paid dearly for her mistakes. She'd trusted and believed. She'd loved with the worshipful adherence of a true naïf. And she had been, like the child warned of a hot stove nevertheless reaching out to test its scorching surface, thoroughly burned.

Dreams could be dashed in a day. A heart could be so easily broken.

Nothing was forever. Nothing was certain.

She'd finally realized she had no choice, no option as a female dependent upon her father and his endless wealth and equally endless cruelty, and she had fashioned herself into a new Daisy. This Daisy knew how to dress, knew how to style her hair, knew how to flirt with a man and lure him into a dark alcove for a stolen kiss. She kept her heart from her sleeve. She was brazen and bold, and she used every weapon in her arsenal to get what she wanted.

Last night had been no different. Today would be no different.

The only thing that mattered was that she would finally achieve what she wanted most. She would be free from her father's rule and free from being forced to marry the repugnant Lord Breckly.

"Everything will soon change for me, I think," she told her lady's maid with a confidence that was only slightly shaken by the knowledge that she knew precious little about the man to whom she would soon bind herself. Two meetings and a passionate embrace was hardly enough for her to call him an acquaintance, let alone marry him. But her father's edict had been clear, and his return, along with the announcement of her betrothal to Breckly, imminent. Placed in such a position, what could she have done differently?

Where else could she turn in London, a relatively strange city to her, with no funds and no friends to speak of? She could sell her king's ransom in diamonds, try to run free and start a new life somewhere else. But the only other time she'd attempted such a feat, her father had found her with ease. Selling a magnificent cache of diamonds had a way of rendering one's anonymity impossible. Her homecoming had earned her a broken rib.

As she quit her chamber and made her way downstairs to meet Aunt Caroline in the salon, the relief inside her slowly withered, leaving in its wake a stern sense of misgiving. So much could yet go wrong. Her father could still refuse the match and demand that she wed his chosen bridegroom instead. The duke could decide not to offer for her. Or, worse, he could turn out to be a man who was violent against women. Or a lecher. Or something else equally odious.

By the time she entered the salon to find not only her aunt but the Duke of Trent within, she was wringing her hands at her waist, a dreadful habit she could never seem to shake whenever she was ill at ease. No matter how unladylike it was. When her gaze met the duke's, she stopped, halfway over the threshold, and tore her hands apart.

An unaccountable burst of nervousness assailed her. He was early. Or perhaps she was late. It didn't matter. All that did matter was that he was here. He had come. And he stood at her half-entry to the chamber, debonair in his gray jacket and silver waistcoat, tall and brooding and even more handsome than he'd been last night. His expression possessed an intensity that seemed to call for her entire attention. Her every sense focused upon the gorgeous man who just last night had pulled down her bodice and taken her bare breast into his mouth as though she was already his.

No man had ever been so daring with her.

Thinking of the wet heat of his mouth upon her nipple sent an ache between her thighs. Dear heavens, had she actually just thought about such a thing in the bright morning light, with her aunt as an audience? How shameless.

"Daisy," Aunt Caroline said then, her tone tight with the same disapproval she had used to dress Daisy down during the carriage ride home the night before. "You kept His Grace waiting."

Daisy couldn't tear her eyes from the duke, who pinned her with a similar, rapt stare. "My apologies." Belatedly, she realized she had yet to enter the room. She forced herself to move forward with as much grace as she could muster while his eyes all but consumed her. "Good morning, Aunt Caroline, Your Grace."

"No apology is necessary, Miss Vanreid, as such loveliness is more than worth any wait," said the duke with smooth charm.

Daisy seated herself on a settee at her aunt's side. "You're too kind, Duke."

He inclined his head, as if his manners wouldn't allow him to argue the point. The air became stilted as silence fell upon the sunny chamber. A mantle clock ticked. At last, Aunt Caroline disrupted the uncomfortable quiet.

"As I was informing Your Grace before my niece arrived, Mr. Vanreid will be arriving in London soon. He was attending business in Liverpool, but he has been apprised of the…situation. He telegrammed this morning to say that he alone will conduct all further matters with you directly upon his return, Your Grace."

Her father was in Liverpool? Daisy had thought him still traveling across the Atlantic. The knowledge that he wasn't both troubled and surprised her. Apparently, Aunt Caroline was privier to her father's business than Daisy was. The realization made Daisy look at her aunt with new eyes. No one knew better than Daisy just how ruthless and cruel her father could be.

That her father wanted to conduct matters with the duke, however, distressed her even more. For he hadn't sent an outright acceptance of an impending marriage. A fist of dread closed on Daisy's heart.

She refused to believe that she could be so close to freedom, only to be thwarted.

*No.*

Two sets of eyes swung to her.

Had she said that aloud? Apparently so. She flushed. "Aunt Caroline, can you not act in Father's stead?"

Her aunt's eyebrows nearly touched her hairline. "You cannot be serious, young lady. We find ourselves in an untenable situation brought about by your own thoughtless recklessness and wicked behavior. I would not presume to speak on your father's behalf. I can imagine he has a great deal to say to you and His Grace both, and I cannot think any of it will be good."

Well. It seemed Aunt Caroline was decidedly not in her corner. She supposed she ought not to be surprised, for her aunt had been ever touting the illustrious match her father planned for her with Lord Breckly. It wasn't as if they had ever shared anything more than each other's company. Certainly never a warm embrace.

Aunt Caroline had no children of her own, and there was nothing maternal about her. Daisy felt the familiar, old pang of loss whenever she thought of her own mother, who'd been gone for so long she was nothing more than a lock of hair pressed behind glass on a mourning pin and a shadowy remembrance.

The duke cleared his throat, his expression growing pained. "Mrs. Stanley, I'm afraid the fault of this 'untenable situation,' as you've called it, must be laid upon no one but me. I've been smitten by your niece ever since I first saw her, and last night I allowed my base nature to prevail. The only way to rectify the insult I've paid Miss Vanreid is by offering marriage, which I fully intend to do upon Mr. Vanreid's arrival."

Aunt Caroline wasn't so easily swayed. In the absence of wine, she was an absolute stickler. She directed an expression of extreme displeasure in the duke's direction. "I'm sure you were dazzled by Daisy's beauty. Everyone is. However, there is the matter of her impending betrothal to Lord Breckly to be considered now. Mr. Vanreid remains set on his lordship."

The duke smiled, but it didn't reach his eyes. "I'm sure you will agree that, given yesterday's turn of events, a match between Lord Breckly and Miss Vanreid is no longer possible."

He didn't appear any happier than Aunt Caroline to be engaged in this early morning audience. Perhaps he regretted his actions and wished he could extricate himself by more impermanent means than marriage.

But it was too late. The dye had been cast. And Daisy had no intention of becoming Lady Breckly. *Mr. Vanreid remains set on his lordship.* However, surely her father would agree that a duke, even one who had compromised her, was a far better catch than a mere viscount. Surely in this one instance, if none other in her life, her father would see reason.

For an instant, the memory of the last time she'd been set on marrying a man returned to her. She shook it from her mind, tucking it back into the past where it belonged. The bruises on her body had long ago faded. The bruise on her heart had taken far longer to disappear.

"I cannot presume to know what my brother will agree to, Your Grace," Aunt Caroline said then, further churning up Daisy's fears. "He wishes the best for my niece."

That was a blatant falsehood. Her father wished what was best for himself in all things. Her aunt's words suggested what Daisy began to suspect—that her father would not necessarily abandon his plan of marrying her to

Breckly. What was it that the man had over her father? Daisy wished she knew. Wished she understood the tangled web in which she'd found herself. With each day, she grew more and more convinced that her father was involved in something nefarious.

And that Padraig was as well.

She didn't know how the pieces of the puzzle slid together, but all she did know was that she didn't want to be a part of any of it. The mere thought of her father's arrival was enough to make her queasy. She'd been free of his presence, living a charmed life in London, for two months. His return threatened to change everything.

The duke's gaze was once again fastened upon her, and she couldn't help but think he assessed her, taking in far more of her than she would have preferred. Whatever he saw in her expression, it made him turn back to Aunt Caroline with a stern frown.

"Mrs. Stanley." His accent was perfectly modulated, crisp. "I feel quite certain that Mr. Vanreid will find my pedigree faultless. Until he arrives and we can be assured of his blessing, however, I would like your permission to formally court Miss Vanreid, beginning with a turn about the gardens. Are you amenable to that?"

Aunt Caroline appeared very much the opposite of amenable, but she was faced with a prickly conundrum: insult a duke or adhere to her misplaced loyalty to her brother. Her lips compressed into a firm line. "Very well," she relented. "But you may not go out of sight of the window, Your Grace. I'll be watching."

A smile quirked the corner of his sensual lips, his first true sign of levity thus far. "Naturally, madam. I wouldn't have it any other way."

* * * * *

Sebastian guided Miss Vanreid into the crisp morning air, all too aware of the glare trained on his back by the aunt. She was a deal more formidable when not befuddled by drink, that much was certain. Just as it was also certain that the woman clutching his arm in a manacle-like grip feared her father.

And unless his instincts were mistaken, she feared her father a great deal. He recognized the flash in her eyes, the tense set of her shoulders, the way she'd seemed to withdraw. All the boldness, daring, and brilliance that was Daisy Vanreid had withered and died before him in the salon at the mention of her father's return.

Part of him knew he shouldn't give a damn about what past terrors haunted the flirtatious beauty alongside him. But another part of him, a part he didn't care to examine too closely, suggested that learning the story behind Miss Vanreid's distress would aid him in his cause.

The more information he could uncover about Vanreid, the better. Perhaps earning his daughter's trust would also garner some additional information. If she was involved in the dynamite plots, showing her kindness could be a way to sidestep any barriers she'd seek to erect between them.

There was also the troubling matter that he had actually felt…something when he'd noted Miss Vanreid's subtly quelled terror. That he'd felt anything at all irritated him. He'd been trained, damn it. He was meant to feel nothing. No emotion, no pity, and certainly not kindness. Not concern or worry.

Absolutely not *protective*.

He refused to believe any of those emotions were the source of the odd tightness in his chest as he stopped with her now, just before a dormant rose bush and still within full view of her disapproving aunt. Where was a bottle of champagne and the Duke of Carlisle when he needed him? he wondered grimly.

Sebastian stared unseeing at the desiccated gardens for a beat before turning to Miss Vanreid. He tried not to notice how comely she was, even from the side. Outdoors, away from her aunt and the looming specter of her father, she outshone the sunshine. The purple of her gown heightened her creamy skin and the burnished coils of her thick hair.

Everything about the gown, from its cinched waist to its lace trim, was designed to call attention to her impeccable figure and the sweet curve of her bosom. The dolman she'd donned to ward off the chill air did little to conceal her fine figure.

Damn it, he thought as he surveyed her profile, a wardrobe of dresses that buttoned to the throat wouldn't be enough to tame her beauty or its effect upon him. Bloody hell. Maybe it would be unwise to see this assignment through.

But no. He had a duty. He'd sworn an oath. The lives of so many innocents were at peril.

"Miss Vanreid," he bit out, displeased by the tumult she set off within him. "You seemed ill at ease back in the salon. What causes you such grief?"

She was silent, seemingly engrossed in a study of the dormant rose bushes. "I don't wish to marry Lord Breckly, Your Grace." Her voice was low, toneless. "Is it your intention to wed me?"

Wed her? Everything within him screamed *no*. Bed her? Everything within him screamed *yes*. His cock surged against his trousers and he shifted slightly to minimize the evidence of her extreme effect on him. She was an anomaly. Enigmatic, beautiful, seductive, but also quiet and imbued with a sadness he didn't yet comprehend. He would learn her. Would learn every one of her secrets before he was through.

"It would be my honor, Miss Vanreid, to make you my wife," he lied.

She turned to him finally, subjecting him to the full force of her undeniable beauty. "Have you ever hit a woman?"

Her question took the air from his lungs. What kind of a woman asked such a thing? The kind who had been abused, his instincts told him. The kind who sought to avoid entanglement in a situation similar to the one in which she already found herself.

"Of course not," he answered past his shock, pausing a

beat to read her expression. "Do you trust me?"

She pursed her lips together, taking her time to answer. "I know little of you, Your Grace, so to say that I trust you implicitly would make a liar of me."

Ah, there was candor, he supposed, pointed as a dagger. "Such wisdom from one so young is a rarity."

As the words left him, he realized how pompous he sounded. How ducal. He hadn't meant to imply she wasn't intelligent. Far from it—her intellect and her daring were the two traits that attracted him to her the most. Anyone could be beautiful. But not everyone could be bold and smart and fearless. The lady before him—duplicitous enemy of the Crown or no—was all of those things.

She was the sort of woman who, in different times, he would have been proud to call his duchess. Given the circumstances, the dubious cloud of her associations, and the fact that he'd been charged with viewing her as an enemy, his feelings for her in this moment could not be rooted in anything less rational than duty. For the spy, control was everything. Emotions had to be carefully excised, as infection from a wound, else the entire limb would require amputation.

Grim thought, that. But fitting.

She stiffened, oblivious to the unsettling bent of his thoughts, her chin tilting up in ravishing defiance. "Age is a fallacious indicator of intelligence, Your Grace."

"So it can be," he acknowledged, taking a step toward her. Her skirts billowed into his trousers. Her scent enveloped him. The morning was yet again unseasonably warm, yet still cold, and so he couldn't be certain whether the scarcely discernible tremble that passed over her just then was from the chill or from something else. "You're wise to withhold your trust until it's earned. But know that I would never intentionally cause you harm."

Was that even true? Hell, he didn't know any longer. He would never hit her. Would never bring physical pain upon her. Anything else? He couldn't promise. His time with her was as ephemeral as life itself.

Her wide, green eyes, vibrant in this sleeping garden of drab browns and withered moss, plumbed his. "You must know that I haven't a choice, Your Grace. If you are a dishonest man, no pain you could visit upon me would surpass that which I've already endured. Forgive me for my honesty, but you are the lesser of all evils, as far as I can discern."

Her gaze didn't flinch from his, and he knew then that some of the enigma that was Daisy Vanreid had been revealed to him. An unfamiliar sensation, troubling and tense, rose within him as full realization settled. There was only one conclusion here that made sense.

Gently, he touched her elbow, not wishing to cause her further distress. "Has your father hit you, sweet?"

She looked away in a clear sign that he had guessed correctly. "Of course he hasn't."

"Miss Vanreid," he pressed, catching her stubborn chin and guiding her face back to his. "Daisy. If I'm to help you, then you must be honest with me. Has your father inflicted violence upon you?"

She closed her eyes and took a deep breath. "Yes." Shame steeped her tone.

There it was again, that coiled sensation in his chest. The tightening in his gut. A grim, raw fury lit within him. Her father had struck her. More than once. He'd caused her pain, done her violence. A primitive urge to defend her rose, battling to supremacy over every other emotion. Even over his work as a spy. He didn't question it. Didn't think twice.

"He will never raise a hand to you again once you're my wife," he vowed, his voice shaking with the furor trapped inside him. "This I swear. Nor will I ever abuse you in any fashion."

These were promises he could make her.

Jesus, they were the *only* promises he could make her.

Miss Vanreid—the vibrant, flirtatious beauty who had never stepped down or batted a lash since he'd been watching her—trembled beneath his touch. The cynic in him reminded him that it could all be a ruse. Someone as bold and *laissez-faire* with her reputation as she was seemed at odds with the vulnerable, frightened woman before him now.

His training, however, led him to believe in her sincerity. Perhaps the true act was the Daisy Vanreid she showed the world, because inside she was terrified and desperate to escape her father's clutches. So desperate she'd throw herself into the arms of any man who'd catch her.

"I can't be certain he will allow a union between us, Your Grace," she whispered, as though she feared her aunt could somehow distinguish their dialogue even from within the elegant townhouse at their backs. "For some reason, he has been determined that I should marry the Viscount Breckly. Aunt Caroline says they've reached an understanding for my hand. The announcement of the betrothal was only awaiting my father's arrival."

There was something suspicious indeed about Vanreid's determination to wed his sole daughter to an aging reprobate. He would hazard a guess that the impetus had something to do with Breckly's ancestral estate in Ireland. He was quite an influential man in his home country. Clearly, Sebastian would need to further investigate the connection between the two men.

Miss Vanreid seemed to be the sacrificial lamb binding them. And reluctantly from the looks of things. He couldn't blame her. No one as lovely, youthful, and alluring as she ought to be saddled with an elderly oaf for a husband. The mere thought of Breckly in her bed was enough to make Sebastian bilious.

"I find it curious that you believe your father would prefer a mere viscount to a duke who is much nearer in age to you." He searched her expression for any sign that she knew more than she let on.

But her mossy eyes never wavered from his. "As do I, Your Grace. There seems to be a reason for my father's preference in suitor, but I cannot think of anything to recommend Lord Breckly at all."

"Nor can I." He noticed that a small tendril of hair had willfully escaped from her coif to curl against her ear, and before he even realized what he was about, he caught it in his fingers. It was every bit as silky and soft as he'd imagined it would be, and damned if he didn't conjure up an image of her with her hair unbound, those golden waves falling past her shoulders. Nude. In his bed.

Good God.

He went rigid in his trousers. It was an effect she seemed to regularly have on him. One that he couldn't control regardless of the serious nature of his assignment or the fact that he still couldn't trust her and had no intention of being a true husband to her. The sooner they could be granted an annulment, the better. But first he had to manage to marry her.

"I don't want to marry Lord Breckly," she said suddenly. "My father...when he returns, I don't know what he will do."

Her words effectively chilled his ardor. He tucked the errant curl behind her ear, severing their physical connection, for it clouded his judgment. "Do you have reason to fear him?"

She closed her eyes, her breath hitching. Her lids fluttered open again, unshed tears glistening and turning her eyes an even brighter shade of green. "I cannot be here when he returns. I won't. Neither will I marry Lord Breckly. I will do anything, Your Grace. *Anything*."

Her vehemence struck a chord within him. The truth was that Carlisle had procured a marriage license by registrar. The cagey bastard had already had it in hand before he'd even deigned to inform Sebastian of the necessity for marrying Miss Vanreid. It would never cease to amaze him just how much could be accomplished—how many laws and rules could be ignored, cast aside, and broken—in the name of keeping England safe. The League was shadowy yet omnipotent.

He made up his mind. There would be no courting of Vanreid as Carlisle had wanted, no ingratiating himself to Miss Vanreid's father in the hope of winning her hand in a rushed but nevertheless proper manner. Sebastian was a spy, and his allegiance was to England, but he was also a gentleman. And there was no bloody way he would stand idly by knowing she would be brutalized for actions that were of his own making.

There were pawns and then there were *pawns*. He had never been asked to stoop to this level before, to risk his own progeny, the line of the Trent duchy, in the name of Crown and country. To marry a woman he knew nothing about, a woman who could either be a traitor, a spy, or worse. To turn a blind eye to the fact that her father had clearly beaten her often enough and badly enough to terrify her.

That he wouldn't do. He wouldn't consign Daisy Vanreid to any hells that were greater than those she'd already visited. "How much freedom do you have here?" he asked curtly.

"None unless Aunt Caroline is otherwise distracted."

He knew the sort of distraction that would appeal to dear Aunt Caroline. Carlisle had a face the ladies swooned for. Christ knew why, for most of the time, Sebastian longed to plant a fist into the man's supercilious chin. Only his oath kept him from mayhem.

"If Aunt Caroline has sufficient distraction tomorrow afternoon, do you think you could leave without anyone's notice?" he asked, relishing the prospect of informing Carlisle he'd need to dance attendance on a middle-aged harpy with a weakness for liquor and cock. Mayhap not in that precise order.

Miss Vanreid's eyes widened. "I believe I could. What do you have in mind?"

"Two o'clock tomorrow, and you shall find out." He forced his eyes away from Miss Vanreid's lovely, upturned face just in time to see her aunt storming toward them, skirts flapping with indignation. It would appear he had tarried too long in the sunshine and Miss Vanreid's decadent presence. "I'll be waiting in an unmarked carriage. Bring only what you require."

"My conscience demands that I warn you that my father will almost certainly rescind my dowry should I defy him, Your Grace," she began, only for him to interrupt her.

"I don't require your dowry. While it's a well-known fact that many of my peers are pockets to let, I need not fear penury. I've a substantial sum of my own, so you needn't worry yourself on that score." He paused as the aunt stalked ever closer. "Trust that I'll make certain your father can never lay another hand on you again."

She heaved a sigh of relief, as though he'd just rescued her from the maws of certain ruin.

Little did she know that her downward spiral was only just beginning. There would be no fists or brute strength leveled against her. But there would be a reckoning. He would determine how much she knew, and whether or not she was complicit. And if she was complicit, her father would be the least of her fears.

*chapter five*

"I'LL BE BACK IN A TRICE," Daisy told her Aunt Caroline later that afternoon as their carriage came to a halt outside a milliner's. Fortunately, the duke's departure had left her aunt so overwrought that she'd imbibed several glasses of port. As a result, Daisy had convinced her to allow an excursion that Aunt Caroline wouldn't have ordinarily approved of. Especially since Daisy's honor had been so recently compromised.

But Daisy didn't care. She needed to see Bridget, and she'd do so by any means.

Her aunt hiccupped. "I don't think you ought to venture inside unchaperoned. Your father would not approve."

"I have Abigail," she argued of her lady's maid. "We will be back in the carriage in a blink of an eye."

Of course, there was the natural possibility that her aunt just may doze off in the warm confines of the waiting carriage before Daisy returned, which would only make matters much simpler. She wisely refrained from saying so.

Her aunt grumbled. "Very well. But I will give you five minutes, and five minutes only. You know that girl is not—"

"I'm aware," Daisy interrupted curtly, lest her inebriated aunt let any family secrets slip from her lips before her lady's maid. "I'll return posthaste. It's all very proper, Aunt."

Aunt Caroline's mouth tightened into a knot of disapproval. "Be quick about it, then."

Daisy didn't tarry a second longer before alighting from the carriage with her lady's maid following in her wake. She sincerely hoped that Bridget was on duty today, for she hadn't enough time to send word.

Inside the milliner's, the scene was familiar—a bevy of hats on display, all the first stare of fashion. The shop was a fine one, and Bridget held a senior position, though Daisy would have preferred she'd listened to reason and come to stay with her and Aunt Caroline. Bridget, of course, had been equally stubborn in her refusal and vehement in her dislike of Daisy.

But Daisy was nothing if not determined, and so she continued to pay visits to the milliner's as often as she could to see the half sister she'd always known existed an ocean away but had never met until her arrival in London. As a lonely girl, Daisy had dreamt of meeting the older sister born out of wedlock, conceived during the early years of her parents' marriage. To her father, Bridget was a sign of shame. To Daisy, she was family. Daisy had sought her out immediately, but she had not met with the welcoming she'd hoped.

Time, she reminded herself. Her sister required some time to warm to her. Daisy knew Bridget's early years in Ireland had not been easy. Her mother had died when she was but a girl, and she'd come to London to eke out her existence. While Daisy's life had not been easy either, she had nevertheless known wealth and privilege.

Madame Villiers herself was on the floor today, her mahogany curls artfully arranged, a fashionable fringe of bangs cut across her high forehead. "How may I help you,

52

mademoiselle?"

Daisy smiled. "I would like ten of your newest creations, if you please, Madame, delivered immediately to my address. I trust your impeccable sense of fashion implicitly."

Madame Villiers's eyes lit up. "But of course, Mademoiselle Vanreid. We will give nothing but the best, *les meilleurs chapeaux*. Our designs rival Parisian fashion plates."

"I've changed my mind, Madame," Daisy said in a voice loud enough to carry to her fellow patrons milling about. "I'd like fifteen of your best."

The woman smiled, resembling nothing so much as a satisfied feline. Her creations, though sought after, were dear. An order of fifteen hats was worth a handsome sum.

"*Naturellement*. We will be more than happy to send fifteen of our finest to the celebrated heiress Mademoiselle Vanreid, whom all of London admires. We are *trés* honored."

Perfect. Fortunately for Daisy, Madame Villiers didn't require much flattery to resort to bombast. In a much quieter voice, she said for the milliner's ears alone, "And, of course, if Miss O'Malley is on duty, I would appreciate a word."

"Ah, *oui*," said Madame in an equally subdued pitch. "I believe you'll find Miss O'Malley at her usual post, working with the feathers."

"*Merci*," Daisy said, *sotto voce*, before instructing her lady's maid to await her in the main shop. Her half sister needed her, and Daisy owed her so much. She had been raised in a life of privilege and plenty while Bridget had suffered. She had vowed to see that her sister was always provided for, and a union with the duke could call that promise into question.

It was something she hadn't considered in her selfish desire to gain her own freedom from an insupportable marriage with Breckly. But she wouldn't forget her sister, nor would she turn her back upon her. So much depended upon her now. The weight of it all threatened to consume her.

She retained hope that Trent possessed a softer side, an understanding. He had sworn to protect her against her father's wrath, hadn't he? However, it almost seemed too good to be true, the prospect of freedom from tyranny and violence.

Nevertheless, it hung there, a lure tenuously within her faltering grasp. Hers if she but took it.

Daisy slipped discreetly into the room that Madame Villiers had indicated. Within, her half sister was alone. Bridget, toiling over the proper placement of an ostrich feather, paused at her entrance. Despite her raven hair and the fact that she'd had a different mother, Bridget's features closely resembled Daisy's own. They were three years apart in age and worlds apart in every other way save appearance.

She pinned Daisy with a forbidding frown now. "And what are you doing here, Miss High-and-Mighty heiress?"

When the Duke of Carlisle held a private party at his Belgravia address, he put elite dens of vice to shame. Sebastian took in the decadence before him with a jaundiced eye. Some of the most powerful men in the *ton* thronged the ballroom, twirling with the crème de la crème of London Cyprians. Champagne flowed aplenty. The ladies were painted and scantily clad, the men already deep in their cups. And damn if he didn't smell the cloying scent of opium in the air.

The opium likely emerged from one of the surrounding chambers where the duke kept rooms devoted to sin. On his slow perambulation, Sebastian had noted a chamber where a nude woman acted as a serving platter for charcuterie, a shrouded, low-lit room with pillows on the floor, and yet another where couples were coming and going in various stages of *dishabille*.

Sybarite fêtes such as these were what Carlisle deemed

"hiding in plain sight," one of the best means of achieving communication and maintaining his façade without arousing suspicion. If all the polite world thought him a dissolute rakehell, none would be inclined to question the company he kept. For his part, Sebastian adopted the same voluptuary lifestyle, sans the hedonistic all-night parties.

Unlike Carlisle, he required sleep.

He accepted a flute of champagne from a servant bearing a gilded tray and pretended to take a long gulp. In truth, he needed a clear head tonight, for the last of their plans would be laid in motion. And he would sure as hell need a clear head on the morrow when he faced the matrimonial equivalent of the gallows.

For as much as his body reacted to the notion of Miss Daisy Vanreid becoming his wife, his mind couldn't help but feel the exact opposite. He'd learned long ago that his body was weak. His mind was stronger. He could harness his inconvenient attraction to her into a more focused energy—pursuing the plotters at large before they injured or murdered hundreds of innocent civilians.

Feigning another sip of his champagne, he stole a discreet look at his pocket watch. Thank God. The appointed time had come. Careful to blend with the boisterous revelers, he slipped from the ballroom and decamped for the secret portal hidden in the elaborate Rococo wood panels gracing the great hall beyond. He made certain he was alone before locating the mechanism behind a scroll that allowed the door to open inward.

Carlisle already awaited him within as the panel clicked closed at his back. The hidden room was kept intentionally sparse lest a servant ever inadvertently discover its existence: a desk, two chairs, a lamp, decanter, and tumblers. It resembled nothing more than a place where an aggrieved man might have escaped from his harridan wife for a peaceful drink.

Except Carlisle didn't have a wife, and the sole purpose of the hidden chamber was of a far more clandestine nature.

It had been through the last two dukes, and would be carried on should Carlisle ever bear a son. The League swore oaths that extended to their progeny. With the title came the burden. And before that, a lifetime of preparation.

The duke was seated, a tumbler of whisky at hand. "You met with her?"

No greeting. No pretense of friendship. But Sebastian was accustomed to Carlisle by now. "I did," he confirmed, striding across the small room and folding his body into one of the uncomfortable wing chairs facing his superior in command. "According to the aunt and the girl both, it is unlikely Vanreid will alter his course of a union between Miss Vanreid and Breckly. I'll be meeting her clandestinely tomorrow afternoon and we'll wed immediately. But are you utterly sure it's necessary for me to marry the girl?"

Carlisle remained impassive. The man had no conscience, of that much Sebastian was certain. Very likely no soul either. "The marriage is a necessity, so do what you must. We need a reason to keep close to her and to Vanreid, McGuire, and the rest of the plotters. Arresting them now will only undermine our efforts, and as it stands, we haven't enough against them to keep them in prison for long. We need more information."

"Information you expect me to acquire," Sebastian finished for him.

Carlisle inclined his head. "You've done well entrenching yourself in the life of a scoundrel. After you marry the girl, you'll approach Vanreid about a dowry, making it seem as if you ruined her intentionally so that you could benefit from the union. Press him for information about his firearms factory and the illegal arms trade he's engaging in here."

The ruse seemed dashed transparent. "You expect him to confess he's engaging in the illicit selling of weapons on the streets of London to a man who compromised his only daughter and ruined the match he intended for her? Forgive me, but that seems deuced unlikely."

"Greed is never unlikely, particularly not with Vanreid's sort," Carlisle said. "I understand your aversion to this mission, but you cannot allow that to stand in the way of what must be done. As unpalatable as such an arrangement may be, we are fighting a unique battle. We've men in civilian clothes, blending in with ordinary folk on the streets, intending to kill innocents. Extraordinary times call for extraordinary measures. If we can put Vanreid in prison for the illegal firearms, it stands to reason that we can bargain with him for a great deal more information. The names of all the plotters could be within our grasp."

Damn. There would be no eleventh hour reprieve for him at all, it seemed. "I will be granted an annulment without any repercussions? I don't take my familial duty lightly. One day, I'll need an heir."

He would not—could not—sacrifice the future of the duchy to a forced marriage with anyone, let alone someone as inscrutable as Daisy Vanreid. A woman who could be plotting against his country and its people.

The duke inclined his head. "Your service to the Crown will be rewarded. I have every suspicion that this operation will end in Miss Vanreid's arrest, which will only aid your cause."

A chill of foreboding traveled mercilessly down his spine. No matter how much he distrusted her, the thought of Daisy imprisoned made his chest feel tight. "Her arrest?"

"Yes." The duke's expression hardened to rival marble. "I have several eyes on her. This afternoon, she met with an Irish shop girl who is believed to be connected to the plots. The girl has been seen meeting several suspected Fenians here in London."

Jesus. He allowed the information to sift through his brain. Of course, he wasn't at all shocked to learn that Carlisle had other operatives following Miss Vanreid. Sebastian was tasked solely with trailing her at social events and learning as much as he could about her habits and associations, all of which he had loyally done. But evidence—true evidence—of her complicity in any dynamite campaign seemed implausible at best.

"Miss Vanreid has not presented any indication of guilt to me," he said stiffly. An odd surge of something streaked through him. Defensiveness? On behalf of a woman he scarcely knew? How bloody absurd.

And yet, there it was, lurking like an unwanted guest. Undeniable.

Carlisle raised a brow, his expression resembling nothing so much as a vulture who'd scented carrion. "If you've developed a weakness for the chit, perhaps it would be best to send another man in your place tomorrow. Briarly would do just as well, I should think."

Damn it to hell. Briarly was a callous son-of-a-whore, League member or no, and the thought of him supplanting Sebastian on the morrow didn't sit well. Not at all. The man had allowed six people to burn to death inside a merchant's building in Cheapside and had nearly killed Sebastian in the process. The fire had gutted the premises, resulting in a spectacle so severe that even the Prince of Wales had visited the charred ruins the next day. The general public would never know the true story of what had happened, but Sebastian would never forget. Since that day forward, he had never again tolerated Briarly's presence. And Carlisle knew it.

"She's a lady, Carlisle. You can't just marry her off to whomever you like."

"She's a pawn, and you'd be wise to remember that." The duke's voice was frigid as Wenham Lake ice. "Moreover, she may be dangerous. Don't let a pretty face and a luscious pair of bubbies distract you from your main aim, Trent. I saw the way you pawed at her last night, and I know you want her, but you cannot have her. She's poison to you. Lives are at stake. I repeat: if you cannot carry out your mission, I'll pull you off the assignment. Briarly is more than qualified. The incident in Cheapside couldn't have been avoided, and his record remains sterling in the eyes of the League."

Sebastian clenched his jaw. Sterling, Briarly sure as hell was not. But he didn't need to be taken to task or reminded of the risks they all took in the name of keeping England safe from the bloodthirsty miscreants who sought to despoil it. Nor did he appreciate being rebuked and threatened, even if part of him inwardly admitted it was deserved. He was a good spy, damn it, one of the best.

What was it about Daisy Vanreid that afflicted his mind? It wasn't her undeniable beauty, for he'd seen and bedded his share of lovely women. Nor was it her fortune, for he possessed a formidable sum himself thanks to his father's service to the Crown and generations of temperate investments. It wasn't his unwanted attraction to her. Other women had made his cock hard before her. Others would after her.

What the devil was it, then? Self-disgust warred with irritation. "I haven't given her tits a second thought," he lied with an icy hauteur that matched Carlisle's. He had touched them, by God, has kissed the creamy swells he'd bared in the moonlight. And they'd been softer than silk. The sort of temptation he could ill afford. The sort of temptation that thundered through his veins with a potency far more alluring than any drug or spirit.

"Daisy Vanreid is a means to an end." The duke took a slow drag of whisky, prolonging the air of reproach that hung heavy between them in the tiny secret chamber.

"She's been beaten by her father," he informed Carlisle, hoping the revelation might offer an explanation for the both of them as to why Daisy Vanreid, by all accounts an untrustworthy siren potentially abetting a dangerous coterie of would-be assassins, affected him the way she did.

"According to the lady, I trust?" Carlisle's voice dripped with derision. "Good God, man, did the fire erase all memory of training from your mind? Gaining the sympathy of your mark is one of the oldest gambits in the bloody book."

Of course it was, but his training and his experience had both shown him how to recognize true emotion and true fear when he saw it. Fear could be capitalized upon, manipulated to gain an advantage over one's opponent with relative ease. In Miss Vanreid's case, her fear had only made him weak. Because something—some instinct deep in his gut—told him she was innocent. That she was ignorant of any dynamite plots and wanted no part of whatever insidious dealings in which her father was embroiled.

It wasn't lost on him either that Carlisle would refer to the Cheapside fire in such a cavalier fashion, as though it had been nothing more than a ride in the park. Sebastian bore scars on his hands and arms that attested to that. It took every bit of the training to which Carlisle had alluded to maintain his calm.

"My *training* suggests her fear of her father is genuine."

Carlisle stared at him in that penetrating, disconcerting way again. Almost as if he could read Sebastian's mind. "Whether or not she fears her father and whether or not he beats her is irrelevant to the matter at hand. You'd do best to watch yourself, Trent. Any sign of weakness for the chit, and I won't hesitate to pull you off this assignment."

Sebastian held himself rigidly. Perhaps he had earned his superior's scorn, but he couldn't shake his gut feeling. In all his years of service, his instincts had never failed him. Still, he had no choice but to kowtow, because the thought of any other man—Briarly in particular—wedding Daisy Vanreid appalled him. "Understood, Your Grace."

The duke nodded, seemingly mollified. "You'll marry her tomorrow, then?"

"Yes," Sebastian ground out with great reluctance.

Marriage to anyone, let alone to a pawn, and especially to Daisy Vanreid, did not appeal to him in the slightest. Binding himself to a woman Carlisle intended to throw into prison, a woman suspected of treason, was an intensely personal sacrifice, and one he didn't make easily. And yet he had to acknowledge that there was some rogue part of him that wasn't entirely sad at the prospect of shackling himself to her.

What the hell was the matter with him?

"Our plan will proceed without further alteration?"

Disgust sliced through him with the bite of a blade. He couldn't help feeling that he was just as much of a pawn as Miss Vanreid, a chess piece maneuvered about the League's board. It didn't sit well with him that his every interaction with Daisy—from following her into the garden last night to proposing marriage earlier, to wedding her—had been plotted and mapped out by Carlisle like a general working out a battle strategy.

Only one part hadn't been predetermined, and that had been the animal lust raging through him with Daisy in his arms. His desire for her was not feigned or planned. And certainly not controllable.

The duke awaited his response, so he inclined his head. "Our plan will proceed. I'm secreting her away at two o'clock tomorrow."

"Excellent." Carlisle took another sip of spirits.

"There's only one problem," he took great pleasure in adding.

"Jesus, Trent. You're tipping the scales tonight, and it isn't in your bloody favor," the duke warned.

"The lady's aunt will need to be distracted." He grinned. "And she rather took a liking to you. Ply the biddy with some drink and she'll be all yours. If you don't, I can't promise Miss Vanreid can manage an escape."

With that parting shot, he ducked back out of the room, Carlisle's growled curses trailing after him.

## chapter six

$\mathscr{T}$HE DUCHESS OF TRENT.

Her Grace.

How odd. How absurd. She, Daisy Vanreid, who'd earned her carefully honed London reputation as a bold flirt and a rebel, who had been snubbed by New York's Knickerbocker elite and an untold number of haughty aristocrats, had just married a *duke*. And not just any duke, but the most handsome duke she'd laid eyes on since landing on England's dreary shore. Sebastian Fairmont, the Duke of Trent.

Daisy stared at her reflection in the strange mirror in the equally strange chamber. She didn't look any different. Her hair remained styled in the same Grecian plait Abigail had fashioned for her before she'd managed to flee Aunt Caroline's home. She still wore her afternoon gown, a vibrant emerald silk trimmed with lace, navy cording, and a cluster of crushed velvet roses on the bodice. Not her finest dress, and certainly not the dress she'd envisioned as her wedding frock, but a more inspired choice would have roused Aunt Caroline's suspicions. Daisy hadn't been willing to take the risk.

Sacrificing her vanity for the sake of her future had been the wisest decision to make. And in a life that had been marked by a series of unwise decisions, to Daisy, the handsome afternoon gown—not nearly as impressive as most of her wardrobe—was a sign that she was ready to turn over a new leaf. To begin again. To live a life unencumbered by fear or threats of violence.

To be…her true self, something she had never had the opportunity to be. Under her father's watchful gaze, she had been quiet and reserved, her every action above reproach lest she earn his rage. With Aunt Caroline as her chaperone, she had been someone else, a desperate flirt whose confidence was largely pretense.

And now here she stood, stripped of both roles. Plain old Daisy. Daisy who didn't know what to do. Should she be bold? Should she be coy? Goodness, she didn't even know the duke, the man she'd just wed. She had shown so many different faces to so many different people—all in an effort to escape her father's violence and disapproval in one fashion or another—that she wasn't certain *she* even knew who she was.

Her hands shook as she smoothed an imaginary wrinkle from her skirt and pinched her pale cheeks to lend them a hint of color. She had no lady's maid. No portmanteau. No other gowns. All she had stood reflected in the glass: herself, the duke's unadorned gold band he'd slipped on her finger, the gown and undergarments beneath it, the heavy weight of the diamond jewelry she'd carefully filled her hidden pockets with.

That was all.

*Bring only what you require*, the duke had instructed, and Daisy had followed his directive. The sole exception was the king's ransom in diamonds her father had bestowed upon her, most of which had been gifts after he'd hurt her and all of which had been his means of showing the world just how immeasurable his wealth was. No, the diamonds weren't required, but something within her—that old instinct for survival—had told her to take them just before she fled.

Her dowry, she thought with a grim smile, for she very much doubted her father would grant her another penny after she'd flaunted and defied him in such a public, irrevocable manner. Earned by every bruise she'd ever worn, each slam of a fist into her body.

She had borne his cruelty. She had allowed herself to be paraded before New York high society first and then London, clothed in the most luxurious Parisian silks and satins. Adorned by enough riches to rival any queen. She had accepted his slaps, his shoves, his brutal beatings when she disappointed him or went against his strict edicts.

But she had finally reached her limit. Consigning herself to the life he'd chosen for her had been the last outrage. Bearing his rage one more time when her freedom hovered within her grasp had been an impossibility. Leaving hadn't been a difficult decision. She'd never known a true home or family in her life. Aunt Caroline cared only for the attention chaperoning Daisy brought her. Her father cared only for the wealth and connections she could give him with her marriage.

How ironic it was that a near stranger—now her husband—was the only person in her life who didn't want to use her for his own selfish gain. And there was no doubt about it, Trent had nothing to gain by marrying her. Even the lure of her immense dowry could not be enough since her father would revoke it and she'd made no secret of the fact.

Daisy read the gossip sheets, which often spewed thinly veiled venom toward her. For a duke to wed an American girl who had flouted convention and courted ruin—even if her motivation for so doing was justifiable—who had spent the last month in a desperate bid to kiss as many bachelors as possible in the hopes she could land a proposal, for the Duke of Trent to marry the notorious Daisy Vanreid, he would have to be motivated by only two things. His desire for her and his honor.

Her conscience pricked her then, an unwanted reminder that she had forced his hand, had encouraged him when no lady would have. It didn't matter that he'd been circling her like a shark for the last month. She needn't have lured him into the moonlit garden. Needn't have dared him.

*Take your turn.*

And his response? *I believe I will.*

The reminder sent a frisson of something foreign down her spine. Something delightful and frightening all at once. She clasped her hands tightly at her waist. At any moment, a knock would sound on the door adjoining the chamber in which she now stood to his.

She could not think of the handsome room surrounding her as hers. Not yet. Perhaps not ever. Everything had happened with far too much haste, and now Daisy couldn't help but feel herself mired in a dream from which she would soon wake.

After their simple vows at the registrar's, they had ridden in awkward silence to the duke's home. Now her home. He'd performed a perfunctory introduction to his domestics. They'd shared tea and some muffins Daisy had been too nervous to sample beyond a tiny nibble.

The duke had hardly touched his tea and muffin either. Instead, a flush had stained his throat, drawing her attention to his pronounced Adam's apple. The absurd thought had flitted through her mind to press a kiss there, to bury her nose in his neck and inhale deeply of the strong, masculine scent of him.

"We will need to…render this union," he had announced abruptly. "I'm sorry, for I know this has all transpired with unaccustomed rapidity. But given your father's treatment of you, and the fact that he will oppose an alliance between us, I cannot think of any other way."

His words had rattled about in her mind like pins in a seamstress's box. A noisy jangle until they found their home in her skin. *Render. Union.* He meant they would consummate. And of course they would. After all, they were married. She was his duchess. Everything had been properly done.

Except he remained a stranger to her. Likewise, he little knew her. Daisy had been wearing the mantle of accomplished flirt for so long in the absence of her father's tyranny that she'd neglected to contemplate the ultimate consequences of her actions.

Playing a role was one thing. Becoming a wife was another.

"Can we not delay, Your Grace?" she had asked.

His regard had been frank, verging on grim. "Do you wish to give your father any means of dissolving this union?"

"No," she had whispered, staring down at the perfect circle of fragrant tea awaiting her consumption. The porcelain of her teacup was thin and delicate, at least a century old, and embellished with his family coat of arms. A reminder that regardless of how much wealth her father had amassed with his tireless greed, the Trent duchy was the sort of ancient privilege the Vanreids could never aspire to reach.

The duke had replaced his cup in its saucer with nary a sound. "Then we would be best served to rule out any means as expediently as possible."

Such a cool, emotionless method of announcing to her that they would consummate their marriage, Daisy thought now as she continued to stare at her reflection. And just then, the much-awaited knock sounded at the door.

"Enter."

Her voice lacked its ordinary note of confidence. Gone too was the sensual, almost smoky quality that inevitably led to him thinking the wrong sort of thoughts. Thoughts that involved creamy skin, lush breasts, a prettily nipped waist, and full hips. Thoughts that wondered at the precise shade of her nipples. It had been dark, after all, in the gardens at the Darlington ball. The moonlight had bathed her in an ethereal silver, goddess-like glow.

Damn it to hell. What was he doing, waxing on about her in such a fashion? He wasn't meant to consummate their union. He was meant to keep up the pretense before his household so that there would be no question. So that her bastard of a father couldn't attempt to delegitimize the marriage.

So that their falsehood of a union would appear genuine. A love match rather than a means for him to gain access to Vanreid and any information Daisy possessed about his businesses.

Sebastian hesitated for a few breaths, willing his fierce arousal to abate, before opening the door to the chamber adjoining his. The duchess's chamber. Somehow, it was easier to think of it in those terms than to call it hers.

To call it Daisy's.

For given the circumstances, that seemed altogether wrong. And far too intimate for a woman who was a pawn, a woman whose presence and memory both would eventually be expunged from the home. From Sebastian himself.

How? Something—some inner devil—asked the question before he could dismiss it. How could he ever forget her? Jesus, he was very much afraid that he could not, no matter how he tried.

It took every bit of training he had to maintain his calm and purpose as he entered the room. She stood, completely dressed in the same, smart green gown she'd worn to wed him. Her golden tresses were still confined in an elaborate coil of braids. Her eyes widened as he crossed the chamber to her, and her fingers laced together at her wasp waist as though in prayer.

Two thoughts struck him in rapid succession.

Her beauty made him ache.

She was nervous.

He stopped with only a few paces between them, near enough that he caught a whiff of bergamot. Suspicion sliced into him, mingling with lust. She appeared as jittery as a wild hare, about to race away for a hiding place should he make one false step. Were her nerves those of a chaste bride who'd just married a stranger? Or was her conscience bringing her an unwanted pang of guilt at her deception? The possibilities were plain, an odd dichotomy. Either she knew what her father planned and she was a part of an intricate scheme to infiltrate the League, or she was an innocent being used by both sides.

But he mustn't think about the last, for his duty wasn't to question. It was to carry out the missions presented him. To keep home and hearth safe for all. It sure as hell wasn't sympathizing with the woman before him. A vibrant, lovely, luscious woman he couldn't trust. A woman whose father planned death and destruction.

"I neglected to assign you a lady's maid," he realized aloud. He'd never had a woman in his residence before, under his care. His mother had passed away when he'd been a lad of fifteen, and his father not long after that. He'd spent half his life as a bachelor. Likely, his oversight had been the cause of his housekeeper's request to meet with him. A request he'd denied in his need to see the task before him accomplished as expediently as possible.

A pretty pink flush crept over her creamy skin. "Mrs. Robbins saw to that, Your Grace. I was too caught up in my thoughts to ring for her. I apologize. Would you like me to ring for her now?"

Ah, Mrs. Robbins was a more than capable woman. He should've known she'd tie up all his loose ends as always. Not even his unannounced arrival with a new bride had thrown her.

"Sebastian," he corrected Miss Vanreid gently.

Not Miss Vanreid, he reminded himself. For she was his wife now, even if their union wasn't real or meant to last.

He couldn't very well think of her as his duchess, could he? Daisy, he decided. A flower that symbolized innocence. How ironic.

"Sebastian," she echoed, her color deepening. Her clasped fingers tightened until her knuckles protruded in stark relief. "Should I ring for the lady's maid to aid in my…preparation?"

Either she could rival the greatest actress to ever tread the boards, or she was every bit as innocent as her namesake. In matters of the flesh, if nothing else. "There's no need to ring for her now. I have no intention of consummating the marriage."

Her wide, sensual lips fell open in surprise, her golden brows snapping together. "You don't?"

"No." Every base, uncouth instinct in his body thundered for him to go against his better judgment. To take her in his arms and taste that pliable mouth once more. To find the hidden buttons on her bodice and slide them from their moorings. To strip away all her layers until every inch of her soft, sweet flesh was revealed to him. To finish the plundering he'd begun in the moonlight.

His cock went completely rigid at the images such unworthy thoughts produced. Good Christ. This was not part of the bloody plan. Why did she have to be so damnably tempting?

Her expressive face betrayed her confusion. "I'm afraid I don't understand."

"We need time to get to know each other," he elaborated. "The unusual haste with which our nuptials took place has robbed from us the chance to court."

"You wish to court me?" She stared at him. Her gown heightened the emerald hue of her eyes. The fingers that had been laced so tightly together now plucked at her skirts, adjusting the fall of silk over her crinoline dress shaper. Some of her signature bravado returned. Here was the woman who had dared him to take his turn. "Have you taken a woman to bed before, Your Grace?"

He nearly swallowed his tongue. Jesus. She thought him a virgin? He didn't bloody well kiss like a virgin. And just what sort of woman asked such an insulting, prying sort of question? His skin felt unaccountably hot. Dear Lord, he couldn't possibly be flushing, could he? A gentleman didn't blush. *He* didn't blush, goddamn it.

He cleared his throat. "Yes, though I daresay this isn't proper discourse for…husband and wife. In a marriage, it's best to leave the past where it belongs."

Referring to them as such, a married pair, made his entire body tighten. It sounded so intimate. In truth, it *was* intimate. A man couldn't be closer to any other woman. And yet, their marriage was a lie. Everything about it was false. He had to remind himself. She stood before him, his for the taking. And yet he could not have her.

Ought not to want her.

Wanted her with a fiery desperation anyway.

"Forgive me if I've insulted you," she said then. "Gentlemen do not frequently act with honor toward me. I've cultivated a reputation, you understand."

Her admission had him clenching his jaw so tightly that his teeth hurt. What man had dishonored her? He wanted to feed any bastard who had touched her his teeth. But of course, he hadn't the right. And it was ludicrous to entertain such a feeling of primeval possession. She wasn't his. Not truly. Nor would she ever be.

He tamped down the primitive emotions surging through him. "Daisy."

"I don't mean to suggest that my reputation is anything but a reputation," she prattled on. "I…I have kissed a few suitors, and I don't deny it. I do realize what you must think of me, but I was desperate to escape the marriage my father wanted for me. I would have done anything, even marrying a man I scarcely know."

Brilliant. She thought him a virgin, and she'd only agreed to marry him to escape being shackled to Breckly, her father's choice. How grim. His mind and body were at odds, scrambling for control. The thought of another man kissing her, the recollections of the times he'd spied her in the arms of her suitors, made him want to thrash them all. No one should kiss her but him, damn it.

Ridiculous thought. Foolish to even entertain such idiocy. He couldn't shake it. The notion clung to the deepest part of him, a part he'd buried beneath years of exhaustive work for the League. Years of never allowing anyone close. It wasn't just that she was his wife. It was that she was *his*. He knew it in his bones.

He took a step closer to her. Then another. Her warm scent enveloped him fully: bergamot, vanilla, ambergris, and *Daisy*. His fingers itched to take the pins from her hair, relieve it from its careful braids, to see it cascade in silky waves down her back. His mouth longed to feel the soft heat of hers beneath it.

This was dangerous territory indeed. He wasn't supposed to want her. Wasn't supposed to touch her or take her. But he was only a man, after all. And she had pushed him. Very far. Perhaps over the brink.

He caught her waist and hauled her against him. Her hands settled on his shoulders, her eyes even wider. So green. The green of moss in early spring. So beautiful.

"Are you suggesting you only agreed to this marriage to escape a match with Viscount Breckly?" he demanded.

"N-not entirely."

"Why did you marry me, Daisy?" He hungered for an answer. A truthful answer. Maybe he could rattle her. Rattle the both of them. He didn't like the idea of harboring an enemy of England beneath his roof.

Or of wanting said enemy beneath him.

She blinked. "You asked."

He couldn't control his body. Couldn't stop himself from cupping her lovely face, swiping his thumb over her lower lip. "The truth, Daisy."

Her mouth fell open, the hot wind of her breath scorching him. "I trapped you. There, I've said it. I apologize, Your Grace. I noticed you. You'd been watching me from the perimeter of every ball. And I was running out of time."

Her words took him aback. He hadn't expected an admission. Hadn't anticipated honesty. But his instincts told him that was what she offered him now. Sweet Jesus, the woman thought she'd tricked him into marrying her. Little wonder she seemed so ill at ease. "You trapped me?"

"In the garden. I had decided that I would scream, bring others down upon us. And I would have, even if my aunt had not come upon us. I wanted you to follow me. I wanted you to ruin me." Her voice broke on the last sentence, but her gaze remained unwavering. "I'm sorry. I felt as if I had no choice. Do you forgive me, Your Grace?"

Bloody, bloody hell. He stared at her, bemused. "Sebastian. If I'm your husband you must dispense with formality now. Call me Sebastian."

"Sebastian then." Her eyes shone.

Christ. Was she about to cry? This couldn't be an act. Could it?

His hands tightened on her waist. "I forgive you. Unless there is something else, something you aren't telling me?"

Her nostrils flared, her color paling. Her gaze darted away to a corner of the chamber before returning to his. "Of course there isn't anything else."

The tell was there. She was lying. A grim sensation settled over him, displacing the lust. Superseding everything except his duty. Duty to Crown and country. Duty to innocents. Duty to everyone but the lovely, deceptive woman currently in his grasp.

His goddamn wife.

He set her away from him. "Thank you for your candor, my dear." It took everything in him—all his years of training—to keep his tone even. Rage ricocheted through him, chasing away the last strains of ardor. Clearing his befuddled mind.

Not his. She was not his. Could not be.

He bent down then and extracted a knife from his boot, flipping it open. "We will make certain the servants believe our marriage has been consummated." He pressed the blade to the thumb that had touched her lip, a fitting punishment, cutting into his flesh. He didn't even feel the pain.

"You've cut yourself! What in heaven's name are you doing?"

He ignored her startled question and stalked to the bed, dragging back the bedclothes. Squeezing his wound, he smeared a liberal amount of blood onto the crisp white sheets to blunt any questions. Keeping up appearances was an essential component of his mission. Double agents could be anywhere, from the lowliest scullery maid to the butler, though he trusted Giles implicitly.

"Sealing our fates," he said at last, his tone harsh, even to his own ears. She had followed him and he caught yet another hint of her scent. Damn if it didn't skirt his defenses, threaten to lure him back into the haze of lust. "No one, not the domestics, not your father, not anyone will question the veracity of our union after this."

"Your Grace?"

He turned away from the brilliant streaks of scarlet marring the sheets and flicked a gaze over her. A scant two steps separated them now, and the animal in him wanted to lash out, to haul her against him and ravage her mouth. To bend her over the bed and raise her skirts.

He hissed out a breath, willing his hunger to calm. "Sebastian," he reminded.

"Sebastian, then." She lowered her gaze, emanating a sudden and uncharacteristic shyness. "I fear there's one problem with your plan."

His *plan*. He raised a brow, his gut clenching. He didn't like her choice of phrase, and suspicion warred with the desire that had plagued him ever since he'd first laid eyes on her. "Oh?"

Her eyes met his, those cheeks flushing an even deeper shade of red. "I'm still clothed."

# chapter seven

*P*ERHAPS SHE COULD HAVE WORDED THAT BETTER, Daisy reflected as the duke gawped at her with searing intensity. Her skin felt unaccountably warm. Her entire body, in fact, felt feverish, a state that could be owed in part to her blunt observation and in part to her reaction to him.

He was beautiful, her husband.

*Sebastian*, he had insisted, though it still seemed odd to think of him in intimate terms. To be standing in such proximity to him that his scent, hints of pine and musk, washed over her. To be alone with him in a bedchamber— her bedchamber.

Odd and somehow intoxicating. Her every sense was heightened, her body awash with anticipation. She could feel his stare like a caress, from her hardened nipples to the ache between her thighs. She wanted him, but he didn't want her. His blood sullying the sheets, the cut on his thumb, the hard set of his jaw, all bespoke antipathy. And she couldn't blame him. He was a man whose hand had been forced, who'd been saddled with a sudden, unwanted burden.

Except that he wasn't staring at her now with the same rigid expression he'd worn since crossing the threshold. No, indeed. He was looking at her rather in the same fashion she imagined a mountain lion appeared just before clamping its jaws around its prey.

He was looking at her like he wanted to consume her.

"You want me to help you disrobe?" he asked, his voice a low, gruff rumble that sent a thrill skittering through her.

"Yes," she blurted. Dear Lord, she was only making things worse. "That is, of course I will require assistance. If you want the servants to believe we've…consummated the marriage, then you cannot propose to leave me standing alone in my chamber, with my *toilette* intact. I'm afraid I can't undress myself, given the construction of this gown. Therefore, it stands to reason that you'll need to aid me."

More than anything else, she didn't wish to give her father any reason to attempt to prove the marriage invalid. She hardly knew what he'd do when he realized that she'd not only ruined herself but disobeyed him, dashing any chances for his much-desired connection with Lord Breckly. No one defied her father without suffering deeply for their daring.

The memory of the last time she'd done so cut through her with the precision of a blade and every bit as much pain before she chased it from her mind. She wouldn't think of Padraig now or ever again if she could help it. He was her past, and the man standing before her was her future. They couldn't have been more different.

She couldn't afford to allow one questioning maidservant who noticed Daisy was still perfectly, impeccably dressed—bloodied sheets or no—to open the door for her father. She would not return to live beneath his roof. Nor would she suffer one more of his rages.

"Very well." Sebastian closed the distance between them in two long strides. "I assume this bloody frock has buttons on it somewhere?"

Her breath caught as his fingers traced the front panel of her bodice, beginning just beneath her breasts and then down over her ribs. Through her stiff corset and layers of undergarments, she could still feel the heat of him. She watched his large, capable hands tracing downward, over her waist. The buttons were hidden on her back, and some wicked part of her longed to hold her tongue, to make him continue his fruitless search just for the delicious slide of his fingers over her body.

"On the back." Her gaze traveled from his hands to his mouth. What would it be like to have those sensual lips angling over hers again, this time with no one to interrupt and no encumbrances?

He seized her waist and spun her about so abruptly that she lost her balance and fell into him. A distinct ridge prodded the small of her back, and she fought and lost the urge to rub herself against him like a cat. His fingers bit into her waist, pulling her back and anchoring her to him completely. A dark, carnal sound tore from him. His mouth was on her in the next breath, kissing the same sensitive skin behind her ear that he had brought to life that night in the moonlight.

His lips grazed the shell of her ear, then skimmed lower, trailing a series of decadent kisses down her throat. When he stopped to lick and nibble there, a pang of something new started from her core and radiated throughout her entire body. The heady, magic spell that had descended on her at the Darlington ball returned.

She yearned for something she didn't entirely comprehend. All she knew was that she ached with a need that only he could slake. Sebastian. Her husband. Self-preservation was the last thing on her mind as she writhed against his powerful frame, wanting more of his mouth, more of his kisses, more of his touch.

Daisy felt pins being plucked from her hair, the heaviness of her braids loosening and opening. One of his hands had migrated from her waist, and was buried in her half-unbound locks, fisting in it, angling her head back so that he could feast on her neck.

"Christ, you smell so bloody good," he growled against her throat.

So did he, and she would have told him as much if she could have managed to utter a single, coherent word. But he had robbed her of the ability to conduct intelligent conversation. To think of anything that wasn't him, his wicked lips, his knowing touch.

She inhaled deeply, her fingers reaching back to sink into his dark hair. Perhaps they didn't need pretense. Some wild impulse within her imagined him stripping her gown away, covering her body with his on the bed. Consummating their union. It was such a tepid phrase, a bloodless way of describing the intense pleasure he gave her. What would it be like to give herself to him? To become his wife in deed as well as name? Her pulse pounded.

But just as curiosity mingled with desire, he tore his mouth from her neck and set her away from him. "Jesus," he muttered, sounding as shaken as she felt. His fingers skated over her spine. "Where are the goddamn buttons, Daisy?"

The spell was broken. Reality returned to her. It was daylight. The rumbling of conveyances on the street below reached her ears. What had she been thinking to allow herself to get so carried away? He was a stranger to her, even if he was her husband, and he clearly resented her.

Of course, how could she find fault with him after confessing the way she'd schemed against him? And then, even a breath later, when he'd asked her if there was anything else she needed to unburden, she had misled him again. Had lied to him. Part of her had wanted to tell him about Bridget, but another part reminded her she didn't know what sort of man she'd married. She would like to believe he would never hurt her, but she had suffered many disappointments in her life, and the cynic in her wouldn't allow for blind hope or trust.

"The buttons, Daisy." His voice cracked like a whip through her jumbled thoughts.

With trembling hands, she reached behind her to find the line of buttons cleverly disguised beneath a velvet placket. "Here."

His fingers brushed against hers for a brief moment, and the contact was like a spark of electricity. Hastily, she snatched her hands away to pluck some more of the pins from her coiffure. Cool air kissed her bare shoulders above her chemise and corset as he peeled open the back of her gown.

"There now." He pulled her sleeves down, her bodice going along with it. "I'll loosen your corset. I trust you can manage the rest?"

His tone was cool once more. Almost impersonal.

It was as if he had two opposite parts of himself at war. He was frigid one moment and scorching the next. A cold, imperious man she couldn't read at one turn and a sensual, wicked lover the next. Which one was he?

She swallowed, confusion warring with the lingering remnants of desire. He must be angry with her for her deception despite his claim to the contrary. "I can manage the rest, Your Grace. It was merely the laces and the buttons that I couldn't reach. Thank you for your help."

"Sebastian." The laces of her corset went slack as he undid the solid knot Abigail had tied earlier and plucked at the crisscrossed strings to loosen them. "Wait another twenty minutes or so before ringing for your lady's maid."

"Yes, Your—Sebastian." She swallowed, holding her bodice to her chest as he swept past her, stalking in the direction of his chamber.

"I'll be leaving shortly. Settle yourself however you like," he called over his shoulder, not even bothering to glance her way.

His callous treatment after such an intimate moment stung more than it should. It wasn't as if she loved him. Goodness, it wasn't as if she even knew him. But somehow,

78

none of that mattered as she watched him walk away. He wanted her to call him by his Christian name, but he didn't want to consummate their marriage, and he couldn't wait to remove himself from her presence.

"Will you be home for dinner?" she called after him.

He hesitated for a moment just before crossing back into his chamber. "It's doubtful. Should your family call or cause any undue trouble for you, inform Giles to have word sent to me at once. He'll know where to find me."

And then the door snapped closed behind him, leaving her standing alone in her new chamber, half-naked and more adrift than she'd ever been in her life.

He was going mad.

He'd trained to withstand water torture, to suffer broken bones, plucked fingernails, mind tricks, and beatings. He'd learned the art of defending himself with his fists and dexterity, with an expert crack of a pistol or the deft flick of his wrist and a sharp blade. He'd spent nights in brutal cold, days in the company of the most sadistic men and scurrilous criminals in the land. Had survived an assassin and a deadly inferno.

He damn well ought to be able to resist one woman. Even if she was a beautiful goddess of a woman who smelled delicious, whose soft skin made him want to taste her everywhere, whose mere presence in a room made him want to take her so hard and deep he didn't know where he ended and she began.

"Fuck," he muttered, glaring at the half-empty glass of whisky in his hands before downing the remainder of the contents in one fiery gulp. The burn distracted him but for a second, and the liquor did nothing to soothe his jagged nerves.

"Jesus, Sebastian." Griffin, the Duke of Strathmore and one of Sebastian's oldest and best friends in the League, pinned him with a pitying look. They were seated in Strathmore's billiard room, sipping whisky. "I can't believe you agreed to marry the chit."

That made two of them.

Sebastian slapped his glass down on the carved mahogany table between their chairs and took up the decanter to refill it with another hearty dose of amber-colored liquid. "I took an oath. I do what's asked of me."

Regardless of how preposterous it was. Regardless of how much he loathed being the sacrificial lamb. And regardless of how doing what he'd been asked had felt wrong for the first time today.

His oath and his sense of honor were currently at odds, wreaking havoc upon his conscience. Everything within him had wanted to claim Daisy Vanreid as his earlier that afternoon. Even though she was a woman he couldn't trust. Even though doing so would be akin to using her, manipulating a woman he'd soon no longer even be married to. If she was innocent, he'd never forgive himself. But if she was guilty, there would be hell to pay. None of it—not the way he felt or his reaction to her—made sense. Indeed, nothing about this entire mission did, and it sure as hell didn't help that Carlisle was keeping him largely in the dark.

Griffin took a drag of his cigarette and exhaled slowly. "I don't know if I could do the same. The thought of marrying anyone—let alone a saucy American wench suspected of treason—is enough to make me ill."

*Treason.*

Hearing the word in correlation with Daisy was like a dagger's honed blade into his gut. "I don't think she knows anything Carlisle suspects her of knowing."

His friend stared at him, his look speculative. Almost suspicious. "You don't think so? Did you bloody well read the report he sent to the League?"

Of course he had. The letter had arrived transcribed in careful code that to the outside observer would have seemed unassuming as a maiden aunt's tepid scrawl. But in truth, it had contained privileged information. The same information about Daisy that Carlisle had fed him previously. Connections to an Irish shop girl suspected of working with the dynamitards, a broken betrothal to a Fenian leader. Nothing new, and nothing substantial.

His friend's probing gaze made him take another swig of spirits. "I read it."

He'd read it twice and then burned it, just as he did with all League correspondence.

"And?" Griffin raised a brow, raising his cigarette back to his mouth for another puff.

Sebastian fought the absurd urge to take one of his friend's cigarettes from the paper sleeve on the table and smoke it himself. Perhaps it would calm him, but ever since the fire, he hadn't been able to countenance bringing any sort of smoke into his lungs. It made him cagey, took him back to the day he'd almost died.

He settled for whisky instead. "And it's flimsy evidence at best, Griff. I'm not saying I trust Daisy, but neither do I believe it's in her nature to plot to kill innocent civilians."

No, he realized as he spoke the words aloud. Nothing in his dealings with her had shown she possessed the capacity for cruelty, or the ability to hurt others without compunction that he'd witnessed in so many other foes over the years. She was an odd woman, sometimes bold and blazing with daring and passion, other times haunted by the brutalities she claimed to have received from her father. He longed to believe her innocent, to accept everything she'd told him as truth, and the knowledge was an unwanted revelation to him.

For there was something she was keeping from him. She had lied to him earlier, boldly and without compunction. That small hesitation had given her away.

"Have you bedded her?" His friend asked baldly into the silence that had descended upon them.

The need to defend her honor rose within him. He was an oxymoron if one ever lived. "No," he snapped. "Not that it is any of your concern."

"You want to bed her," Griffin concluded.

Correctly, damn his hide.

"No," he lied. "I don't bed pawns. I never have."

The last bit was truth, at least.

"She's a beauty." Griffin ground the nub of his cigarette into a silver ashtray. "Had half the men of the *ton* sniffing her skirts. Christ, you must have heard the rumors about her. She couldn't be an innocent maid by this juncture. No one would blame you for wanting a taste yourself."

Of course he'd heard the rumors. Had seen with his own two eyes the way she led men on a merry dance, lured them in with her wiles. Kissed them. But something uncoiled within him then, some burning need to defend her, a searing outrage on her behalf. The Daisy Vanreid who had asked him if he had ever hit a woman had been desperate. And she didn't deserve the scorn of any man. He believed her. Against all reason and ration, he believed her.

"You go too far," he warned his friend. "The lady is my wife."

"Not truly." Griffin's expression turned from scornful to incredulous as he scoured Sebastian's countenance. "Bast. You're defending her like a man who's smitten. Are you mad?"

How ironic that his friend had reached the selfsame conclusion as he. What was it about Daisy that undid him? His mouth curled into a grim, mirthless smile. "Likely."

"Bed her then." Griffin took a long pull of whisky. "Get her out of your blood. But you'd best sleep with a dagger under your bloody pillow."

Sebastian finished the dregs of his second glass. By now, the stuff had finally begun to do its work, filling his veins with a calming languor. Drinking himself into a stupor seemed like a good course of action for the evening of his wedding day. Perhaps it would keep him from making any greater mistakes than those he'd already committed. "Griff?"

Griffin stared into the fire in the grate, seemingly mesmerized by the dancing flames. "Aye?" he grunted without looking up.

"Go to hell," he said without heat.

His friend's dark eyes met his, as he raised his glass for a mocking salute. "Already there, old chap."

Though Griffin spoke the words casually, Sebastian knew his friend suffered from demons wrought by what he'd seen and done, just as they all had. Griffin had never been the same after returning from Paris. He had been a young, optimistic operative caught up in the siege and taken hostage by the French. When Sebastian and another spy had finally located and freed him, Griffin had resembled nothing so much as a beaten, emaciated corpse.

In the Special League, there was always a price to pay, and each member had paid their fair shares in pounds of flesh.

The heaviness of the moment settled into his bones. He searched for something flippant to say, some manner of distraction for them both. "Hell has some damn good whisky."

Griffin grinned and downed the rest of his glass. "That is does. Care for a game of billiards?"

Sebastian finished his whisky as well. Had it been his second or his third? The fourth? Who gave a damn. He was getting soused tonight. It was the only panacea he had left. "Prepare to lose, my friend."

## chapter eight

*W*ELL. THIS GAVE NEW MEANING to the tired old phrase *drunk as a lord*. Though perhaps in this instance, it would be more apt to say *drunk as a duke*.

Daisy stared at her bleary-eyed husband, who had just appeared as she was *en route* to her lonely breakfast. He wore the same trousers, coat, and waistcoat he'd left in the day before. He was rumpled, his hair disheveled, dark half-moons marring the flesh beneath his eyes. The undeniable scent of spirits perfumed the air.

"It seems I've arrived just in time," he announced as though he hadn't a care in the world. "Giles tells me you're about to break your fast."

She'd far prefer to break a vase. Over his arrogant noggin.

Her mouth tightened as she surveyed him further. How dare he, the cad? Where had he been? What had he been doing aside from plundering London's whisky cache? Yesterday, she'd thought he resented having to marry her with such haste. She'd felt guilty at her part in the entire affair. Had known a keening despair at his taciturn demeanor. When he had left her alone, she had wanted very much for him to stay.

But he had attempted to brush her off with some feigned sense of honor and disappeared. What had he said? *We need time to get to know each other*. Ah yes, and her favorite: *the unusual haste with which our nuptials took place has robbed from us the chance to court*.

What nonsense. The only thing he'd been courting was a thorough sousing. How foolish of her to have known a moment of remorse for using him to escape her father's clutches. The man before her—somehow still handsome even in his disgraceful state—didn't deserve a drop of pity. Was he a drunkard, or had he found the prospect of wedding her so loathsome that he'd needed to find solace in a bottle? She had asked if he had ever hit a woman, but perhaps there was a more salient question she ought to have posed.

He stalked toward her when she maintained a frigid silence. "Haven't you anything to say to me, wife?"

There, before the footmen waiting to dance attendance on a formal breakfast, she raked the duke's person with undisguised disdain. "You're sozzled."

His brows crashed together. "And you're impertinent. I assure you, I'm nothing of the sort."

"You're wearing yesterday's attire." She was so vexed with him that she didn't care that it wasn't done to speak her mind, and that it was decidedly *de trop* to do so in front of servants.

He made a show of inspecting his person before meeting her gaze once more with an indolence she found particularly infuriating. "Since I'm wearing it now, I daresay it's today's attire."

A closer look at his wrinkled coat and trousers suggested that he'd slept in them. She wasn't sure why such an observation would bring her relief. If he'd spent the evening in the arms of a mistress, it was no concern of hers. Theirs wasn't a love match. He didn't even seem to like her. And for her part, she had only chosen him because she was desperate.

And because she enjoyed his kisses.

Daisy struck that aberrant thought from her mind.

The compulsion to remove herself from his presence was strong. How could she be affected by her inconvenient attraction to him when he had spent the entirety of their wedding night drinking himself to oblivion and committing Lord knew what manner of sins?

That was it. She needed to escape. "If you will excuse me, Your Grace, I fear I've lost my appetite. I'll be retiring to my chamber for the remainder of the day."

"No." His expression was mulish.

The devil. She skewered him with a glare. "Pardon me, Your Grace?"

"I do believe you heard me, *Your Grace*," he drawled.

The obvious sign of the manner in which he'd been frittering away the evening—and perhaps early morning as well—stiffened her spine. For a moment, she thought of the woman she'd been before, in New York, under her father's watchful eye and stern edicts. That Daisy would never dare to gainsay any man. Not her father. Not her husband.

But her time in England had changed her. The Daisy she had become wouldn't be insulted by the man she'd married. A man who seemed to delight in leaving her at sixes and sevens, one moment smoldering, the next ice, and the next a reprobate.

She spun on her heel, presenting him with her back and a silent impression of what she thought of his boorish behavior. Daisy Vanreid—strike that—Daisy Trent, as she was to call herself now, would not meekly obey an order. From anyone. Ever again.

At that precise moment, Giles, who had been unflappable from the instant she'd first met him the day before, hurried into their midst at a clipped pace, his expression uncharacteristically pained.

"Your Graces, forgive me, but I'm afraid we've a guest who refuses to leave without an audience," the butler said.

"We aren't at home," dismissed the duke without a second thought.

How accustomed he was, she thought, to his life of aristocratic privilege. A duke commanded a certain respect from everyone. From his fellow peers, from his servants. It seemed Daisy was the only one who didn't hold her husband in awe.

"The gentleman in question claims to be Her Grace's father," Giles informed in hushed tones, his gaze darting from Daisy to the duke.

How odd this entire tableau must appear, she thought wryly as a sick feeling of foreboding unfurled within her. She tensed in the same way she always had before a reckoning with her father. This time, he would not be able to strike her.

Would he?

She swallowed, and everything around her seemed to slow to a torpid pace. She was hyperaware of every sound, from the uncharacteristic shuffling of a footman's feet to the footsteps approaching down the hall. The angry, heavy footfalls of her father.

Daisy would recognize them anywhere.

He stalked around the corner, his gaze lighting on her, fury blazing from his every pore. "You disgraceful harlot!" he shouted.

The world became small all of a sudden. Everything revolved around the white-haired man tearing toward her like a wild bull. A black circle clouded her vision. Dizziness assailed her. A rushing sounded in her ears. She'd thought she'd prepared herself for seeing him again. But she had not. Her reaction was as terrifying and helpless as ever.

"Father," she whispered. He came toward her, faster than she would have expected, while she stood rooted to the floor, gasping in air, panic making her heart pound and her mouth go dry. She couldn't move. Couldn't defend herself. He raised his fist. And she closed her eyes, bracing for the inevitable blow.

Sebastian remained rather foggy from his nocturnal drinking session with Griffin. Not to mention that his head was pounding. But he could still throw a goddamn punch like the warrior he was. Boxing sessions kept him at peak performance. So when he saw Daisy's bastard of a father storming toward her with the clear intent of striking her, his instincts went into action.

He threw himself in front of her, unadulterated rage charging through him as he caught Vanreid's fist in a manacle-like grip midair. His other hand caught the son-of-a-bitch's necktie and yanked, closing off his air supply. Carlisle's careful instructions regarding the man vanished from Sebastian's mind, dispelled by a combination of drink and raw emotion.

It didn't matter that he risked his cover and reputation both. Nor did he give a damn that he wasn't meant to bring undue attention to himself since doing so could endanger their mission. All that did matter was the need to protect Daisy, fierce and swift and all-consuming.

"You will never again," he bit out, stark fury sharpening everything into focus, "raise a hand against my wife. Do you understand me, Vanreid?"

The man was tall, strapping as an ox, but he was no match for Sebastian's superior strength. His face went red as he choked for air and struggled to unsuccessfully remove Sebastian's hand from his necktie. He wondered how a delicate, graceful beauty like Daisy had come from such a beast.

"Never again," he repeated, watching with grim satisfaction as his opponent continued to fight for breath. For a moment, some wild fiend deep within him imagined tightening his hold and not relenting until the swine succumbed. There was a quicker, cleaner manner of choking a man, however, one that required far less effort. And in general, it was a poor plan to commit murder before one's servants.

He released Vanreid at last, stepping back and drawing Daisy into a protective embrace at his side. They faced her father as a unified front, and though nothing was as it seemed, Sebastian knew that he'd do anything to keep her from ever returning to this brute's dubious clutches.

Vanreid gasped for breath, his eyes burning them both like hot coals. "You've married her?"

Belatedly, it occurred to Sebastian that—like committing murder—engaging in sensitive dialogue was not well done before servants. Their current audience consisted of a wide-eyed chambermaid, two footmen, and Giles. Perhaps consuming a vast quantity of spirits the night before had been ill-advised after all. His head began pounding, and everything else had vanished in the face of Vanreid's ugly intrusion.

He cleared his throat and cast a meaningful glance toward his domestics. "Perhaps we should adjourn to a more private chamber, Mr. Vanreid."

A stern look from Giles was all it required for the servants to disperse with quiet but respectful haste. Sebastian, Vanreid, and Daisy stood alone in the eerie quiet, each reeling in a different fashion, he suspected, from the events of the day.

Vanreid's color had returned to normal, but he was still quite obviously livid. "I would prefer to have an audience with my daughter alone."

Sebastian cast a glance at Daisy, who had been markedly silent during the entire exchange. She was wide-eyed and wan. Being in the presence of her sire had taken the wind from her sails. The hand he had placed on the small of her back absorbed a tremble.

"There will be no audience with my wife," he snapped. No chance for the blighter to punish Daisy. No chance for him to harm her ever again. "You will speak before me or no one."

Vanreid's lip curled into a sneer. "Who do you think you are? I could have you arrested for your conduct! Pawing at her in a public place, abducting her for a secret wedding. Good God, I haven't even any proof this marriage is valid."

Sebastian took a menacing step forward, bringing Daisy with him. The desire to plant his fist directly into Vanreid's nose was overwhelmingly strong. "Our marriage is legal, binding, and consummated. You will speak to my wife before me or you will not speak to her at all. Furthermore, you will address her with courtesy. You will give her the respect she is due as the Duchess of Trent. If you dare to say a word against her, I'll have you removed at once."

Daisy's hand, resting in the crook of his elbow for support, tightened on him then in unspoken gratitude. But he didn't want her gratitude. He wanted her freedom. Their marriage was complex, their circumstances even more so. Of one thing, however, he was certain, and it was that he never again wanted to see Daisy Vanreid cower to filth like her father.

"Leave now, Father," Daisy said, finally using her voice and reclaiming the power that had so long been denied her. "I don't wish to speak to you."

Vanreid had eyes only for his daughter, and Sebastian didn't like what he read within the sinister depths. "You betrayed me. I paid handsomely to garner you a husband, and you disgraced yourself, acting the trollop. I always knew you had your mother's sinful nature."

Daisy blanched, her fingers biting into Sebastian's flesh. "You paid to have me do your bidding, to marry me off to a decrepit scoundrel whose cruelty matches your own. I did what I needed to in order to secure my freedom from such an appalling union. As for my mother, you aren't worthy of speaking her name. Leave now, and never return."

"You will depart of your own accord," he ground out when the bastard hesitated, looking as if he wished to spew more acidic rage, "or be forcibly removed, Vanreid. The choice is yours."

Vanreid's dark eyes glinted the obsidian of the harshest, darkest night as he stared down first Daisy and then Sebastian. "I will go. But mark my words. This shall be your greatest regret."

Sebastian had faced far more worthy opponents than a ruddy-faced tyrant with a penchant for abusing his innocent daughter. But even so, something about Vanreid's countenance chilled his blood.

Keeping his expression carefully rigid, he called out for Giles, who had strayed far enough for propriety but not too far. The butler appeared, two burly footmen at the ready.

"Your Grace?"

"See Mr. Vanreid to the door, if you please," Sebastian instructed Giles, careful to keep his tone languid. His training had been stamped into his marrow. *Show no weakness. Bend to no one. Offer no mercy.* "I shouldn't think he'll be returning."

"You will regret this," Vanreid hissed, his tone as dark as his expression. Those dark, devil's eyes of his focused on Daisy alone. "Mark my words. One day, you'll regret this, but by then it will be far, far too late to save yourself."

Daisy swayed into Sebastian, and he steadied her with ease. It was a natural gesture, instinctive reaction, being her support. Something deep inside him wanted to tear out Vanreid's throat. To beat him to a bloody pulp for daring to harm the woman at his side. For daring to attempt to control her and foist her lush, vibrant beauty and mind off on an old lecher for his own benefit.

"Go to hell," Sebastian growled as the footmen—who were in truth far more than mere footmen—crowded Vanreid, prodding him to begin his retreat.

"You'll join me there one day, Trent," Vanreid swore before turning on his heel and stalking away.

Daisy's father disappeared from view in the great hall. So too the footmen and the ever-vigilant Giles. The moment he was gone, Daisy tore herself from Sebastian. He felt the abrupt departure as if some part of himself had been suddenly removed.

"He is gone now," he said to his wife, unnecessarily. And because the silence between them was awkward and because he was acutely aware that he'd spent their wedding night tippling whisky and because he knew she was displeased with him.

It didn't matter that he didn't know who Daisy Vanreid truly was. That she was a cipher to him. A woman he was warned against, and yet ordered to keep close. A woman who could be capable of incredible deceit and depravity if the information he'd received about her was to be believed. A woman he was drawn to more than anyone else before her, against all good judgment and certainly against all reason.

She faced him, as august as the queen. "You never returned last night."

He clasped his wrists behind his back, unapologetic because he could not afford to be. Feeling like a cad anyway. "No."

"You smell of spirits," she accused. "Tell me, Your Grace. I would hope that our marriage could at least begin in honesty. Do you have a mistress? Is that where you spent the night?"

He stared at her, not knowing what to say. Ladies weren't meant to be so forthright. His father had kept his position in the Special League from his mother for the entirety of their union. He had also kept a mistress for fifteen years. His mother had never been aware of either fact.

But Sebastian had. His mother had been a good woman, kindhearted and gentle. She'd deserved far more than his father's callous deception. Sebastian had thought it then, and he thought it now. The only difference was that now he understood what it was like to bear the onerous burden of membership in the League.

It fostered deception. It took a man's life from his own hands.

"I do not," he answered Daisy truthfully. *Not that it is any of your concern.* "This is not the sort of dialogue we ought to have here."

Not with the servants about. Not when he was still half in his cups, head still pounding like the devil's blacksmith himself was using his cranium as an anvil. Better yet, it was a conversation they ought never to have, for what could he say?

How was he to explain himself to her when he could not? When he could not even trust her? When she was his bloody wife, and there was nothing he wanted more than to strip her from her layers and lose himself inside her softness, but he could not touch her? Yesterday had been a mistake. He had no right to touch her, to kiss her, to long for more. Today was a mistake. Standing here, now, in the same space as her, breathing in her exotic scent, was a grievous error.

Misery slithered through him. He wasn't meant to feel anything for her. She was a means to an end. So why the hell did her stricken, pale face rattle him? Why did seeing her so vulnerable make him want to take her into his arms?

"Where should we have such a dialogue, Your Grace?" she asked quietly into the silence that had fallen between them. "Because I wish very much to know where I stand."

An odd, tight sensation began in his chest and settled low in his gut.

*Guilt.*

Surely not. He was trained to never empathize. His capacity for emotion was tainted by years of living a secret life, of never allowing anyone to breach his defenses.

He swallowed, unable to look away from her. Daisy. The woman he'd married. The woman Carlisle wanted to throw into prison. Jesus, as if she hadn't already suffered enough. It was guilt, alright. He felt lower than a goddamn worm.

He was lying to her. Manipulating her. Using her.

She could be innocent. Or she could be guilty as sin.

"Come to my study in two hours' time," he bit out, tamping his conscience firmly back down to the furthest, unreachable depths of himself. Precisely where it belonged.

## chapter nine

AISY WOULD HAVE SWORN SHE FACED a different man entirely as she entered the duke's study.

He stood at her arrival, steeped in his customary arrogance once more. Not a wrinkle was to be found on his jacket, not a dark hair on his head out of place. He looked handsome and refreshed. For a moment, it was difficult to recall her earlier ire at being abandoned on their wedding night in favor of a bottle of whisky.

Difficult but not impossible.

"Daisy," he greeted, his tone formal rather than warm. "Do sit, my dear."

She didn't know which version of the man she'd married to expect. He was at times forbidding, at times unbearably sensual, others remote and aloof. This morning, he had arrived the dissolute wastrel and metamorphosed into her champion before once again closing himself off to her. Who would he be now?

Arranging her skirts with care, she seated herself opposite his imposing desk. "Have you breakfasted?" she asked, instantly wishing she could call the words back as soon as they left her lips.

She'd had her breakfast alone, and she'd thought to send him a tray but had not at the last moment, deeming him unworthy of such an act of consideration. Guilt had been a gradually growing knot in her belly ever since, even if he didn't deserve it. Such an odd thing, to have another person to fret over. To be living in a strange house with a strange man, with servants whose names she couldn't all yet remember, and yet to *belong*.

An odd expression flashed across his face, as though she'd startled him but also displeased him at the same time. "I took a tray in my chamber. Thank you for your concern."

She swallowed, laced her fingers together in her lap, and tried not to appear as awkward as she felt. "It is my duty as your wife to look after you, Your Grace."

His jaw went rigid. "No it is not. I shall look after myself just as I always have."

He was angry with her, but she didn't know why. Wouldn't most men expect a wife to make certain they were well pleased and well fed? In her father's household, keeping him content had been her chief concern. Over time, she'd found it helped to assuage his tempers. Little things, like making certain each meal contained only his favorites, served at the right temperature, the right time of day.

But this man was not her father. Nor, she hoped, was he anything like him. Naturally, that would remain to be seen. He had promised never to harm her, but she still knew so little of him. And what she did know left her with nothing but questions and consternation.

Then again, perhaps her revelation that she'd sought to entrap him was the source of his disquiet. It was a sin she owned fully, for she alone had led him into the moonlight. He was equally as responsible for what had occurred next, but the initial lure had been her doing.

She pressed her lips together, considering her words with care. "It is not my intention to displease you."

As much as he had hurt her, she was willing to forgive. After all, she had manipulated him. Having to wed in such an abrupt manner could not be easy for anyone. Lord knew it had not been for Daisy, though she found her union to Trent infinitely more palatable than a forced marriage with Breckly.

His vexing actions aside, she wanted them to have a fresh start. For their unorthodox marriage to have a chance to flourish rather than to founder. While she'd spent most of her life motherless, she longed for children of her own one day. The notion filled her heart with a bursting, airy sort of joy as she stared at the forbidding stranger before her.

Her children would be his, as odd as it seemed, and she would not bring children into an unhappy union. She had been the product of one, and she didn't wish to visit the same sin upon an innocent. At the very least, she felt certain they could achieve mutual respect for each other, if the duke was but willing.

He frowned then, but the severity of it only seemed to intensify his looks rather than detract from them. "You do not displease me, Daisy."

And yet his every reaction to her suggested the complete opposite. "Clearly I have or else you wouldn't have left me on our wedding day only to return the next morning smelling of whisky, wearing the same clothes you departed in."

There. She'd said it. And a humiliating tear was poised at the corner of her eye, drat it all. She would not allow it to fall. Would not. When he didn't immediately speak, she launched into another speech, fearing the silence and what it would do to her. "I understand you resent me for having trapped you. It wasn't fair of me to place my own wellbeing and desires before yours. Fear of my father is not sufficient excuse. If I could redo what I've done, I would, knowing how wrong it was. But I would very much like our marriage to be a cordial one...pleasant, even. I think perhaps we might be friends, if you'll but grant me your forgiveness and a second chance. Do you think you can, Your Grace?"

"Sebastian." He stood so abruptly that his chair flew back, nearly toppling over.

She should have stood as well, but something about the man and the moment kept her rooted to her chair, incapable of motion.

"Sebastian," she repeated hesitantly as he circled the desk and approached her.

He was inscrutable yet determined. He slid between her skirts and the front of his desk, bracing his big hands on the polished arms of the chair and lowering his head to meet her gaze. "Daisy."

His eyes were twin pools of hot, blue fire, burning into her where she sat. "Yes?"

"You didn't entrap me."

"Of course I did," she argued. "It's the reason you've been so cold. The reason why you don't want to consummate our marriage. I understand. Truly, I do. What I've done is despicable. I would not want me either."

"I want you." His tone had softened. He leaned down, clasping her hands with his and pulling her to her feet. One tug and she fell against him. "I followed you. I kissed you. I dishonored you. I married you. My behavior last night was...regrettable. I'm sorry for leaving you here alone to wonder. All I can say is that my mind has been whirling ever since I first laid eyes on you."

She liked the feeling of his body burning into hers. And she wanted to believe him, even if a troubling undercurrent she couldn't quite identify tinged his words. His gaze devoured her with a hunger that threatened to light an answering fire within her. How she wished she could know his heart. Hear the inner workings of his capable mind. Was he being honest with her now? Or was he, as she suspected, withholding some part of himself?

"You're only seeking to assuage my guilt," she dismissed, trying to disentangle her hands from his grasp. "You mustn't, Sebastian. What I did was unconscionable. I can only think it was a moment of weakness, fearing my father's imminent return, which led me to act as I did."

He wouldn't allow it, holding firm, the connection of his bare skin on hers sparking the ever-present need within her into a full, engulfing flame. "You will cease, my dear. An apology is not what I require at this moment."

She shouldn't dare to ask what it was he required. Everything about his demeanor had changed. He fairly smoldered. But he was her husband now, some wickedness inside her reminded. He was hers. She could dare as she pleased.

Daisy rocked to her tiptoes, bringing her mouth nearly flush with his. His breath was hot, ghosting across lips that tingled with anticipation. Lips that longed to be claimed. "What do you require, Your Grace?"

A wolfish smile pulled at his sensual mouth. "Sebastian. What do you require, *Sebastian?*"

"Sebastian," she relented. And then her mind returned to her, piercing the rose-colored haze wrought by her foolish need. He had abandoned her last night, only to return this morning. Inebriated. "If you want me as much as you claim, and if you aren't angry with me for forcing your hand, then nothing makes sense. Why did you leave me last night, *Sebastian?*"

He inhaled sharply, almost as though she'd surprised him with her boldness. *Good.*

Those beautiful lips frowned at her. "Honor."

Here, at last, was something torn from him with a ring of truth. The rest, she was beginning to suspect, was pure, masculine seduction. But she had faced many a handsome rake, and having lived twenty years in fear of her father, she could harden herself better than anyone. She'd spent her entire life reinforcing herself against everyone—it was something of a talent by this juncture.

And it was that same inurement that led her now. She could not forget that regardless of how handsome and alluring her husband was, she didn't know him and couldn't trust him. Just as she had never been able to trust anyone other than herself. Ever. "Honor made you lose yourself into a decanter of whisky and only return by breakfast?"

"Not precisely, buttercup." His frown turned into a smile, though it held little warmth. "But I suspect you already know that, being the intelligent, resourceful woman that you are. Which begs the question: what do you want from me?"

She didn't hesitate. "Honesty."

By all the heavens, she hadn't escaped one untenable situation for another. And if she'd somehow misread the signs, she would remove herself as expediently as possible. Since their vows, a new sense of understanding had dawned upon her. For the first time in her life, she was unencumbered by the watchful tyranny of her father. During her season, Aunt Caroline had perpetuated the crime by proxy. But now, she was free.

Free to be herself. Whoever Daisy Vanreid was.

Strike that, she reminded herself again. Whoever Daisy *Trent* was. For she was married now. Daisy Vanreid had become the Duchess of Trent. Like it or not. Disappointing wedding night or no. They were bound forever. She would make do with the devil she had chosen rather than the devil she knew.

"Honesty," he said slowly, as if it were a menace. "Do you mean to tell me that *you've* been entirely honest with me, wife?"

No. She had not. She thought of Bridget. Thought of flirtations and meaningless kisses, all unwanted, enacted in a desperate ploy to escape the fate her father had chosen for her. Should they matter now when they never had? Somehow, everything she'd ever done returned to her conscience in that moment, mocking her. Her foolish betrothal, Padraig, young love that hadn't been love at all.

"You are not the only man I contemplated entrapping in marriage," she confessed, for she still wasn't certain she ought to confide in him about her sister. "I kissed other men, as you know. I played the role of the flirt. I'll not make excuses for my actions, save to say that I did everything I could to escape the fate consigned me." She had said as much before, though not with such candor.

A growl tore from him, and then his hands were cupping her face, forcing her to gaze upon only him. As if her eyes would ever venture anywhere else. He was all she saw. All she wanted to see.

Forever.

"There are no others," he told her ruthlessly, his hands hot and demanding upon her, "from this moment forward. The mere mentioning of them makes me want to tear them limb from limb."

She wished his touch didn't feel quite so delicious upon her. "Is that what bothers you, then? Is that why you left without word and drowned yourself in drink?"

His mouth hardened. "Nonsense. I know a great deal about you, Daisy. Far more than you think, I'd wager, and yet here I stand."

He had been watching her, hadn't he? How many times had their gazes snared? On how many occasions had he cleverly toppled a vase or trod on a creaking floorboard at just the right moment to keep her from ruin? There had been Wilford, and how many others?

An emotion, thick and dark and indefinable—something resembling suspicion—unfurled within her. "Why were you watching me? I had always assumed it was because you were interested in me yourself. That wasn't why, though, was it?"

It had never occurred to her until now that he'd been the cause of each interruption that had spared her ruining. Like a protector. Or something else. Something troubling. Something very troubling indeed.

He met her gaze now, unflinching. "I watched you because I wanted you for myself." His thumb traced the corner of her mouth. "You were correct in your assumption. So you see, my dear? I am not angry with you for entrapping me as I am the one who entrapped you. It was my guilty conscience that sent me from you last evening, and my guilty conscience that kept me away."

"Your guilty conscience," she repeated, for it was difficult indeed to make sense of anything when his thumb worshipped the bow of her upper lip, lingering with a delicate caress that made her heart race into a steady gallop. He thought he had entrapped her?

"Yes." His gaze was fastened upon her mouth now, hungry and bright. But a hint of frown lingered between his dark brows. "My guilty conscience. Just when I thought I hadn't one."

His admission struck her, and she couldn't help but feel it was the most candid he'd been since she met him. It only lasted for a flash, and then the practiced seducer had returned. His thumb followed the seam of her lips, once, twice.

She kissed the fleshy pad, allowed her tongue to dart out against his skin for a taste. Salty and delicious and Sebastian. She wanted more. But she also wanted a conversation. Some idea of who they were and where they were headed.

"It would seem, then, that neither of us ought to bear the weight of a guilty conscience any longer," she observed, allowing herself to touch him for the first time since their awkward interview had begun. Her hands slid inside his coat, across the silk of his waistcoat, the firm, muscled flesh rippling beneath his layers of civility. He felt, in a word, divine.

So good that she couldn't keep herself from slipping the whole way around his taut abdomen until she reached his back. Here, he was rigid. Warmth blazed from him. She pressed her palms to the hollow just above his hips. Forced them higher, gliding along muscle and bone, the starch in his bearing, absorbing him, learning him, marking him as hers.

Such freedom, the ability to touch him as she wished. To admire the solid masculinity of him, so different from her soft curves. She was lush where he was spare, and he was strong and strapping where she was small. What a delectable dichotomy was man and woman.

It had never occurred to her before this moment how incredibly perfect it was, how she fit to him and he to her. But now, she felt it, and it was…incredible. His breathing went harsh, matching hers. His mouth was very near. She tried not to stare at those perfectly chiseled lips in longing. Tried not to want him.

But she failed miserably.

"Daisy." One word—her name—torn from him. He sounded as if he were in pain.

Perhaps he was. His beautiful face was all rigid lines when she wrenched her eyes from his mouth. She didn't know what to say in this moment of intense possibility, desire humming in the air like a current. Her mind raced, tangling itself in knots, and all she could think was it was wrong to feel such sweeping emotion for a man she scarcely knew.

She wanted to know him. All of him. Wanted to know what his laugh sounded like, how his skin would smell if she pressed her nose to the bristle-shaded angle of his jaw. "I don't know anything about you." She tried to understand the effect he had upon her. "It makes no sense that I should feel the way I do for you."

He stroked her cheek with a tenderness that belied the scorching heat of his stare. "Nothing makes sense, buttercup. Not you, not me, not what we're doing here or how we found ourselves where we are. Tell me, what do you feel? For me?"

For some reason, her overburdened mind thought first of physicality: his deceptive strength, corded muscle, not a hint of spare flesh over bone. He was larger than she'd even realized at such proximity. Capable of doing her harm if he wished. And yet, she didn't fear him. He lowered his head, bringing their lips ever closer. Near enough that she could rock forward, take his mouth.

"Longing," she whispered. "I long…and I ache. No one

has ever made me feel as you do, Your Grace."

"Sebastian." With one hand, he cupped her face, positioning her as though she awaited his kiss. His other hand roamed. His fingers traveled down her throat, lingering for a beat at the hollow where her pulse pounded. "That is gratifying to hear, considering I'm your husband."

The grimness in his tone wasn't lost on her. Oh dear. She had made a muck of it, hadn't she? But how was she to think properly when his hands were on her and he stood in such proximity, his touch so knowing and delicious, weakening any resolve she'd had remaining?

"You're a stranger to me," she reminded him. "My surprise stems from the fact that I've known you for so short a time, and already you've changed many things for me."

"More than you know, buttercup." His mouth tightened as his fingers trailed over her décolletage, across the twin swells of her breasts. She hoped he wouldn't notice she was still wearing the same gown she'd worn yesterday. At some point, she would need to fetch her belongings if indeed her father would even allow it.

She swallowed, trying to tamp down the desire clamoring inside her as he skimmed the lace and bead-trimmed bodice before slipping beneath her corset. "Tell me about yourself, Sebastian."

"There isn't much to tell." He found her nipple, rolled it between thumb and forefinger.

Daisy couldn't quite suppress her gasp. The heaviness between her legs pulsed with each pluck of his clever fingers. "How old are you?"

"I have thirty years." He leaned closer, pressing a kiss to the skin just beneath her ear. "How many have you, sweet?"

Good heavens, his tongue was upon her. Licking. Scalding. His teeth nipped gently. She couldn't think. Here was the man she'd been drawn to, in her arms at last. The seducer. The wicked lover. What had he asked?

Years, she recalled belatedly. He had inquired after her

age. "Twenty." She steeled herself against his potent allure. "Have you any siblings? A mother?"

He paused, his lips against her throat. "None in this world."

She recognized the pain in his voice, the regret. A glimmer of the true man, raw and real, showed through his arrogant façade. "I'm so sorry, Sebastian." She ran her hands over his back in gentle caresses, seeking to soothe.

"Bloody hell." Abruptly, he straightened, whisked his touch away, and clamped firm hands on her waist, setting her from him. His breathing was labored, his eyes dark and unreadable. "I promised you a courting, not a fuck on the desk in my study."

His words made her cheeks burn. She had heard coarse speech before, enough to know what such a word meant. But for the first time, it held a previously unknown appeal for her. The appeal of the wicked. Truth be told, she wouldn't have objected to a *fuck on the desk* in his study, and whatever unknown delights such a thing would entail.

She wisely refrained from saying so aloud, even as she felt the loss of his touch as keenly as if he had taken away an intrinsic part of her. She crossed her arms over her chest, watching him as he transformed yet again before her. He was as changeable as the weather, it seemed. Sunny, drizzling, a torrent. She could not predict which version of himself he would be from one moment to the next.

"Jesus." He raked a hand through his hair, pinning his gaze on something over her shoulder as he attempted to compose himself. "I'm sorry, Daisy. I should not have said something so profane to a lady. To my wife."

"I daresay I've heard worse." She sought to assuage his concern even as she noted the odd inflection in his voice as he'd called her his wife. As though it were somehow unfathomable. Or perhaps even unwanted.

She had not been raised to be a delicate flower. Though her name was Daisy, she'd never related to her namesake—spindly stems and bright, cheerful blooms that withered in

105

no time. All that brilliant show and heads hanging as if in shame within a few days' time. Her father had wanted her to be that sort of woman. Pretty on the outside but meek and mild, easily bent. She had defied him time and again, bearing the ugly consequences. He had not crushed her yet. And perhaps, she was beginning to realize, the real truth was that she was uncrushable after all.

"All the same," he said stiffly, "I beg your forgiveness. Now if you'll excuse me, my dear, I do have some matters that need my attention. I shall see you at dinner, yes?"

She was being dismissed. A chill ran through her. Uncrushable, but she had her pride. "Yes, of course. Forgive me. Undoubtedly, there are any number of things I must see to as well."

Yes, she was sure there were. She had a household to manage. A house and domestics to familiarize herself with. Somewhere, there was a library brimming with books she might read. And yet, what she wanted more than any of those things was to remain here, basking in the Duke of Trent's presence. How confounding he was.

Perhaps this was how marriage was handled amongst the aristocracy. Having spent most of her life in New York without a mother, Daisy hardly knew what to expect. No one had prepared her. Aunt Caroline had told her some nonsense about always being a dutiful wife, heeding her husband's every whim. Never voicing a contradictory opinion.

She turned to go, realizing she stood there staring at him like a green country girl gazing upon the first handsome man she'd ever seen. She knew when her presence was no longer desired, and she had no wish to linger where she wasn't wanted. Had she made a mistake in marrying the duke? Trapped by circumstance, she may have been. Foolish, she was not. It would seem that only time could decide.

Daisy's hand was on the intricate knob to his study door when he called out to her.

"Daisy."

She spun to face him. He stood where she had left him, standing before his desk, so handsome her heart gave a pang in her breast. "Yes?"

"Your dress." He waved a hand to encompass it, from her head to her hem. "You look stunning in it, but one cannot help but notice it is a repeat of yesterday's. Ironic coming from the woman who berated me for a similar crime."

She pursed her lips. "The crime was not similar in all senses. Moreover, the plain truth is that I only arrived here yesterday with this gown and not a stitch else. I'm not certain my father will even allow me to return to retrieve my wardrobe."

"You'll not return there," he ordered with the air of a man well-accustomed to issuing commands. He was a duke, after all. "Send an intermediary, and if Mr. Vanreid is unwilling to allow you to have your possessions, commission new dresses. Dresses that button all the way to the throat. I'm told that's the rage these days."

He had noticed after all.

"Thank you, Sebastian." She turned to leave again with one thought foremost in her mind.

How odd that he should pay special attention to lady's fashion. Particularly when high-necked bodices were decidedly *de trop*. Yes, that was very odd indeed.

## chapter ten

*S*HE WAS LATE.

Sebastian paced as he waited for Daisy to join him for dinner. He pulled out his watch to find that only a bloody minute had passed since he'd last checked. Damn it, she had him in an uproar. His mind was as jumbled as a field after battle and every bit as dark and desolate.

Her tardiness was not the only sin he could lay at her door. She was making him go mad, goddamn it. Mad with guilt, mad with frustration, mad with self-disgust, and worst of all, mad with lust.

His need for her was like a pulsing, raging beast inside him that wanted to spring free of its cage and devour her in a single, voracious bite. What was it about Daisy Vanreid that made him want to lick and kiss and nibble, to plunder and grind and fuck until he filled her with his seed?

The thought was enough to make him stiff as a fire log, even dressed for dinner and irritated, stalking the polished parquet as he awaited her. He willed his lust to cool. Counted his steps. *One, two...ten...fifteen.* Stared at the portrait of the Third Duke of Trent, sometime Lord Privy

Seal. Thought about how much of a blessing it was that men were no longer required to wear wigs in the name of fashion. Recalled what Paris had looked like after the siege, its citizens reduced to eating rats, buildings turned to rubble, dead bodies everywhere.

*Twenty-two...twenty-nine...thirty-four.*

It wasn't working, goddamn it.

Nothing could distract him from her. From what he'd done. From what he wanted to do and what he'd *almost* done. Jesus, he'd nearly taken her. On his desk. In his study. Knowing she was suspected of treason. Knowing Carlisle intended to see her cast into a prison. Everything in him had been calling for him to turn her around, lift her skirts, and slide home. It was appalling to realize just how well and truly depraved he'd become over his years serving the Crown.

What the hell was the matter with him?

And Daisy? She'd been kind. Sweet, actually. Genuine, too. Like him, she wore many roles and showed a host of different faces to the people around her. But she had been giving and true. He'd heard too clearly the unadulterated sympathy in her voice when he'd revealed he had no living family remaining save himself. Had felt the comfort in her gentle hands, her embrace.

Bloody, bloody hell.

Sympathy was the last thing he wanted from her. What he wanted more than anything was her body beneath his. Taking him, shuddering against him, relishing his claim upon her. He did not want to like her. Did not want to be troubled by the fact that for a woman who had suffered brutal abuse at the hands of her father, she was quick with compassion and concern. That he was manipulating her, deceiving her, and she could be an innocent. That nothing—no amount of conscience or reasoning—lessened how much he wanted to claim her. Even if it was wrong. Even if it was pretense. Even if everything between them was a lie carefully crafted to betray her and make her vulnerable.

None of it made a whit of sense.

Just as it made no sense that here he was, pacing the hall like a caged tiger, waiting for her, when he very well could have gone to have a glass of whisky and had Giles call him when she finally deigned to join him for dinner.

At long last, she appeared at the top of the staircase, beginning her graceful descent as though she wasn't—he consulted his watch again—thirty-three minutes late. When he glanced back up at her, his mouth went dry and a hunger that had nothing to do with dinner and everything to do with her slammed straight into his chest.

Her gown was purple brocade with full, tiered skirts that were pinned with flowers and trimmed with lace. Her ivory shoulders were mouthwateringly bare above small, delicate sleeves. But the most arresting feature of her gown was the ribbon that crisscrossed over a bodice that hugged her ripe bosom and trim waist to perfection. The ribbon tied into a pretty bow just between her breasts.

He had never wanted to untie a ribbon more in his life than he did now as he wordlessly drank in the sight of the most beautiful woman he'd ever seen. His woman, and he felt that possession of her in his bones as though it was just as right and natural and necessary as his own blood. Some devil in him, some wild impulse, wanted to keep her.

Forever.

What the bloody hell?

He frowned, feeling like a volley of cannon had exploded in his head. "You're late," he barked out, his voice a tad more sharp than he'd intended.

She faltered on the last step, losing her balance and pitching forward. Like a child drawn to a sweet, he'd already stalked to the base of the stairs, his body subconsciously seeking proximity. When she fell, it was directly into his arms. He caught her, soft and warm and bergamot-scented and unbearably fucking lovely.

Her golden curls brushed his jaw.

"Sebastian." She sounded breathless.

Her small hands splayed against his chest, twin brands through three layers of cloth. When she would have taken a step back, he held her firm. He told himself it was so that he could ascertain she was steady on her feet. The truth of it was that he wanted to hold her. He craved her. Had to have her.

"Dinner was set for half an hour ago." Some churlish part of him, that part at war with himself, forced him to issue the cool admonishment. He could have said so many other things. Told her how blindingly lovely she looked, for instance. Demanded she spin on her heel and return to her chamber so he could strip her out of the gown she'd just spent half the evening donning.

The push and pull inside him was like a gong. Had to have her. Couldn't have her. Shouldn't. Wouldn't. Needed to. Longed. Damn it, when had this mission become so complicated? The first moment he'd ever laid eyes on the dazzling, complex goddess that was Daisy Vanreid. That was precisely when.

She tilted her head back, considering him with that signature, intense regard of hers. A frown creased her brows, the only imperfection on her face, and he wanted to smooth it with his lips. "Forgive me for keeping you waiting. It took rather a great deal of…persuasion on the part of the footmen sent to my father's house. By the time my gowns arrived, it was already quite late."

Her voice, dulcet and warm, slid through him like honey to the senses. By God, looking and smelling and sounding as she did, he could forgive her anything. *Even treason*, whispered an insidious voice inside his mind.

Conscience? The devil? He didn't know.

He forced himself to clear his suddenly thick throat and form a response. "Dinner is served at eight here. Now that you've the fripperies you required, I trust your tardiness won't happen again."

Her expression shifted, her smile disappearing. He felt the loss of that sunshine as viscerally as a tooth extraction.

He was being a cad. He knew it. But damn it, he'd never before been so torn between duty and what he felt. He wasn't meant to have *feelings*. He was bloody well meant to feel nothing. At. All.

"Since my tardiness has so disturbed your good humor, perhaps you ought to release me so that we may attend dinner without further delay." Her tone was tart. The depths of her eyes sparkled with something indefinable.

She was fierce. And right. Jesus, he was still holding her in his arms as if he couldn't bear to release her. He hadn't let her go. That was how perfect she fit, how much the beast inside him needed to keep her there.

He set her away from him as though she were made of flame rather than the most tempting feminine flesh he'd ever touched. "Of course. I wished to be certain you were steady on your feet."

The look she gave him was knowing. "Yes, naturally. Thank you for ascertaining my…stability."

What could he say to such cheek? He would dearly like to put her stability in peril once more by sweeping her off to the nearest chamber, lifting her skirts, and running his hand up her thigh to the slit in her drawers. He'd stroke her pearl until she cried out for him, slide his fingers inside to test her tight sheath and ready her for his cock.

Dear God, the fire in him was burning out of control. Had she poisoned his afternoon tea? He swallowed. Bowed to her with a formal precision that was the antithesis of the raw crudity roiling inside him. "Allow me to escort you to dinner, Duchess?"

She took his proffered arm. "I thought you'd never ask, Duke. Dinner is to be served at eight, you know."

Though she appeared as poised and regal as any lady born to play the role of duchess, there was an unmistakable tinge of laughter in her voice. She mocked him. The daring of the woman would never cease to astonish him. As he led her to the dining room, he realized, quite belatedly and much to his consternation, that he too was smiling.

Mad it was, then.

The descent had begun.

Daisy barely tasted the *potage aux choux*. The soup course was savory yet sweet, unutterably delicious even though she didn't take more than five full spoons to her lips before nodding to one of the footmen in attendance to whisk it away. Her eyes were only for the man seated opposite her.

Sebastian. Duke. Husband.

He was all of those things and yet he remained, more than any of those descriptors, an enigma. A man she could not quite understand, but one to whom she was drawn with the madness of a child staring into the sun. Such folly could only lead to a bad end. Blindness? A headache? Worse?

It didn't matter. She wasn't hungry for soup.

She was hungry for him.

For his hands on her, for the way he held her, as if she was as necessary to him as air. Such gentle strength in that touch. Not an ounce of anger, not even when he waged a silent battle within his mind. He couldn't hide himself from her as well as he imagined he could.

Silence stretched, awkward and interminable, as the next course was laid before them. Salmon à la Chantilly—a fine piece of fish smothered in decadent sauce. Daisy forked a bite but didn't bring it to her lips. For most of the meal thus far, Sebastian had studiously avoided her gaze.

Conversely, she couldn't seem to keep her eyes from him. Strange how she had never before noted how tempting the cords of his neck were. An errant impulse to set her lips to him there, absorb his pulse, to taste his skin, struck her. He glanced up from his dinner at that moment and their stares clashed. Awareness sizzled between them even as she flushed at being caught gawping at him as if she'd never before seen a man in the flesh.

"Are my manners remiss?" he asked in a teasing tone,

his earlier ice melted.

Her cheeks flamed hotter. She longed to press her palms to them. "Forgive me. I've never been adept at silence."

That much, at least, was true, though she'd been ogling him merely for the pleasure it gave her. No need to tell him that, however. She'd already made a fool of herself.

A half smile curved his lips. She felt its sensual effects in a swell of desire that flooded her as sudden as sunshine filling a darkened room. "How reassuring. I thought perhaps I had béchamel on my chin."

Daisy pressed her lips together, suppressing a smile of her own. How enjoyable it was to banter with him. This relaxed, charismatic side of him—a side he seemed to reserve and reveal only sparingly—made her feel as if all the wine she'd sipped had gone to her head.

What had he said again? Ah, yes. Now she recalled. She quirked a brow at him. "I'm sure you must know that the sauce on the fish course isn't béchamel at all, Your Grace."

He flashed her a devastating, full-blown grin. "I've never been adept at French cuisine. I daresay that makes us even, buttercup."

*Buttercup.*

She liked when he called her that. "My tardiness for dinner and your sauce confusion?"

His gaze searched hers before settling on her lips. "Just so. A fair exchange, no? I'll forgive you for making me wait for my dinner, and you'll forgive me for being an ignorant clod."

"I can think of many ways to describe you, but 'ignorant clod' would never be one of them," she confessed before she could think better of her admission. It wouldn't do, after all, to allow him too much power. To let him know how easily he affected her.

"Oh?" His stare slid from her mouth, snapping back to her eyes with so much heat that her nipples tightened right there at the table with servants standing sentry and a table of china and cutlery and fine food between them. "Would you care to enlighten me?"

*Gorgeous. Alluring. Arrogant. Mysterious. Sensual. Dangerous.*

She forced her mind to stop unleashing the torrent of possibilities upon her, none of which she would speak aloud. So many adjectives in the English language could be applied to the singular man before her. If her cheeks had been hot before, they were positively aflame now. The way he looked at her—such frank hunger and barely leashed civility—took her breath.

She settled for a few with less damning connotations. "Distracting and occasionally vexing."

He laughed then, and it was pleasant and deep. His laughter filled her belly with warmth. She hadn't heard it before, and she couldn't shake the impression that he didn't laugh often. Perhaps she could bring more levity into his world. His eyes crinkled, a heretofore unseen dimple making an appearance in his right cheek. Only the right. She wanted to kiss it.

How silly, and yet her lips longed to learn that groove as much as her heart yearned to make him laugh again. To make him laugh often. Her life had been one of much misery and loneliness, forever trapped beneath someone else's rule, forever forced to accede to the expectations of her father.

Now, she was free, and she felt that newfound liberation in truth for the first time as she sat there with her uneaten salmon and the man she'd married in a whirlwind laughing across from her. Hope was a delicate, airy thing rising inside her like a hot air balloon.

"I object to vexing," he said at last, still grinning at her even after his mirth had subsided. A hint of that precious dimple lingered, bracketing his supple lips. "Distracting, however, I will happily own."

His tone was intimate and sincere. She swallowed, thinking it would be most unwise to fall in love with her husband on the second day of their marriage. "I suppose it depends on one's definition of the term," she said tartly to distract herself from how handsome he was and how easily he could woo her when he was charming. "Hangnails are also distracting. As are splinters and headaches."

He threw back his head and laughed again, the sound rich and uncontained. The dimple had returned in full force and she couldn't tear her eyes away. "You may not be adept at silence, sweet, but you have a knack for a proper setdown."

She would never have dared to speak with such abandon before. Life under her father's strict rule had taught her to hold her tongue and eradicate any hint of audacity or opinion. But she was not beneath her father's thumb any longer, and she was beginning to appreciate that fact in new ways.

She found herself smiling back at her too-handsome husband. "I was exercising logic, Your Grace. Make of it what you will."

He sobered, his gaze becoming intense, his expression one of unguarded hunger. "I believe we've finished with the fish course," he announced to the servants without even glancing in their directions. "Bring the next in twenty minutes. Anyone who disturbs us before that time has passed shall be sacked without reference." His gaze held hers, molten and hungry, rife with meaning.

Daisy felt the full force of that look, beginning with a pulse of need between her thighs and radiating throughout her entire body. Her already hard nipples tightened even more, and she felt a sudden urgency to once again have his mouth upon her there. Sucking. Nipping, perhaps even.

Good heavens. His stare was doing wicked things to her senses and mind both. She tore her gaze away to watch as the servants dutifully departed, closing the door behind them with judicious grace.

They were alone, with twenty minutes to call their own. Perhaps she should have been embarrassed that he had delivered such a blatant edict to the servants. Twenty minutes alone, between courses. His motivation would be obvious to them, of course. One didn't stop a dinner in medias res. Not unless one's intentions were scandalous. Impure. Dangerous. Another adjective rattled to the forefront of her mind as she swung her eyes back to her husband in time to watch him unfold his tall, muscled length from his chair.

*Delicious.*

"Why have you stopped the dinner, Your Grace?" she asked, breathless despite her best intentions. Hadn't he just shamed her before his servants? Strike that. Before *their* servants? "I thought your hunger was the reason for your earlier pique with me over my tardiness."

He moved to her with the cagey grace of a predatory cat. A big, predatory cat. A tiger, she thought, before thinking better of the choice. No, he was a lion. Proud and strong and savage. And handsome. Yes, he was undeniably that.

"I appreciate punctuality," he said, as if that explained his behavior. "And it's Sebastian, buttercup, as I've already told you. No more formality between us. I don't like it."

He skirted the table, never taking his eyes from her. No lord she had ever seen dignifying London's ballrooms had been anything like him. It was as if he were a breed of his own, even if she couldn't quite determine just what it was that set him so apart from all the rest. Wealth and titles had never meant anything to her. Kindness did. Compassion as well—two things she'd seen precious little of thus far, whether at home or here in England.

But that wasn't it. Anyone could be compassionate. Anyone could be kind if he chose. The duke—Sebastian, she must think of him as now—had been both to her at times. And still, there was something else about him that marked him as different. The mystery, the shadows in his eyes, the potent strength, the way he doled out parts of himself in such tiny increments that she was sure she'd only gotten to know the equivalent of a thimble-full...it was all those things and more. He was like a summer storm: aggressive, sudden, and beautiful in his harsh, powerful way.

He didn't stop until he stood behind her. She sat frozen, waiting, her heart pounding faster than a spooked horse's hooves on a road. Every part of her clamored for his touch. At last, his hands, large and warm, settled on her bare shoulders, just above the layered sleeves of her evening gown. Just a touch, his skin on hers, and yet it felt unbearably intimate. Desire ricocheted through her.

His breath was hot, his lips brushing over her ear as he spoke. "A true gentleman should never stand in the presence of a lady while she remains seated."

She knew as much, of course. She had been trained, after all. Her father had done his utmost to see that she would be wedded to the husband of his choice. A titled, born-in-the-purple aristocrat. Perhaps she should have stood when he had, for the sake of manners. But she had been too preoccupied by watching him to take note of anything else.

*Breathe*, she chided herself, *breathe*. And she did, inhaling slowly, refusing to give in to the temptation of turning her head and meeting his mouth with hers. They were courting, after all, were they not? Moreover, he remained a man she little knew, despite the fact that they were now husband and wife.

"Are you not a true gentleman, then?" she forced herself to ask as his thumbs began to run a lazy pattern of circles over her collarbone.

"Would a gentleman follow a lady into the moonlight, intent on her seduction?" Something hot and wet and firm—his tongue, she realized, traced the ridges of her ear.

She trembled, though it wasn't with fear. It was with something else, something far more authoritative. Her own need. Her hands remained in her lap, but now she grabbed fistfuls of fabric, clenching the brocade to keep herself from touching him.

"Would a lady lead a gentleman into the moonlight?" She injected a lightness into her tone that she hardly felt. After all, she wasn't blameless in the situation in which they now found themselves mired. She hadn't forgiven herself yet, even if it seemed that he had.

His hands slid lower, to the swells of her breasts, continuing their careful, steady seduction. Swirls on her skin. Circles of desire that threatened to set her aflame. The tips of his fingers brushed the ribbon trimming her décolletage. Though she knew it was wanton and she ought not to, she arched her back ever so slightly, as if in offering. Her nipples longed for his touch. She felt as coiled as a spring, her entire being a pile of dry kindling about to be set aflame.

"Perhaps we are a perfect match, buttercup." His words were low, tinged with desire, rendering them almost a feral growl. "I'm not a gentleman, and you're not a lady."

Either they brought out the worst in each other or the best. Daisy still hadn't decided. All she knew was that he was setting her on fire in a slow burn, and she couldn't bear much more teasing. Her body longed—no, hungered—for something, anything deeper and more meaningful than what they'd already shared. She didn't know what it was, what he could give her that he hadn't already, but her instinct told her it would far surpass anything she'd experienced thus far.

She wanted him to claim her. To do wicked things to her. To make her his.

He slipped beneath her bodice then, between her chemise and her skin, beneath her corset. Those knowing fingers found her nipples with unerring persistence, rolling them, pinching, plucking. Drawing a moan from her. His lips pressed to her throat, just below her ear.

"Why did you call off the servants?" the question left her, a re-asking of the query she'd already posed. It was a desperate attempt at self-preservation. Because every part of her longed for him to continue doing what he was doing to her and then more. So much more. Anything he wished. Good heavens, this man was pure, blissful torture.

"Cannot a man long to be alone with his wife?" He dragged his teeth slowly down the corded column of her throat. When he reached her shoulder, he gave her a playful bite as he pinched her nipples again.

The ache between her thighs heightened. Her body felt boneless, breath held in anticipation, the core of her wet and wanting in a way she'd never before known. It was shameful, how much he could make her desire him.

"You said we should court," she reminded him as his mouth opened over her flesh, sucking and biting before soothing the sting with his tongue.

"This *is* courting." He removed his left hand from her bodice and lowered it to her lap, settling over hers where she clasped her skirts. Their fingers tangled while his right hand continued to play with her nipple. "If I had my way, I'd have you bent over this table right now, buttercup, with your skirt up around your waist and my cock so deep inside you that—"

A discreet knock sounded at the door to the dining room just then. How had the time passed with such swiftness? The butler's calm, utterly proper voice cut through the moment. "Your Grace? Forgive the interruption, but the next course will arrive in two minutes."

"Damn it." Sebastian exhaled against her throat.

*Yes, damn it*, she echoed inwardly. Some wicked part of her she hadn't known existed still longed to hear the rest of what he'd been about to say. Such wicked, wanton things. So low and base, she ought to take umbrage as any properly bred lady would. But what he had said would taunt her all night long. His cock inside her. The mere notion was enough to make her come out of her skin.

His hand retreated from her bodice. "I should have asked for a whole bloody hour."

His tone was grim. As grim as she felt. The loss of his touch was an ache pounding through her wherever his skin had last met hers. Acting on instinct alone, she released her skirts at last, reaching behind her to still him when he would have disengaged. She caught his cheek to her palm, the bristles of his whiskers a welcome abrasion upon her palm. She had chosen not to wear gloves on occasion of the intimacy of the setting and she was heartily glad for it now.

Daisy turned finally, so that their mouths nearly brushed.

Her eyes met his, challenging the sparks she saw. The heat. The want. "Yes," she agreed, "you should have."

And then she pressed her lips to his.

## chapter eleven

$\mathcal{S}$HE HAD KISSED HIM.

And it had been inexperienced. Not at all artful. No hint of seduction. No teasing. Daisy's mouth had simply turned to his, seeking. But if anything, her approach had only made the beast raging inside him hunger for more. And so, he'd met her halfway, claiming, obliging her.

He'd thrust his tongue into her mouth, moaning his appreciation for her boldness, his hand fisting her skirts of its own volition and raising them higher. Up, past her knees, almost to her thighs. He found his way back into the inviting warmth of her bodice where the fullness of her breast made him long for more.

He'd caught her lower lip between his teeth and bit. He'd almost been to the sweet slit in her drawers, his tongue taking her mouth the way he longed to claim her cunny, his fingers skimming past stockings and satin ribbons, over soft thighs she parted just for him. And then another knock had come at the door. Giles again. Ever discreet. Ever circumspect.

It was a final warning. To postpone the servants yet

again would set tongues belowstairs wagging more than they already had. He and Daisy were newly wed and allowed some latitude. But calling for a twenty-minute break followed by another, followed by only-the-Lord-knew-what was testing the bounds of propriety more than he ought to do, and even Sebastian knew that. There was also the concern, nipping at him, that Carlisle's eyes and ears could be among his domestics.

With a final, thorough kiss and a tweak of the sweet, tight bud of her nipple, he had withdrawn. The willpower required to disengage himself from her had been proportionate to the size of his cock, both of which had rendered his sudden retreat back to his seat a decidedly painful endeavor.

They'd blithely moved on to the next course, feigning an unaffected air that was as honest as paste gems on an actress's throat. *Filet de bouef sauce Madère aux haricots verts*, as it happened. It was the first time in Sebastian's life that he'd had a perfectly cooked steak on his plate and hadn't wanted to eat a goddamn bite.

Because all he wanted—the only bloody nourishment that would satisfy him—was the gorgeous, unpredictable, untrustworthy woman he'd been forced to marry. How the hell had Carlisle ever imagined he could marry a goddess like Daisy Vanreid off to a man, whether he be a loyal, oath-swearing member of the League or no, without her tempting him to ruination?

Sebastian had a glass of whisky in hand now as he stared at the door adjoining his chamber to hers, and he couldn't fathom anyone not wanting to fuck Daisy to oblivion. She was that alluring, that sensual, that innately beautiful. She was also bold and daring, witty and brave, smart and warm and soft, slow to rile, easy to laugh.

Ordinarily, he didn't imbibe often, and especially not during the course of a mission, but something about the situation in which he currently found himself made him want to drink an entire barrel of liquor if only it would quiet the demons eating away at him.

The demons that told him to throw open the door between them, go to the woman he'd married, and take her. To tear away every scrap of fabric keeping her body from him until she was completely nude. To throw her on the bed, spread her luscious thighs, and take her for his own.

He groaned. Beneath his dressing gown, his cock was harder than ever, raging and pulsing at the thought of burying himself in soft, wet, womanly flesh. But not just any woman's. Daisy's. Christ yes, there was something about that golden-haired American minx that fashioned him Odysseus and her one of the Sirens. A beautiful, undeniable lure leading him into the treacherous rocks of the shore.

His ship was bound to crash if he followed her. Yet somehow, he couldn't seem to stay away. Didn't want to. Her skin had been softer than silk where he'd tasted her, kissed her, felt the rapid drum of her heartbeat. Whatever it was that sizzled between them, it was undeniable, and she felt it every bit as much as he did.

Without even realizing he'd moved, he found himself across his chamber, hand on the doorknob separating him from her. Jesus. This was getting out of control. He tossed back the contents of his glass, relishing the burn that only fine whisky could provide, and then set it aside. There was nary a sound on the other side of the door as he took a few breaths and willed his raging arousal to subside.

Going to her chamber was foolish, and he recognized it. But he couldn't seem to keep his distance from her. *One breath, two breaths.* His cock was harder than a marble bust. *Three, four.* Still not lessening. Christ, this propensity for counting was all her fault, and it needed to bloody well end.

He thought of the queen. Thought of his maternal grandmother's funeral. *Five, six.* Attempted to recall some Shakespeare, but the only lines that came to mind had her name in them.

*When daisies pied and violets blue.*

Damn it all to hell. More words returned to him,

mocking. *The cuckoo, then, on every tree, mocks married men, for thus sings he...*

Bloody, bloody hell. Leave it to Shakespeare to taunt him as well, with a well-placed barb. She wasn't his. Not to keep, no matter how much he desired her. This was all foolishness. Ridiculous. Unutterably stupid. And yet, he couldn't excise her from his mind.

The scent of her—bergamot, vanilla, ambergris—still filled his senses as if she stood before him. His fingers burned with remembrance of the feeling of those hard little buds of her nipples.

Distraction wasn't working. Neither was tarrying. Or breathing. He needed to see her. Needed to touch her. He rapped sharply on the door. Waited for her to respond. Hoped she would tell him to go to hell.

Instead, he heard her dulcet voice, so calming and pleasant to the ears. "You may enter."

And enter he did. Damn if hearing her issue such an invitation didn't make the blood pound harder through his veins as he thought of another sort of invitation. Another form of entry he might make into her territory. He was an unconscionable bastard, but he strode across her chamber just the same.

She stood near her bed, clad in only a silken dressing gown trimmed with ruffles and belted at the waist. It was cream, and the pallid color didn't do her a bit of justice, but it looked like the sort of thing a young lady might have commissioned for her wedding trousseau. He couldn't squelch the deep-seated satisfaction that took root within him at the realization that he was the one to see her in that robe and not anyone else.

The full effect of her beauty hit him then, visceral and raw. Left him reeling. He took her in, the woman he'd married, the vixen who was meant to be his dupe but somehow always seemed to hold him in the palm of her dainty hand. Christ, she was lovely.

Her hair was unbound, sending long, burnished waves

cascading down her back. He longed to bury his face in those locks, to grab a fistful of golden skeins, wrap them around his hand, drag her head back, and hold her tight while he ravaged her mouth with his kiss. Her waist was small even without her corset, her breasts full and high, hips as lush as he'd imagined they would be. Her bare feet and trim ankles peeped out below the hem of her gown to tease him.

This was how he should have seen her last night. How he wanted to see her every night for the rest of his life. The thought struck him before he could tamp it down.

One word echoed in his mind. Triumphant. Blistering. Wrong.

*Mine.*

Horribly wrong, and yet somehow also right. She was his. Maybe not forever, but right now, in this moment, she was his wife. He was her husband. His body wanted hers, and her body...her body sang for him. It was as if she was made for his touch. He'd never before shared desire of this magnitude with another woman.

But there was a reason she was his, a reason he had married her, and duty wouldn't allow him to forget, regardless of how badly he needed her. He'd been ordered to use her for information. Glean any bits of knowledge about her father from her. Unravel what, if anything, she knew about Fenians, plots, and bombs. Possibly see her sent to gaol, and the mere notion was enough to make him feel the sting of shame to his bones. How could he know the truth, deceive her, yet want her so?

"Good evening," he forced himself to say, playing the part of gentleman when all he longed to do was tear her dressing gown away, take her in his arms, and pin her to the bed where he could leisurely kiss, lick, bite, and fuck every part of her all night long.

He stopped with a safe distance between them. And the distance felt somehow unimpeachable and cavernous all at once.

Daisy appeared nervous. Her fingers caught the knot of her belt, plucking at it as if she sought to learn every tactile sensation from it she could. "Good evening, Sebastian," she returned, a shy smile curling her generous lips.

She had used his name without his prompting, and he took it as a good sign. He stepped even closer, which proved a mistake the moment that her scent hit him like a punch to the jaw.

He swallowed, tamping down his arousal with an inner, iron fist. "I'm sorry for yesterday," he apologized again, and he didn't know why. The words left his tongue before he could recall them. He should leave. Buss her on the cheek and go back to his chamber where he belonged.

"Yesterday is already forgiven." The smile on her full lips deepened, blossoming across her face in a way that struck him directly in the groin.

"Generous of you," he gritted, irritated with himself for the way she affected him. How was it that the simple act of being in her chamber, within her charmed sphere, could reduce him to an untried youth about to drown in his own lust?

Daisy raised a brow. "Hardly. I count myself equally in need of forgiveness."

Her confession stirred a dormant part of him. The spy came to life. In his experience, there was always a grain of truth to be found in everything. Was there some sin for which she needed forgiveness? Did a heavy conscience hide behind her beautiful, goddess-like façade? He could not dismiss her tangential associations with McGuire and Fenians no matter how much he longed to. Though sadly, not even suspicion diminished his rampant arousal.

He kept his tone smooth. "Forgiveness, buttercup?"

A becoming flush of pink tinged her cheekbones. Her gaze never wavered from his. "For my part in forcing this marriage upon you. I know you claim to have wanted me for yourself, but you've no notion of how much guilt I feel. I was so selfish, so desperate to escape what my father had planned for me, and I took your freedom of choice from you."

Ah. The spy within him was suitably mollified. She still—naïf that she was—imagined she had been responsible for their hasty vows. If what she claimed was true, how appallingly little she knew of the world in which she lived. He could have swept their little scandal beneath the rug and moved on with his life. In such matters, a man didn't shoulder the blame. But for a woman, ruination was thorough and forever. He had owed her—a beautiful and brazen American heiress with an already diminished reputation—nothing. No one could have forced him to make her his duchess save the Crown.

And, put to it, the Crown had done just that, albeit for none of the reasons Daisy would have supposed.

"Your guilt is misplaced," he told her solemnly, his gaze traveling over every curve and hollow of her face. If he was searching for a flaw, he found none. "I've already told you that the fault lies with me alone."

Another lie, but he had already told her so many. Even in this unguarded moment in her chamber, where they should be nothing more than man and woman, he was manipulating her. Forced by circumstance, his duty, and his mission to keep her in the dark.

Still, though he had his orders, they didn't require him to seduce her. To use her. To slake his needs in her receptive, gorgeous body. His presence in her chamber was a sin that he alone could own. He'd thought himself a man of honor until Daisy had swept into his life. She brought him to the periphery of his limits.

Beyond them now, for the motivations driving him in this moment sure as hell weren't borne of honor or duty or good. No, his impetus was base and deep, dark and damning. Lust. Need. Hunger. The physical ache to claim her, to possess her. Christ, he felt it all the way to his bloody bones.

"I think you are too generous," she said then.

He squelched the bark of bitter laughter that threatened to emerge. Generous. Ha. He was nothing of the sort. He was greedy. Selfish. Sinful. His sometime conscience re-emerged, reminding him that there was a mission at hand. A mission of far greater importance than sinking his aching cock inside the cunny of the ethereal beauty before him.

No matter how much the need clawed him apart inside.

"Your father," he pried, taking advantage of the opening in their dialogue. His sense of duty refused to allow him to miss this moment, regardless of how much he wanted her. "Were his intentions for your marriage always transparent? Did you come to London knowing what he expected of you?"

Her long lashes lowered over her brilliant eyes for a moment, fanning against her cheeks. "I knew that he wished for me to marry an aristocrat. I had foolishly believed that coming to London would grant me a modicum of freedom. And I had somehow imagined I'd be given a choice in who my husband would be. How foolish I was to think he would ever do anything but control me. I should have known."

Her voice hushed to a near whisper at the last. Jesus, if she was an actress, then she was possessed of a far greater talent than any actress he'd ever witnessed treading the boards. He thought he saw her—the real Daisy Vanreid—for the first time. She had lived a life of terrifying oppression under her father's brutality. Coming to England was to have been her escape. Instead, it had turned into her prison in more ways than she had yet to even realize.

There it was again, that goddamn conscience he'd sworn he didn't have, tearing into him with the precision of a well-sharpened dagger. She had been kept beneath her tyrant father's thumb. She thought she'd somehow managed her independence. Thought she was married to a good man, a man deserving of her apology, a man who could be a real husband to her.

He was not that man.

And he had used her already—intended to use her far

worse—than her father ever had. In the name of Crown, country, the League, and his own bloody desires. He was a bastard, a sinner, a liar, and a spy.

*Walk away*, the voice inside him, a voice that still contained a shred of honor, warned. *Bid her good night and walk away before you do something you will regret.* And yet, he couldn't. Couldn't force himself to spin on his heel. Couldn't make himself utter polite pleasantries before wishing her an agreeable sleep and retreating to his chamber.

Instead of leaving, he stepped closer. *One steps, two steps, three.* There it was once more, the goddamn counting. And he couldn't stop it. Couldn't stop what he wanted to do. Couldn't stop the way she made him feel. His hands clamped on her waist, hauling her against him.

She fell into him with the rightness of a homecoming after a long journey. Vivid green eyes widened, lush lips falling open in surprise at the abruptness of his action. Her hands fluttered to his chest, and he was glad he wore a robe only, for it meant there was one fine layer of cloth between her skin and his.

He should press her for more information about her father, but he couldn't. Couldn't go another second without crushing her mouth beneath his. He took her lips with all of the turmoil churning through him and none of the finesse she deserved. His tongue traced the seam of her lips once before pushing inside to plunder. She tasted decadent, like the raspberry sauce that had been served over the biscuit pudding at dinner, and like something dark and delicious that was innately Daisy.

Her body was lush and warm beneath the silken splendor of her dressing gown. Tempting him. He wanted to tear the impediment away, to fill himself with her. To fill her with his cock. Instead, he slid his hands down her waist to cup the round swells of her pert derriere. Without a thought for her innocence, he ground her against him, his cock straining between them, hard and ready.

*You cannot have her.* Carlisle's words came back to his mind suddenly, slamming through him along with the lust. A pointed reminder, taunting him. He had a duty to the League and his country, oaths to uphold. What the hell was he doing, kissing Daisy, about to tear off her robe and sink himself inside her? Fuck, this was foolishness. He risked so much. *She's poison to you.*

Yes, she was, just like a buttercup. His buttercup. Beautiful, bold, alluring, and poisonous. But Daisy's was the sort of poison that would kill him slowly. Leave him euphoric until he finally succumbed. And he wanted that poison. Wanted her so much the need of her threatened to split him apart.

He couldn't trust her. She was the daughter of one of England's most dangerous enemies, the former betrothed of a vile bastard hell-bent on death and destruction. Carlisle believed he had enough evidence against her to eventually see her in prison.

And none of that mattered one bloody whit when she was in his arms.

He kissed her harder, seeking to punish her for making him want her so much that he was willing to forsake everything he'd spent his life building just to have her. But he also wanted to mark her, brand her. To make certain she knew that whatever came to pass between them, some part of her would always be his, would always long to return to this night when they were wild and wicked together.

She moaned, straining against him, the hard peaks of her breasts digging into his chest. She had such sweet, responsive nipples. Her hands caressed over his chest, higher, linking around his neck as she kissed him back with abandon. Tongues dueled. Blood thundered straight to his cock, his balls tightening as if having her like this was enough to make him spend like some callow youth. His heart pounded.

Bed.

He needed her on the bed. Now. Needed her stripped

131

of every scrap of fabric keeping her from him, the beauty of her body laid bare, legs splayed. He wanted to taste the essence of her, give her a crashing, body-shaking release with his tongue alone. Hell, yes.

*One, two, three.* He led her backward without breaking the kiss. Jesus, there it was. Counting again. Not many steps keeping him from what he wanted. His tongue in her mouth. His teeth biting her lower lip. Delicious. She was so bloody delicious.

And he was mad, his head swimming with lust, body drenched in unquenched desire, conscience in turmoil. Wrong, being with her like this was wrong. Unfair to Daisy. A betrayal of his oath. She could be dangerous. She could be deceiving him. Christ knew he was deceiving her.

He didn't give a damn about anything other than Daisy as he took another step, then another until his leg wedged between her soft thighs. Her dressing gown parted. Sebastian released her bottom with one hand and caught his robe, dragging it to the side. Nothing but naked skin would do. He pressed into her farther. Silken inner thighs slid against him, setting him aflame. Farther again, slowly. The kiss deepened. He didn't stop until she rode his thigh, trapped between him and the bed at her back.

Nothing could have prepared him for the first touch of her slippery heat. Wet, so wet. And on fire. Bloody hell, she scorched him. On a shocked gasp, she arched, dragging herself over him, leaving a trail of her dew.

Sweet Christ.

Madness. Sheer, unadulterated madness was what made him catch her up in his arms and deposit her on the bed's edge, her legs still spread, dressing gown open. His thigh was wet, and he felt the loss of her heat in a pang that tore through him. Breaking the kiss, he stood to his full height, allowing himself the pleasure of seeing her so thoroughly undone.

Lord was she a sight to behold.

Her mouth was swollen from his kiss, lips red and

succulent as raspberry syrup. Her robe gaped, the knot at her sash gone loose in their frenzied lovemaking, leaving her breasts partially freed as well. His gazed traveled lower, to the vee of her dressing gown. Twin slices of the creamy flesh of her inner thighs beckoned, her cunny nearly exposed.

He'd never seen a more beautiful woman.

Or a woman he wanted more.

Jesus, she unmanned him.

"Sebastian?" Daisy was breathless, her eyes searching his. She appeared dazed, flushed. Consumed by the same torrent of desire coursing through him like a bloody flood.

He didn't know what her question was, but the answer was yes. Absolutely. Undeniably. Yes. To everything. To anything. To whatever she wished. For Daisy, the answer would always be yes.

He recognized the truth of it as she sprawled across the bed, waiting for him to lay his claim. So much hung in the balance, so many words unspoken, so many falsehoods and blockades between them, seemingly unsurmountable. But he was seizing this moment because he was a bloody selfish bastard, and he was going to give her what she wanted. What he needed so badly to give her.

Release.

He swore to himself that he wouldn't take her, no matter how much he longed to. It wasn't right or fair to her, not when she didn't know the truth behind their union. Not when he intended to procure an annulment. But he could give her pleasure. Just this once, even if doing so ended him in the process.

"Take off your dressing gown." The command was torn from him.

She swallowed, gaze searching his, a pretty pink flush tingeing her high cheekbones. "You wish to consummate the marriage after all?"

*Yes*, cried out every bloody part of him.

"Not tonight," he reassured her instead, leaning forward and catching her waist. Slowly, he lifted her onto the center of the bed and lowered her until her head nestled in pillows, a bounty of golden curls spilling everywhere. "Tonight we will get more acquainted with each other."

*Acquainted.* Such a mild, silly verb for what he intended to do. He nearly smiled at the absurdity of it as he joined her on the bed, readjusting to keep the barrier of his own robe intact. Stretching his body alongside hers, he lay on his side, an elbow propped on one pillow to give him purchase. Sebastian couldn't resist sinking his fingers into the lush strands of her hair. Like burnished silk, it fell back to the pillow, teasing his senses with a fresh wave of bergamot and ambergris.

"Can you not acquaint yourself with me while I'm wearing my robe?" Daisy asked, finding her starch amidst a renewed sense of modesty.

He did grin then, skimming a slight caress over her cheek. She was still flushed, and damn it if she didn't look utterly delectable lying there, shy and beautiful as sin. "I can, but it won't be as enjoyable for either of us, buttercup."

Her fingers remained on the knot securing her robe in place, gripping tightly. "Enjoyable, Your Grace?"

He winced at her reversal, the habit of using his title as though they were strangers in a drawing room exchanging pleasantries. She seemed to revert to formality whenever she grew nervous.

"Sebastian," he prompted her for what was surely the hundredth time, cupping her cheek in his palm and brushing his thumb over that irresistible lower lip of hers.

She would need some coaxing, it seemed. The bravado that had led her to defiantly urge him to take his turn at the Beresford Ball had been precisely that. He was beginning to understand her a bit, this wild summer storm wrapped up in luscious female form. An inner layer hid beneath the fierce face she showed the world, one that was vulnerable.

"I'm not certain I'm in agreement with that statement." She eyed him warily, her gaze dropping to his right cheek for a moment before settling once more on his.

His rogue dimple, he realized, and it occurred to him that he'd seen her staring at it on more than one occasion. Clearly he would need to make use of it more often. For some mad reason, he imagined her lips pressing to the groove in his skin. The mark of happiness, as his mother had once called it.

A blessing, she'd said, her sweet voice redolent with maternal love. Sebastian had always fancied it a curse, an imperfection that rendered his face asymmetrical. But the way Daisy's gaze stole to it with such a rapt expression, he was beginning to think perhaps his mother had been right after all.

"Which statement don't you agree with, darling?" he asked Daisy with cheeky intention. "That getting acquainted with each other without your dressing gown as an impediment will be enjoyable, or my name?"

"Your name," replied the minx, surprising him with a teasing smile of her own. "I'm sure your name is something sensible and suitably haughty, something more along the lines of William or Alistair."

A strange sensation, heavy and warm and altogether unfamiliar, slid through his chest as he shared a smile with her. What the hell was it? Some odd sensation of…rightness? Was that the proper word? No, he decided instantly. More than likely, it was something else, caused by frustrated lust.

"Is Sebastian not a sensible name?" He traced the bridge of her nose with his index finger.

Strange how even touching her there, in such a seemingly innocent location, made his ballocks tighten in anticipation. He hesitated at the tip, the two of them connected by such an infinitesimal touch and yet the torrent of need between them so deep and raging. She could feel it too, this inevitable attraction they shared, sparking and threatening to burn into a full-blown flame. He could see it in the way her eyes flared, her pupils dilated, her lush mouth dipped open and her raspberry-dessert breath ghosted over his lips.

Raspberry had never been so bloody intoxicating.

"I've never thought it a sensible name," she said into the charged silence. "Though perhaps it does bring to mind the sort of man who gets churlish when his wife is late for dinner."

The chuckle burst forth from him before he even knew it was there. He had been an utter boor to her, hadn't he? And solely because he found it so goddamn difficult to keep her at arm's length when all he wanted was to keep her here, like this: warm and smiling and beautiful, her eyes laughing into his, her decadent pink mouth just a dip of his head away from being kissed.

Bloody hell.

Before thoughts of duty and loyalty and doubt could stop him, he dropped his hand to its natural home on the nip of her waist and lowered his mouth to hers. Fitting his lips to hers, he kissed her, coaxing her to respond with gentle pressure. He took his time with that kiss, drinking her in, savoring her.

"I'm certain," he added against her mouth before kissing her again. This time, his tongue teased the seam of her lips, requesting entrance. She opened to him, and he swept inside. Raspberry-sweet and all that was delicious. Their tongues dueled for a moment before he broke the kiss to drag his mouth down her throat.

As much as he loved kissing her, reveling in the unexpected closeness this night had brought upon them, he couldn't deny that his self-restraint was growing thin. He needed to remember the promise he'd made to himself. He would not take her. Not, at least, until...

Jesus, until what? He pressed his mouth to the hollow at the base of her neck where her pulse pounded the strongest. And then he couldn't resist tonguing the soft flesh. He had to still his wayward mind. There was no future in this, in the Duke of Trent and Daisy Vanreid. All there could be was tonight. This one night where he allowed himself to be a selfish bastard and forget about his oaths to the League for the span of an hour and no more.

Never again.

"I'm beginning to think you were correct," Daisy said on a sigh.

He stilled, looking up at her and raising a brow. "Which statement, buttercup?"

The grin that curved her mouth was blinding. It took his breath. "Both."

## chapter twelve

E WAS A HANDSOME DEVIL, the Duke of Trent.

Not the duke any longer but Sebastian, and she really must remember that.

Her husband, she thought again. It was still so new, a fresh connection to which she'd yet to grow accustomed. How sudden and foreign her married state was to her, though not without its own allure. Having a husband who kissed the way Sebastian did was no hardship. But that she was installed in his home, laughing with him in bed, seemed a dream from which she would wake too soon, finding herself back in her chamber at the rented Belgravia home with Aunt Caroline.

It wasn't a dream, however, for he smiled back at her now, unleashing his rakish dimple while his fingers closed over hers at the knot on her robe. "I'm glad we're in accord."

That was one way to describe the molten sensations rushing through her. So dry and chaste sounding, and not at all a proper means of conveying the way he made her flush hot, every part of her tingling as though jolted by an electric current. The flutter of her pulse, the ache in her womb, the frenzied way her body longed for his, all made a blatant lie of *accord*.

Without employing much effort, he brushed her hands aside. She didn't protest this time, for any initial embarrassment she may have felt at being completely nude before him had been extinguished by the raw, aching need he evoked within her. She liked this side of him, the darkness she sensed within him dashed away by rare light.

The knot came undone. He stared at her intently, his grin fading, and she reached out to trace his fleeting dimple. With the pad of her index finger, she worshipped that lone groove until it was gone. His whiskers proved a shiver-inducing abrasion against her skin.

He turned his head to press a kiss to her palm. "Now it's time for me to do penance for being a churl."

She bit her lip, feeling not a hint of contrition for making light of his earlier arrogance. "At least you admit it."

Oh how she reveled in this newfound freedom. Living in the absence of fear, no longer beneath someone else's thumb, exhilarated her. Sebastian had helped her to achieve such liberty. The man who looked at her now as if she were a present he dearly longed to unwrap.

As if on cue, her dressing gown parted, exposing her flesh to cool air and her husband's smoldering gaze. His hand lowered to the bare skin of her waist, sweeping slowly upward until he cupped her breast. She followed his lead, arching into him, her already hard nipple pressing into the center of his palm. He rewarded her by rolling his thumb over it in lazy circles before gently pinching and pulling.

"They do match your lips," he murmured, flicking his gaze over her bare breasts in a manner that felt like another sort of caress.

Her cheeks went hot. Good heavens, was he talking about…

"Your nipples." His drawl was languid. "They're the

color of wild rose blossoms just like your mouth." As he spoke, his free hand found her other breast, visiting the same sensual torture upon it. "The loveliest shade of pink I've ever seen."

The way he spoke, the way he looked upon her, a blend of reverence and raw desire, undid her. She framed his handsome face with her hands, needing to touch him as well. Something shifted inside her, and she knew she would never again be the same. Nothing would.

"Sebastian," she said, loving his name on her tongue, one word that had come to encompass her entire world in the span of a few days.

The old Daisy would have questioned her feelings, would have been incredibly guarded with her heart and her honesty and her body. The new Daisy, however, had blossomed, and she was unafraid and bold. She was a married woman now. He was her husband, she was his, and nothing between them was wrong.

She wanted to begin again, to rise from the ashes of the woman she'd been. To believe in tender touches and gentleness. She wanted happiness and safety and even love to be within her reach. Because she deserved those things, and she always had, but she'd been too frightened to know it.

She pulled him to her, and she couldn't care if her actions were rough or gauche. All she cared about was his mouth crashing down, warm and supple, skilled and insistent. He fitted his lips over hers, and no other kiss had felt as right as this one, in this moment, with this man. She knew instinctively that she would remember this kiss for the rest of her life.

It was the kiss that changed everything.

He seemed to sense the sudden shift as well, for his mouth pressed harder into hers, his tongue sinking inside her mouth on a rough groan she felt between her thighs. His hands left her breasts, one skimming up her throat to the base of her skull, fisting in her hair and angling her to better receive his kisses. The other traveled down her belly to her hip bone, learning every curve and shallow and dip. He touched her as no one ever had, in places no one else had seen, and with such attention and care that her heart couldn't help but notice. His tender reverence filled her with wonder.

Farther still that wicked hand went as he fed her kisses, trailing across her mound and dipping into her folds where he found the part of her that clamored for his touch the most. That secret little nub she'd found on her own. It had been wicked of her, and she knew it, but like all iniquity, it had called her back for more. And more was what she yearned for now. How could she have imagined the bone-melting pleasure of a man's hand replacing hers?

And this man—good, sweet heavens. He knew what she wanted, his fingers working over her in a back and forth motion, softly at first until she jerked her hips upward, seeking. The time for reticence was gone. She wanted Sebastian, wanted him in ways she couldn't even fathom, ways that her body knew better than her mind. He understood her wordless plea, applying more pressure, and it was her turn to moan into their kiss, her tongue playing with his before slipping into his mouth for the first time.

He tasted of whisky and sin and Sebastian, and she couldn't get enough. His fingers continued their expert play, working her into a frenzy. Her heart raced, her body humming with energy and desire. She held her breath as the first wave of release threatened to break over her, pleasure sparking from her center and burning outward until every bit of her—even her toes—tingled.

He tore his mouth from hers and buried his face in her throat, his breathing harsh, lips against her skin. "Yes, love. Fly for me."

Harder, faster. She thrust her hips against his hand, helpless and mindless in her need. "Sebastian," she bit out, and she wasn't sure if she meant it as a plea or a curse. One word thundered through her lust-fogged mind. *More.*

She didn't think. Didn't question. The time for reserve and fear was long gone. That lone word spurred her on. More. More of him. More of anything he would do to her. Simply *more*.

She caught the knot of his robe and tore it open. The twin sides of the fine fabric went slack, falling open to provide a glimpse of his bare chest from the way he'd angled his body. And oh what a glimpse it was. Daisy hadn't ever seen a bare male chest, and Sebastian's was a sight to behold. Perfectly sculpted, slabbed with muscle, lightly dusted in hair. His nipples were dark and flat, so different from hers, and she couldn't resist touching one.

He groaned and kissed her neck. "Curious little buttercup. You're playing with fire."

She traced the circle, rubbed her thumb over the tip as he'd done to her. He withdrew his hand from its task of pleasuring her and flattened her palm over his chest before guiding it lower. Down over his taut, ridged abdomen and lower still, until together they reached something long and hot and hard.

Surely it could only be his manhood, but it wasn't at all as she'd imagined it would be. Here was a part of him that was firm like the rest of his body and yet soft as velvet. Her fingers closed over him, and he was large. Impossibly large. She was not ignorant of what passed between a man and a woman, thanks to Aunt Caroline. How would they ever fit together?

As he showed her how to touch him, moving her hand up and down, tightening her fingers over his shaft, she cast the uncertainty from her mind. For touching him, feeling his strong body jerk against hers, hips thrusting, hearing his gravelly moan, sent an answering pulse of heat and wetness flooding between her thighs.

And then his fingers were once more upon the flesh he'd so tortured, circling and playing, at first lightly and then harder. Her entire body tightened, anticipation a delicious trill up her spine. He kissed a path to her breast, closing his mouth over a nipple and sucking, nipping, licking until she thought she'd go mad. Every part of her was unbearably aware, from the way his scent engulfed her to the sensation he rung from her with his mouth and fingers. It was too much.

It was everything.

And she wanted…

"Sebastian," she whispered his name again, almost a benediction. Lord, how she wanted. For the first time in her life, she felt alive. Felt it with such exhilaration, that wild surge of something primal and invigorating speeding through her.

He tore his mouth from her breast, breathing heavier even than before, his gaze meeting hers. "Spend for me, love."

There was something about his command—laden with authority, knowing and dark and decadent—that sent her crashing over the edge. A burst of violent, delicious pleasure assaulted her. She cried out, fingers tightening on him reflexively, twisting her lower body into his. Tremors seized her, little bursts of dark stars flashed through her vision, and she came undone as she never had before. Shaking, heart hammering in her breast, the world swirling around her, she clutched him to her in a half-embrace.

"My God, you're so bloody beautiful." His fingers slipped from her pearl down across the seam of her folds, seeking. He kissed his way back up her throat, worshipping every part of her with that wonderful mouth of his. Her chin, her cheek, her jaw, the tip of her nose. "I want you so bloody much I ache with it."

"Yes." She stroked him the way he'd shown her, knowing that even with the release he'd already given her, she wouldn't feel complete until he had fully joined with her. She wanted him inside her. She was hollow and aching. Needing. "I want you too."

His tongue found the dip behind her ear, that miraculous place only he had ever discovered, and when he ran it over her skin, she nearly climaxed all over again.

"I shouldn't," he muttered, alternating between kisses and licks.

She didn't know what he meant, but she was also sure she didn't care. Her capacity for reasoning, logic, and any sort of thought that didn't involve him and what he was doing to her, had long since fled. "Please, Sebastian."

She wasn't even certain what she pled for. It didn't matter. Nothing mattered but him and her and the depraved passion they unleashed within each other. She didn't want a courtship. She wanted him. The absence of fear was a thrilling, ridiculous thing. She felt so giddy that she would have laughed if he had not taken her fingers from his shaft and if he had not run his length over her wet, sensitive flesh where she wanted him most.

"Forgive me," he said into her ear, and then the head of him, hard and thick and demanding, thrust inside her.

His entry robbed her of breath. Pain, burning and sharp, stabbed through her. Her body stiffened beneath his, a gasp tearing from her throat. She'd known there would be pain. Aunt Caroline had warned her, but it had still taken her by surprise, lost as she'd been in the heady pleasure he'd already visited upon her.

"Bloody hell," Sebastian swore, holding himself over her and scouring her face with his concerned, dark-blue gaze. He remained still within her, rigid and hot and not at all unwanted in spite of the unfamiliar intrusion and its accompaniment of discomfort. "I've hurt you."

In truth, she had been more startled than anything. Her father's fists and boots had inflicted far more damage upon her over the years than Sebastian ever could. With this pain would come great pleasure. With the other pain had only come the fear of more, inevitable pain and suffering

"I shall survive. I've been hurt far worse in my lifetime." She blinked away the tears stinging her eyes.

"I'm sorry," he pressed his forehead to hers for a moment, his warm breath fanning her lips. "I'm so sorry, buttercup. It will only ever pain you the first time. Let me make it better for you. Please?"

Sebastian raised his head again, searching her eyes. He trailed the gentlest of touches over her cheek. His beautiful face had softened, his expression tender, etched with concern. She would have given him anything in that moment. There was a darkness inside him that she sensed, for she had the same darkness dwelling within her. Sebastian was the first person who had ever made her want to drench the darkness in light—both his and hers. She couldn't shake the feeling that somehow, as strange and incomprehensible as it seemed, they had been meant to come together. Just as she couldn't shake the feeling that he could and would make anything better for her.

He was the man who had rescued her from ruin, and she would never forget that.

"Yes," she told him, for in truth, she wanted him still. The pulsing pain had abated. She moved beneath him tentatively, drawing him deeper, and though some lingering discomfort remained, her need for him revisited her in a great flood of sensation. "Yes, Sebastian."

He kissed her, long and lingering, plundering her mouth as he moved. Tentatively, slowly. His fingers dipped between them, finding the nub at the center of her folds again. The burning gave way to small licks of pleasure that began at her core and radiated throughout her body. Her inner muscles adjusted, her body naturally becoming accustomed to his. He stretched and filled and claimed.

And she liked the feeling of him, potent, male, demanding. His mouth took, his kisses bruising and carnal, wild with need, open, hungry, and unashamed. He bit her lip, thrust his tongue against hers. His body gave, those wicked fingers on her knowing where to touch, how much pressure, when to increase his pace and when to slow to a torturous rhythm that left her gasping into his mouth and arching against him.

He tore his lips away, as breathless as she. "Daisy, sweet

Christ, you're going to be the death of me." He kissed her neck again, tongued the hollow behind her ear. "Spend again for me, buttercup. Make it worth everything."

There was an undercurrent in his words, a hint of accusation, a whole lot of fire. She didn't know what he meant, and further examination would need to wait, for he was moving again, faster and deeper. It consumed her. He consumed her. She angled her hips against him, allowing her thighs to fall open more, bringing him even deeper. Nothing had ever been more right. He was everything, and she was everything, and the world was exploding with color and light and sound and smell, and oh dear Lord...

"Again, buttercup." There was his voice, low and demanding, his tongue resuming its exploration of her skin as though she were a delicacy laid before him. Behind her ear, down her throat, probing against her pulse, the curve of her breast, teasing a nipple. He caught the stiff peak in his teeth, nipping, his fingers working faster over her pearl, his manhood sliding in and out with delicious friction.

She gasped. Moaned something. Perhaps it was his name. She didn't know. Didn't care. Her breath came faster, heart galloping, entire body aflame, and she was hyperaware of every connection between his body and hers. Ready to come undone.

Bliss crashed over her, sudden and overwhelming, like the sea in the grip of a hurricane. It was fierce, magnificent. Nature at her most violent and passionate. Daisy shook, crying out, gripping his broad shoulders, sinking her nails into him, straining upward, seeking more as pleasure burst within her.

He gave her what she wanted, sliding home deep and quick, moving in long, pleasurable thrusts that had her tightening around him even more. And then, his large body went utterly stiff as he drove himself into her again, a curse slipping from his lips before his mouth came down on hers once more. A new sensation, hot and wet, blossomed inside her.

He rocked into her a few more times, prolonging the moment and the pleasure both, before breaking the kiss to stare down at her. "Damn it."

And then he withdrew from her body, rolled away, and left the bed.

"Sebastian," she protested, feeling the loss of his touch—the loss of him—like an ache.

He stalked away from her, his dressing gown billowing behind him like a dark, angry cloud. She realized belatedly that neither of them had entirely removed their robes. As he opened the door joining their chambers, she flipped the ends of hers back over her, covering her nudity.

How foolish, an attempt to preserve her modesty after sharing her entire body with him. After he had known her and pleasured her so intimately. But as she watched him leave, she was acutely aware that, husband or no, he remained very much a stranger to her, and she was beginning to fear that it wasn't just her body he had claimed.

The thought left her more chilled than the cool night air and the London damp combined. Indeed, it chilled her straight to the marrow.

## chapter thirteen

W HAT IN THE BLOODY HELL had he just done?
Sebastian breezed into his private bathing
chamber. The gaslights remained lit, for he'd
intended to perform his nightly ablutions before going to
sleep. But instead, he'd gone in search of the one woman in
the goddamn world that he should stay farthest from. The
woman he couldn't seem to stop touching, kissing, wanting,
and lusting over.

The woman he had just bedded.

Had he actually believed he could withstand the
temptation of being in Daisy's bedchamber again without
taking her? More fool, he, for all it had taken was the wet
heat of her cunny and the sweetness of her lips to make him
risk everything he sought to preserve. His loyalty, his oath,
his country, his honor.

"Fuck," he cursed once with feeling, and then thrice
more for good measure. "Fuck, fuck, fuck." This latest
manifestation of counting he blamed upon her as well.

She had infected him like a disease. Burrowed beneath
his skin like a tick. Had somehow managed to do what no

other woman before her ever had. And in one night of allowing his prick to rule his head, he'd just done what he'd sworn he wouldn't do.

He washed her blood from his cock, and he had never performed another task that made him feel lower. There it was, the evidence of their union. How the hell would he annul their marriage now, after he had so selfishly and stupidly taken her innocence? Oh, he had no doubt that Carlisle would still pull the proper strings to accomplish such a feat, but could Sebastian, in good conscience, do it?

One answer belonged to that question, and one answer only.

*No.*

He pulled his robe together and knotted the belt. Then, he seized the bowl he ordinarily used for shaving and filled it with warm water, still cursing himself. He took up two small towels before turning back toward the chamber where he'd left Daisy, thoroughly deflowered. He lowered all the lights save one.

Carlisle was going to have his head. Married for the span of one day, and he'd consummated. Had more than consummated. He'd spent inside her. Jesus Christ, his stupidity and raging lust now meant that there was the chance that Daisy could bear his child.

The notion didn't curdle his blood as it ought. Instead, an odd, foreign surge of warmth flooded his chest. What in the name of all that was holy? Ruthlessly, he forced the sensation to go the hell away. She wasn't meant to be his duchess. He still didn't know which side of the damn fence she stood on. He had deceived her, had dishonored her, and under no circumstance should the thought of Daisy growing heavy with his child and bearing him a daughter with sprightly golden curls and green eyes make him feel anything other than revulsion.

When he strode back into her chamber, determination and self-control firmly once more at the reins, a pang of some indefinable emotion nevertheless stabbed through him. She lay where he'd left her, the long, beautiful strands of her hair in disarray, her robe closed, hands laced together in a protective gesture. Her expression wary, her cheeks flushed a becoming shade of pink as she made eye contact with him.

She looked so small and alone, delicate and frighteningly lovely all at once, that his hands trembled, sending some of the water splashing from the sides of the bowl. It landed on his bare foot and the thick carpet with a splat. Damn it to hell, how could this woman who was a stranger to him, this dainty, elegant creature he didn't dare trust, shake him to his core?

It made no sense, but she did.

He continued across the chamber, not stopping until he'd reached her bedside. Everything in him had meant to upkeep his honor and preserve her virginity. Yesterday, he'd stood at this same spot, slashing his thumb and smearing his blood into the bedclothes to maintain both.

He loathed himself.

"Your Grace?" she asked, her tone hesitant, wide eyes going from his hands to his face.

Her guard was down, it was plain to see, and she looked every bit like a woman who'd had to live her life by the whims of a violent man. She was a wary thing, his buttercup.

Surely not his, though?

*His*, answered something deep inside him, just as quickly.

"Promise me something?" He deposited the bowl on the bedside table with care, his gaze never leaving hers. "You will dispense with the formality between us forever. From this moment forward, I am only Sebastian to you."

A frown creased the creamy perfection of her forehead. "I'm sorry."

His self-loathing increased tenfold. "You have done nothing for which you need apologize. I, on the other hand, have. This...consummating our union...I should never have come to you tonight. And for that, I must apologize to you. I promised you a courting, and within a day, I've made a liar and a cad of myself."

And worse, he added inwardly.

A man without honor was not a man at all.

"Sebastian." A soft smile transformed her features, and if she had been beautiful before, there was only one word to describe her now. Radiant. She glowed. Daisy was a force.

"As we've already established." He found himself smiling back at her like a bloody escapee from a lunatic asylum. "The sort of churl who doesn't appreciate his wife's tardiness at dinner."

"Yes." Her smile widened, and so did his, and for a beat, he fell into her green gaze, mesmerized by that simple way she had of making him see levity where he was certain none could be had. "Then you must promise me not to apologize for what happened tonight. A churl you may be, but a cad and a liar, surely not."

Christ, she didn't know how wrong she was.

He had not returned to her side to make a confession, however. He jerked his attention back to the bowl of water. Best to act while it still remained warm. And there was utterly nothing to be gained by mooning at his beautiful pawn of a wife. A woman suspected of treason.

For some reason, the reminder didn't hold as much ice and warning as it once had. He dipped one of the towels into the bowl, saturating it, before wringing out the excess. Slowly, he joined her on the bed.

"What are you doing?" she asked, eyes going wide.

Curious that she would only question him now, when the damage had long since been done. With his free hand, he nudged her knees open. "Tending to you, buttercup. Let me, please?"

She resisted. "I'm perfectly capable of—"

"Of course you are," he interrupted, not at all surprised. Something had told him that she would be independent to the last. This was a woman who had been relying on herself and herself alone for far too long. "But I want to do this for you."

Her flush heightened as her eyes searched his. At long last, she nodded, her jaw tensing, the only outward show of her nervousness. "If you must."

It was a means of doing penance, and a small one at that. He guided her thighs open, swept aside the fabric of her dressing gown once more, revealing her mound in all its perfection. Blood smeared her thigh. Her cunny was pink and wet with the evidence of their lovemaking. His cock surged anew at the sight, some primal force in him relishing his claiming of her.

She was his, by God.

He moved the wet towel over her, cleaning her. First her thigh, then her pretty pink flesh, washing her, worshipping her. She didn't attempt to close herself to him or push him away, simply remained still and silent, allowing him to complete this torturous task he'd assigned for himself.

Two sets of bloodied sheets in two nights. He hadn't an inkling what the servants would think, but it was too damn late to worry about such trivial repercussions now. The most damning consequences of all would follow if Carlisle ever got wind of it.

"I hurt you," he said again, because he still recalled the way she'd gone rigid beneath him when he'd torn past the barrier of her innocence, and because he hated himself for giving her any sort of pain at all, for deceiving her even now.

He dried her with the other towel and kissed her inner thighs. Would have continued, kissing all the way to her cunny, tasting her where he longed to taste her the most, but her hands flitted to his shoulders like twin butterflies, urging him upward. He allowed her to move him where she would. He wouldn't dream of pushing her too far, and he'd already taken far more than he had a right to take.

"It was nothing." She gripped his elbows and drew him toward her.

But it wasn't nothing. He hadn't liked hurting her. Hated that he was hurting her still with every action, each small deception. He would make up for it the only way he knew how.

As though it was the most natural thing in the world, his mouth connected with hers. The kiss was long and slow and deep. Leading once more to the path of ruin. With great reluctance, he tore his mouth from hers and returned the towel to the bowl.

He had never before spent an entire night in bed with a woman, but he had also never deflowered an innocent before either. It was bloody peculiar, but he didn't want to leave her. Before giving his rational mind the chance to confuse matters for him, he turned down the lights and shucked his dressing gown. With her help, he made short work of Daisy's as well.

She didn't protest when he drew her body against his and pulled the bedclothes atop them both. They were joined from ankle to shoulder, his arm banded over her waist in a possessive grip he couldn't restrain. Soft, womanly heat burned him alive. The scent of bergamot and vanilla and ambergris blended into one heady note. Christ, but everything about her drove him to distraction.

"I'm sorry for hurting you," he said into the darkness and the silence that had fallen between them. He meant that in every way possible, so much feeling and emotion packed into that sentence it could have been a bloody ocean-faring merchant ship loaded from bow to stern and it still would not have contained more.

Her hand found his where it tightened over the curve of her waist, their fingers tangling. "I've promised to call you Sebastian and you've promised to cease all apologies for tonight. If you mean to go back on your word, I'll have to refer to you as Your Grace forever. That could prove a lengthy sentence indeed, *Your Grace.*"

He detected the smile in her words and realized he was grinning back into the night, like some besotted fool. Staying in her chamber had been another mistake in a series of grievous errors. But he hadn't the willpower to move from her side now, and what was one more sin in a catalog of so many?

"Touché, buttercup." He paused, his smile fading as he thought again of her earlier words. *I've been hurt far worse in my lifetime.* Part of him probed her now because he knew he must, and part of him probed her because he was the man who had taken her innocence, and he cared for her regardless of the glaring fact that he should not make such a neophyte mistake. "You said you've been hurt worse. Your father…what did he do to you?"

He heard her swallow, the steady, even pace of her breathing increasing in increments. Without light to illuminate her face, he read her on tells and body language alone. The fingers tangled in his tightened. She didn't answer.

"Daisy," he tried again, careful to keep his tone gentle. "I'm your husband. Won't you tell me?"

"Why would you want to know?" she asked at last, her voice small, marked by some indefinable emotion. Shame, perhaps?

Why, indeed?

Because he needed to know.

Because he needed to believe her, to understand her story, where she'd come from and who she was.

And also, because he needed to know just how badly he'd have to hurt her son-of-a-bitch of a father in reprisal.

"I want to know what he did to you, Daisy, because I'm going to do each one of those things to him in return, only with ten times more depravity." It was as honest a reply as he could manage.

"You mustn't say that." There was her voice again, lilting and haunting in the night's inky stillness.

"Tell me, buttercup," he urged, pulling her tighter to his side, as though he could somehow absorb her, take on any pain she'd ever experienced just to lessen her burden, and keep her forever safe from harm. He would have gladly done so had it been possible. All the disgust he'd felt at betraying his duty had somehow faltered in the blinding brilliance of the feeling of her trusting form next to his.

She was silent for an indeterminate space of time. No sound but busy London outside, clacking hooves, her steady breathing, vehicles traveling, so many people all around them, and yet, there they were. Two naked bodies pressed against each other. Connecting in a way he'd never before imagined possible, a way that transcended the physicality of a mere joining. He'd bedded his fair share of women. But he didn't lie to himself that any of those occasions could compare to this.

"It began after my mother died," she said, quietly at first, and then with more authority as she continued. "I was four years old, and I'd spilled ink on the new rug in his office, where I wasn't meant to be. He whipped me with a riding crop. As I grew older and began acting as his hostess, the punishments he meted out changed. Fists and kicks mostly, though he was always careful never to strike me where anyone else could ever see the mark."

Jesus.

The air felt as if it had been sucked straight from his lungs. She spoke calmly, with a matter-of-fact acceptance that disturbed him. Daisy had mettle, the sort he couldn't even begin to fathom any other fine lady of his acquaintance possessing.

"His fists." His voice was toneless. Vanreid's fists were practically the size of ham hocks. And he had used them upon a helpless woman, whose bones were as dainty as a bird's. Sebastian's blood went cold. And *kicks*. By God, the man was built like an ox, and he'd kicked Daisy. To manage such a feat, she would've had to have already been on the floor, struck down by him. "Where? Where did he hurt you?"

He had to know, and yet the knowledge would make him ill.

"Sebastian," she protested. "It doesn't matter."

Oh, it mattered. Retribution would be his. Vanreid

would be made to pay.

But he didn't wish to push her too far, or upset her by asking her to relive such viciousness, and so he tucked her head against his chest and kissed her crown. "I would take each of those beatings for you, buttercup. If I could, I would remove every memory of them."

She burrowed closer, rubbing her cheek against his bare chest like a cat, trusting. "Thank you, Sebastian."

She had no cause to offer him gratitude.

Already, she had given him far more than she should this night. She had given him everything she had. And he'd taken it. Every last shred. Her innocence was his. Her future was in his hands. But she didn't know that. Naïf that she was, she hadn't an inkling that he was the last bloody man in all of London she should have entrusted with such a priceless gift.

He stroked her hair, sweet-smelling and luxuriant as silk, a new surge of protectiveness settling heavy in his gut. The devil of it was that, given the opportunity, he'd do it all over again.

"Sleep now, buttercup," he told her.

Soon, the steady, rhythmic sound of her breathing filled the chamber. Sebastian stared into the black void of the night, still stroking her hair, unable to find the same solace that only slumber could provide.

## chapter fourteen

$\mathcal{S}$HE WOKE AS DAWN SLIPPED THROUGH THE WINDOW dressings, painting drowsy shadows and golden swaths of light over her chamber. For a moment, she blinked, thinking herself back at Aunt Caroline's. But no, the size of the room was disproportionately large, and she lay on a firmer bed, quite on the wrong side. Where had the striped wallpaper gone?

It took her disoriented mind a thorough scan of the chamber from left to right until she recalled where she was. Who she was. What she had done. Beneath the bedclothes, she wore not a stitch, her body sore and tender in new places.

Good heavens. She pressed a hand to her scalding cheek as memories of the night washed over her, a foreign lick of anticipation trilling down her spine. He had been *inside* her.

How would she face him today?

The question took on a rather poignant significance when her eyes adjusted better to the dim light and she realized he was still in her bed. She clutched the counterpane to her bare breasts as her hungry gaze absorbed him. He lay on his back, bedclothes hugging his hips to reveal the breathtaking beauty of his bare chest and torso.

Even in repose, he exuded masculine strength, from the defined slabs of muscle on his abdomen to his broad chest and shoulders. His hair was swept back from his forehead, his brow for once unmarked by a frown, his nose a flawless line to match his equally perfect mouth. His lashes fanned over his high cheekbones, the dark growth of a beard stippling his jaw.

She ought to look away.

Her eyes traced the dents near his hip bones, the dark trail of hair that went below the blankets and straight to his hidden manhood. She remembered the way he'd felt, thick and smooth and hot in her palm, the way he'd felt thrusting into her. They had been as close as a man and woman could be.

They were husband and wife. Consummating the marriage was only right. But how odd it was that he had seen and touched every part of her body. Why, she didn't even know what he liked to read, what he preferred for breakfast, or how he took his tea.

And that was when she noticed the faint tracery of something on his hands and arms. Not raised scars, she noted, but a discoloration scarcely even noticeable in the early morning glow. She'd seen markings like that once before, on the face of a man who had been burned in an incident at one of her father's factories. Her gaze lingered on her husband's strong arms. Had Sebastian been in a fire?

"They're scars, buttercup."

His words, low and intimate as velvet, dragged over her bare flesh. She couldn't suppress the undignified squeak that rose to her lips. Flushing hotter still, she dragged her gaze back to his face to find him watching her, heavy-lidded and sensual. He didn't seem disturbed by her unabashed examination of him, but she knew a pang of embarrassment at being caught.

"Scars?" she asked, gripping the bedclothes even tighter

as she thought of how she must appear.

Her hair was unbound, trailing wild down around her face, and she was sure she looked a fright. This was her punishment for ogling him. She could have slipped from the bed, thrown on her robe, taken a brush to her unmanageable locks. Instead, he'd caught her at her frumpiest while she looked upon him the way a caged lion watched a hunk of raw meat on the other side of the bars.

He watched her intently, his sensual lips tightening as he appeared to weigh his next words. "I was in a house fire as a lad. Fortunately, I survived almost unscathed."

*Almost unscathed.* She wondered if he referred to the scars he bore or to something he didn't wear on his skin but carried inside. A fire must have been frightening, and for a small child to have experienced…well, her heart ached for the boy he must have been.

She ran her fingertips over the evidence of that long-ago inferno. He didn't move away from her touch, simply allowed it. His skin felt smooth and warm, every bit as perfect as the rest of him.

"I'm sorry," she whispered, and her apology was twofold. She was sorry for what had happened to him, sorry for staring.

"I'm not worthy of your pity, buttercup." His tone was wry.

"I don't pity you," she said quickly, for she didn't. Empathy and pity were two different beasts. Touching him was having a strange effect on her heartbeat and her ability to concentrate. Her body hungered for his, but she was keenly aware that she didn't wish to appear overeager. "I'm curious. There's so much I don't know about you."

And she wanted to know all of it, all of him. Already, she knew his scent, his body, the way he moved in her. But she wanted more from him. She wanted their marriage to be more than a necessity.

"Curious." He watched her in that predatory way he had that sent a thrill straight to her core.

"Yes," she forced herself to say with as much feigned nonchalance as she could muster. "I find myself wondering whether you prefer poetry or prose and whether or not you take sugar in your tea."

"Poetry and tea?" The frown returned, furrowing his brow. "If those are your most pressing bloody thoughts this morning, then I've been terribly remiss."

Of course they hadn't been her first thoughts. She searched his face now, wondering if he was dismayed or he was teasing her. "You haven't been remiss, Your...Sebastian."

A slow smile curved his lips, his dimple reemerging to taunt her. "I must have done something right in order to only receive half a Your Grace."

He was teasing her, alright. She was certain of it. This was a different side of her husband, one she'd yet to see. He seemed at once self-possessed and perfectly at home, yet vulnerable. His customary ice had thawed. And here, in this distrait morning light, she felt as though she were perhaps seeing the true Sebastian for the first time.

"You've done many things right," she told him, blushing even more furiously as the words left her lips. Sweet Lord, what was she saying? She'd meant that he had been kind and honorable, had rescued her from an intolerable situation when he hadn't owed her anything, and that he'd stood up against her father on her behalf. That he'd touched her with the sort of worship she'd never imagined possible.

But as his deep, blue gaze bored into hers, the air between them was suddenly heavy, charged with sexual innuendo she hadn't intended.

"I could do more things right," he told her with unrepentant cheek. "Perhaps we could pare it down to a one quarter Your Grace by the time we break our fast."

A one quarter Your Grace.

Truly.

She laughed. Threw back her head, embraced it. Laughed as she hadn't ever done before. Her life had not held much room for mirth. Perhaps the time had come to change that, in the most unlikely form: a man she'd married out of necessity and desperation. A man who carried a burden on his shoulders he'd yet to share with her, who hadn't any living family, and who had defended her in the face of her father's wrath.

Her heart felt…light.

Whole.

She was still laughing when he rolled atop her, pressing her to the bed.

His hands cupped her face, and he rocked his hips into hers so that she felt every marvelous part of what was hidden by the bedclothes against her now. He was hard and demanding, and answering sensation blossomed between her thighs where their skin met. She wanted him. Her laughter dried up.

His gaze bored into hers. "I like the way you laugh, buttercup."

And just like that, her heart felt…full.

A new awareness budded within her as she caressed the taut muscles of his upper arms and let her legs fall open to welcome him. "Perhaps you can even manage to make it a one-eighth Your Grace," she teased him back.

He undulated against her again, running his length over her slick mound, grinding against the bud of her sex that he'd plied with such delicious torture last night. Slowly, he fitted his mouth to hers, his upper lip nestling into the seam of hers. He bit her lower lip, swiped away the sting with his tongue. Her fingernails sank into his arms, urging him in silent plea.

He broke the kiss at last, running his nose alongside hers and inhaling deeply of her scent, as though it pleased him. "I'm aiming for one-sixteenth, buttercup."

His mouth, swift and knowing, swallowed her laugh. And then his fingers dipped between their bodies to toy with her pearl, sending need shooting through her, and she stopped laughing and kissed him right back with all the crazy tumult bubbling up inside her. She embraced it, embraced him, and he made love to her as the sun rose over London and the world came back to life.

And Daisy's world was irrevocably changed.

# chapter fifteen

*W*HY DID THINKING ABOUT HER BLOODY
LAUGH make his cock go rigid in his trousers?
And where was the scent of bergamot
originating from?

Why was it making him harder?

Sebastian sat in his study, flipping through the efficiently
ordered correspondence his secretary had presented him
with, numbers and letters blurring before him. Even spies
of the realm still needed to manage their empires at home,
and sometimes that proved the devil of a task, particularly
when he was supposed to focus on the price of wheat and
the cost of stone masons and the growing influx of
American cheese.

A week had passed since he'd married Daisy. He'd given
up any pretense at honor and had given in to his need of
her, reasoning that having his fill would slake the all-
consuming desire she'd fanned to fire within him. Night
after night, he'd gone to her chamber. Not just nights, if he
were honest.

He'd come upon her in the library one afternoon, and

on another occasion, he'd brought them both to earth-shattering orgasm right here on his desk. There had been the morning he'd lifted her skirts and fucked her in the hall, where anyone could have come across them. The wickedness—in the open, on the verge of being caught by a stray servant at all times—had only propelled them both into a crescendo of pleasure.

Each time his body left hers, he was certain it would be the last, that it would be enough. And the next time he came across her, he couldn't stop from touching her, kissing her, wanting her.

Even now, beneath the watchful eye of his secretary, he wanted her so much his teeth ached. He had left her abed hours ago. She should have been well purged from his mind, exorcised from his body. A bloody week of losing himself inside her, and he was only left needing her more.

He should never have bedded her in the first place.

Yet how could he not have?

And how could he stop, when he'd already had her so many times and yet his yearning only increased rather than sputtering out like a tired old flame? How many times had it been? *Once, twice, perhaps a dozen?* More counting, there he went, spiraling deeper into the abyss. *Thirteen? Fourteen?* With each number, he strummed his fingers on the surface of his desk as though the tactile sensation could somehow shake him free of this infernal torture. Free of this insatiable need to have her again warring with the overwhelming sense of disgust that he'd taken her at all.

That he'd spent the last week the happiest he'd ever been in his entire life, and that he didn't want it to end.

Bloody hell, Carlisle would have his head on a pike if he ever learned the truth.

None of these thoughts were doing him any good. He crumpled the letter he held in his fist. "Simmonds?"

"Yes, Your Grace?" His eternally efficient secretary interrupted his grim musings.

"Where is the letter from my agent at Thornsby Hall?"

he demanded, and if his voice was harsh as a whip it was only because he was doing his damnedest to hide the ridiculous state of his trousers.

Tight. Too bloody tight. He shifted in his chair, but that did him no good, so he forced himself to stare at Simmonds, which would surely force his cock to return to its normal state of order. His secretary was all angles, all male, arms disproportionately long so that his fingers hung to his knees, and a scar on his upper lip rendered his mustache preposterously off-center. He didn't have golden hair or pink nipples or smell like a sultry combination of dessert and sexual congress.

Christ, that last, rogue thought wasn't helping. Not a goddamn whit.

Simmonds cleared his throat, his expression growing ill at ease. He was an easy read, and Sebastian liked that about him. It wouldn't do to have a man he couldn't see straight through involved in his personal and estate matters. Simmons was trustworthy, dependable, and he never asked questions.

"Your Grace, I believe the letter in question is currently…in your hand," Simmonds said then.

Sebastian's eyes narrowed. Perhaps he ought to sack him. Did he think he was daft? "Of course it isn't, or I wouldn't be asking you for its whereabouts, now would I?"

"Forgive me, Your Grace. It is merely that I know the order of the correspondence. They're arranged by level of import, and your concern over the cost of suggested improvements at Thornsby Hall led me to place it atop the stack."

He stared at his secretary, who stared back at him, unrelenting. This was Simmonds' only fault, his inability to kowtow. And truly, it wasn't a fault in Sebastian's book. Not ordinarily. In this moment, however, it was, because he was beginning to fear Simmonds was correct and that he'd been so distracted by thoughts of his glorious American minx that he couldn't even bloody well read.

His gaze lowered to the crumpled sheet in his hand, and he recognized the familiar slanted scrawl of Carnes, his Thornsby land agent, peering from between his fingers. "Simmonds," he said without looking up.

"Yes, Your Grace?"

"That will be all," he dismissed.

Far better to wallow in his humiliation and shame on his own, he reasoned, than with his secretary watching over him. With his broad shoulders on his otherwise narrow frame, the man looked like a bloody upside-down triangle.

He waited for Simmonds to take his leave before releasing the letter and spreading it over his desk in a futile attempt to smooth out the many wrinkles. Thornsby Hall was his family seat and his chief concern these days when he wasn't otherwise engaged in duty. His father had allowed it to fall into disrepair, and Sebastian had begun to undertake the tremendous investment of restoring it to its proper glory. A great, sprawling estate of seven thousand acres, it contained some of his fondest boyhood memories. Thornsby Hall was to be his reward when he retired from service to the League.

Or when he was removed from service, which seemed far more likely given his recent carelessness. He forced himself to read the correspondence from Carnes in full, but his mind remained diverted.

Fifty thousand pounds for this year's needed improvements. The leaking roof had been repaired, thank fuck, but the crumbling southern wall needed to be addressed. Something about an increase in the turkey flock. Fodder cabbage, turnips, and sheep.

There it was again, damn it all.

Bergamot.

And her laughter the first morning after he'd made love to her. Her laughter had been like a gift: unexpected and treasured, a joy to his soul. That beautiful, mellifluous sound had wound its way inside him, imprinted itself upon his very memory, so that he would never again hear another woman's levity without thinking of her. Of Daisy with her spun-gold hair and her sad eyes and insuppressible daring. Of how he had once laughed with her and it had been the best fucking morning of his life.

The only morning in as long as he could recall where he'd allowed himself the luxury of being. He had been Sebastian, and she had been Daisy, and none of the mire surrounding them had intruded.

Realization struck him then, with the force of a fist straight to the jaw. He didn't just lust after her. Bedding her had not been based upon basic sexual need alone in the same way it had with his past lovers. It had been necessary, yes, but in the way that filling his lungs with breath was necessary. Why else would he have been caught up in her for an entire week and still more lost than he'd ever been?

Bergamot hit him again.

He lowered his nose to his shoulder and took a discreet sniff. Jesus, his neck smelled like her. It was as if she'd planted her scent on him as another method of feminine torture. He must have been remiss in his morning ablutions, but he couldn't say he minded now, for he liked the way she smelled.

He liked Daisy.

A knock sounded at his study door, and unless he was mistaken, it wasn't the knock of any of his servants. Which could only mean one thing.

Her.

She wasn't satisfied with invading his mind and imprinting her scent upon him, but now she intended to infiltrate his inner sanctum as well. He would ignore her, he decided, flipping past the Thornsby Hall letter to the next. She was his temporary wife, he reminded himself. Their union wasn't meant to last. It was a falsehood. A ruse. They needn't play at being husband and wife. He wasn't required to invite her into his study. And he bloody well ought to stop spending every night in her chamber. He would, just as soon as he could bring himself to look at her without needing to tear aside her fripperies and fill her with his cock.

That didn't seem likely any time soon.

The knock came again, followed by her voice. "I've been wondering all week and have yet to reach an answer. What follows a one-sixteenth, Your Grace?"

The woman was mad.

He should continue ignoring her. Turn her away. Begin to erect a sensible distance between them. But he was grinning, and that meant he was just as mad as she.

Fit for the lunatic asylum, the both of them.

"You may enter," he called out, and it wasn't solely with resignation. No indeed, there was also a most unwanted note of anticipation underlying his words.

The door opened, and she swept inside, a vision in a pink-and-red-striped frock with lace underskirts peeking through. Her hair was styled differently today, worn in a loose twist atop her head with curls framing her face. She looked like a goddess he'd seen in a picture at the Grosvenor Gallery once: luscious, romantic, purely feminine.

The air fled from his lungs as he stood in deference and bowed. How was it possible that she was even more beautiful, more vibrant and magnetic, than she'd ever been? How was it possible that he wanted her more than ever?

She offered him a formal curtsy as well, but her full lips quirked into a confident smile. "Sebastian."

"One thirty-second," he answered, skirting his desk and going to her. Suddenly, he couldn't be in the same chamber as she without having her in his arms.

He tried to remind himself that he was a spy with a duty to the Crown, but that argument had grown increasingly muffled as he'd gotten to know Daisy better. She made him recall what he'd forgotten over the last dozen years: that beneath the façade he was forced to present to the world, he was also just a man. His training had prepared him for torture and death, had taught him how to defend himself with or without weapons, to kill with his bare hands, to read a man's face, to anticipate his enemy's every action. But none of his training had prepared him for the onslaught of one small, daring woman.

The warm tones of her gown enhanced the moss of her eyes as he approached her, and he won a laugh from her that settled somewhere in the vicinity of his heart. "Good heavens, that is quite a small fraction. Would one even pronounce the 'Y'?"

"I can't be certain." He caught her waist and pulled her against him, savoring the already familiar crush of her breasts into his chest. "But one could rectify the matter by referring to one's husband by his given name."

"Oh?" She raised a brow in feigned innocence and batted her long lashes. "And what is that? My memory is appalling, I'm afraid, and I've forgotten."

"Perhaps I can stir it for you, buttercup." He gave in to temptation and lowered his mouth to hers. How naturally they fit together. How easy it was to slide his hand into the soft confines of her neat coiffure, cup her perfectly shaped head, and angle her just as he wanted her. His tongue traced the seam of her lips, demanding entrance, and she opened for him without hesitation, her tongue tangling with his.

She tasted of chocolate and decadence, and he wanted more. Always wanted more. And that was the problem, wasn't it? His hands tightened on her waist, and he led her backward until they reached his desk. He could never have his fill of her.

He dragged his mouth from hers and trailed a fervent line of kisses to her ear, tonguing the silky patch of skin behind it. She tasted of vanilla and the light salt of her skin. She moaned and clutched at his shoulders. So responsive, his Daisy.

"You've bewitched me," he accused softly into her ear. "I'm meant to be attending estate matters and all I want is to lift your skirts and feel if you're as wet for me already as I suspect you are."

She would be drenched when he touched her, and this he knew by the way she strained against him, as if she desired all points of her body to be in simultaneous contact with his. He felt the same. He wanted every inch of her flawless skin naked and pressed against his, from her hard, pink nipples to her pale, curved legs.

"Shall I leave you to estate matters?" she asked, breathless.

He tore his lips from her neck to survey the contents of his desk. Correspondence. A stack of news. Some pens and sheaves of paper. His ledger. To hell with all of it. With one swipe of his arm, he sent it raining to the carpet. Papers flew, somersaulting over themselves, pens clanging together, the news crumpling into a heap.

"I do believe I've had enough of estate matters for the nonce," he decided, grinning down at her like a lovesick fool.

No, surely not lovesick. Nor a fool, he corrected himself hastily. It had only been a week, after all. Love didn't come upon a man so precipitously, and especially not when the lady in question was suspected of treason. He was sure of it.

In an effort to ward off further maudlin sentiment, he took her mouth with his once more, and this kiss was unapologetically demanding. He sucked on her lower lip, then caught it between his teeth and tugged. Frantic, fierce need speared him. The need to have her, to consume her. His cock twitched against his trousers, his balls already drawn tight in anticipation of flooding release.

Her palms, which had dropped to his chest and had been conducting a slow, torturous exploration over his waistcoat and shirt, gently pushed, putting enough distance between them to break the kiss. Her gaze sparkled into his, the green of early spring rebirth after the barren death of winter.

"You've a duty, Sebastian," she said then.

For a heartbeat, he stilled, the blood pumping through his veins turning to ice. Was it possible that she somehow knew after all? Jesus, why would she repeat the words his own conscience riddled him with every day?

And then she tilted her head in that way he'd come to

know meant she was being earnest, cupping his jaw in her hand. "I don't wish to distract you from your work. I missed you, but I don't wish to be unfairly demanding of your time. I'll leave you to it, then. I need to go over the menu with Mrs. Robbins, and I've yet to make myself at home in your library. Father thought reading invited sloth, so I haven't read as much as I would have preferred."

He released the breath he hadn't realized he'd been holding. She was babbling, and she was adorable, and he was going to come out of his skin if he wasn't buried deep inside her in the next five minutes.

"Daisy." He pressed a kiss to her open palm, and held her to him when she would have attempted to make her retreat. "You may distract me any time you wish, buttercup. My time will always be yours, and if you want to buy an entire new library's worth of books that are to your liking, I won't blink a bloody eye. Read until you need spectacles. But you're not leaving this room until I've made you spend."

Her eyes widened, cheeks going rosy. Lovemaking remained new to her, though she'd proven an apt and willing pupil. She was still very much an innocent, however, and he would enjoy debauching her for the rest of their lives.

*The rest of their lives.*

The unbidden thought sent something profound streaking through him. And it wasn't dread or a sense of futility. It wasn't guilt or duty. It was…Christ, he didn't know what it was.

Rather than further complicate matters, he lifted her onto the desk. His hands fisted in her billowing skirts, crushing the fine silk, but he didn't give a damn. Slowly, his gaze never leaving hers, he drew them to her waist, petticoats, chemise, and all, and lifted them so that they lay atop his desk.

As he surveyed his handiwork, his mouth went dry. She was perfectly coiffed and demure from the waist up, her bodice in place, hair as elegant as when she'd entered the chamber. But from the waist down, she was pure, unadulterated siren. Lacy drawers hugged her hips. Narrow ankles clad in silk stockings peeped from beneath, and her heeled black leather shoes dangling over the floor somehow rendered it all incredibly erotic.

He wished he could keep her here, in this moment, forever.

Beautiful and bold and undeniably his.

"Sebastian," she said his name quietly, and it held a wary note of protest.

"Buttercup," he returned, his fingers finding the button on her drawers, just below the point of her corset. He slid it free of its mooring and pushed the undergarment down her legs, leaving her nude from the waist down except for her stockings, garters, and shoes.

He nearly came right then and there as he drank in the sight of her. She was so fucking beautiful it hurt to look at her. His chest physically ached. And his cock, well, Jesus, that was another matter entirely.

He sank to his knees on the soft carpet, ignoring the startled sound she made, and urged her legs apart. "Open for me, darling?"

He had seen her before, had tended to her intimately on their first night. But this was different, in the undeniable daylight of his study, in the midst of the afternoon, and he was intending to dance a different sort of attendance upon her.

She hesitated only a moment before giving in to him, sliding her legs apart so that he could see the heart of her, as pink and beautiful as her full mouth and hard little nipples. He hummed with pleasure as he ran his hands along the soft expanses of her inner thighs and lowered his head.

His tongue traced over her pearl slowly, allowing her to get accustomed to him. One swipe, then another, and another. He ran circles over her, teasing and leisurely, listening for her intakes of breath, attuned to the tilt of her hips and the rocking of her body against his mouth as he learned what pleased her.

A lilting moan tore from her, and it was his name, and he felt it all the way to his cock. He sucked then, loving her on his tongue, in his mouth, and nipped her with his teeth. She tasted musky and sweet and like the affirmation, it seemed, of life itself. He ran his tongue over her seam, finding her wet and hot, and then let his tongue find its natural place inside her. He filled her as deeply as he could, thrusting, worshipping, claiming.

She surrounded him, enveloping him, her fingers in his hair, her cunny soft and wet and so bloody sweet he never wanted to stop. With one hand, he cupped her pert derriere, angling her against him to maximize his ability to pleasure her. His other hand splayed over her mound, his thumb finding her pearl with unerring accuracy. Again and again, he sank his tongue inside her as he worked her clitoris. Her cries of pleasure grew in crescendo, raining around him so that he was completely surrounded in nothing but Daisy. Her scent in his nostrils, her taste on his tongue, her moans in his ears, her slick flesh beneath his touch.

She was going to come. He sensed it, reveled in it as her body jerked into his with increased insistence until all at once, she was arching against him, trembling and crying out, her release liquid and sweeter than honey on his tongue. He lapped it up, his cock so hard he feared he wouldn't even make it inside her before he lost himself.

Tearing his mouth away, he stood and in one swift motion, he pulled her from his desk and spun her around so that she faced it. He couldn't look at her for one moment more. He'd never felt closer to another woman in his life. Had never wanted anyone the way he desired her. And yet everything was a lie. He was a lie. But as much as he couldn't face her, he also couldn't bear to let her go.

"Sebastian?" Her tone held a note of question.

"Hush," he soothed into her ear before pressing kisses to her throat. He clamped his hands on the sweet curves of her waist and guided her forward, grinding his hips into hers from behind. "I'm going to make you fly again, buttercup."

He hefted her skirts out of the way and tore open his trousers, pulling himself free of his smalls. He dipped his fingers into her silky heat and then smeared her wetness over his aching cock. One swift undulation of his hips brought him inside her.

"Oh," Daisy said.

He kissed her ear, her throat, stilling though he was half certain stopping now would kill him. "Do you want me to continue, love?"

"Mmm," she hummed, arching her back and bringing him even deeper inside her tight sheath. "Please."

He didn't need to hear it twice. Burying his face in her hair, he pounded into her. His fingers sank into her folds, finding her pearl. She met him thrust for thrust, her head back, her breath coming in pants as she cried out his name. She came before he did, tightening on his cock with so much force that he lost himself in the next instant, sliding home within her as he exploded.

There wasn't time for him to withdraw, and in truth, he didn't want to. He let out a hoarse cry of his own as her body milked him dry. Deep inside her, he came, filling her with his seed, sealing their fates.

She was his, and that was that.

He collapsed against her, kissing her throat, still inside her, and he had never known another experience in his life that had been as true and real. "My God, Daisy," he rasped into her skin. "My God."

There was nothing else he could say.

# chapter sixteen

"YOUR GRACE, THERE'S ANOTHER DELIVERY OF BOOKS. Where would you prefer them to be placed?"

At the sound of Giles' crisp, perfectly modulated voice, Daisy turned away from the wall of spines she's been attempting to organize. His expression was placid, unflappable as always. If he thought it odd that his employer had purchased half a dozen crates of books for his new duchess, the butler didn't show it for a moment.

"More books?" she repeated in question, though she needn't have. The first delivery had come just after breakfast, followed by another and yet another. She should have expected that Sebastian wasn't finished. That he executed this gift as he did all things, with a complete disregard for half measure. "You may as well send them up. What is it they say, Giles? In for a penny, in for a pound?"

But the staid butler didn't answer. He bowed. "As Your Grace wishes." And then he disappeared, leaving Daisy alone in a sea of books once more.

Alphabetize, or shelve the books according to subject

175

matter? That had been the question troubling her the most until Giles' return to the library. But given the number of deliveries they'd already received, another question was beginning to supersede. Where to put them all?

Following their conversation in his study—and the sizzling interlude that followed it, the likes of which still made her cheeks heat several days later—Sebastian had surprised her with a trip to a book shop. How marvelous it had been to be surrounded by walls of books, their heady leather and paper scent, and to know she could read any of them she liked.

"There are three crates' worth, Your Grace," Giles confirmed then. "I didn't wish to presume and have them brought here immediately given the library's current state."

Daisy cast a wry glance about her at the butler's apt observation. Crates littered the elegant carpet, some half-empty and others yet filled to the brim. Although the scene had the appearance of mayhem, she was methodically working her way through all the books on Sebastian's shelves, deciding which books to keep, which to store, and which others might be donated.

"The library is yours," Sebastian had told her at the book shop. "Remove whatever displeases you. Fill it with whatever you like."

"It's your library," she had said. "I wouldn't dream of encroaching."

"It isn't encroaching when you've been issued an invitation, buttercup." He'd touched the tip of her nose then, and she had felt his heat even through his gloves. His expression had been serious, almost sad. "The library is filled with musty old tomes from the last three dukes, and I haven't done much to make it my own. It is only right that you should make it yours."

His soft words and solemn regard had made her heart pang. How was it, she'd wondered, that she could have been so wrong about him? He had seemed arrogant and aloof. On the first night they'd spoken, they'd matched wills and wits, and she'd been so certain he was an autocrat like so many of his fellow lords. Like her father. But in truth, he was multifaceted and complex, and he'd appeared in her life when she'd needed him most, setting her free.

"Your Grace," she had protested.

A ghost of a smile had flitted over his sensual mouth then, and he'd brushed her bottom lip with his thumb. "A full 'Your Grace.' Where have I erred?"

She had frowned back at him, looking about to make certain they hadn't an audience. "You are too generous."

And he'd shaken his head slowly. "I'm selfish. Far too bloody selfish. I enjoy your happiness, Daisy. It occurs to me you've had far less of it than you deserve. Buy all the books you want. That's why I've brought you here."

In the face of his disconcerting kindness and the temptation of pages waiting to be turned, she gave in. She had lovingly browsed the entire shop, lingering over her choices as she narrowed her selections down to eight books. Sebastian had followed her, watching, making several recommendations. He'd urged her to purchase more but she'd refused, not wishing to overindulge in his generosity. She'd left the shop thrilled, thinking the matter settled.

Until the first delivery had arrived that morning. And the second. Then the third. Each opened crate revealed more than the last. Here was a treasure trove of literature waiting to be devoured: Shakespeare and Chaucer and Trollope and Dickens, Browning and Tennyson and Byron and Austen. History books, books in French and Latin, the two languages she'd told him she was well-versed in.

Best of all had been the single book, wrapped in fine paper and delivered by hand. She'd opened it to find an edition of *Gulliver's Travels*, Sebastian's bold scrawl on the first page.

*A favorite for a favorite—*
*S.*

If her heart had been Pegasus, it would have galloped and flown from her chest. But her heart was only mortal, formed of weak flesh, and it had pounded instead. Pounded with the knowledge that the mysterious feelings flitting through her over the last fortnight had solidified into something tangible and definable. Something quite frightening and altogether unexpected.

Love.

Daisy stared at the row of spines before her, unseeing. Over the past few hours, she'd had a great deal of time to think. Alone, in this vast chamber with nothing but a cheerfully flickering fire in the grate and hundreds of small worlds confined in pages and words, she had realized that she loved Sebastian.

It didn't matter that their marriage was new, that there was so much of him she had yet to discover. The heart knew what it wanted, and it stubbornly wanted the man who had listened to her, who had rescued her, who had made her feel at home for the first time in her life. It wanted a handsome duke who could make her laugh or make her melt with equal proficiency.

The door opened, and with it came three strapping footmen, bearing crates laden with more books. "Over there, if you please," she directed, enjoying the task laid before her. It was good to finally have a sense of purpose.

A sense of belonging.

She felt it here.

Now, if only she could manage to conquer Sebastian's heart the same way she meant to surmount his library. As she watched the footmen gingerly make their delivery, she realized she was still holding the Swift volume. She'd carried it about all morning, unable to relinquish it to the shelf.

And of all the words waiting to fall beneath her eye in the cavernous chamber, there were only five that mattered to her the most.

*A favorite for a favorite.*

## chapter seventeen

*T*HE REALIZATION STRUCK SEBASTIAN, much as he suspected lightning might, on a cold, foggy March morning as he reconnoitered with Griffin for the first time since his wedding night.

Then again, it wasn't so much a realization as it was a revelation. Or perhaps, to be more accurate, a fallacy. For it was improbable, foolhardy, and altogether wrong. He said it aloud into the mists anyway because he couldn't contain the words in his mind any longer. Not for one moment more.

"I'm going to keep her," he announced, aware that his awkward phrasing made it sound more as if he'd decided to keep a racehorse rather than a wife and mother to his future children.

But there it was just the same, poor delivery aside. Saying it felt equal parts alarming and freeing. And also right. So very, very right. Daisy was his. She was his, and she was innocent of any and all Fenian plots. She was kind and good, sweet and giving, and everything a woman who had spent most of her life being abused by her father should seemingly *not* be. She was the part of himself he'd been missing. The part of himself he hadn't known existed until he'd recognized it in her eyes.

"Bloody hell, Bast," Griffin bit out. "You know it's impossible."

Sebastian kept his eyes trained forward as he rode, pretending as if he hadn't heard his friend speak. It was early, and Hyde Park was not yet teeming with the scores of horsemen and parade of the fashionable that would inevitably clutter it. Dawn rides had long been their habit— the perfect cover for relaying sensitive information that was best not entrusted to paper.

Impossible? No. Improbable? Yes.

But as it happened, Sebastian wasn't inclined to give a damn. For the first time in his life, he felt…at peace. He'd dedicated his life to the League, but he had finally reached his limit. He would not send an innocent woman to gaol. He would not misuse her after she had given so freely of her body, mind, and heart. By God, he would not treat her as a pawn for another moment more.

Because she wasn't a pawn.

She was Daisy, and she was strong against all odds, and her laughter was infectious, and she had changed him in a way he'd never imagined possible. She had opened a door into a life he might have, and God help him, he intended to walk through that door. With her at his side. He intended to take that life and make it theirs.

"Sebastian," Griffin said again, and this time his tone was grim.

Grim because he could read Sebastian better than anyone else could. But Sebastian didn't want to hear any of his friend's sermons. He didn't need any further reminders and warnings concerning Daisy. His mind drowned in them. The only thing keeping him afloat in this vast ocean of self-loathing and confusion threatening to consume him was the same person Griffin warned him away from.

Daisy.

And that was why he wanted her as his true wife, for the rest of their lives. She was everything he wanted, and nothing he'd ever imagined he'd needed. He'd realized that he couldn't get her out of his life until he got her out of his blood, out of his head, and out of his bed. But he couldn't do that. Wouldn't do that.

She was his, full stop.

"Sod off," he said conversationally.

He didn't want to hear what Griffin had to say. Not a word.

"You took her to the opera," his friend countered. "A book shop, the museum, hell, Sebastian, you're courting the chit. Have you lost your goddamn mind?"

He continued to ignore Griffin, urging his mount into a faster pace. Eyes and ears everywhere, he thought bitterly. Apparently, Carlisle's little birds had been following him about with more dedication these days. Was Griffin one of those birds? The thought was akin to a knife to the gut. He was like a brother to Sebastian. The brother he'd never had.

Griffin's gelding matched his mare pace for pace. "You're bedding her," he called out, "and it's turning you into a fool. Do yourself a favor and find someone else to fuck."

That was bloody well the wrong thing to say to him. The wrong fucking thing to say to him.

Sebastian reined in his horse and dismounted, forcing his sometime friend to do the same. They squared off like a pair of prize fighters, staring each other down. Rage coursed through him, tightening his jaw until his teeth gnashed together. Sebastian broke the uneasy silence first.

"Never speak of her that way again," he warned in a voice that vibrated with barely suppressed fury. He had never before wanted to smash his fist into Griffin's nose the way he did now, so much that his knuckles ached with it.

"You want to hit me, Bast?" Griffin sneered. "Over a set of skirts you haven't even been bedding for the span of a month? Go ahead, you prick. Choose a treasonous tart over our brotherhood. Hit me. See what happens."

*A set of skirts.* That was the phrase that did it. Or perhaps it was *treasonous tart.* Sebastian would never know for certain. All he did know was that in the next breath, his fist collided with Griffin's jaw.

His friend's head snapped back, and he stumbled before regaining his footing. "Jesus, Sebastian. What the bloody hell?"

He stared back at Griffin as pain seared his knuckles, and as a reddish-purple bruise blossomed on his friend's jaw. "Fuck. I didn't intend to strike you, Griff. I'm sorry. It's merely that she's…"

He allowed his words to trail off for fear of where they'd been headed. *She's the woman I love.* Had he really been about to say such a ludicrous thing? Of course not. There was a vast difference between desiring a woman as his companion and having her in his bed and *loving* her. He'd only been married to her for the span of a fortnight, Chrissakes.

"She's colluding with the Fenians," Griffin finished for him. "Tell me you don't think she's innocent, Bast."

"Her father is colluding with the Fenians," he corrected coldly. "Her father who beat her savagely from the time she was a wee, defenseless girl of four. Her father who she never wants to see again. Vanreid is the enemy we seek to bring to heel, not Daisy."

Griffin's expression remained hard as stone, unreadable. "I suppose we'll find out the truth of that soon enough."

There was something his friend hadn't said, and he knew it. "Meaning?"

"It's time, Bast." Griffin rubbed his bruised jaw. "Carlisle wants you to proceed with approaching Vanreid about a dowry. He expected you to do it sooner than this, and he isn't pleased. You're to invite him to your home. We need to pin the firearms to him. We've word from our American agents that an attack is imminent. They've commissioned a bloody submarine, Bast. It's built and seaworthy, and they have every intention of using it to bombard one of our vessels. This is war."

Sebastian's blood went cold. He knew what was expected of him, but he'd been hoping like hell that there would be another way. That Carlisle would change his battle plans and leave Sebastian with a more palatable option.

The thought of having Vanreid present in his home made his skin crawl. The son-of-a-bitch ought to be disemboweled for what he'd done to Daisy, and that was a bloody, nasty business. Sebastian had seen the aftermath of just such a killing, and though it haunted him to this day, even an end as ghastly as that would be too merciful for Vanreid.

Now he was to pretend as though all was roses and rainbows, to invite Vanreid to his study and play the part of dissolute rakehell. To bring the bastard close enough to Daisy to hurt her once more.

He didn't know if he could do it. He needed time. Time to think. To clear his mind. He had hit the one man in the world who was like a brother to him. But Griffin had not hit him back. For some reason, that troubled Sebastian the most.

"Thank you for the message," he said tersely, and then he spun on his heel and threw himself atop his horse once more before riding hell for leather away from the only person he'd ever believed he could trust. Away from unwanted duty. Away from everyone and everything.

Griffin's words echoed in the staccato of his horse's hooves.

*This is war.*

Yes, bloody hell, it was.

Daisy descended the stairs for dinner at precisely a quarter past eight that evening, just as she had every night since her first dinner with him. What had begun as a small assertion of her independence had quickly changed. She kept him waiting, and he took her to task, though increasingly with more sensual heat than genuine irritation. It had become rather a diversion of sorts between them.

He pushed, she pulled. He was inflexible and disciplined where she longed to experience life free of the constraints that had once contained her. She wanted to soak up every moment of every day in this new life she led, while Sebastian seemed somehow restrained. The sadness in him remained, haunting his beautiful eyes. It was only when she teased him that he came to life at last, shedding his armor and allowing himself to simply be.

She'd come to realize that her husband was a rigid and disciplined man. He woke before dawn, breakfasted early, devoted himself to his estates and other matters, took his exercise, and then awaited her at dinner. And she liked keeping him waiting, even if it meant she secretly paced the floor of her chamber, sneaking glances at the mantle clock, as she made certain not to be punctual.

But there was an undeniably different air about him tonight as she glossed her right hand lightly over the polished balustrade, holding her skirts slightly aloft with her left. She'd become adept at sweeping down the staircase as though she glided, and she'd chosen a seafoam blue silk evening gown trimmed with rosettes and a revealing décolletage, but none of those trivialities mattered when her eyes found him as she was halfway down the stairs.

He wasn't pacing tonight. His back was to her, head bowed forward as though in prayer, hands clasped at his back. She didn't know him to be a particularly pious man, and in the fortnight they'd been married, he'd never missed the opportunity to unleash his caged energy on the parquet floor as he awaited her.

Something had changed, and she felt it the same way she'd experience a chill running straight down her spine. She paused, on the fourth stair from the bottom, watching him. This was not the reunion she'd anticipated after receiving a library's worth of books, all carefully chosen with her interests in mind. And especially not after an inscription that called her a favorite.

*A favorite.*

As though she were someone to be cherished. Perhaps loved, though that was a finer emotion that she didn't expect from him after only a fortnight of marriage. Hearts did what they would, and just because hers had stubbornly decided to fall for him didn't mean his in turn could be expected to feel the same.

Still, those words had worked their way deep inside her to a place she hadn't even known existed, making her smile all day long. Those words had been responsible for the soft hums of pleasure emerging from her as she made herself at home in the library. Those words were what caused the frisson of desire to glide through her even now, accompanied by the swift fluttering of her heart.

But he still hadn't turned to face her, and he must have heard her footfalls on the stairs by now. "Sebastian," she called softly.

He turned to her at last, his expression grim in the moment before he appeared to collect himself and don one of his many facades. A sensual smile curved his lips with ease. "Late again, buttercup?" he asked, but there was no bite to his words, only a bittersweet resonance.

Her heart clenched in her breast as she forced herself to descend the remainder of the stairs. "Forgive me for keeping you waiting," she said tonight the same as she had each night before, taking extra care to maintain the flippancy in her tone. This time, she had a new explanation for her tardiness at the ready. "Someone sent me the contents of an entire book shop, and I spent the course of the day attempting to reconcile the shelves, the existing literature, and the new volumes."

He strode toward her with a confidence that was purely his, all ducal, and somehow elegant and sinful at once. His dark hair was swept back from his high forehead, and he wore a black coat, black trousers, and a crisp white shirt beneath a gunmetal brocade waistcoat. He looked dark and lethal and delicious.

And hers.

He *was* hers, she reminded herself as he took her outstretched hand in his and guided her down the last step. The guidance wasn't necessary. His touch, however, was.

She was smiling at him like a foolish girl, but she didn't care. "Have you nothing to say, Your—"

"Sebastian," he intervened, drawing her closer. He lowered his head, and their lips nearly met. His scent swept over her, pine and man and husband. "A one-half Your Grace is all I'm willing to allow tonight, Duchess."

Her fingers tightened over his. He was ever an enigma, keeping a part of himself from her. The part she wanted the most. His eyes were blue, so blue, bluer than the brightest country summer sky of her childhood before her father had moved them to the city.

"Thank you," she told him. "For the books."

He raised her hand to his lips for a kiss, his gaze searing hers. "I would have far preferred for you to select them yourself, but you were stubborn as ever."

His extravagance still did strange things to her insides. When he'd attempted to convince her to buy half the book shop, she had objected. Of course she had. What sane woman would want her husband to empty his coffers over her literary whims? Her father would never have allowed such a thing.

That thought had ultimately rendered her acceptance of Sebastian's somewhat high-handed gift all the more acceptable to her. Sebastian wasn't attempting to control her with his gift. He wanted to please her, and that was the difference.

"I'm a simple woman," she said then. "I don't require crates of books, fancy houses, or servants to satisfy me."

He squeezed her fingers, his expression inscrutable. "What does satisfy you, Daisy?"

You.

She nearly said the word. She almost revealed herself to him, made herself as vulnerable as she could possibly be. Instead, she shook her head, unwilling to give him everything. Uncertain if she could. Her feelings remained too new and strange. The notion of telling him she loved him made her mouth go dry and her heart pound.

"I look forward to reading," she told him instead. "Thank you. Thank you for listening to me, for choosing books to my liking."

"Are they to your liking, buttercup?"

His question was unexpected. No one had ever been as concerned with her happiness and satisfaction as Sebastian was. Sometimes, his attentiveness threw her. Other times, it made her sigh.

In this instance, her smile broadened. "The selections were most judicious. You somehow know what I would want to read most."

He hesitated, and she couldn't suppress the sensation that he wanted to say more. Instead, he inclined his head and offered his arm. "Dinner, my darling?"

It was a tired phrase, she thought—*my darling*—as she clenched his muscled forearm. She wasn't his darling, was she? That phrase, so easily rolled off his facile tongue, didn't mean what her imprudent heart longed to believe it did.

The truth was that she hadn't the slightest inclination of what, if anything, he felt for her, aside from desire. The way he looked at her, the way he touched her and held her, told her all she needed to know on that account. But though he'd warmed to her, she mustn't fool herself.

And right now, he watched her in that way of his that was intimate and assessing all at once. While here she stood, wishing he'd meant to call her his darling in the truest sense. Wishing he'd forego all manners and formality, sweep her in his arms, and take her upstairs.

Oh, foolish, foolish heart.

"Dinner," she forced herself to say, for it was far wiser than blurting her feelings. "Yes, let's."

By the loin of mutton à la Brétonne, Sebastian realized that it was no stroke of chance that all his favorites were being served in the course of one dinner. And he knew instantly that it wasn't the redoubtable Mrs. Robbins who was solely responsible. Though Mrs. Robbins had been a retainer for his entire life, she had never in all her years of service orchestrated such a dinner on his behalf unless he had specifically requested it.

He met Daisy's gaze over the lovely table setting—fresh hothouse blooms carefully arranged amidst new table linens, silver, and china, candles flickering with a pleasant glow, all of which he was certain was her doing as well.

"Leave us," he told the servants dancing attendance upon them without ever taking his eyes from her.

They remained silent until they were blessedly alone.

"Buttercup," he said then, his throat going embarrassingly thick. He would have said something else, but he didn't wish to further embarrass himself by wearing his heart on his bloody sleeve.

His heart on his sleeve?

Christ.

From what hell had that rogue thought emerged?

The answering smile she gave him was so blinding that it robbed him of his breath. For a moment, he stared, basking in her beauty, forgetting all about the untenable mire in which he currently found himself. Submarines, dynamite, and the Fenian menace—not to mention the goddamn League itself and his unwanted mission—dissipated like a storm chased away by the sun.

"Is the dinner to your liking?" she asked him, repeating his earlier question to her.

Jesus. He devoured her with his gaze, from her golden hair carefully plaited and styled high atop her head to her high forehead, the dainty slashes of her brows, her elegant nose, and those wide, luscious lips he loved to bite and lick and crush beneath his, then lower for just a beat, over her full, creamy breasts. Suddenly, he was no longer hungry for dinner.

"You arranged this." If his voice sounded rusty and deep, it couldn't be helped any more than his reaction to her could. He hadn't bloody well wanted to marry her. He hadn't wanted the all-consuming attraction he felt for her. He hadn't meant to burn whenever he looked upon her. To want—nay, need—her so much that he was willing to do damn near anything to keep her at his side, as his duchess.

But he did.

She tilted her head, considering him and—he feared—seeing far too much. "With the aid of Mrs. Robbins, of course. You've been unfailingly kind to me, and I wished to convey my gratitude in some small way."

The beast in him instantly thought of other ways she might convey her gratitude as well. None of them involved mutton or potatoes à la Lyonnaise. Fighting a groan, he shifted in his chair as discomfort settled in the vicinity of his trousers. A familiar affliction whenever he was in her presence.

And then he thought of how she didn't owe him her gratitude at all. She didn't owe him a bloody thing, and if she knew the half of it, she'd never speak to him again. Over the past fortnight, he'd done his best to compartmentalize his duty and the way he'd begun to feel for Daisy. But eventually, the twain would meet, and his meeting with Griffin earlier had made that stark fact all the more real.

He had a duty. Even if he'd fallen in love with the woman he was duty-bound to distrust. Even if he was still trapped in the emerald depths of said woman's eyes. He couldn't tell her the truth. Not yet. Perhaps not ever.

Guilt sliced through him with the precision of a bayonet. "You needn't feel beholden. I'm not the Galahad you think me."

It was as much of a warning as he could issue to her

without giving himself away and putting his mission and the League at risk. The reminder of what he was expected to do—lure in her bastard of a father, pretend as though he'd married Daisy for her fortune, bring him close enough to hurt her once more—made a swift stab of nausea ride through his gut. The mutton was delicious, and it was his favorite dish, but he couldn't stomach another bite of food.

"You're a good man, Sebastian," Daisy said, her cheekbones flushing a charming pink beneath his scrutiny. "It's futile to try to convince me otherwise."

"A good man wouldn't have ruined you in the moonlight without a care for your reputation."

Bitterness unfurled. How could she be so innocent and good, so blind in her trust of him, she who had been only mistreated and used for her entire life? He had kissed her, ripped her bodice, in the gardens of a ball where they could have been seen by anyone. He had shamed her, used her, all in the name of duty, and without a care. From the beginning, he had deceived her. Knowing that she was suspected of treason, he had still lusted after her, had taken her bloody maidenhead while he was meant to annul their marriage. And he had done all this as he knew there remained a chance she could be cast into prison.

He hated himself. Hated lying to her. Even now, he couldn't tell her what he so desperately longed to tell her. He had sworn an oath to the League before he'd ever sworn an oath to her. But now the two were hopelessly at war with each other.

Daisy held up her hands, palms facing the ceiling, a teasing smile flirting with the lips he longed to claim. "Ruined and yet here I sit, perfectly well. Your conscience may feel otherwise, but believe me when I say that my ruination was my saving grace. I don't regret that night, Sebastian. I wanted it, and not just because I wanted to be free of Lord Breckly, but because I wanted you."

Her words sank straight through him, leaving a path of fire in their wake. By God, he wished he were free. For the first time in his life, he was no longer content to be a part of the League. For the first fucking time, he wanted to be...Sebastian. Simply himself. With no secrets, no lies, no danger, no worry, no allegiance to anyone other than the woman facing him across the expanse of snowy linens and gleaming cutlery and delicious-smelling mutton.

And that was when he recognized it in full, this restless feeling sliding around within him, this sense of incompletion and confusion. The life he led—secrecy, collusion, danger—had ceased to fulfill him long ago. He wanted something more, something real.

He wasn't going to bring Vanreid into his home or within striking distance of Daisy. Not today, not tomorrow, not the next day. On this—the safety of his wife—he wouldn't hesitate to defy Carlisle. He wouldn't risk her. She was too precious to him.

And when this mission was over, he was going to retire from the League. If Daisy forgave him after he told her as much of the truth as he was able, they would go to Thornsby Hall and raise half a dozen children.

Children with Daisy.

Something warm settled in his gut. The thought of planting his seed in her, watching her grow with his babe, took his breath and made his cock even harder than it already was by being seated across from her, in her charmed presence.

"Sebastian?" her voice was hesitant, questioning. "Won't you say something? I fear I've shocked you with my confession."

He shot from his chair so quickly that it thudded backward, tipped on its side on the carpet behind him. He didn't give a damn. "You could never shock me, buttercup," he assured her as he stalked around the table.

Being in the same space as her without having her in his arms was suddenly insupportable. He had to have her. Right. Bloody. Now. Everything else could be dealt with another day—the League, her father, his mission, the lies between them. But here, in this moment, he was going to give her the only honesty he could. It wasn't what she deserved, but it was all he had.

Her eyes went wide as he hauled her from her chair before making a thorough swipe of the table behind her with his arm. China, silver, and the fourth course all went crashing to the center of the table. He didn't give a damn if every last monogrammed plate was smashed to bits. Didn't care if the mutton went to waste. His hands went to her waist, spanning it easily.

She ought to eat more, he thought absently as he lifted her up and deposited her on the table at her back. Her hands went to his shoulders, and she still hadn't said a word, her shock rendering her speechless.

When her derriere settled on the table linen and he caught her billowing skirts in his fists, she found her tongue at last. "Sebastian! What are you doing? We haven't even finished dinner or had dessert. Cook has prepared cocoa biscuits and strawberries."

She was breathless, flushed, and she smelled better than anything ever had. He wanted to inhale her, trap her bergamot and vanilla and ambergris in his lungs so that whenever he wasn't in her presence he could still breathe her.

His gaze fell to her mouth. "You don't like strawberries."

"You do." Her fingers tightened on his shoulders. "How did you know I don't like strawberries?"

He didn't answer her. Instead, he rucked her skirts up to her waist, pooling their voluminous layers on the table. And that was when he made the most astonishing, delicious revelation. His duchess wasn't wearing any drawers. Nothing but silk stockings and garters and well-curved legs.

And the most tempting cunny he'd ever seen.

She was his.

"To hell with the cocoa biscuits and strawberries, love." He sank to his knees in appreciation, his hands on her hips, gliding over warm silk until they reached warmer flesh. "All I want is you."

"Sebastian." She sounded equal parts scandalized and breathless. "You mustn't. We're in the midst of dinner. The servants…"

*Mine*, he thought as he kissed the tempting skin above her garters. First her left leg, then the right. "No one will disturb us." He had made it clear to his staff after their first dinner. There would be no discreet knock, no hesitant interruption.

He had all the time in the world to savor her. And savor her he would. Sweet Christ, but her thighs were glorious. There was something delectably carnal about all that ivory: garters, silk, skin, and the way she attempted to press her legs together to preserve her modesty. *Mine*. There it was again, unbidden, the claim he staked upon her.

He'd meant what he said to Griffin. He was firm in his decision. This woman, who was soft and kind and beautiful, who made him laugh as much as she made him lust, she belonged to him now, just as he belonged to her. There would be no annulment.

"Sebastian." Her hands flitted to his shoulders first, then to his hair. But instead of pushing him away, her fingers tunneled a path to his scalp. "This is wicked."

"Mmm." He hummed his satisfaction as he kissed higher, caressing her thighs with slow, languorous strokes as he urged her to open to him. "I want to taste you, love." Another kiss, then another, and she allowed him to nudge her legs apart.

A noise emerged from her throat as well, half moan, half mewl, and he'd never heard a sweeter sound than Daisy losing the tight grip she attempted to keep on her control. Slowly, he spread her legs, inch by torturous inch. He kissed each inner thigh. *Mine*. Nipped her with his teeth, making her jerk as her fingers tensed in his hair. *Mine*. Licked the soft skin to soothe it. *Mine*. Higher he went, his mouth dragging over her, worshipping, loving.

And then she was open to him completely, and he slid his hands to cup her bare bottom and drag her closer. He was like a man lost on a desert plain who had just stumbled across a babbling stream, sinking to his knees to cup that life source and bring it into his body with a desperation borne of pure necessity. He ran his tongue over her seam, once, twice, again and again. Teasing. Tasting. She moved beneath him, moaning, twisting, her legs clamping down on his head.

He removed a hand from her bottom to stroke her thigh, calming her, letting her adjust to the onslaught of sensation. Sweet. She was so bloody sweet. Musky and feminine and something else uniquely her. She filled his senses, surrounding him, until there was nothing else that existed. There was only Daisy on his tongue, Daisy's breathy sounds of helpless desire, Daisy's fingers in his hair, her thighs soft against him, the wet, delicious heat of her.

*Mine.* He found the prize he sought, his tongue probing through her slick folds to discover her pearl. He flicked over that exquisite bundle of sensation, working it with his tongue. *Mine.* He blew a stream of hot air over her.

"Oh," she said, and then, "oh, Sebastian."

Very gently, he bit, catching her between his upper lip and his teeth before raking over her pearl again and again. He sucked her, looking up to find her watching him, her expression slack and unguarded, her lush mouth partially open, her chest heaving with each labored breath.

Their gazes clashed and he allowed her to slide from his lips with a lusty pop. "Spend for me, Daisy. I want to make you come with nothing but my tongue."

This was all he could offer her until he was free of the League: his body and her pleasure. He could make her fly, could give her release, and he wanted that for her now more than anything. She deserved so much more, so much better. She deserved his honesty and his love, and he would give her both as soon as he was able.

For the moment, he could only run his tongue over her

slit again—once, twice, five times, more—before sinking it inside her as deep as he could. Pointing his tongue, he thrust it inside her again and again. His hand traveled up her thigh to the skin revealed beneath her corset, directly above her womb. Here, she would carry their babes. He flattened his hand over her. *Mine.* And her hand came to rest upon his, their fingers tangling.

"Please," she said.

Her plea spurred him on. Back to her pearl he went, licking, sucking, nipping, learning what she liked best. The particularly sensitive spot below that sweet bud and slightly to the right made her buck and go wild. He closed his mouth over her, raking her with his teeth until finally, she exploded. He watched her as she came, her back arched, head thrown back in ecstasy to reveal the graceful column of her throat, her breasts straining against her bodice.

"Sebastian," she cried. "I love you."

The rush of her release was liquid and instant, and he lost his ability to form coherent thought.

*Mine. Bloody, fucking hell. Mine.*

Had she said that? Those three words? He didn't dare to hope, to believe. Just when he was convinced he'd been mistaken, he heard her low moan, and it was undeniable. *I love you, I love you, I love you.*

Ah, Christ. This woman would be his undoing. He tore his mouth from her at last, hauling her into his arms for a tight embrace. If he'd been able to pull her inside himself, he would have, so fierce and unexpected was his reaction to her words and his need of her.

"Thank you, my love," he said into her ear. "Now let's get the hell upstairs so we can finish what we've started."

She kissed his jaw, her arms tightening around him. "Yes," was all she said.

He withdrew and helped her restore her dress into a semblance of order. Wordlessly, he took her hand and led her to her chamber. Once there, he made love to her twice, once with frantic abandon and once with slow, tender passion. With his body, he told her the words he wasn't yet free to say. Words he wouldn't say until this godforsaken mission was over and he could be truthful with her. Words she deserved to hear after he was freed of the shackles of his oath, and his only duty was instead to her.

When at last he lay in the darkness with her curled against him, both of their bodies spent, Daisy's even breathing indicating she was asleep, he kissed her bare shoulder.

"I love you, too," he whispered into the night.

## chapter eighteen

$\mathcal{T}$ HE NEXT MORNING, SEBASTIAN BROKE HIS FAST in his customary fashion: close to dawn, alone, and with *The Times* ironed and laid out beside his plate. He forked up a bite of *oeuf cocottes* and chewed thoughtfully as his mind drifted from parliamentary matters and news of the world abroad.

To hell with everything ordinary. Today was no ordinary goddamn day. Today, everything had changed. The sun rising to break London's bleak fog had seemed unnaturally bright. His coffee tasted better than it ever had. His chest felt lighter, and he couldn't bloody well stop grinning like a fool.

Daisy loved him. And he loved her.

Yes, Christ help him, as sudden and strange and ill-advised as it seemed, he had found the woman he wanted to spend the rest of his days loving. His relationship with Daisy was cordial and easy. She possessed intelligence and determination and wit, all enhanced by a lively sense of humor. When he was irritable, she made him laugh. When he was arrogant, she subtly reminded him. When he reached out his hand, she took it.

She'd been tardy for dinner every bloody night, and he hadn't even minded, although he was certain she kept him waiting by design. When she arrived, a teasing smile on her lips, resplendent in her evening finery, it was all he could do not to take her in his arms, carry her back up the staircase, and make love to her all night long.

She was like sunlight after a torrent of rain. Something about the woman was impossibly charming, and it wasn't just her beauty. It was some indefinable quality he'd never known another female to possess. Or perhaps, it was her, *Daisy* who affected him so. She'd had him at war with himself, from the start, half of him wanting her desperately and the other half of him determined to keep her at arm's length where she belonged.

But as the days had progressed, the words "pawn" and "annulment" had found themselves unceremoniously thrust into the recesses of his mind. He'd watched her, of course, and had sifted through her personal effects, not without an organ-piercing stab of guilt each time. He'd located her journal and had painstakingly read every entry. All he'd managed to discover was that she was thrilled to begin reading the contents of her library and that her penmanship was surprisingly slanted and imperfect.

He frowned at his newspaper, the words blurring before him. Aside from the deficiency of her handwriting, Daisy was exactly as he'd suspected: a kindhearted, vivacious young lady who'd been mistreated by her father and had been desperate to escape him and the decrepit lecher of a match he'd chosen for her.

The most pressing task at hand for him was amassing evidence of her innocence to provide to Carlisle. The sooner he could remove Daisy as a suspect, the better. Troubling questions remained, of course. Her connection to the Irish shop girl and Padraig McGuire, chief among them. He recognized that his love for her did not exculpate her. Of course, the hardened spy within him even had to acknowledge that there was a chance she was guilty as sin after all, and he had allowed his feelings to cloud his judgment.

Either way, there was only one conclusion to the situation in which he found himself. Daisy was either guilty or she was innocent, and Sebastian was either a fool or he wasn't.

To that end, he would continue to follow leads and build a case for Carlisle. He had every hope that they'd bring him to the inevitable conclusion that Daisy had no parts of her father's plotting with the Fenians. That the woman he was so bloody drawn to—the woman he'd fallen hopelessly in love with against his every instinct and all his years of training combined—had no more to do with dynamite plots than the queen herself.

"Pardon the interruption, Your Grace, but you've some correspondence this morning," Giles interrupted, his tone faultlessly formal.

He lowered the neglected paper and acknowledged his butler, accepting the correspondence as though it was likely as harmless as a letter from a maiden aunt. Sebastian waited until Giles had discreetly resumed his place by the sideboard before tearing open the seal of the letter. His eyes scanned the familiar, brief scrawl, that old, worn knot resurging. His blood went cold.

The message was coded, its contents seemingly innocuous enough.

*Would you care to meet for a morning ride? The skies look too ominous to wait until afternoon.*

It was unsigned, but that hardly mattered. He knew the note's author just as he knew he had a pair of hands and the sun glinted in the sky above him even though he couldn't see it from where he sat.

Carlisle wanted to meet at once.

And nothing about a sudden summons from the Duke of Carlisle was ever a matter for rejoicing.

Dread, heavy and hard and unpalatable as hell, twisted

in his gut. This brief idyll with Daisy was bound to be disrupted. But damn it if he hadn't enjoyed every moment of it while it had lasted.

The devil, it seemed, would always collect his due. He may love Daisy so much that it made his chest physically ache, but he wasn't free to pursue that love just yet. For now, he was bound by his honor, his word, his loyalty to the Crown, and his family legacy. He felt them all like steel manacles circling his wrists. Keeping him prisoner. From the moment he'd taken his vows, his life had ceased to be his own.

Everything had changed, but just the same, nothing had.

He folded the note in thirds, carefully keeping his expression bland for the sake of the footman and butler dancing attendance on him. He should have remained in Daisy's chamber, her body sleek and soft and warm and naked in his arms. He could have woken her with his kiss and then slid his cock home inside her.

Instead, he had risen early and dressed in customary fashion, requesting the papers and his breakfast. He had done all this because despite the fact that he would like nothing more than to pretend as if he was free to love Daisy the way he wished and the way she deserved, he was not. And lingering in her bed only prolonged his own torture and inner torment.

Ah, but if only he had stayed, kissed her sweet lips, rolled her onto her back…

But no. He supposed the note would have found him anywhere. Still, it would have been a damn sight more pleasurable to have spent the morning sucking his wife's pretty pink nipples than reading a piece in *The Times* about the Government of India and the Ameer of Cabul before running off to do Carlisle's bidding. Sebastian slid the note into the pocket of his coat, resumed breakfast for several more bites, and then announced that he would need his mount saddled while he changed into riding dress.

Yes, it was time for the devil to collect his due.

The ride to Carlisle's personal residence was chilly, made more miserable by a ceaseless damp that had descended upon the city. For such a summons as this, his instructions were to always rendezvous at Blayton House. As they traveled in the same circles and feigned friendship as often as possible, two dukes might quite easily and inconspicuously call upon each other. More of Carlisle's hiding in plain sight, as it were.

It didn't take long to reach Blayton House, and before he knew it, Sebastian was handing off his reins to a groom and being led deep into Carlisle's inner sanctum by his forbidding, hoary-haired butler. Carlisle stood upon Sebastian's entrance to his study.

"Trent." Carlisle was the face of genial civility. "Fancy a drink?"

It was the role he played for the world—drunken lothario, hardened rake, lighthearted man about town. In truth, the Duke of Carlisle was an odd fish—severe, harsh, dark, and deadly. Sebastian had once witnessed him gut a man with his blade before calmly wiping it clean with a monogrammed handkerchief.

For some odd reason, the sight and scent of that long-ago moment returned to him now. France, ten years before, on the outskirts of Paris. They'd been on a mission to free Griffin, and they'd been beset by a small party of German soldiers. The odds had been against them—Sebastian and Carlisle against five—but they'd prevailed. Carlisle had been a savage, killing two of the Germans with his bare hands and a third with his knife. Sebastian had dispatched the other two. Strange, so strange, that he should recall that day just now.

The butler disappeared, the door clicked closed.

Sebastian faced his superior. "Will I need a drink for whatever reason you've ordered me here?"

"Two minutes," the duke muttered, his expression

turning as grim as a death mask.

It was highly unusual for Carlisle to reveal he had the capacity to experience emotions. Seeing this side of him disturbed Sebastian, who watched as his superior stalked to the sideboard, snatched up a decanter, and poured whisky into two glasses. Not even after killing the three Germans had Carlisle been this disjointed.

Sebastian extracted his pocket watch, heeding Carlisle's warning that it would not be safe to speak freely until two full minutes had passed. He accepted the whisky the duke offered him, tilted back his head, and swallowed the contents in a fiery gulp. It burned a path straight to his gut.

He flicked another glance at his watch. "Two minutes has passed."

"A bomb was discovered early this morning by a night constable," Carlisle said, taking a hearty swallow of his own spirits before continuing. "It didn't detonate, thank Christ. The poor sod saw a smoldering box and was foolish enough to extinguish the flame. Thanks to his foolishness, the residence of the lord mayor still stands."

A desolate streak of despair snaked through him. They had heard whisperings from their operatives stationed in America for many months now that London was a target. The explosion at the armory in Salford had been but the beginning. The Fenian foe had been growing in numbers, power, and audacity. But until now, the threat had seemed nothing more than that—a threat to be monitored and obliterated before it manifested itself in far more dangerous means than chattering amongst spies, ebullient rallies, and incendiary articles. London, the League had been sure, would be far too risky of a target for the Fenians to pursue.

It would seem that was a grave fallacy.

At long last, their greatest fear had become a reality in the heart of London.

"Jesus," he said slowly, passing a hand over his face. The whisky had begun its pleasant, detached warming of his senses, but it did nothing to dull the urgency of the matter facing them. Griffin's warning of the day before churned through him: the bloody submarine. *This is war*. Fuck. "What information do you have?"

"Not much at this juncture. The constable took the box to Bow Lane station. There was almost forty pounds of gunpowder filling the damn thing, along with some foreign newspapers and two addresses, one in London and another in Liverpool." Carlisle stalked back to the sideboard, slamming his half-full whisky glass on the carved mahogany with such force that Sebastian was shocked it hadn't shattered. "Our men are investigating the addresses as we speak. If the constable had not walked by when he did, the bomb would have exploded. He's bloody fortunate he wasn't killed. Another thirty seconds, perhaps, and he would have been."

Forty pounds of gunpowder. Holy God. The bastards who had fashioned the bomb had intended to cause a great deal of destruction. They needed to be stopped by whatever means necessary and as quickly as possible.

A sickening sense of inevitability slid home inside him. He thought of Daisy, then, and how he'd allowed himself to believe that he could actually be free of the burden of this life and all its duties and encumbrances. Griffin had been right. This was war, damn it, and the enemy had infiltrated London, prepared to maim and kill as many innocents as possible. How could he possibly leave the League now, in such a time of need?

Had he imagined that he could ever leave this life? That he could simply be a man in love with a woman? That he could retire to Thornsby Hall and raise golden-haired babies with Daisy? In the span of an hour, everything had changed. A bomb had been set. Lives were in jeopardy. This was bigger than all of them. Bigger than his own selfish desires.

He knew what he must do.

He stiffened in his seat. "How can I be of service?"

"The Home Office wants you in Liverpool immediately." Carlisle's answer was quick, decisive. He'd likely spent the dawn hours crafting his strategy.

"Why Liverpool?" he asked, recognizing that such an assignment would take him from Daisy when the last thing in the world he wanted to do was leave her side, especially with so much unfinished business between them. Just last night, she had told him she loved him. He needed to tell her the truth, to beg her forgiveness.

But first, he had an oath to uphold.

And he would loyally uphold that oath until he met his end or until he was relieved of his duties, whichever came first. The last fortnight aside, he was capable of thinking and acting like a rational, loyal subject of the Queen. Like a man who had been tasked with defending England and her people from all supposed threats, whether or not they happened to be lovely, golden-haired, luscious-lipped sirens who smelled of vanilla and bergamot.

Carlisle's gaze was on him, hard and assessing. "Liverpool is where Vanreid just spent a great deal of time. We suspect him of bringing supplies and funds to aid the Fenians already planted in England. The address inside the box could have been planted to mislead us, or it could be a valuable asset to our cause. Either way, we need one of our best men to be our eyes and ears there for the next month at least. If there is a dynamite ring based in Liverpool we will run them to bloody ground before they can set one more bomb."

Sebastian nodded. Vanreid again. Why could Carlisle not accept that Vanreid, a corpulent animal who had beaten his own daughter and attempted to marry her off to an aging reprobate, was the source of the evil they wanted to defeat? That Daisy had no part in it? That she was an innocent victim who deserved far more than a false marriage to a man who had done nothing but deceive her from the day he'd met her? For his part in this travesty, Sebastian could not keep his gorge from rising each time he thought of it.

But his was not to question. He owed his loyalty to the League and to his country first, regardless of how unpalatable he found his present task. "I'll need to inform Daisy of my plans."

"No." Carlisle stalked forward again, dark as a thundercloud. "You will inform her of nothing. Her part in this plot remains unclear, but she is not to be trusted. Indeed, you must not even think of her as your wife. She is a means to an end. Nothing more. Am I understood, Trent?"

The words tumbled about in his mind, settled into his veins, cold as winter's ice. *A means to an end. Nothing.* He saw her face, lovely and expressive. Thought of the way she came alive in his arms, all innocent fire. Heard her words. *I love you.* She had slipped past his battlements and crept beneath his skin, and he could never do what Carlisle asked. Not any longer.

For as long as he lived, the taste of her—sweet, wild, delicious—would remain with him. Some long-overlooked restlessness inside him hungered for her. He could kiss her senseless on a thousand nights under a hundred different moons, and he would still want her more than he had the night before.

She was not—could never again be—just a means to an end.

"She is an innocent in this, Carlisle." Sebastian met him halfway, unafraid and unapologetic. Yes, he had a duty but he also had a mind of his own, and everything in him told him that Daisy was not a part of whatever evil her father sowed. Maybe it was what he wanted to believe. Something had changed for him from the moment he'd met her, and it left him questioning everything: his loyalty, his oath, the League, his instincts, his own bloody honor.

Everything.

The duke considered him. "You've been bedding her against my orders, then."

It was not a question, but a statement. Rage swarmed through him to hear Carlisle speak so cavalierly of her, as if she were no better than a tavern doxy. He clenched his fists at his sides to keep from smashing one of them into his superior's jaw. "Go to hell."

"Jesus." Carlisle stared at him, his expression for once undisguised. It was pure, unadulterated disgust. "I never would have expected it of you, Trent."

He didn't wish to discuss Daisy with anyone, and especially not the Duke of Carlisle. It felt like a betrayal of her. "Goddamn you, Carlisle, the League doesn't own my cock, and I'll do with it what I like. Furthermore, I swear to you that I have uncovered nothing to suggest she has even an inkling of the Fenian plots. She cannot abide by her father, who beat her and wanted to marry her off to Breckly despite her own vehement objections."

"That is what she wants you to believe. I daresay this wouldn't be the first time a good man has fallen prey to a traitorous cunny." Carlisle snorted. "Certainly won't be the last."

He had never longed to thrash a man to within an inch of his life more. Sebastian took a menacing step forward. "Do not dare to disparage her in my presence again."

Carlisle met him halfway. They squared off, boot to boot, of a height with each other. Sebastian was a bit leaner than Carlisle, but he was sure he could win handily in a bout of fisticuffs.

"Push me at your peril, Trent," Carlisle warned, his tone soft yet somehow as harsh as a whip. "Forget whatever spell she's cast upon you with her wiles. We have far more important tasks at hand. More bombs will be fashioned and lit in the streets. They've already blown apart a building and killed a child. Innocent lives will be taken unless we act, goddamn it."

Yes, damn it all to hell. Sebastian took a breath, his superior's stern admonition recalling the stakes to him. Dynamite. Death and destruction. So many lives were in danger. How many more innocents would shed their blood and lives at the hands of these monsters unless they were stopped? He had sworn to defend his country, and regardless of the way he felt for Daisy, he had to stay true to his oath.

"Liverpool," Sebastian muttered, flexing his hands. He would not beat Carlisle senseless. Not today. Another day, perhaps. For now, there remained a different sort of war to fight.

"Yes." Carlisle's eyes blazed with something akin to madness. "I need you in Liverpool. I need you clearheaded and alert. You've always been one of the best, Trent, and we can't afford to lose you now."

He would go, though the notion left him cold and hollow. Curious feeling, that. For the entirety of his years serving in the League, only one other mission had given him pause. And that one had been marrying Daisy Vanreid.

"You'll not lose me," he said hoarsely. "I'll uphold my duty to the end. I'll travel to Hades if the League but asks, and you know it."

Carlisle gave him a fleeting smile. "Not Hades just yet, Trent. But you must leave at once."

At once. The words echoed through him, unwanted as ice going down his spine. "I'm to leave now?"

He thought of Daisy, curled on her side, naked beneath the bedclothes, warm and sweet-smelling. She loved him. He loved her. And now, he would have to leave her as if she meant less than nothing to him.

Carlisle nodded. "I trust it won't be a problem. You cannot tell Miss Vanreid where you're going or for how long you'll be gone. She isn't to be trusted. You will send her a note advising her that a matter on one of your estates requires your intervention."

He wanted to argue that Daisy was no longer Miss Vanreid. He was proud to give her his name, to blanket her in the protection of his family. She was Daisy Trent now, and she belonged with him, at his side. But how could he even claim her when he was about to abandon her, to leave her with a note and nothing more?

The notion left him cold. His mouth went dry. He didn't

want to do this. Not today, not ever. No part of him wanted to leave Daisy behind. But he was torn as ever between his duty and the woman he'd inexplicably come to love.

What were more lies in a steadily growing sea of them?

"A matter on one of my estates?"

"Cholera," Carlisle bit out. "Tell her she must remain in London for her own safety. Everything you need will be waiting for you at the rendezvous point in Cheapside. When you arrive in Liverpool, send me a telegram telling me the weather is fair. I'll join you there as soon as I'm able."

Sebastian nodded. This was a role he had played before, and perhaps all too well. Being a spy was in his blood. He could do anything he must. Would do anything he must. Being nearly burned alive hadn't been enough. Why stop now? Indeed, why stop when there were others, far more vulnerable than he, to be protected? Daisy included. Perhaps this would be the way he could finally prove to Carlisle that she had nothing at all to do with the Fenians or their plots.

"I'll do as you ask," he said finally, though he still refused to be the first to take a step in retreat. Sebastian Fairmont, Duke of Trent, did not fall back from a challenge, and neither did he step away from his oaths and his duty. Sworn to protect, at all costs. He had known that the day may come when he would have to sacrifice his own happiness for the greater good.

This was that day.

And suddenly, the day was grim, and nothing was as it had seemed.

Carlisle, as it happened, was a man who knew when to switch tactics. He would've made a bloody brilliant general. He sidestepped Sebastian and stalked back to the sideboard, hands clasped behind his back as if he hadn't a care in the world. "Good man, Trent," he called over his shoulder.

Sebastian still itched to hit him. He needed to leave the chamber before he did something foolish, like charge his superior and feed him his irritatingly even teeth. "Your

Grace," he said instead, keeping his voice carefully modulated with a blend of respect and formality. Not even Carlisle could fault him. "I will take my leave."

"Do, Trent." The duke called dismissively over his shoulder. "Get whatever you require, and hie yourself to Liverpool at once."

Grinding his teeth against a further, most unwise retort, Sebastian spun on his heel and strode to the door of Carlisle's study. Putting space between himself and the duke was essential. Too much longer in the heartless bastard's presence would nullify the remaining shreds of honor and dignity to which he currently clung.

His hand hovered over the filigree knob when Carlisle's voice stopped him.

"Oh, and Trent? Do yourself a favor when you reach Liverpool. Find a whore and fuck her raw. You can thank me later."

There went the last thread of his sanity, clipped like a scissors attacking a fine embroidery thread. *Snip.* He was about to come undone. To explode as surely as the dynamite they chased. But no. He would not. Carlisle loved to goad. To push a man to the edge of reason and then boot him off the ledge.

Sebastian wouldn't fall into his trap. He forced out a breath, controlled himself. "Go to hell, Carlisle," he threw back with a calm he little felt.

Growling another feral curse, he tore open the door like the savage roaring to life within and slammed it behind him. Still, the small show of violence wasn't enough. He would have to leave Daisy behind today. And Jesus Christ, something within him wasn't sure if he could.

He rode away with an aggression that matched the roiling fury inside. Duty called. He had an allegiance to his country and his queen, and that far outweighed the selfish whims of the human heart.

Nothing mattered but this mission. Not what he wanted, not the indelible connection he felt to the woman he'd married, and certainly not his own needs. He had broken the cardinal rule of the spy and had allowed himself to forget he'd been playing a role, that the pleasure of his days with a pawn had been manufactured and temporary.

Time seemed to pass in a blink, and he was back where he'd begun, his imposing town home presiding over him, mocking him. So many deceptions had built that home. And he was yet another duke living a life of secrets, a life that would never be his own.

He knew a deep pang of resentment at the realization before he banished it. He had no right to feel as if he was owed anything, for he had known what being a member of the League would entail when he'd sworn his oath. He'd forfeited the right to make his own choices. He did what the League ordered. He protected the Crown and the people at all costs.

He did not, damn it all, put all his years of training and loyalty in jeopardy for the sake of one golden-haired American woman, even if his stubborn heart loved her, and even if she made him laugh and even if being in her presence reminded him of the life he wanted, the one that was just beyond his grasp. He couldn't be selfish now, even if every part of him wanted to tell Carlisle to go to the devil so that he could stay right where he was, familiarizing himself with the lovely enigma he'd married.

No, it wasn't meant to be.

Perhaps Daisy wasn't meant to be, and he'd only been fooling himself to imagine this would end any differently. With grim intention, he handed off his reins to a groom. He would return to his chamber, write a note to Daisy, and leave before she even knew he'd gone. In the end, a clean break would be easier for them both. Far preferable, it seemed, than facing her and delivering a protracted lie. Carlisle could bloody well stuff his cholera nonsense up his meddling arse.

Love and duty didn't bloody well mix, and he was hopelessly adrift.

# chapter nineteen

*D*AISY SLEPT FAR LONGER than she ordinarily would have. When she woke, the day was bright and bold, shining through her window dressing in a pointed reminder that she ought not to have lazed about as long as she had. Part of her expected Sebastian to be lying next to her in bed, but that same part was destined for disappointment, for the side of the bed he ordinarily occupied was empty.

She rolled onto her side, swiping a leg and an arm over the place where he should have been. It was cold, which meant Sebastian had been gone for some time. Had she expected him to linger? Had she expected him to reciprocate after her embarrassing declaration yesterday?

The mere thought of what had occurred was enough to make her slap the back of her hand to her forehead. Sebastian had…good heavens, she couldn't even form words in the privacy of her own thoughts for what he'd done to her. During the midst of dinner. On the table. With the servants likely aware of just what he'd been about.

And what had she done? Not only had she reveled in it,

but she'd brought the entire, deliciously wicked interlude upon herself by not wearing drawers. She still hadn't enough undergarments. It was silly, and she felt utterly ridiculous, but when she'd sent for her wardrobe from her father's home, not all of her undergarments had arrived. As it was, she was frightfully short on drawers. She did need to acquire more, and last night had been ample proof of that.

Then again, if eschewing drawers meant that her husband would treat her to such decadent lovemaking, she might be tempted to leave them off every night. She could grow accustomed to such treatment.

The wanton thought made her cheeks go hot.

That was it. Time to rise and see to her day.

She wished she hadn't embarrassed herself by telling Sebastian she loved him. In a weak moment, the words had escaped her, one big rush, before she'd been capable of tamping them down. There had been no calling them back.

Lord have mercy. They'd been married a fortnight. What had she been thinking? Daisy threw back the bedclothes and forced herself from bed, into the chill morning air. Of course, she knew what she'd been thinking. Here was a man who was capable of great kindness and gentleness, who kissed and touched her as if she were precious to him, who laughed with her, who took the time to know her.

He paid attention to the smallest detail where she was concerned. Before him, the only other man she'd ever been close to in the same sense had been Padraig, her betrothed, and that had not ended well. Padraig too had been kind and gentle. He'd made her dream of a world in which she didn't live beneath her father's thumb.

Then had come the day when her father had decided that her marriage to Padraig was no longer beneficial to him. Daisy crept across the carpet to the bell pull, yanking to summon her lady's maid as she shivered into the morning air. Why was she thinking of it now, when her happiness with Sebastian filled her heart to near bursting?

It was silly, really, but for some odd reason she recalled

the day her father had told her she would not be marrying Padraig McGuire. Her father had called both her and Padraig into his office, and he had given Padraig an ultimatum: marry my daughter or run my empire. Of course, Padraig had chosen the latter. Who wouldn't have? Her father owned half of New York City and enough factories to start his own country. Any man would have chosen the empire.

Those old hurts had healed, as a bruise, with time. Now, she was fiercely glad to have discovered the sort of man Padraig was before binding herself to him. No, Padraig's choice didn't bother her any longer, even if her ribs recalled every moment of what had happened after that awkward interview when her heart had been broken. For her defiance, she had received her father's wrath. Broken ribs, as it turned out, were a great deal more painful and infinitely more difficult to recover from.

But recover, she had. She didn't regret her past, for all of it—the good, the bad, the painful, the sad—had fashioned her into the woman she'd become. Her past had made her strong, had shown her that in spite of everything, there was still good in the world. There was still a dashing rake who had rescued her, who laughed with her, who knew she didn't like strawberries, who made love to her with such tenderness that the mere thought sent an ache straight through her.

Her door opened to reveal Abigail's familiar form bustling into the chamber, and Daisy was once again glad that she had been able to retain her lady's maid. Her father had dismissed her from her post without reference following Daisy's elopement, and she'd found her way to the duke's residence where Daisy had instantly hired her.

"Good morning to you, Your Grace," Abigail greeted.

"It is a fine day, isn't it?" Daisy returned her smile in spite of the turmoil of her emotions. There was no sense in dwelling on the past or worrying about the future. Both existed, an unavoidable axis of her life.

Abigail held up a folded sheet of paper that bore a seal. "His Grace directed this to be delivered to you."

How odd, Daisy thought as she accepted the note. A brief, naïve hope flitted through her that it was a declaration of his love. She opened it to scan its contents. A love letter, it most assuredly was not.

*Dearest Daisy,*

*A matter most private and urgent has necessitated my immediate departure from London. I shall return as soon as possible.*

*Yours, regretfully,*
*Sebastian*

She read the note six times before her shocked mind finally began to absorb the words it contained. Her eyes kept returning to two in particular: *immediate departure*. Departure. Immediate. They played in her mind like a taunting song, sending a cold, hard knot of dread into her stomach.

She swayed, catching her balance on the footboard of her bed.

Sebastian was…gone?

"His Grace has left?" she asked her lady's maid, feeling disoriented, as if she'd woken from a long sleep and couldn't make sense of where she was.

"Earlier this morning, Your Grace," Abigail confirmed with a cheerful smile, as though Daisy's heart wasn't breaking right then and there in her chest.

She had told him she loved him, and the next morning, he had left her with nothing more than a two-sentence note. He hadn't even woken her before he'd gone, had disappeared from her bed in the predawn light and ridden out of her life with no explanation. A private and urgent matter. What did that even mean? Where had he gone, and when in heaven's name would he return?

"Your Grace?"

Abigail's voice reached her as though from the opposite

end of a long hallway. Daisy blinked. The note fell from her fingers, sailing to the floor. Tears stung her eyes, and a queasy sensation stole over her.

"Your Grace? Is something amiss?" Abigail asked again. "You've gone pale."

Sebastian had left her.

He was gone.

And she was going to be ill.

She raced across the chamber, just barely making it to the chamber pot before casting up her accounts.

## chapter twenty

*24th March, 1881*

*Dearest Sebastian,*

*I hope that this letter finds you in good health. A week has passed and I've still yet to receive word from you. The note you left behind was rather terse and imprecise. Indeed, you neglected to mention just how long your absence would be and what your destination was. At your leisure, might you apprise me? I do hope you won't be away for long.*

*Your loving wife,*
*Daisy*

An entire week passed without word from Sebastian. Each day seemed more interminable than the last. Daisy felt like a sleepwalker, going through the motions of the passing hours without being aware of what she was doing. She met with Mrs. Robbins to plan menus and oversee the household as though nothing was wrong. She greeted Giles at breakfast. She continued organizing the library.

But the house was dreadfully quiet and cavernous

without Sebastian. She missed him at dinner. She went into his chamber just to smell the lingering scent of him, walked into his study in the hopes she'd find him there. At night, she longed for him and hated herself for the weakness. She had no one to laugh with, no one to surprise her with kisses or meet her gaze in a wicked glance over the table.

It was unshakeable, this feeling she had as if a part of her had gone missing. She wanted that part of her back. Two weeks after a lifetime of waiting had not been enough. She wanted to rail against the unfairness of it, to rail against him, to find him—wherever he'd gone—and bring him back to her.

But she also wanted to deliver the most blistering, crushing dressing down in the history of dressings down. She wanted to demand that he face her, that he explain to her how he could have disappeared from her life as suddenly as he'd entered it. How could he have left her like this, leaving her to think she meant less than nothing to him? Had he gone to a mistress? Had he left because she'd confessed her feelings?

The questions plagued her, day after day. She woke up and wondered. Traveled through the day in meaningless attempts to distract herself, all while wondering. Laid down to bed at night, wishing he was with her, wondering still. Where was he? When would he return?

As the first week of his absence melded into the second, the sadness permeating Daisy began to harden into resolve. On Monday morning, she and Mrs. Robbins sat together for their customary planning of the week ahead.

"Would you care for some Root's Cuca Cocoa, Your Grace?" the kindly housekeeper asked. Her hair was steel gray, and fine laughter lines bracketed her eyes and mouth. She was sincere and kind, and always smelled of fresh soap and powder.

Daisy had come to appreciate her steadfast presence, but she could hear quite plainly the sympathy steeping the elder woman's voice. It was the same sympathy she'd seen in

Giles' expression when she'd asked if he knew where His Grace had gone or when he might return. *I'm afraid not, Your Grace. Though I'm sure he shall return as soon as he's able. Such matters do occasionally call His Grace away.*

Such matters. Private and urgent matters. The mere thought made her curl her lip as she sat in the sunshine-stained salon with her husband's housekeeper.

She straightened her spine. "Whatever for, Mrs. Robbins?"

"It's just the thing for those who suffer from bouts of worry or sleeplessness," Mrs. Robbins said gently. "There now, Your Grace. I know you're fretting over His Grace, and it's plain to see you aren't getting as much rest or sustenance as you need. I'll have Sally brew a cup for you, shall I?"

"No," she bit out, watching as the housekeeper's smile faded before adding, "thank you. Perhaps I will try some later."

"Of course, Your Grace." Mrs. Robbins nodded. "Forgive me for my presumption. I wish to see to your comfort."

Daisy forced herself to smile, for none of this was the housekeeper's fault, and she was a dear heart. "There's no need to ask for my forgiveness, Mrs. Robbins. I greatly appreciate your concern as well as all your guidance in household matters. I do realize that my presence here has been rather unorthodox and unexpected. You've been an invaluable asset. Truly."

The housekeeper flushed with pleasure. "Thank you, Your Grace."

The questions bubbling up within her crowded onto her tongue then. Just the night before, she'd gone into his chamber, determined to scour it from the highest shelf to the lowest point beneath his carved oak bed in hopes of finding any clue as to where he'd gone. Nothing had seemed out of place. Everything had been in immaculate order, not a piece of furniture out of place. Nothing, that was, except for the note she'd located, slipped between the pages of a book, folded three times and dated the day he'd left. *Would you care to meet for a morning ride? The skies look too ominous to wait until afternoon.*

That note, unsigned and written in a bold, masculine scrawl, was the key to his abrupt departure. Daisy was certain of it. If only she could discover its author and what it meant. He had said nothing of plans to meet anyone for a morning ride. She would have recalled.

"Mrs. Robbins," she began delicately, seeking the proper words, "has His Grace ever abruptly departed London in the past?"

A rare frown firmed the housekeeper's lips. "I've instructed the kitchens to keep all the plates hot. Do you find their temperature to your liking, Your Grace?"

Daisy blinked. "The plates are always appropriately warm. But His Grace…is this a habit of his? None of the household seems particularly surprised. As a relatively new bride who had no inkling he'd planned a trip, you can appreciate why I might wonder, can't you, Mrs. Robbins?"

Mrs. Robbins swallowed. "The chestnuts yesterday. Were they to your liking? I told Monsieur Gascoigne that chestnuts ought to be boiled prior to the roasting, but he disagreed with me and proceeded with the roasting. Are you growing tired of *haricots verts*? It seems to me that Monsieur favors them far too frequently. At least he has the sense not to chop them the way some cooks do."

The housekeeper was babbling, and it was most uncharacteristic of her. It was Daisy's turn to frown. "Mrs. Robbins, the chestnuts were lovely, and I must say that I'm not partial to beans, but you haven't answered my question."

"Oh dear me." Gray eyebrows rose over eyes the color of sherry. "Are you certain you wouldn't like some Root's?"

Good heavens. Why would Mrs. Robbins insist on evading her questions? The insidious suggestion rose inside her again, that he had a mistress hidden away in the

219

countryside. Perhaps he'd gone to her.

"No Root's, Mrs. Robbins," she said grimly. "You've been a retainer here since the last duke, have you not?"

The servant's lips tightened. "I have been so honored, yes, Your Grace."

"Then you've known my husband the duke for his whole life."

"I have, and a finer gentleman doesn't exist, Your Grace," Mrs. Robbins said firmly.

There was a note of truth in the housekeeper's voice, but it didn't satisfy Daisy. "Then surely you can say whether or not he has previously disappeared in so sudden and unexpected a manner. You must appreciate that I am…concerned for his welfare. He left no indication of where he might be going or for how long he would be gone."

Mrs. Robbins sighed. "It isn't my place to say, Your Grace."

Daisy stared, frustration rising within her, mingling with anger and despair. "Does His Grace like asparagus?" she asked suddenly.

The housekeeper blinked, looking startled by the abrupt shift in discussion. "Why, no, I don't believe he does, Your Grace."

"Excellent," she gritted through a smile she didn't feel. "Please see that it is served every day this week."

"Of course, Your Grace." Mrs. Robbins' expression was one of blatant confusion.

"I like asparagus," she explained. She would have gone through every vegetable she enjoyed until she'd reached one he didn't like, and that was the truth of it.

*5ᵗʰ April, 1881*

*Dear husband,*

*I've taken the liberty of sending copies of this letter to each of your estates should you find yourself at any of them. You are missed in London. While I understand the nature of your departure was both "private" and "urgent" as you stated, I believe that as your wife, I am at least entitled to know when you shall return. May it be sooner rather than later.*

*Yours,*
*Daisy*

Liverpool was a city of dead-ends.

At least, that was the way it seemed.

Sebastian had been firmly ensconced there for over a bloody fortnight, and he'd precious few leads. In the small, nondescript rooms he kept over the Barrel and Anchor, the din of the seedy tavern reached him as a raucous assault on his ears: roaring laughter, music, and female squeals. His rooms smelled of stale ale and cheroots, and yesterday he'd interrupted an assignation between a dock worker and a whore in the hall.

He found himself in a grim sort of purgatory here, where he was Mr. George Thompson rather than the Duke of Trent and he came and went from his rooms without anyone giving a damn whether he lived or died. Hiding in plain sight was one of his gifts as a spy, but that didn't bloody well mean he liked it, particularly when every speck of information he'd managed to glean from his days of scouring the city and questioning chemists had turned out to be worthless.

He'd yet to uncover evidence of the dynamite factory Carlisle suspected was being run from the city. No large purchases of glycerin, nitric acid, and sulfuric acid—the ingredients required for the creation of dynamite—had been recorded at any of the chemists he'd visited thus far. He was becoming convinced that either Vanreid was using his ships to somehow secret dynamite or the bastards had chosen another city as their base.

With a muttered curse, he stalked to the chipped pitcher and bowl atop an equally battered washstand and splashed water on his face. The man staring back at him in the cracked mirror was a forbidding stranger. Wincing, he peeled away the false mustache affixed to his upper lip.

The removal smarted, but not as much as being away from Daisy did. Each day he was gone from her, unable to contact her, far from her side and her bed where he longed to be, was like a bare blade finding its home in his gut.

Two sharp knocks at his door, followed by a pause and then three more in rapid succession interrupted his thoughts. Using the scrap of toweling by the pitcher and bowl, he dried his face before pivoting and striding back across the chamber. He hesitated only a moment before knocking once on the door.

The person on the other side knocked back in the sign they had prearranged.

Griffin had arrived at last. Feeling a small surge of relief that his friend and comrade had finally joined him, he pulled open the door, careful to keep out of sight lest anyone should see him sans mustache.

His friend raised a golden brow at him as he stepped over the threshold and the door snapped closed at his back. Like Sebastian, he wore plain trousers and a work shirt and jacket. He'd grown a beard, and he rather resembled nothing so much as a Whitechapel thug. "Brother George, is that you?" he deadpanned.

"Of course you must know that it is I, brother John," he returned, grinning.

They clapped each other on the back solidly.

"It's good to see you, Bast," Griffin said. "I'm deuced glad Carlisle decided to pair us up on this one."

"As am I." Though they were the best of friends, they

had not worked together on many missions. When he'd received word from Carlisle two days prior that Griffin would be joining him, he'd been more than pleased, in spite of their last clash. Griffin had a sharp eye, keen wit, steady hand, and the cool calculation of a seasoned warrior. "Even if it means I'll be stuck in bloody Liverpool for another fortnight at least."

Tomorrow, they would move to a new part of the city, take different rooms, and begin Thompson Brothers Chemists. Since Sebastian's work had thus far uncovered precious little, they were going to act as a lure, selling their goods wholesale below market price. Either the Fenians were purchasing their acids and glycerin in small quantities from a variety of chemists to avoid detection, or they were not in Liverpool at all.

Thompson Brothers should—within a relatively short time frame—give them the means to determine the answer. If the plotters were in Liverpool, it stood to reason that they would purchase more affordable supplies, and it was down to Sebastian and Griffin to monitor the customers and their purchases.

"Liverpool is where we need eyes and ears the most," Griffin said then. "We've word from the consul in Philadelphia that there are plots in the works to blow up public buildings here in the city."

Sebastian's blood went cold. "Jesus. The information is reliable?"

Griffin nodded. "It comes directly from the Pinkertons."

Hell. The Pinkerton Detective Agency's work was always sound. "I've still no evidence that the dynamite is being manufactured here. I've run every lead I had to ground, and I've come up with nothing."

"I'm here now, old chap. We'll find these bastards one way or another and put a stop to them." Though Griffin's tone was congenial, his countenance was anything but. His expression was fairly murderous.

"That we will." He paused then, his thoughts going, inevitably, to Daisy. Christ, what must she think of him? He had wedded her, bedded her, and left with nothing but a terse note and no indication of when he might return. Though he knew his actions were borne of duty rather than callousness, she did not, and the notion had been driving him mad this last fortnight. He longed for her as he never had for another, and though he cursed himself for his weakness, he couldn't deny it. "Have you any word from London?"

"Bloody fucking hell, Bast. Is this about your American tart?"

His head felt as if it may explode. "She. Is. Not. A. Tart," he bit out.

"Oh, Christ." Griffin studied him in his signature, penetrating manner that had made far more worthy opponents than Sebastian tremble in fear. "Never say you fancy yourself…in *love* with the chit."

He spat the word "love" as though it were a dirty word, something to revile, a bitter taste he couldn't wait to remove from his tongue.

Heat climbed his throat. Good God. He didn't flush, and yet…how else to explain the warmth searing his flesh, reaching to even his cheeks? He cleared his throat. "The chit is my wife."

Griffin's lips thinned. "Have you forgotten the circumstances that made her your wife?"

"No, goddamn it," he growled.

Of course he hadn't forgotten. How could he, when the deceit he'd perpetrated swallowed him whole each time he thought of it? He had spent his entire adult life as a spy, lying to everyone around him. Manipulating, dissembling, using, donning whatever name and disguise he required in the moment. But for the first time, the credo by which he'd lived—anything in the name of the League—no longer sufficed.

"I saw any number of cheeky wenches in the tavern

below. You could have your pick of the lot for the night, if that's what ails you." Griffin's gaze was steadfast, unrelenting.

Damn him. "I don't want to tup a whore," he bit out. "I'm *married* to her, by God. I owe her my fidelity, if nothing else."

"Fuck." Griffin shook his head. "I told Carlisle it shouldn't be you, but he was adamant you were the man for the task. He doesn't know you the way I do. You're too bloody softhearted for it, and now she's managed to cozen you into thinking she's not the deceptive bitch she truly is."

Sebastian didn't think. Indeed, his brain seemed to take leave of the rest of his body, for it was almost as if the two were disconnected as his fist swung wildly, finding rigid purchase in his best friend's jaw for the second time in as many weeks. He watched as Griffin's head snapped back, almost from a dream. A bloody nightmare.

But Griffin had pushed him too far, and this…he would not be insulted. Wouldn't allow his loyalty to be called into question, not by anyone and especially not by the man he considered a brother. The way he'd spoken of Daisy, disparaging her, as if she were a siren who'd bewitched him, and as if any other woman might easily take her place. It was not to be borne.

Griffin was a seasoned fighter, and he was cold as ice. Always. So the fist meeting Sebastian's jaw a scant few seconds later was no surprise, though the burst of pain and stars marring his vision took him aback for half a second. There. He supposed they were even this time around.

"Have you no word on her?" he asked ruefully, rubbing the place where his friend's right hook had connected with his face.

"Fucking hell," Griffin snarled, staring at him as though he were a stranger.

"Who watches her?" Sebastian pressed, undeterred in his quest for some word of Daisy, however small and insignificant. By God, he missed her, and with a desperation that was utterly humiliating. "Surely someone, if not you. Is she safe, at least?"

Leaving her had been difficult enough, but leaving her behind knowing that her bastard of a father was within the same city, still capable of reaching her and hurting her…that was a different kind of torture. The sort of torture that none of his training could have prepared him for.

"She's safe." Griffin's lip curled into a sneer. "What's next, Bast? You're going to secret her away to the country and start getting brats on her? Men like us aren't meant for that life. We're bound to put the League first."

Sebastian met his gaze, unflinching. His friend wasn't wrong, not about any of it, and he was being torn apart from the inside out, stretched in two opposing directions. Love versus loyalty, duty against want. "I'm putting the League first or I wouldn't be here, damn it."

Griffin's expression became dazed. "This isn't like you."

No, it wasn't. But he'd never been in love before. "Maybe you don't know me," he said evenly.

Because the truth of it was that he'd begun to realize not even *he* had known himself. The man he'd believed himself to be had been an island in a vast ocean, accountable to no one, untouchable and unbreakable. The man he thought he was would never have fallen in love with a slip of an American girl who was stronger than anyone he'd ever met. He was not himself without her, and she was the part of him that had been missing all along. With Daisy, he was whole.

"I'm beginning to think I don't," Griffin said, sounding weary. "But we've a duty to uphold and a mission to carry out."

Yes, they bloody well did.

## chapter twenty-one

*15th April, 1881*

*Your Grace,*

*Over a month has passed without word. I find myself fearing for your wellbeing. None of the staff knows of your whereabouts or the reason for your abrupt departure. Indeed, it is quite as if you have disappeared. If your absence is due to me, perhaps you could be kind enough to inform me so that I may make amends.*

*I do hope to hear from you soon. In the meantime, I hope you don't mind my recent increase in expenditures. I've commissioned an entire new wardrobe and have begun making a few, much-needed alternations to our London home. I'm sure you will agree that the paintings of the former dukes were decidedly de trop and much in need of replacement. I've had them sent to the attics.*

*Sincerely,*
*Daisy Trent*

Daisy found herself being ushered into the salon of the Duchess of Leeds by a butler who looked as if he'd be more at home on the docks than he was in his formal attire. He possessed none of the formidable starch of Giles, and he seemed far too young for the position, tall and broad and commanding, with a head of black hair and a wicked scar running down his right cheek.

He was almost handsome, though not in the classical sense. Rather, his was a raw, brawny attractiveness that was most disarming in a servant who was meant to blend into the wallpaper unless he was required. This man would never blend into wallpaper. Damask could not possibly contain him.

The invitation from the duchess had arrived two days before, disarming Daisy, for she didn't recall ever having much discourse with the Duchess of Leeds. And precious few invitations had been forthcoming for the American who had eloped with the duke who'd subsequently disappeared.

Daisy read the gossip sheets, even if she knew she shouldn't. She was more than aware of her reputation and what was being said of her. It wasn't pretty.

"Her Grace, the Duchess of Trent," the man masquerading as a butler announced.

Daisy entered the salon to an unexpected sight. The Duchess of Leeds sat on a gilded settee, surrounded by a bevy of dogs, an orange cat curled on her lap. One dog, a handsome terrier with an under-bite, rose and sauntered toward Daisy, sniffing her skirts.

Daisy didn't think twice before lowering herself to the dog's level, offering him her hand for a judicious sniff. He sniffed deeply for a few moments, pressing his warm nuzzle into her palm, before delivering a lick.

"Your Grace," said the duchess, drawing Daisy's attention back to her with a smile that only served to heighten her exotic beauty. She had rich chestnut hair, high cheekbones, and flashing green eyes. "It seems as if you've met with Hugo's approval."

"He is a dear." Daisy removed her glove to rub Hugo's satiny head. He rewarded her by getting onto his haunches and licking her directly across the mouth.

"Oh heavens, Hugo. Down, boy." The duchess's voice rang across the salon, cutting and authoritative. "My dear duchess, please do stand else I fear the little mongrel will stuff his tongue down your throat."

Daisy laughed as Hugo licked her cheek. "I don't mind."

As a girl, she'd longed for a dog, and that same longing returned to her in a rush now, likely compounded by an entire month of loneliness and isolation. March had turned into April, the weather warming, spring blossoming over the city, and still her husband had not returned. No word. No indication he even still breathed. The pang in her chest tightened, and the little dog seemed to sense her distress, for his simple lick turned into a frenzy of wet, overzealous canine kisses.

"Oh dear heavens, you little scoundrel," the duchess chided. "Down, Hugo!"

The dog at last obeyed, settling himself on his haunches and blinking up at her with large, chocolate eyes. Daisy gave his head another pat before she stood, recalling her manners as she swept into a curtsy.

"Pish, none of that now," the duchess said, an open and friendly smile curving her lips and rendering her even lovelier. "I don't believe in standing on ceremony." She gestured about her airily. "I'm somewhat of a collector of strays, you see."

A collector of strays—yes, it made sense, from the dogs, to the cat, to the butler. Daisy couldn't help but wonder if the odd woman before her viewed her as yet another one.

"How kindhearted of you." Daisy strove for diplomacy. "Thank you for your invitation, Your Grace. I find myself something of an outsider in London."

"You mustn't thank me. Do come in and get settled," the duchess ordered. "And please, you must call me Georgiana, I insist. Ludlow will bring tea shortly."

Daisy hesitantly found her way to a chair that flanked the duchess, Hugo trailing happily along with her and sitting on the hem of her skirts after she'd found her seat. They chatted politely until the unlikely butler returned, looking almost ridiculous as he bore a dainty silver tray in his meaty paws. Daisy didn't miss the look the duchess exchanged with the man before he quietly retreated from the room once more.

Innocuous chatter continued over tea, Daisy grateful for the companionship and the distraction both. Georgiana, as it turned out, was a fellow American heiress. Having grown up largely abroad, she possessed the cultured accent of any lady to the manor born. Daisy felt herself warming to the garrulous duchess, who was quick to laugh and equally generous in her smiles. During the course of their tête-à-tête, she almost forgot the misery of her current situation.

Until Georgiana eyed her sympathetically over her tea and uttered the observation she least wished to hear. "You seem dreadfully in need of a friend, Daisy."

Daisy nearly spat her tea all over her silk gown. Yes, she supposed she was dreadfully in need of a friend. But who was this odd woman she scarcely knew, who kept a menagerie of small animals and had a terrifying butler, to say so?

"I'm perfectly content," her pride forced her to say.

The duchess wasn't fooled. She tilted her head, considering her. "You look perfectly miserable, dear."

Daisy firmed her lips, stifling the unwanted surge of emotion evoked by her would-be friend's words. "I'm…" *Lonely, wretched, dejected, heartbroken.* She swallowed. "A friend would be lovely."

"Excellent. You may be surprised to learn that we have a great deal more in common than hailing from the same homeland." Georgiana settled her teacup into its saucer. "I too have a husband given to abrupt disappearances and secrecy."

Daisy considered her newfound friend, struggling to make sense of the implications of what she'd just revealed. During the time she'd flitted about fashionable London society, she had never seen the Duke of Leeds himself. "Is

His Grace not in residence?" she asked hesitantly.

Georgianna's sunny expression went uncharacteristically dark. "He claims to be in America on a prolonged hunting expedition. Naturally, I don't believe a word of it."

Daisy frowned, feeling uncomfortable with this glimpse into the marriage of two virtual strangers. "You don't?"

"I found some correspondence in the fire grate of his study, half burnt. It was nothing but a few sentences, meaningless observations on the weather, and I couldn't fathom why he would've gone to the trouble of burning such a thing." Georgiana paused. "It was only later, when I found some other letters stuffed amongst his books, that I realized they were written in code. It wasn't at all what it seemed."

Letters written in code.

What in heaven's name...

Daisy's mind returned to the odd note she'd found in Sebastian's chamber, folded in thirds. *The skies look too ominous to wait until afternoon.* A shiver went straight down her spine. "Were you able to translate them?" she asked.

Georgiana nodded slowly. "My husband isn't hunting game, Daisy. He's in New York City. I haven't yet worked out what it is he's doing or why, but it's something to do with the Fenians. What's more, there was a name on one of the letters."

Dread crept through her, uncoiling and then snapping tight around her heart like a manacle. Somehow, she knew what Georgiana was going to say next. "It was my name, wasn't it?"

The duchess nodded. "So it only seems fitting, you see, that you and I ought to join forces and bring our miserable husbands to heel."

Daisy set down her teacup with numb fingers as suspicion, hurt, and confusion warred within her. "What do you propose we do?"

Georgiana smiled, but this time, the smile didn't reach her eyes. "We'll wage a campaign of our own. Men are not so different from dogs in some ways, you see. Both are quite territorial. By the time we're finished, they'll be begging to tell us the truth."

*30th April, 1881*

*Your Grace,*

*If you would deign to answer any of my letters, or to return to London where I await you, you would do me the utmost kindness. Your silence is as disheartening as your abandonment.*

*I do so fervently hope you won't mind the soirees I've been hosting, which are sometimes quite dear in cost. I confess that I was startled to realize I'd spent nearly a hundred pounds on ice sculptures over the course of the month. To be fair, however, the sculptures were exquisite.*

*Sincerely,*
*Duchess of Trent*

April bled into May.

By day, Sebastian and Griffin oversaw the chemist's shop, keeping their wits about them and their eyes and ears open. Their clientele was steady and predictable. No large-scale purchases of acids or glycerin. Nothing that would be cause for suspicion or alarm.

By night, they scoured the streets of Liverpool. Their intelligence from the Pinkertons in America was concise and clear. There would be an attack. The devil of it was that beyond knowing a bomb planting was imminent, they were helpless to stop the destruction from unfolding without evidence leading them to the origin of the conspiracy.

"All roads lead to Vanreid," Griffin pointed out needlessly as they stood alone in their empty storefront one evening.

Sebastian stilled in the act of tallying their ledger from the day. Though he'd never been interested in trade, here was a part of his duty that he enjoyed. Numbers were so precise. There was no confusion when it came to arithmetic. One was either correct or incorrect, and there was not a bloody subjective thing about it. So unlike every other part of his life that he almost found peace in working over the leather-bound book with his pen. It was a diversion, at any rate, from missing Daisy and wondering what the hell she must think of his sudden disappearance.

Duty was a hell of a thing.

"Of course all roads lead to Vanreid," he said at last, measuring his words with care as he finished a sum. "He is the primary source of funds. He owns the arms factory, the boats. He hides his every evil action beneath the pretext of innocent business. And yet, for all that, he remains the wily fox who has outsmarted us, gotten into the henhouse, and eaten every last fowl, for we cannot buy evidence against him."

"Do you not think it odd, Bast, the way he can seemingly predict our moves?" Griffin asked from across the room.

He stiffened. Acting on information from American operatives, they had raided Vanreid's ships on four occasions, only to be met with legitimate goods each time. Not a hint of dynamite or dynamite-making ingredients to be found.

"Do you mean to suggest I shared sensitive information with Daisy?" he calmly asked, his pen still scratching away on the ledger. It was better to involve himself in such tasks than to dwell on the growing doubt his best friend levied his way each passing day. As their mission had proved increasingly fruitless, the strain between them had only gotten worse.

"I would never question your loyalty, Bast." Griffin's tone was quiet, contemplative. "That, I think, is rather the point. Is your loyalty to her as strong as your loyalty to the

League?"

He didn't know the answer to the goddamn question, nor did he wish to consider it. *Ten carboys of nitric acid*, he read, and then he froze. "Did you arrange for a large sale of nitric acid today?"

"No," Griffin snapped. "Don't seek to distract me, Bast. It's high time we had this out between the two of us. You haven't spoken a word about her since the night I arrived."

No, he had not. Daisy was a private matter, and to his mind, she had nothing to do with his obligations in Liverpool. She was, simply, his. And he would not discuss her as if she were an enemy or a suspect when she was the woman who owned his heart. But that was neither here nor there at the moment, for he was staring at a blank line where the scrawl of their assistant shop boy, James, indicated an inordinately large purchase of nitric acid, along with fourteen carboys of sulfuric acid.

They were to be delivered the following day to an address not far off. The lure had finally worked, damn it.

He jerked his head up to find Griffin pacing the shop floor, a scowl hardening his features. "I believe we need to pay a visit to one Reginald White."

"What are you on about?" Griffin stalked over to him.

Sebastian pushed the ledger toward his friend, pointing to the entry in question. "Have a look for yourself. It seems to me that Reginald White purchased far too great a quantity for a mere painter. Indeed, it rather seems to me that the bastard bought enough to make dynamite."

Griffin scanned the ledger, his jaw clenching. "Bloody hell. What do you know? It looks like we may have found our canary after all."

Sebastian raised a brow. "Let's go."

The sun had long since set, all storefronts closed. Liverpool's night denizens had come out to play in full, raucous effect. It was nigh onto midnight, which meant they hadn't a moment to waste. Working with haste, they closed down the shop for the night, locked everything away, doused the lights, and moved on foot to their destination.

Number three Castle Street was a fairly nondescript building. No lights burned within. By the streetlight, Sebastian read the sign hanging over the small storefront. Reginald White, Painter & Decorator. They had reached their quarry, and he knew a moment of pure, unadulterated thrill. Here was the part of his work in the League that called to him, that felt like home. Danger excited him.

And yet, for some reason, tonight the excitement felt, after its initial rush...hollow. Perhaps it was because he knew that back in London, the most exquisite woman he'd ever known was organizing his library and wondering where in the hell he'd gone. Jesus, she was probably cursing him, hating him. When he finally did return, there was no telling if he would be able to win her back.

But this wasn't the time or the place for that thought. For now, he was a pledged member of the League, and he had a mission to see through. For Daisy, and for every other innocent who would be an unwitting victim, he needed to cast Vanreid into gaol forever.

*That's it, old chap. Wits about you. Time to move.*

"We'll canvas the perimeter, make certain no one's within," he told Griffin lowly. You take the east, I'll move from the west, and we'll meet in the rear."

"Done," Griffin agreed, his hand going to the pistol he kept beneath his jacket.

"God go with you, brother," they said in unison.

And then, they parted ways and sank into the night. Some twenty minutes later, they reconnoitered by a locked back door.

"No one's inside," Griffin grunted Sebastian's thoughts aloud. "We need to gain access, see what's within."

Sebastian lit a match to illuminate the lock on the door. "Have you your bloody keys?"

"Does a stag shit in the woods?" Griffin asked triumphantly, extracting the ring of skeleton keys he always kept at the ready from his pocket.

He would have laughed had the situation been any less dire. Griffin's gift was picking locks. He had seven keys, and if none of them fit a lock, Griffin could muscle the closest match into working. He'd never seen a door the Duke of Strathmore couldn't break through with his innate feel.

Griffin turned his attention to the door. Sebastian's match sputtered out, but it little mattered. In less than two minutes, Griffin had the door open. They stepped inside, shutting the portal behind them, and lit the gas lamps on low, walking with as much care as possible lest anyone let the rooms above the shop. The storefront seemed innocent enough.

Sebastian followed Griffin into the back room, and that was the precise location where innocent morphed into something decidedly evil.

"Carboys of nitric acid," Griffin reported quietly. "Seventeen, in all."

"Ten of sulfuric," Sebastian added grimly.

The evidence grew more damning as they continued. On the boiler, a vat of nitroglycerin simmered.

"Bloody hell," Griffin rasped.

It was in that precise moment that Sebastian's gaze found a scrap of paper bearing a nearly illegible scrawl. He snatched it up, reading it thrice, sure he was wrong. Sure that no one, especially not the sort of enemy who had been brewing dynamite beneath the nose of England's most elite spies for the past two months, could be so foolish.

"Fuck." He scanned the contents again for good measure. *Midnight. Dale Street.* "There's to be an explosion tonight at the police station."

"Jesus. We've got to get there to warn them," Griffin said needlessly.

Taking great care to leave the premises just as they'd found it, they backtracked together, turning down all the lamps, leaving and locking the door. Dale Street wasn't far by foot, so they took off at a run. They'd almost reached the station when the explosion struck. The earth rumbled, the sound of the detonation reverberating in otherworldly fashion, blasting through his chest. Glass shattered. A woman screamed.

And at last, the war they'd been warned of had arrived at Liverpool. But Sebastian and Griffin had been too goddamn late to stop it. They halted in their tracks, watching the smoke rise in the wake of the blast, and the resultant commotion unleash.

"Fucking hell," Sebastian breathed, smoke and the bitter ascent of sulfur burning his lungs.

"Hell on earth," Griffin agreed bitterly. "Damn their hides. We'll get them, Bast. We'll get every last one of the rotten bastards."

Sebastian watched the glow of flame, the smoke billowing into the air. He thought of Daisy, her innocence, the way he'd last left her, and his heart ached. Then he thought of her father, the duplicitous son-of-a-bitch who financed these godforsaken plots. And a part of him resented her, for being so innocent and good and naïve. For being the woman he loved and yet also the daughter of the enemy he needed to destroy. It wasn't fair, damn it. Life was not fair.

Because nothing was as it seemed, and everything was about to change.

## chapter twenty-two

*23rd May, 1881*

*Your Grace,*
    *You will perhaps be happy to learn that I've made a great number
of friends in your absence. There are ever so many gentlemen eager to
make my acquaintance now that the Duchess of Leeds has taken me
under her wing.*
    *In particular, the Earl of Bolton is a noble and generous man, and
not at all as you described him. It is such a pity that your "private"
and "urgent" matter keeps you from London, as I think you would get
on with him as well as I do.*

*Sincerely,*
*Duchess of Trent*

Daisy stared at the man who had once been her betrothed
and fought back the familiar burst of nausea that had been
striking her on and off for the last month. Tall and lanky,
with black hair and flashing blue eyes, he was just as
handsome as he'd been the day she'd first met him in New
York at one of her father's dinner parties. Padraig McGuire,

with his lilting accent from Ireland's shores, his easy smiles, and wicked charm.

She'd fallen for those charms once upon a time.

Strange where life had led them, their diverging paths bringing them to this moment. Now, when she looked upon him, she saw a stranger. What a naïve girl she'd been to think she'd been prepared for marriage to him. She knew now that the girlish fancy she'd felt had been predicated by the burning desire to escape her father more than any other emotion.

And some two years later, here she stood, an abandoned duchess in a foreign land, no happier as the Duchess of Trent than she would've been as Mrs. Padraig McGuire. Two years, and she'd learned nothing about entrusting her heart to the care of men. How sobering.

"Why have you come, Mr. McGuire?" she asked into the silence that had fallen between them.

She stood by the window in the small salon where she received callers, a sliver of sun warming her face. The chamber was filled with flowers, a testament to the last month's efforts. Her arrangement with Georgiana was proceeding with success. Together, they had managed to set the *ton* on its ear with all manner of gossip in the hopes that they would cause enough furor to bring their husbands home and get the answers they so badly deserved.

Hugo sat at her feet, guarding her as was his wont. The boisterous pup had proved far more devoted to her than any person had ever been.

Padraig took a step closer to her, and Hugo growled.

"Bloody hell, Daisy. Must you have that mutt present?" He cast a jaundiced eye toward her beloved companion.

Her chin rose. "Yes, I must, and you're far too familiar, Mr. McGuire. You may address me as 'Your Grace' or you may leave."

Another step brought him nearer, and for a moment she wondered if she should fear him. After all, he ran her father's businesses. She should not have received him again today, his fourth visit in the last fortnight since his abrupt reappearance in her life. And especially not since he was using a false name for reasons he refused to divulge. Indeed, she would not have had he not dangled the one lure before her that she couldn't resist.

Bridget.

Her sister had abruptly quit her position with Madame Villiers, and she had disappeared. Daisy had not heard from her, and she was dreadfully worried. Madame had no notion of where she'd gone or why, leaving Daisy adrift.

"Forgive me, Your Grace." Padraig's tone was mocking, but he stopped where he was, the boldly patterned replacement carpet she'd chosen between them. "Are you happy then? As a duchess? Is it the life you wanted?"

Her own husband had abandoned her as if she were of no greater import than the newspaper he'd discarded the day before. And she had given her heart to him, or at least to the man she'd imagined him to be. For the real Sebastian was an enigma to her. A mystery she could not seem to solve. Of course this was not the life she wanted, spending each day in frivolous amusements, working with Georgiana to cause as much gossip as possible in the hopes she might get the answers she so desperately sought.

*Where are you, Sebastian?* she wondered silently. *And, more importantly, who are you?*

She forced a smile to her lips. "This is the life I've been given. I am…content. But that is enough idle chatter, Mr. McGuire. You said you had news of my sister that required an audience. I don't wish to hear anything you say if it doesn't concern her. May I remind you that your other visits have been fruitless? That each time you claim to have information regarding her whereabouts, they lead to dead-ends?"

Padraig's mouth flattened into a harsh line. "You loathe me."

Did she? Once, perhaps, she had, but time, distance, and knowledge could heal any wound. Now, she looked upon him and felt nothing. He was not the man she'd believed him to be, and she was no longer the girl he'd once known. "You are my father's emissary. My distaste for you stems from that fact alone."

"I've told you I'm not here at his behest." Padraig's gaze searched hers as a frown furrowed his brow. "He doesn't know I've been speaking with you, though I've made no secret of it. I don't answer to Vanreid."

She wasn't sure she believed that, but she didn't wish to discuss her father with him. Her every tie to him except her sister had been severed, and she intended to keep it that way forever. "Have you news of Bridget or not?"

"Yes."

His single-word response did little to quell the apprehension unfurling within her. "And? Where is she? What has happened?"

Padraig strode toward her, closing the distance. Hugo growled again, making him stop short of reaching her. "She's no longer in London. Her precise location is unknown, but I fear she's in danger."

Danger. The apprehension iced into fear. Her hands clenched in her skirts. "What sort of danger?"

"Bombs, Daisy," he said simply.

And she didn't bother to correct his familiar address this time, for her inundated mind was too busy attempting to make sense of what he'd just told her. "Bombs."

"Dynamite, to be specific." His expression tightened. "The danger is grave."

Good, sweet heavens. The papers had been abuzz with talk of the explosion in Liverpool and talk of Fenian uprisings. Daisy had never imagined such evils had anything to do with her sister's disappearance. "Do you mean to say she's involved with the Fenians?"

Padraig inclined his head. "I cannot say. All I will say is you should trust no one, including me."

He caught her hand then, and Hugo gave a small yip of protest as he raised it to his lips for a kiss. Daisy snatched her hand from his grasp, staring at him, questions and dread rushing through her like flood waters. "Why are you telling me this? Padraig, are you connected to this? Is that why you've come calling using the name John Greaves instead of your own?"

He shook his head slowly. "The danger is grave," he repeated, bowing to her. "Be wary of those closest to you, and take care of yourself."

She watched him turn to leave, clutching her hand to her madly thumping heart. Just before he reached the door, he turned back to her, a brief ghost of a smile flitting over his lips. "If it had been within my power, I would have kept him from hurting you," he said in an odd tone. "Know that. Goodbye, Daisy Vanreid."

As quickly as he'd re-emerged in her life, Padraig McGuire was gone, the paneled door clicking closed at his back. She stared at the space where he'd been, knowing somehow that this was the last call he would make upon her.

"Daisy Trent," she corrected, not that it mattered.

*25th May, 1881*

*Dear Sir,*

*As we prepare to enter the third month of your absence, I write you with unexpected news. I am expecting your child. Though you've amply demonstrated your lack of sentiment for myself, I cannot help but hope you may be somewhat less reticent in regards to an innocent.*

*In other matters, I hope you don't mind that I've recently replaced all the carpets with a fine Axminster at 8 shillings a yard. Redecorating the old nursery will prove even more costly, I fear.*

*Sincerely,*
*Duchess of Trent*

"Surely even you can concede she's become a liability now, Trent."

Scowling, Sebastian looked up from the Home Office report the Duke of Carlisle had offered up for his perusal. Following the blast at the police station, Carlisle had joined Sebastian and Griffin in Liverpool. They'd arrested three Fenians responsible for the dynamite operation on Castle Street, but there were literally hundreds more suspects and clues to pursue. The last fortnight had been a blur of running more leads to ground.

But now, a different sort of blur descended upon Sebastian. Words rattled about in his mind, attempting to form into coherent thoughts. The anger crashing through him wouldn't allow a complete sentence to form. The words, separately, meant little.

*Trousers.* That explained the fortune she'd spent at an establishment owned by a Madame Blanc. *Wild parties.* And that absolutely explained the thousands of pounds in expenditures he'd noticed disappearing from his accounts. He read on. *Scandal. Artists and playwrights. The Earl of Bolton.*

*Trousers.* Goddamn it. *The Earl of bloody Bolton?*

The image of Bolton touching Daisy—of taking her in his arms and kissing her soft pink lips, of hearing her satisfied sighs and stripping away her layers and losing himself in her delectable body—made him want to smash his fist through the table. Through a wall. Through the Earl of Bolton's fucking face.

What had she said that first night at the Beresford ball?

*Thank you for your unnecessary concern, Your Grace, but foxes don't frighten me. They never have.*

The devil. If she had allowed Bolton to touch so much as her hand, he'd… What would he do? Hadn't he left her behind without a word? He'd been gone nearly three months, a far longer span of time than the fortnight he'd known her. His fault. He had pushed her away. He had chosen duty over her.

But if the contents of the report were to be believed, she was faithless. A soul-crushing ire seared through him at the thought. She could have waited for him to return. By God, she'd claimed to love him. *Lies*, whispered a voice inside his mind. *She lied to you. What other lies did she tell?*

He tamped down the bile. Forced himself to calm. Took a breath. Two.

There. He felt nothing. Thank Christ Carlisle had chosen to deliver this report in private while Griffin was out reconnoitering with some men from the Home Office. And then, he felt something again. Sudden and explosive, directly in the vicinity of his chest.

"The Earl of Bolton? Tell me, Carlisle. Is she fucking the Earl of Bolton?" He hadn't meant to snarl out those particular questions to the brick wall of a man staring him down. But they'd emerged, raw and visceral, from somewhere deep within him.

"Likely bewitched Bolton the same way she's bewitched you," Carlisle said, his tone sour. "Does she have a magical cunny?"

Sebastian clenched his fists. He would not strike the leader of the League. He would not. "Go to hell."

Carlisle raised a brow. "Perhaps we ought to ask Bolton."

Sebastian launched himself from his chair so forcefully that it toppled over behind him. He was going to beat Carlisle to a pulp. "Fuck you, Carlisle."

"I once thought you unshakeable." Carlisle whistled, cocking his head to consider him as though viewing him for the first time. "The man who survived a fire and an assassin's blade brought low by a conniving bit of American skirts. But do read on, Trent. It would appear there's someone else who may have enjoyed her ample charms as well."

Damn Carlisle. He was like a lion pawing at a mouse, and Sebastian couldn't shake the feeling that part of the man enjoyed this. Enjoyed tormenting him. His body teemed with fury and the need to smash something or someone. Belatedly, his training returned to him. He forced the tight muscles of his body to relax, his face to become expressionless. If Carlisle meant to provoke him into doing something stupid, he wouldn't facilitate the bastard.

Sebastian caught the report back up and hurriedly scoured the contents, returning to the last three paragraphs he'd missed. The blood turned to ice in his veins.

*Padraig McGuire called upon Her Grace and was received upon four separate occasions, the first lasting one quarter of an hour, the next lasting twenty minutes, one-half hour the third…*

The remainder of the report swirled before his eyes. She had been closeting herself with her former betrothed. A dangerous man, and one that perhaps she had never stopped loving. Betrayal, sharp and sudden as any blade, twisted through him.

He was going to kill McGuire.

When the time came, he would savage him and take great pleasure in it. A knife to the gut, maybe, after water torture. But Daisy… What the hell would he do with his beautiful vixen of a wife if the report was true? Bolton and McGuire? Trousers and scandal? It sounded much like the Daisy Vanreid he'd first met.

Perhaps that was the real Daisy. Mayhap everything had been a lie, from her father's abuse to her fear. Had that sickening scene with Vanreid the day after their wedding been staged for his benefit?

Dear God, his wife was courting ruin and taking lovers. The last few months he'd spent away from her, he'd been a man torn between his duty and the woman he'd married. How many nights had his thoughts strayed to her? How many times had he longed for her scent, the sight of her burnished curls, her mouth and body ripe beneath his? How desperately had he ached for the sound of her voice, the touch of her hand? How thoroughly had his love for her eaten him alive?

And all the while, she'd been scheming and taking other men to bed. In his own bloody home. Was it possible that the entire time he'd thought he was using her, she had in fact been using *him*? The notion was too ugly to contemplate, the implications too far-reaching and severe.

His stupid, bloody heart thudded in his chest. Had everything been a ruse? If it had, he needed to be put down like a lame horse. How could his instincts about her have been so wrong? How could he love someone capable of such deception, he who had been trained better than anyone to recognize even the most cunning subterfuge?

"Trent?" Carlisle's voice—tinged with something he'd swear was concern if he didn't know better—pierced the fog of wrath that had infected his mind.

"What would you have me do?" he rasped.

Carlisle's chiseled face hardened even further. "You'll need to return to London at once. Griffin will accompany you when he returns. According to all the intelligence the Home Office has been able to gather, signs indicate quite strongly that she's been tasked with infiltrating the Special League. It would appear that you are her target."

*Her target.*

The two words echoed in his mind, a taunt. It all made perfect, disgusting sense. A beautiful heiress who'd set the *ton* on its ear. She'd danced her way through a series of suitors and balls, setting off wagging tongues but avoiding ruination. Daisy was the siren meant to lure his ship into the jagged rocks. She'd put on a pretty show of fearing her father. And he'd been sympathetic. His honor had demanded he protect her, even in the face of all logic, reason, and yes, duty.

He was no one's target, damn it. He was one of the finest spies in all of England. There was no way in hell he would allow himself to be outfoxed by a sultry siren who smelled of bergamot and made him hard simply by being in the room.

He straightened, forcing himself to focus. "I return to

London and then what? Wait for those bastards to set off another bomb?"

A strange expression crossed his superior's face. "No. You need to keep a watchful eye on your wife. Find out how much she knows. Discover her connections. Gather as much information for us as you possibly can so that we can send more double operatives to infiltrate their ranks. And do whatever you must to break her and gain the information we need."

*To break her.*

The notion shouldn't fill him with...what, sadness? He couldn't define the sensation hollowing him out. Didn't want to. "As you order, Your Grace." Suddenly, he needed to escape. He felt as if the air had been sucked from the chamber and he couldn't properly breathe. "I will take my leave and begin preparations for my return posthaste."

He pivoted on his heel, ready to flee. Trying not to run from the room. From the demons. From the price of doing what he must. From the burden of duty.

"Trent?"

Sebastian halted, turning back to his superior.

Carlisle had the appearance of a man at his mother's funeral. A foreign sensation crept through Sebastian, filling him with dread. He knew what the duke was going to say before the words ever left his mouth. His entire body tightened, bracing for it.

"Prepare yourself, Trent," Carlisle said finally. "She is a woman, I know, but under the proper circumstances, a bolder course of action may have its merits, if you take my meaning."

He was sure he did, but he wanted to be certain. "You want me to...kill her?"

Asking the question filled him with ice. Dread expanded in his chest. Disgust curdled his gut.

His superior inclined his head, his gaze steady. "I want you to take whatever action you deem necessary as you carry out your duty to the Crown and the innocents under our protection."

Jesus. Sebastian's mouth went dry. The Duke of Carlisle wanted him to *murder* Daisy. He was giving him permission. An indirect order. Even if she was guilty of every crime Carlisle suspected her of and more, women and children were...damn it, they were women and children. Men could be gutted, shot, hanged, or drowned. Burnt alive. Any number of torturous ends could be their fate in the name of duty. But not women.

Not Daisy.

Not *his wife*, regardless of how duplicitous and conniving she may be.

He'd sworn an oath to the League, to his Crown, yes. But he'd also sworn an oath before God. An oath to her. And even if she was the most deceptive viper in all of England, he still loved her. Bloody hell.

Without another word, he stalked away. He made it out the door before he cast up his accounts into the mud and dung-caked street.

## chapter twenty-three

*D*AISY RETURNED FROM YET ANOTHER
EVENING'S ENTERTAINMENT. It was well after
midnight, and she was weary, as much from the
lateness of the hour and the strain of the charade she
maintained as from her delicate condition.

All night long, she had feigned smiles and flirted madly.
Danced with as many rakes and scoundrels as she could
find. She'd laughed, pretended to be a merry wife who
hadn't a care in the world that she'd been left behind.

Pretended that she hadn't been left to gather dust in a
Belgravia townhouse as if she were of no greater import
than the landscapes and former dukes once lining the walls.
That she didn't mind if she had no inkling of her husband's
whereabouts and nowhere to send a proper letter aside from
barraging his estates. That she'd received not one
godforsaken word from him.

It was as if he'd vanished as surely as Bridget had.

Once ensconced in the solitude of her bedchamber, she
plucked the earrings from her ears and slipped off her dress
shoes. They were aquamarine satin, fetching creations that

matched her ensemble perfectly, but hours of clipping about in heels had left her feet aching.

Closing her eyes and releasing a sigh, she rolled her head about her shoulders, seeking to loosen her tense muscles. She had instructed Abigail not to wait up for her, and Hugo was already asleep in the comfortable bed he preferred in the lower salon. She was alone. The silence after such a raucous evening was enjoyable.

With a sigh, she hugged the gentle, almost imperceptible swell of her belly where a child grew. It had taken Georgiana's perceptive observations regarding her wan appearance and frequent bouts of nausea for her to realize she was carrying Sebastian's babe. The notion had initially filled her with hope that he might, at last, return to her. But more days had passed, more letters unanswered, more silence, more waiting, and she had begun to settle into the grim acceptance that her husband didn't give a damn about her.

*Not to worry, little one,* she promised the babe now with a pang in her heart. *I will love you enough for the both of us.*

"Where were you tonight, *wife?*"

The voice, deep and dark and silky with menace, cut into the quiet calm.

An undignified squeak tore from her as she started, eyes flying open. Sebastian stood before her, as if conjured from her troubled thoughts. Wickedly handsome, tall, dark, debonair. Expression as solid as granite, jaw rigid. Blue eyes glittering.

At long last, her husband had returned.

All the air fled her lungs, as if she'd taken a fall from a horse at full gallop. Her heart pounded, the anger and resentment swirling inside her warring against a fragile burst of hope that he was back. Had her letter reached him, then? She drank him in before she could remind herself that he had left her with nary a word or expectation of finding him for nearly three solid months.

"How ironic you should pose such a question," she told

him tartly when she found her voice at last. "For I've been wondering the same of you, *husband*. Where were you these last months?"

But he didn't answer. Instead, he remained forbidding and still, raking her with an insolent gaze. Heat suffused her body. A pang of intense longing began low in her belly and radiated outward before she could ruthlessly tamp it down.

How foolish she was, flesh and heart both betraying her. For she'd missed the husband she'd only begun to know. She'd missed his teasing, his rare smiles, his sensual touch, the way he kissed. Her fragile heart had begun to believe she'd found a future that would not only be preferable to her fate as Viscountess Breckly, but one in which she could find happiness. She couldn't ignore just how bereft his absence had left her.

And now that he was here, within reach, it was as if a missing part of her had been restored.

He was every bit as beautiful as she remembered. More so, in fact. But there was something different about him. Something in the way he held himself so stiffly, in the way he stared at her, his finely formed lip curling into a sneer.

All at once, she knew what that something was. Felt it like a blow that banished her naiveté and her interminable weakness for him both. This was no happy homecoming.

He was furious.

Her earrings, heavy diamonds and hard gold warmed by her skin, bit into her palm. "Sebastian," she said, irritated by the breathless quality of her voice. "Have you nothing to say for yourself?"

He cocked his head, glowering. "Were you expecting someone else, then?"

Daisy frowned. "Someone else?"

"Someone else." He stepped closer to her. He was so near that his scent, clear and masculine and delicious, washed over her. "Someone like the Earl of Bolton, perhaps? Or any one of your other lovers?"

Ah. The gossip had finally reached him wherever he'd

been secreting himself. She knew a brief moment of satisfaction that her endless devotion to flushing him out had succeeded. But the pleasure was hollow, for he had returned a wrathful stranger. And she was angry at him as well. She wanted answers. Wanted to rail against him, demand to know why he'd left her in such haste, nothing but a vague missive to explain. To know the secrets that had taken him from her.

"Well?" he snapped, his voice as sharp as a rapier. "Still holding your tongue, darling? Don't you know that this is the part of our little tragedy where you attempt to explain why you've been welcoming other men into your bed?"

She flinched, steeling herself. "What have you heard?"

"That you've been making a cuckold of me." He took another step closer, stalking her like she was his prey.

Daisy resisted the frantic urge to retreat. He wouldn't strike her. His vitriol was almost palpable. Fear crept its way into her heart as she recalled all the times her father had charged at her. The times he had hit her. The occasion when he'd struck her with so much force that she'd fallen to the floor and his boot-shod foot had connected with her midriff. Her sin? Embarrassing him at dinner by laughing too loudly. She still remembered the sensation of all the air being knocked from her body in a rush, the burning in her lungs.

But she held her ground now against Sebastian's anger, because she was not the girl she'd once been. She was a woman now. Independent and strong. Her chin tipped up in defiance. "I've been doing nothing of the sort."

Two more strides and his long legs brushed the twin falls of her specially tailored trousers. Trousers that would soon no longer fit her with their snug embrace of her blossoming figure. He made a show of raking her with a glance that swept down over her form and left her feeling as though she was bare before him rather than fully dressed. "What in the hell are you wearing?"

"You have functioning eyes," she pointed out with a

flippant air she little felt. "What does it look like I'm wearing?"

Her evening wear ensemble was, she knew, unusual. As part of their campaign to stir up enough scandal to bring their husbands back to them, she and Georgiana sought the aid and creative genius of the talented Madame Blanc, who had been delighted to create beautiful and costly wardrobes featuring cleverly designed trousers and skirted bodices. Daisy adored them, and rather imagined she would wear them even though her original purpose for them—starting enough tongues wagging to bring her husband home—was done.

"It looks as if you're wearing the costume of a whore." His voice was pure ice. "What can you be thinking, gadding about London wearing bloody trousers? Wasn't it enough to take your pleasure with whatever man you could find? You needed to humiliate me as well, is that it?"

His words cut her more than she had expected them to. When she and Georgiana had set their plan into motion, she hadn't considered the full ramifications. She'd been driven by desperation, by longing. By missing him. She'd been prepared to do anything—don trousers, flirt with rakes, incite whispers and disapproval at every turn. Heavens, she had written him a waterfall of letters, desperate for any way to make him come back to her.

But scandal was rather like wildfire. It couldn't be controlled. Once it had begun burning, its hunger for destruction became voracious. Now, it seemed all her frustrated efforts had turned upon her to disastrous effect.

He was home at last, but he didn't believe her. He believed the gossip. And well, why should he not? They were strangers, weren't they? Married for several months, only a fortnight spent in each other's presence. What could she have expected? Her heart felt like a weight in her chest to match the knot of dread spinning in her stomach.

Yet, it was he who had created the chasm. He who had abandoned her with a hastily scrawled missive as explanation. The loneliness, isolation, and confusion of the months without him struck her now with the force of a locomotive. An ire to match his fanned into a flame. Where had he been? What had he been doing? Who was the real Sebastian, Duke of Trent?

"How dare you insult me?" Pent-up emotion made her voice shrill. "You, who abandoned me with no real explanation, no notion of where you'd gone or when you might return?"

"It was a private matter of extreme urgency," he gritted. "I told you I would return as soon as I was able. My departure from London was necessary. Had I been able to avoid it, I wholeheartedly would have."

"A *private* matter. Necessary." The words left a bad taste in her mouth, and the pressing suspicion that had been her constant companion for the last few months returned. What if he had been engaged in a different form of secrecy than what Georgiana suspected? By-blows were common enough, though hardly proper drawing room conversation. A few oddly phrased missives weren't enough to prove some sort of vast conspiracy. "Were you with your mistress?"

"No, goddamn it." Suddenly, his hands gripped her upper arms, large and warm on her bare skin. The contact sent the same fiery need as always licking through her. "I've told you before that I don't have a mistress. I've been bloody true to our vows, which is more than I can say for you."

She wanted to believe him, even as his continued assertion that she had been unfaithful left her cold. "I have not made a cuckold of you."

He pulled her into him and her hands flew to his broad chest, seeking purchase, her earrings falling forgotten to the floor. Her gaze dropped to his mouth. They were so near that if she rose on tiptoe, their lips would meet. How she missed his kiss. For an instant, it didn't matter that he'd been gone, that he had returned a cold and bitter stranger. Her body still longed for his.

Ached for him.

She still loved him.

"Would you care to explain what you've been doing behind closed doors with the Earl of Bolton?" His tone had become deceptively smooth once more. His eyes traveled over her face, studying. "You're beautiful as ever, Daisy. Little wonder half the men of London are waiting in line to lift your skirts. How many others have aside from Bolton?"

She'd known that receiving the Earl of Bolton had been a grievous mistake. At the time, her husband's dislike of the man had served as her primary impetus. "The door was never closed. That was a rumor likely begun by the earl himself."

That much was the truth. Bolton had been clear with his desire that she become his mistress. Daisy had refused and slapped him for the insult, which was likely why he'd spread such a tale—a balm to his wounded pride. The only man she wanted was the one standing before her, and it was a truth she couldn't deny. She had made vows to him and him alone. Her heart beat for him. Broke for him.

"Did you scream the way you did for me, sweet?" His hand left her arm to skim over her jaw, then cup her cheek. His thumb pressed into the fullness of her lower lip with a rough pressure that surprised her. But she liked it. The savagery in him made her pulse leap, her entire body come to life. It was odd and troubling, and yet, there it was. "Tell me. Did you enjoy it when he fucked you? Did you pretend he was me, just for a moment? We both know he couldn't have made you come the way I did."

She swallowed, the memory of their blistering lovemaking coupled with his lean hardness against her—his masculine scent and strength enveloping her—made heat bloom between her thighs. The flesh he'd brought to life became hungry and wet. Her nipples tightened against her corset. His anger should have disturbed her, should have lessened her desire. Such provocative, ugly things, he'd said.

He was being rough and crude, deliberately cruel. The way he touched her—masterful though detached—should have left her cold.

And yet, she couldn't help the way she felt. The way he made her feel. Hot. Restless. Yearning. Her heart still ached for him, and in spite of everything—logic, reason, hurt, common sense—she couldn't deny him.

She nipped at his thumb, tasting him—salt and warmth and man—and he removed it, allowing her to speak. "I did nothing with the Earl of Bolton. Nothing with any other man, for that matter."

"You expect me to believe you?" His tone was frigid. His touch was anything but. It was hot, demanding, seeking. Urgent.

His fingers trailed down her throat, lingering at the diamond necklace she still wore, a weighty reminder of her former life. The caress sent sparks skittering over her skin, need throbbing deep within.

"It's the truth," she whispered.

"The truth. How rich." A bleak smile curved his sensual lips. It was grim, harsh. There was no hint of the dimple she'd once longed to kiss. Not a trace of humor remained within him, it seemed. It was as if a stranger had taken his place. A bitter, broken, angry stranger. Where had he been for the past three months and what had he done? Perhaps, more importantly, what had been done to him?

But she held firm. Stoic. "Yes, the truth. I would never betray our vows, Sebastian."

"You don't think I believe a word that slips past your pretty lips, do you, sweet? Not when you've been carrying on as you have. Wild fêtes, a string of lovers, wearing trousers, for Christ's sake. Were you so foolish to believe that word would not reach me? That I wouldn't learn of your antics and your debauchery?"

She should be frightened. But she was not. Though his language was coarse and his touch lacked the skillful play of slow seduction she'd become accustomed to from him, he would not hurt her. She knew it instinctively.

"How did word reach you?" she asked instead. "Did you get my letters?" One letter in particular. The one in which she revealed the impending birth of their child. The one good that had risen from the ashes of their turbulent union.

"I daresay word has even reached America by now. You made no attempt to hide your lechery." He sneered. "You couldn't even bother to wait until you'd provided me an heir before bedding the Earl of Bolton."

That answered her question, then. He hadn't read a single one of her letters.

Disappointment bloomed as his fingers traveled lower, stopping at the ribbon-trimmed edge of her décolletage. She swallowed against a fresh wave of need. His cruelty should have diminished her body's response to him, but it seemed that nothing could. Her nipples longed for his touch, his mouth. The rake of his teeth. He cupped her breast, and it was a possessive clamp of ownership, nothing sweet about it. Through her corset, undergarments, and silk, his fingers bit into her skin with just enough pressure to arch her back.

She wanted more, and her reaction frightened her. She had not known that darkness and anger could form such a powerful web of seduction. Still, he owed her every bit as much as she owed him, if not more. He was the one who had left. She had been right here, waiting for him, all along.

"Tell me where you've been," she challenged impetuously. "Tell me the truth."

*Care for me enough to give me that, if nothing else.*

"The truth is that even though you've been bedding other lovers, you still want me, don't you, buttercup?" He stilled, his eyes intense and glittering, sparking with unadulterated sexual fire as they burned into hers. "Your pretty pink lips might lie, but your body doesn't."

Damn him. "The truth," she demanded again. "Where were you? Why did you go?"

"Ah, I see the way of it." He smiled without mirth, his tone bitter. "You think you can tempt me with your body, and I'll confess all. But I won't give you the gratification of fucking you, Daisy. You'd like it too much."

The wickedness and arrogance of his words should have repulsed her. He was being a beast, but it somehow made her long for him all the more. Her breasts tingled. The flesh between her thighs hungered for him, for his touch, his claiming. *At last,* her body seemed to say even if her mind couldn't form the acknowledgment, *at last.*

Daisy pressed herself closer to him, her breasts crushing into his hand, into his chest. Their lips were a scant inch apart. His breath ghosted over her mouth, hot and promising. Their legs tangled, free of the encumbrance of skirts, and she felt his arousal, rigid and undeniable, cutting into her belly.

He wanted her, no matter what he said. In that moment, she had infinite power over him, and she knew it.

And she liked it.

She rocked forward, gliding her body along his hard length. Her lower lip brushed his once, twice. "Do you know what I think, Sebastian?" She paused, a wicked urge to shock him rising within, to goad him, push him off the precipice to which he clung. "I think you're lying to me. Lying to yourself. You don't want to fuck me because you're afraid *you'd* like it too much."

There.

One word, raw and vulgar and wrong. His word. *Fuck.* Used upon him as a weapon. But it had the desired effect, and she didn't feel a drop of shame as he growled deep in his throat and forced her backward, guiding her with hands on her waist and long strides. Taking her to the big bed where she'd lain awake so many nights wondering where he was and whether or not he would ever return. Where she'd imagined him joining her, taking his time, kissing her and stripping her bare, learning every bit of her flesh before joining them as one.

But this wasn't going to be anything like her silly fancies, or even like their previous couplings, and she knew it by the harshness in his expression, the wildness of his touch. The backs of her knees bumped into the bed's softness. He didn't throw her on it as she thought he might. Instead, he stopped, stared down at her.

"Explain yourself," he commanded.

She swallowed, not knowing what he wanted to hear. What he meant. She was breathless with waiting, with wanting, with a deep, decadent tide of anticipation. "What do you want me to say, Sebastian? That I've spent these last months wondering where you've been? That I've flirted like mad and courted scandal at every opportunity just so that you would come back to me?"

"No." His nostrils flared.

He was fiercely beautiful, his body leaner against hers, honed to hard, well-muscled angles. Everything about him had become dark and powerful and ruthless. Even his shoulders were more severe and hard beneath her hands as she settled them there to anchor herself.

But she wasn't finished. Let him think of her what he would. There was only one way to win this battle between them. "Do you want to hear how I did everything in my power to find you, and when all else failed, I decided to bring about your return by causing as much scandal as possible? For that's the truth."

"No, goddamn it," he snapped. "No more of your lies."

"My lies?" She rubbed her leg against his, because it felt good and because she couldn't resist the temptation. His proximity did wild things to her senses. But even as she teased him, parried back in this sensual battle between them, she hadn't forgotten that she had just as much cause as he to be angry. More, even. "What of yours, Sebastian? Where have you been?"

Heavens yes, she had every right to be properly enraged. He had disappeared without explanation. Months of no word had passed. Yet he barged back into her life with the grace of a gunboat, raging and bent on destruction. How dare he brand her a liar, accuse her of debasing their vows, when she still didn't have any idea where he'd gone, what he'd done, or whom he'd been with during his lengthy absence?

"You want to ask questions, buttercup?" The grin he flashed her was stark and lethal. Not a hint of merriment. Not a drop of sympathy or contrition. His dimple appeared for a fraction of a moment before it was gone. "Very well. But I get to ask first."

His hands tightened on her waist, her only warning before he lifted her in one fluid motion and tossed her back onto the bed. She hadn't expected his sudden reaction, and so she made her landing in a rather undignified heap, legs akimbo, flat on her back. Her husband's expression was dark and unrelenting as a summer thunderstorm. He stalked forward, between her thighs, and bent forward, planting his palms on either side of her as he pinned her to the mattress. His muscled abdomen pressed into hers, robbing her of breath.

Sebastian lowered his head so that their foreheads nearly touched. His eyes sparked into hers, intense and burning with so much wrath she trembled. "Who the hell is Padraig McGuire to you, Daisy?"

## chapter twenty-four

$\mathcal{S}$HE BLANCHED AT THE NAME OF HER FORMER betrothed, all the color leaching from her beautiful face. Bloody, bloody hell. It wasn't what he wanted to see, even if he'd anticipated it. Even if he'd had the journey between London and Liverpool to reconcile himself to the fact that the woman he'd married—the woman who had forced him to spend the last three months guilt-ridden and torn between his feelings for her and his duty—was a fraud, a liar, and a conniving jade. Possibly even a conspirator and prospective murderess. And then there had been the other part of him, the part that had been desperate to come up with reasons why she could not be, or ways he could save her if she was.

Pathetic of him, really.

His jaw hardened, fingers fisting the bedclothes on either side of her lithe form, a fresh wave of rage bursting through him. Hers was not the reaction of an innocent woman, by God. It was the reaction of a woman who was guilty as sin. A woman who'd just realized the elaborate web of lies and deceit she'd spun had transformed into a trap of her own making.

"Padraig McGuire." He spat the name out as if it left a bad taste in his mouth.

Of course, it did. The thought of any other man touching Daisy, kissing her, running his hands over her bare curves, sinking home inside her... Jesus, it made him livid enough that he wouldn't trust himself alone in a chamber with any of them. Whoever they were. Faceless bastards. Christ knew how many. He wanted to tear them all limb from limb.

Padraig McGuire, however, was the one man above any—even above the Earl of Bolton—that infuriated him to the point of irrational, unpredictable bloodlust. McGuire was a Fenian plotter. A maestro of death and destruction. Most importantly and damning of all, he was a man that Daisy had once loved enough that she'd wished to marry him.

A man she had received in private no less than four times.

Damn it all, he was a fool. For even with the blinders removed, he still couldn't help but want her. His cock was rigid, straining against the placket of his trousers, jutting into the soft warmth of her left thigh. She was even lovelier than he'd recalled during his months away from her. When his eyes had first lit on her tonight as she'd crossed the threshold, he'd been momentarily speechless. Perhaps it had been the trousers, which accentuated her tiny waist and the feminine flare of her hips and trim ankles to perfection. Or perhaps it had simply been her, Daisy.

Goddess. Witch. Siren. Liar.

"I'll ask you one more time," he growled, realizing that she had yet to answer him and his body was growing far too accustomed to his position atop her. His body, in fact, wanted to be buried deep inside her. It was a hell of a thing, how his cock and his mind could fight each other so mercilessly, but there it was. "Who the hell is Padraig McGuire to you?"

She flinched, then swallowed. The thick fringe of her lashes swept down over her eyes. "How do you know that name? He didn't use it when he called here."

Hearing her confirm what he'd already known, that the bastard had called upon her—*at his goddamn home*—as though it had been an innocent social visit, sent another onslaught of fury ricocheting through him. Slowly, the full implications of what she'd said descended.

He'd unwittingly revealed too much to her. To this woman, with her tits straining against her bodice, legs spread wide in satin trousers, with her wide eyes and full, beckoning mouth, who was a deceptive, traitorous bitch.

To this woman, who knew too much, and had always known more than she'd let on. His wife, the woman he had lusted over for three long, interminable months. The same woman who had taken lovers the moment he'd been gone from her sight. The woman he loved.

Bloody hell. The heart was nothing but a weakness. A fool incapable of knowing reason. For there was no reason on this earth—not a goddamn one—that he should still feel this heaviness in his chest, this conflagration inside him by being in her presence.

"You don't have the right to ask anything of me," he snapped at her, feeling an icy cold sink straight into the marrow of his bones. "I pose the questions. You answer them, or tonight won't go well for you. Do you understand?"

She stiffened as she gauged the depth of his rage, bringing her palms between them to shove ineffectually at his chest. The fear in her expression would have made him feel shame on any other day. Regardless of what he'd been ordered to do, and regardless of the depth of her treachery, he would never physically hurt her.

But today was different. Today, he wanted her to drown in dread of what he would do to her. Today, he wanted to make her pay and in so doing, slake some of his own pain. He had believed her. And she had lied. He rose on his knees and caught her wrists in a manacle grip, lowering each to her side and pinning them to the bed. She was helpless. He rocked his body against hers, partly for the simple pleasure and partly to let her know that he was the dominant force. That she answered to him.

"Who is Padraig McGuire?" he posed the question once more, this time with his cock grinding against the part of her he wanted most.

He decided that regardless of how much he would despise himself by morning light, he was not going to stop until he took his fill of Daisy tonight. He would possess her, enjoying the sound of her shameless trousers being torn from her body. He'd rip the bodice to shreds, cut her corset off with the knife in his boot. Then, he'd sink so deep inside her, pound so hard, until she couldn't help but cry out with wild need. Suck her nipples, sink his fingers into the soft bounty of her hair. Yes, by God, he would take her, punish her. And he would enjoy every debauched second of it.

Perhaps he would even bind her wrists. The thought made his cock jerk, and he rolled his hips against hers in instinct, half horrified at himself for being so consumed with lust at the thought of fucking a conscienceless traitor.

But she was still and ashen-faced beneath him, her lips compressed. Not compliant. Not willing as he wanted her to be. The hunger burning within him cooled. He took no pleasure in forcing a woman, regardless of how far she drove him to the edge of sanity. "Who. Is. He?" he pressed.

"Please, Sebastian." She paused, breathless, wetting her lips. "It is not what you must think."

That was a goddamn lie, and he knew it. The report had been forever committed to his memory. *Padraig McGuire called upon Her Grace and was received upon four separate occasions.* She had been alone with McGuire. In Sebastian's own bloody house. Half an hour on the third visit. A scant fifteen minutes on the last, but he wouldn't trouble himself with that now. Perhaps by that time, McGuire had enjoyed his fill and needed only a rushed coupling to satisfy his lust.

The thought of Padraig McGuire atop Daisy much the same as he was now sent more ice through his veins. "The truth," he commanded her, unable to resist pressing his body deeper into hers until her breasts thrust against his chest and his abdomen crushed into the rigid girding of her corset.

Had she forgotten the way it was between them so easily? Or had her introduction to desire only made her hungry for more with the man she almost married? Had nothing they shared been real? Was her body's reaction to him, even now, feigned?

Damn it, not even his disgust for her hampered his raging lust. His cock ground into her in a crude imitation of what he wanted to do, despite the fact that she had allowed the same privilege to others in his absence.

Never mind that she had never been meant to be his wife in truth. As far as she knew, she was his duchess forever. And even if he'd been called away on an urgent matter, she'd sworn to be faithful and obey. How quickly she'd broken her vows. Not to even mention the feelings she'd claimed to have for him. Her protestations of love returned to him now, the remembrance of her sweet, husky voice raining the words down upon him: *I love you. I love you. I love you.*

And he had believed her, fool that he was. Like a starving man hungering for a scrap to put into his empty belly, he had been desperate. Desperate to believe in her and her innocence. How wrong he'd been. His instincts were worthless to him now. And she had done that. She alone had slipped past his defenses, making him fall in love with her, making him want to build a true marriage with her after his mission's completion. Making him want to give up his life's work just to be with her.

What a sodding joke. What a lunatic he was. Perhaps he ought to retire from the League anyway, just on account of his own stupidity. He was useless. Foolish. How could he look any of his fellow League members or his superior in the eye again, knowing what he'd done in allowing this scrap of a woman to control him and lay him low?

Delilah, he thought. She was his bloody Delilah.

"The truth," she said at last, shattering his thoughts, her voice quiet but as decadent as velvet to the senses, just as it always had been. Her lashes swept up, and her gaze met his. That vivid, vibrant, clear green seemed to see straight through him. "I've told you nothing but the truth already. You ought to know that, Sebastian. Just as you know that I was engaged to marry Padraig McGuire in New York City. But he came here for good reason."

Ever perceptive. He could own that she was intelligent. Far too intelligent, for that matter—and wary and cagey—for her own good. Her skills as an actress, however, outshined any other gift she had, even her undeniable beauty. Her protest that McGuire had visited her for good reason almost seemed genuine.

He didn't deny that he was aware of her relationship with McGuire. Why pretend? "Did you not think that word would reach me? That I wouldn't hear of your frequent, *private* visits with a particular gentleman? That I wouldn't then take it upon myself to gather information about who it was that my wife felt the need to spend time with in my absence?"

Private visits with a Fenian plotter. Had they discussed plans for laying bombs and then fucked? Christ, he wouldn't think of it now. He ought to hate her for what she'd done. And yet, somehow he couldn't.

Daisy's gaze didn't waver from his. Aside from the hitch in her breath and the thumping of her heart that he could feel against his chest, she appeared the perfect picture of calm and elegance. "Of course I knew word would reach you, or at least I hoped it would. What would you have done in my place? I'd been abandoned by my husband with no friends or family to speak of, and you certainly didn't answer any of my letters or even bother to send word inquiring after me. You disappeared with just a terse note. Everything I tried failed—no one knew where you'd gone or when you would return. So I decided to attempt to lure you back here by creating so much scandal that you'd have no choice."

There was his brazen actress once again, returning from the ashes of the broken creature she'd wanted him to believe her to be. How bold of her to suggest she'd privately received gentlemen callers in his absence in order to win him back to her side. My God, she lied so swiftly he almost wanted to believe her.

His fingers tightened on her wrists. Her gaze fastened on his, alert and searching. He allowed her nothing, keeping eyes and his expression both cold as the diamonds she wore at her throat. "You expect me to believe that you took lovers so that I would return to you?"

"Of course not." She tugged at her wrists, attempting to free herself. "Sebastian, release me."

He wasn't inclined to listen to her demand. The beast inside him had been caged for too long. He didn't ease his grip. Instead, he lowered his face closer to hers, until her scent flooded him. By some miracle of self-restraint, he refrained from burying his face in the honey-gold strands of her hair. But as he observed her now, he wished he'd taken the pins from her coif before leaping upon her.

"Am I meant to thank you for bedding a string of lovers, including your former betrothed, *in my own home*?" he seethed. The last words emerged as a roar.

"No!" she shouted back at him, turning her weak attempt at escaping him into a full-scale battle. She writhed and bucked beneath him, trying in vain to free her wrists. But all her efforts trapped her more snugly beneath him. "Listen to me, Sebastian."

But he was beyond listening. And in truth, her thrashing like a feral cat only heightened his arousal. Each jerk of her body made the most pleasurable friction against his cock. Her breasts strained against him, her mouth so near to his that he could almost taste her. Her body fitted around him, her lush curves melting into his hardness and angles. A perfect fit. Even half mad with anger and lust, he could still feel the rightness of her beneath him.

Such a bloody shame that the one woman he wanted most in the world was the same woman he'd be sending off to prison along with her lover. First, however, first he would take what was his. What had always been his. And he would take her so fiercely that she would never forget in all of her days that he was the man who had claimed her, body and soul.

"Keep moving about like that, madam, and see what happens," he warned her, his voice ragged and low, saturated by the tumult of the moment. Dichotomies plagued him. He wanted her, but hated himself for his weakness; she was beautiful, but she was a bloody criminal, an enemy of the Crown. His enemy. The woman who had betrayed and deceived him.

She went still beneath him. "You still don't believe me."

"Of course I don't believe you, buttercup." Slowly, he slid her wrists along the bed until they were both held captive above her head. He leaned back to survey his handiwork. She was like an offering before him, breasts outthrust, face flushed, succulent lower lip caught between her teeth.

He wanted to bite her there too. To nip her just enough to give her pain without drawing blood. She needed to pay for what she'd done, for the harm she intended to inflict upon innocents by aiding and abetting Padraig McGuire and her father. For what she had done to him, infiltrating his mind and body as thoroughly as opium. Fury ravaged him, mingling with lust.

Retribution was what this was. He would make her atone for her sins. He would take her one last time so that he could sleep at night when she was gone.

"I'm telling you the truth," she insisted. "It doesn't matter if you believe me or not. Sebastian, you left me. You didn't deserve my loyalty. But I have been here waiting for your return just the same. Even now, I can't deny you because I love you too much."

Bitterness laced through him. "Your manipulation won't work upon me any longer. All those clever little lies, Daisy. You're a brilliant actress, I'll grant you that. But now the time for deceit is at an end."

Her fine-boned wrists were small and delicate enough that he could hold them both in one fist, he discovered, which left his right hand free to do as it wished. He skimmed down the length of her bare arm to the lace at her sleeve. Down over her breasts, and then lower, to her hip, her knee.

"It's true," she said, and there was a tremble in her voice that almost made him feel a trace of compunction. "I love you."

He pressed his forehead to hers. "Liar."

She tugged at her wrists, naively thinking she could somehow overpower him and escape. She could not. "Unlike you, I speak the truth. You still have not said where you were. Will you tell me? Please?"

He ignored her plea. Blood rushed through him, straight to his cock. He didn't want to hear anything else she had to say. No more falsehoods or pretense. No more protestation. One last time. Just this night, he promised himself silently, this night to exorcise her from him.

He kissed her. Took her mouth with his to stop hers from moving. Or at least that's what he told himself as lust slammed through him. She tasted sweet, sweeter than he remembered, and though he'd wanted the kiss to be punishing, the moment she responded, moaning into his mouth, fitting her lips to his, he knew it could not be.

The only one he punished was himself.

Because his body clamored for her, but so did his heart. Damn it, the weakest part of him wanted to believe her when she professed to love him. When she claimed her antics had all been an attempt to bring about his return. That the fortnight they'd spent together had been real—the laughter, the love, all of it. That she wasn't a Fenian. Dynamite, he thought as he dragged his mouth lower, down her throat, across the silky expanse of creamy skin. She was *his* dynamite.

He had missed her. Dear God, how he had missed her. "Do you want this?" he asked before he tongued the hollow at the base of her throat, just above her glittering diamonds.

"Yes." The word slid from her lips on a sigh. "I want you so much I can't bear it."

Thank fuck. He caught her bodice in his hand, and ripped the delicate silk cleanly from her. Or at least half of it. With a flick of his wrist, the bodice was gone. He gripped her corset and used his thumb to work the first hook-and-eye closure free. It didn't take him long to have the red satin, black-lace-trimmed corset open. Her chemise remained, shielding her from him. He rent the fine fabric as well. She was nude from the waist up.

Her breasts were full and high, the sweet pink nipples he'd recalled countless times while secreted in Liverpool hard and inviting, pointing upward. He couldn't resist lowering his head to take the hardened bud of her left nipple into his mouth. He sucked, relishing the way she writhed against him, arching into his body, squeezing his hips with her thighs. She moaned. He caught her between his teeth, tugged.

She begged. "Please, Sebastian."

Need roared out of control. Thundered though his veins. Lit a fire that burned just beneath his skin. His ballocks tightened, his cock grinding against her center. Jesus. He had never wanted a woman more. His reaction to her was ludicrous. He knew what she was, what she'd done. Christ, he probably didn't even know the half of it. And yet there would be no purging her from his blood until he had her this night.

He released her nipple with a loud, wet pop, tilted his head so that their eyes clashed again at last. Deep, intense green pierced him. Her mouth had fallen open, her breath uneven. He blew on her nipple once. Twice. Nipped it again, his gaze never leaving hers.

"What do you want, Daisy?" As he asked the question,

he canted his hips, pressing the demanding ridge of his cock against her more fully. "Tell me. What do you want?"

Her breasts rose and fell, her breathing faster. She swallowed, ran her tongue over her lower lip. "I want you to believe me."

"Make me believe you," he dared. The challenge was a lie, bold and foolish, for he knew there was no earthly means by which she could persuade him that she wasn't in fact the treacherous viper he had discovered her to be. All the evidence led to only one conclusion. She was her father's daughter. She had betrayed him. She was an actress, a manipulator, a faithless liar. And he had fallen prey to her.

Now, he wanted to exact a bit of his own vengeance before she needed to face her inevitable end. Turning her over to Carlisle and League forces would not be easy when the time came, regardless of what she'd done.

But for tonight, she was his and his alone.

"I shouldn't have to make you," she countered, stubborn to the last. That was Daisy—bravado and courage and manipulation, a vibrant flower that was too bold and dishonest for her own good. "I'm your wife. I've never given you cause to doubt me."

Everything she'd done gave him cause to doubt her. The reports from the Home Office made him doubt her. Her own actions made him doubt her. The fact that her father was the puppeteer for an ever-growing web of Fenian plotters made him doubt her. But doubt and need were two separate propulsions.

He tongued her nipple, and she arched on a breathy moan, responsive as ever. And then he nipped her again. Not hard enough to bruise, but enough that she gasped and writhed against him in obvious frustration. A liar she might be, but there was no pretense in the way her body wanted his. Nor in the way he wanted her. His desire for her was all-consuming.

"Release my hands," she said.

He licked the puckered flesh he'd just bit. "No."

271

"I want to touch you."

Fuck. Longing slammed into him at her simple words. He wanted her to touch him. He could overpower her in an instant. What was the danger, the risk?

Only his heart.

Where the hell had that rogue thought come from? He forced it where it belonged, into the dark recesses of his mind. Good and bloody buried. He did as she asked, and then with two free hands, he took his knife from his boot and lowered it to the waistband of her trousers. One quick, careful swipe, and he'd cut straight through the silk and her drawers both. Fabric gaped. He tossed his knife to the floor where it landed with a carpet-muffled thud. And then he caught the rent fabric in his hands and tore it down her body in one, fluid motion.

Her eyes widened. "Sebastian."

He looked down at their bodies, his poised for entrance despite the barrier of clothing he still wore. Hers...bloody, bloody hell. He took in a curved length of creamy thigh, an impossibly perfect knee, a sweetly turned calf and a trim ankle. But that wasn't what made his mouth go dry. No. His gaze skimmed back up her body, lingering on the soft flesh at the apex of her thighs. Ah, yes. He had not forgotten the taste of her, the way she'd reacted to him. Here was his prize at last, what he'd longed for each seemingly endless day of the three months he'd spent away from her.

His fingers slid into her folds, finding her so slick that he couldn't suppress his groan. His cock surged. Wanting. Needing. His heart pounded. "Daisy." He circled her responsive bundle of flesh once, twice, then traced the seam to her entrance.

He was drawn as tense and still as the strings on a violin awaiting the slide of a bow. He needed to calm himself, to slow down. His heartbeat pounded in his ears, his cock so rigid he had to take a few steadying breaths just to regain his equilibrium.

*One, two, three.*

Counting again, blast it all. Blast *her*.

"Sebastian," she said his name again on a gasp, and it bloody well killed him. "I want you so badly I ache with it. I wanted you every day that you were gone, and I want you now more than I ever did though I hate myself for it."

*Jesus.* He knew the feeling. The breath he'd inhaled hissed from his lungs. When he found his voice, it was dark and low with the same suppressed anger that had been guiding him from the moment he'd first caught sight of her, resplendent in her evening finery, trousers and all. "Damn you. How is it that I want you, so badly, Daisy? It makes no bloody sense, but I want you so goddamn much that I burn with it."

Her right palm caressed down his chest, over the taught plane of his abdomen, before traveling lower. Seeking and bold. Her fingers glanced his trousers directly over his cock. He jerked into her, and her fingers curled around his length.

His mouth descended upon hers, bruising, scalding, possessing. This kiss held no quarter. It was meant to ravish her. Take her. Remind her she was his. That he was her bloody husband, like it or not.

*Not in truth.*

There it was again, his sainted conscience, interrupting at the most inopportune moment. But nothing, not the fact that she'd been parading her lovers in and out of his home, nor that she was working for the Fenians, neither her duplicity nor the fact that he was meant to remove her as a threat, could cool the raging fires within him. Not even his conscience would keep him from sinking deep inside her tonight.

He thrust against her hand, caught her lip between his teeth and lightly bit. His free hand cupped one of her full, beautiful breasts, his thumb working her nipple. Everywhere he touched her, she was hot, soft as silk. Her scent, the scent that had haunted him in his absence, went to his head like fine whisky.

He kissed down her neck, licking and nipping. She tasted

sweet, like vanilla with a trace of bergamot, and by God, he could lick every bit of her all night long if not for the painful state of his engorged cock.

"Open my trousers," he commanded against her skin, before playing his tongue over the elegant hollow where her throat and shoulder met and her pulse raced.

She hesitated only a moment before her fingers found the closure of his waistband. Slowly, his trousers came undone and then the placket of his drawers.

He dragged his mouth lower in appreciation, over her breast to the nipple he wasn't currently plucking between thumb and forefinger. His tongue teased the stiff peak, back and forth, wringing a moan from her lips. Unable to deny himself or her any longer, he gave in and drew her into his mouth. He used his teeth against her, a subtle pressure designed to heighten her arousal, before releasing her.

"Touch me," he said, pressing a kiss alongside that pretty nipple. Pink, so pink. The sweetest pink he'd ever seen, rivaled only by her luscious lips. He kissed the tip.

She gripped him then, and the taunt of her fingers over his bare length was enough to nearly unman him. On another night, when he wasn't quite so carried to the edge by his commingling anger and lust, he would've taken his time. He would've removed his boots and his bloody trousers. His shirt.

But this was no ordinary night, and nothing about the passion exploding between him and Daisy felt ordinary. It felt deuced incendiary, in fact. If he didn't sheathe himself inside her in the next minute, he was going to come all over her hand like a lad who'd just seen his first cunny.

And so he swirled her nub, worked it. Ran his finger along her dewy seam, coating his fingers in the evidence that she wanted him every bit as much as he needed to have her. He slicked his digit over her again and again, teasing at her entrance, sucking her nipple, paying attention to the soft sounds of appreciation she hummed, the way she angled her hips to gain more sensation.

Daisy was near to reaching her pinnacle. Her breathing was coming in fast gasps, her body arching from the bed. Finally, he returned to the pearl he'd originally sought, exerting greater pressure, working her into a fine frenzy. And then he sank a finger deep inside her sheath, testing her, teasing her. Wet. So hot and wet and…damn it, everything in him clamored for more. He hooked his finger, pressing against the most sensitive part of her, fucking her in slow, deep thrusts.

He released her nipple, dragging himself back up her lithe body to her mouth. And he kissed her as though she was everything to him, his life source, and he couldn't get enough.

In that stark, mad moment, she was.

Their tongues tangled, and she shuddered against him, more wetness flooding his already drenched fingers as she came. He took her cries with his mouth and swallowed them, his forever.

There was no time to shuck his shirt. Not enough patience to even pull down his trousers and smalls. He guided his cock to her slick entrance. He forced everything—her betrayal, what would come tomorrow—from his mind. In one swift thrust, he was inside her to the hilt. She was so damn tight, her body wet and hot and so bloody decadent that it took his breath away.

"Sebastian," she cried out, drawing him deeper, her body clenching on his as though she would never let him go.

He didn't want her to, damn it all. He surged inside her, again and again until he jerked himself from her, exploding onto the bed coverings.

*Dynamite.*

How the hell could he ever let her go?

## chapter twenty-five

*D*AISY FLINCHED AS THE DOOR JOINING their chambers slammed.

He didn't believe her, even after what they'd just shared. The moment he'd rolled away from her and righted his clothing, his expression impassive, she'd known. She'd created a chasm, and it threatened to engulf them both.

A part of her wanted to rail against him for so easily doubting her. But part of her knew that if she wanted his honesty and his trust, she would need to meet him halfway. She wanted the truth from him, wanted him to lower the walls he'd erected around himself, for the sake of their marriage but most importantly for the sake of their child.

Knowing what she needed to do, she rose from the bed and took up a dressing gown, belting it at her waist. Her feet carried her to the door he'd just closed. She didn't knock, didn't hesitate before turning the knob and crossing the threshold. This distance between them had to end.

He stood at the window, his back to her. The curtains he'd drawn back were clenched so tightly in his fist that his knuckles were white.

"Get out," his deep voice cut into the silence, the only acknowledgment he'd made of her presence.

"No." She didn't stop until she was so near to him that his familiar scent hit her and she flattened her palm against his shoulder. "Look at me, Sebastian."

He tensed beneath her touch but remained otherwise immobile. "I can't bloody well look at you."

Had she thought he would bend? When had he ever? Her chest grew tight as she recalled the charmed fortnight they'd spent together. Laughing with him. Loving with him. A one thirty-second Your Grace. The library's worth of books he'd had delivered to her door. *A favorite for a favorite.* Those two weeks had been the best she'd ever known. She wanted that life with him back, wanted him back. Forever.

"Padraig McGuire was here because of my sister," she told him softly. "I have a half sister, Bridget. She works— *worked*—at a milliner's shop here in London. A few months ago, she left without word. Padraig had information about her. That and that alone is why I received his calls."

Sebastian whipped about, his face carved in hard, grim lines that did nothing to detract from his startling looks. Even in his rage, he was beautiful. "Padraig?"

She took a step back from him, wincing at his furious tone and harsh expression. "Mr. McGuire. I've known him for several years, Sebastian, and yes I was betrothed to him once. But I was young and foolish and desperate to escape my father. There is nothing between us now, nor has there been since our engagement was broken."

A muscle ticked in his cheek. "Do you love him?"

"Of course not." Giving in to the need to touch him again, she moved nearer, reaching up to cup the rigid set of his jaw. When he didn't withdraw from her touch, a brief flutter of optimism beat in her breast. "I love *you*."

He was silent for so long she feared he wouldn't speak. His eyes devoured her, hungrily raking her face and lower, dipping to her mouth. "Damn you," he whispered.

"No, my love." She glided her palm over the prickly stubble of his whiskers, caressing him. "Damn you for leaving. Why did you go? Where? Tell me, please. I want to understand. Let me in, Sebastian. Let me love you."

But he remained unyielding, even if he allowed her touch. "This sister of yours. Tell me about her."

It wasn't what she'd expected him to dwell on, but neither was he pushing her away, so she supposed that, at least, was something. "Bridget was born out of wedlock soon after my parents married. Father was on business in Ireland. Her mother worked at a tavern. When I learned she was here in London, I was overjoyed. I had always longed to meet her, you see."

"She's a shop girl."

"Yes. I wanted her to leave her position and stay with Aunt Caroline, but she refused. My father…he wouldn't acknowledge her or help her in any way." She took a breath, searching his eyes. "I wanted to tell you about her before. I was hoping she might live with us. But then, you were both gone. I'm worried about her, Sebastian. Mr. McGuire told me she's involved with the Fenians."

Sebastian's gaze sharpened. He caught her hand, removed it from his face. "What else did McGuire tell you?"

She focused on their linked hands, the heat of his skin burning into hers. He had not let her go. "He said she was in danger, that somehow she'd gotten caught up with the dynamitards. Why do you ask?"

All her suspicions crowded down on her in that moment. His abrupt departure, the odd note she'd discovered, the length of time he'd been away, the darkness and secrecy she'd always sensed in him. Georgiana's words echoed eerily in her mind. Dizzy. She felt so dizzy.

*My husband isn't hunting game, Daisy…it's something to do with the Fenians…there was a name on one of the letters.*

The name on the letter had been Daisy's.

The day after Sebastian left, the papers had been filled with news of a foiled Fenian bomb plot. The bomb had been discovered prior to detonation. The people clamored for answers and reassurance. The government's response had remained a secret, but it stood to reason that it would not show its hand to the players seated at its table. No, the Crown would keep its emissaries enshrouded in secrecy, all the better to gain the advantage over their foe. Secrecy such as a husband who disappeared without word.

Dear God.

The chamber spun around her. A rushing sounded in her ears, her breath going shallow. She couldn't seem to suck enough air into her lungs. Or perhaps it was too much air. Little pinpricks of light marred her vision. She tried to pull free of Sebastian's grasp, but he refused to release her.

"You're a spy," she accused.

He stared at her, not denying her charge.

And then her world went black.

Bloody, bloody hell.

Sebastian caught Daisy against his chest before she pitched backward and landed in a crumpled heap on the floor. With little effort, he swept her into his arms and carried her across the chamber, laying her on his bed. His mind spinning, he patted her pale cheeks.

"Daisy, love." His fingers found her pulse, steady and thrumming in her throat. Her chest rose and fell in normal breaths. Christ, she had fainted. And in the moment he watched the bloom fade from her cheeks, her eyes going wide as she issued that lone, correct allegation, he had known.

His instinct had not been wrong. The heated interlude he'd shared with her had pierced the haze of jealousy fogging his brain, had undone him in a way nothing else could. He'd removed himself to his chamber, trying to gain some perspective, to objectively study the situation and facts. But she had just lowered the gavel for him.

She was telling the truth. Not even the greatest actress alive could have managed to feign the shock on her face, the ghostly pallor her skin had taken on, the weightless fall. There was no mistaking the limp feeling of an unconscious body to anyone who had ever known it.

Daisy was not a Fenian plotter. The Irish shop girl she'd been in contact with was her bloody sister born on the wrong side of the blanket. The jagged pieces of truth formed together into a perfect puzzle. He ran his hands over her now, rubbing her arms, urging her to wake. For the first time since his return, he allowed himself to relish the feeling of her, warm and soft. Reassuring. Beloved.

He believed her. Believed everything. Her innocence, her recklessness in trying to force his return, her love for him. Guilt slammed through him with the force of a runaway carriage. He had doubted her. Lied to her. Used her. Abandoned her when he should have never left her side.

He was not worthy of her love, and she was lying supine, out cold, so bloody still and pale it scared him. "Daisy, come back to me," he said, patting her cheek again.

A low moan issued from her parted lips. Golden lashes fluttered on her cheeks. Her eyes opened, startling and verdant. "Sebastian?"

"Buttercup." He pressed a fervent kiss to her brow. "Thank God."

Her hands fluttered to his shoulders, tentative at first as she became lucid once more. Then she clutched him, her fingers digging through the fabric of his shirt. "Who are you?"

Christ if he knew. Right now, in this moment, he was a man who loved the woman before him. A man who had wronged her in the name of duty. A man who very much wanted to atone for his sins.

He lowered himself onto the bed alongside her, framing her face in his hands. Somehow, he needed to unburden himself to her. He owed her his honesty. Owed her so much more. "Sebastian Fairmont, Eighth Duke of Trent, Marquis of Sunbury, and other lesser titles."

His attempt at levity met with a frown that furrowed the smooth expanse of her forehead. "That wasn't what I meant, and you know it."

Could he do it? Did he dare reveal the truth to her? A great, gaping fear paralyzed him for a moment. He had been a spy his entire adult life. He traded in secrets. He deceived everyone he knew. He couldn't recall when his life had been his. When he'd been free. He lived and died by his oath. He was bound to the League.

But now, here, in the woman at his side, was a different form of bond altogether. The sort that transcended everything and everyone. As much as she was his, he too was hers.

"Sebastian." Her voice prodded him, ate at him, forced its way through the indecision. Those moss-green eyes plumbed his. "What I want to know is whether or not you're a spy."

A spy.

All he needed to say was one word. One response. The truth.

He closed his eyes, whispered the answer. "Yes."

Silence stretched between them in the wake of his crippling admission. She stiffened. He kept holding her face because he couldn't bear to release her, stroking his thumbs over her cheekbones with tender care. Such delicate bone structure, so refined. Regal as a queen.

"You've been spying on me, haven't you?" she asked at last, a shimmer of unshed tears glistening in the light, making her eyes all the more vibrant, mossy green.

He wanted to lie. Christ, it would be so much easier.

"The truth, Sebastian," she demanded when he hesitated again. "It's why you were following me when we first met. It's why you married me, why you disappeared. How you knew that I was betrothed to Padraig, how you knew he'd called here. I'll wager you didn't earn those scars in a childhood fire, did you? Don't lie to me any longer."

He'd spent nearly half of his thirty years keeping the truth guarded, locked away from everyone who wasn't part of the League. Unleashing it made his chest go tight, as if the air was being knocked from his lungs by a sound punch to the gut. "You are...my mission," he allowed at last.

She pushed at his shoulders, dislodging his gentle hold on her. A gasp tore from her, and it was the raw sound of grief, and he was its cause, and that wracked him all the way to his bloody bones. "Was any of it true?"

Fuck. He swallowed around the bile rising in his throat. This was not how he'd intended to tell her. Her pain was like a knife to his chest. "You and me, Daisy and Sebastian. That was true. Is true. What I feel for you is as real and true as the roof over our heads and the stars lighting the night sky."

Her hand rose to her mouth as if she attempted to contain the sob shuddering from her. "My God. Was...just now, making love to me, was that part of your mission?"

"No, love." Feeling like the world's biggest rotter, he touched her shoulder, seeking to comfort her.

But she didn't want his comfort.

She shrugged away from him and scooted across the bed, not stopping until she threw her feet onto the floor and stood on the opposite side of him, a pale goddess, brave as ever. His heart ached for her. And he hated himself for the deceptions he'd perpetrated against her. He should never have consummated their marriage, not while he'd been dishonest. Not without giving her the choice of knowing who and what he was.

He recognized it now as she faced him with the look of a woman whose world had just been torn asunder. "Do not dare to call me that. And do not touch me. Is our marriage even binding, or was that a part of your lies as well?"

"It's binding. You are my wife, and I'm your husband." It hadn't been meant to remain that way, his conscience needled him. Damn it, he had to tell her everything and hope that he could somehow regain her trust. He skirted the bed, going to her again, taking her cold hands in his. "Do you want the full truth, Daisy?"

"Release me." She tugged at her hands fruitlessly. He wasn't letting her go. Not now. Not ever.

"The truth," he continued, lacing his fingers through hers and forcing her to meet his gaze, "is that I was meant to annul the marriage at the conclusion of my assignment. Your father is deeply involved with the Fenians who are setting bombs throughout England. He is funding them, running ships with his guns and supplies, but he's a clever bastard, and no one has been able to furnish absolute proof of his guilt. I was assigned to get closer to you, glean as much information from you as I could."

"Glean information from me." She jerked her hands from his grip and stalked around him in such fury that her robe billowed out around her. Halfway across the chamber, she stopped and spun back to face him. "And you intended to learn my father's secrets by following me into a moonlit garden? By marrying me? By consummating the marriage you were meant to annul?"

"It is complicated." Damn Carlisle to hell for what he'd forced him to do. Damn himself for doing it. He followed her, stopping only when the hem of her robe brushed his trousers and her sweet scent wafted over him. So near he could make out the flecks of gold in her eyes. "I wasn't meant to do half of what I've done. My mission was to marry you, keep you close, get even closer to your father, and gather enough evidence against him to see him thrown into prison. But from the moment I first saw you, I couldn't stop wanting you. I tried my damnedest to keep from consummating the marriage, but you were no longer a pawn to me the moment I brought you here as my wife."

She gave a bitter laugh, crossing her arms over herself in a defensive posture. "How honorable you were to refrain from consummating our marriage for the span of one whole day."

Well, Christ. When she put it in those terms...he was a bloody beast, and he knew it. How had this golden angel come to earth, entrusted to him, and he had forsaken her? He passed a hand over his face, trying to gather his thoughts, to marshal them into something worthy of her listening. "I'm not an honorable man. When I should have placed my duty first, I followed my own selfish desires instead, and when I should have placed you first, I answered the call of duty. The truth is stark and ugly, but if you must know one thing, buttercup, know this. I married you out of duty, but I fell in love with you somewhere in between you taking me to task for turning up half-inebriated at breakfast and that morning we lay in bed laughing and making love. Do you remember it?"

She shook her head. "Don't."

"Don't what?" Another step brought their bodies together. His hands found her waist, anchoring her to him. "Don't tell you that I love you? How can I not? I love you, Daisy, Duchess of Trent. You sealed my fate from the moment you dared me to take my turn at the Beresford ball. You had such fire, such daring, the likes of which I've never seen in a woman. You humble me. You inspire me. You make me want to be better so that I'm worthy of being your husband."

"No," she cried out, shaking against him. Her palms flattened to his chest. "Stop it, Sebastian."

He couldn't. He held her to him, made her listen, because he couldn't shake the feeling that if he allowed her to walk away now, he'd lose her forever. And he couldn't bear that. Even with the accusations in the report running through his mind, fury and jealousy wreaking havoc on him for the entire trip from Liverpool to London, he had been thinking of ways he could reform her, convince her to see reason. Keep her safe and at his side.

"I've been living a lie for years. I've devoted my entire life to duty and protecting Crown and country. I don't know how to be different than who I am, but I do know that I love you. I love you, and I will change for you. I'll do anything for you, buttercup."

"Don't you see?" She exhaled, her tone steeped in sadness as she touched his face for a fleeting moment. "I don't want you to change. All I ever wanted from you was your love and your honesty. But you came to me in lies. Everything we shared emerged from your deceit. Do you think you can tell me the truth and everything else will fall into place, that I'll swoon into your arms in gratitude? Because I can assure you it won't. *I* won't. I'm stronger than that."

Of course she was strong. She was the strongest woman he'd ever known. He was in awe of her. "I'm telling you all this because I owe you the truth, Daisy."

"The truth or your version of it?" Her eyes flashed as she faced him, vibrant in her ire. More beautiful than he'd ever seen her as she stood up to him. "Because as I see it, the truth is that you returned for me tonight believing the gossip and lies and whatever information you've received. You believed I had betrayed our vows. I cannot fathom what changed your mind, but I haven't forgotten your words earlier this evening. You are a hypocrite, sir, to charge me with deceiving you when you are the greatest dissembler of them all. A hypocrite and a liar, and I want nothing more to do with you! Grant me the annulment I was meant to have."

With that final, parting shot, she spun on her heel and quit the chamber. The door slammed closed, humming on its frame. He remained where he was, in the center of the chamber. He may as well have been in the middle of a bloody wilderness for all that he could find the answers for what to do next.

Because she was right. He was a hypocrite and a liar. And he didn't deserve a woman as good as Daisy. He didn't deserve her at all.

Unfortunately, that realization didn't make him want or love her any less.

"Fuck me," he growled into the night.

*chapter twenty-six*

S THE SUN BEGAN TO RISE OVER LONDON, Daisy reached a painful conclusion.

She'd spent the night pacing her chamber, struggling to make sense of the tumult within her. Shock had rendered it impossible to sleep. Her feet hurt. Her back ached. She was tired and emotionally drained and more confused than she'd ever been in her life. But she knew what she needed to do.

She was leaving Sebastian.

Her hands skimmed over her burgeoning belly. She needed time and space to decide whether or not she was leaving him forever. There was the babe to consider. He had deceived her, manipulated her, abandoned her.

What a fool she was, falling in love with a man who had merely been carrying out his duty. A man who had suspected her guilty of heinous crimes. A man who had believed the worst of her until it was too late. How naïve of her to have imagined he was the only person in her life who hadn't used her for his own gain.

He had used her more thoroughly than anyone ever had.

His betrayal ran so deep she wasn't sure if she could ever recover from it.

She was so caught up in her tortured thoughts that she didn't realize she was no longer alone in her chamber until the distinctive sound of a gun being cocked rang into the silence. Heart in her throat, she spun about to find the last person in the world she could have ever imagined pointing a pistol at her.

Her lady's maid.

A gasp tore from her as a fresh onslaught of shock barreled through her. Abigail, who had always been pleasant and polite and smiling, who had been her steadfast attendant, first as a nurse and later as her lady's maid, was coolly training a gun upon her. She took an instinctive step forward, palms raised in supplication.

"Don't take another step or you'll regret it," Abigail warned, her voice as cold and hard as the frozen ground on a January morning.

Daisy froze, her mouth going dry. "Abigail, what are you doing?"

"Returning you to your father. He's waiting in a carriage below," Abigail said with an eerie calm that belied the heaviness of the moment. As though Daisy wasn't staring down the barrel of a gun. "Come along quietly, and you won't get hurt."

She shook her head, dread icing a path down her spine. "I don't wish to go anywhere with him. I never want to see him again."

"Ungrateful bitch." Her lip curled. "Just like your mother."

"How dare you disparage my mother?" The words rushed from Daisy's lips before she could think better of them. But she was fiercely defensive of her precious mama's memory—the only part of her that remained.

"I dare quite a bit seeing as how I've a pistol." Abigail stalked forward. "You're not worth much to me any longer, so you'd serve yourself best by shutting your mouth and doing as I say."

Abigail's tone as she had spoken of Daisy's mother struck her then. Bitter, laced with rancor and hatred. Suddenly queasy, she flattened her palm over her belly where even now, her babe innocently grew. She would do anything to protect her child. Her instincts told her that obeying the other woman would be a grave mistake.

Her spinning mind suddenly recalled that she was not without a means of defending herself. As she'd paced the Axminster earlier, she'd discovered Sebastian's forgotten knife on the floor and had slipped it into the pocket on her robe. If she could distract Abigail sufficiently, she had a chance of striking with the knife and knocking the gun from her hand.

Yes, she had to distract her. Keep her talking. *Think, Daisy. Think.*

"What do you know of my mother?" she asked.

"She didn't deserve your father," Abigail snapped. "She never loved him as I do. Now get moving to the door. We haven't much time."

Daisy hesitated, grappling with the elder woman's revelation. "You love my father?"

"I've loved him for years."

"And yet he turned you out without reference," she was quick to point out.

"You believed it so easily, didn't you? You ruined our plans by eloping with that blackguard duke, and I needed a reason to stay close to you." Abigail's eyes narrowed. "Now to the door with you! No more tarrying."

Daisy feared she was going to be ill. "What plans?"

Abigail struck her head with the butt of the pistol. Pain laced through her. She stumbled, losing her balance, crying out. Tears stung her eyes. The woman before her, wild-eyed and stern-faced, was not the woman she had known for her entire life. It was as if a stranger had come to inhabit her body. But that was the gift, she supposed, of evil. It could hide in plain sight, waiting for the right moment to strike and lay low the innocent.

"Walk to the door," the woman gritted, "or I'll hit you even harder next time."

Daisy forced herself to move. One foot in front of the other. Step by step. *Think, Daisy. Distract her.*

"What plans?" she asked again.

Abigail grabbed her arm and settled the pistol into her lower back, urging her to move faster. "You were to marry Lord Breckly to solidify your father's position in the Irish Nationalist League. It would have been the perfect foil. Your father would have been rid of you at last, and his influence and power would have grown immeasurably. But you couldn't obey him, could you?"

Dear God. Her father was a Fenian, and so was Abigail. It all began to make horrible, sickening sense. Why had she failed to see it before now? Sebastian's government had suspected Daisy, and all along, the true conspirator had been her lady's maid, the one woman she'd trusted more than she'd even trusted her own aunt.

She forced her dazed mind to churn up more questions, more diversions. "Why are you doing this, Abigail? What use has my father for me now that I've married another?"

"You're leverage, of course." Abigail pushed her forward so roughly that she stumbled again. She righted herself, the gun jamming into her back. "Wasn't hard to dupe the English fools into believing I'd serve as an informant. They already suspected your father, and we knew it and used their suspicion to our benefit. Did you know they paid me five hundred pounds to tell them that you were colluding to gain Irish independence from English tyranny?"

They'd reached the chamber door, and Daisy's heart hammered in her breast, a combination of what Abigail had revealed to her and the realization that she needed to act now to save herself. Whatever Abigail and her father intended for her, she knew without question that it wasn't as harmless as Abigail would have her believe. Marrying

Sebastian was the first time she had ever gone against her father's edicts. She recalled all too well his red-faced rage the morning after her wedding. How furious he'd been that his bargaining chip had been stripped from his grasp.

No, she couldn't wait any longer. The time had come.

She'd never considered herself brave. For so many years, she'd endured her father's brutal beatings. She'd learned not to defy him, to conform to his wishes, to please him so that he wouldn't strike her. She had played the part of doting daughter for his friends and business associates, and she had never once gainsaid him. Sometimes, he had hit her anyway, for perceived infractions. Afterward, he had always rewarded her with diamonds and kindness. It was a vicious cycle, and Daisy was going to end it.

Here. Now. Today.

She'd never been brave before, but now she had an innocent babe growing within her, and she loved that life more than she loved her own. She would protect her child with everything in her, fight until the last breath escaped her if there was no other way.

"Open the door," Abigail commanded. "We'll go to the servant's stair. You'll say nothing. If anyone sees you, you will smile and tell them that I'm ill and you're seeing me to my rooms to make me a poultice. Belowstairs, they already think you're an angel, so it won't be hard for them to believe it. If you say even a word, I'll—"

Daisy reached into the pocket of her gown with her left hand, her fingers finding the hilt of Sebastian's blade. It was time. With as much speed as she could manage, she yanked her right arm from Abigail's grasp and jammed her elbow into the other woman's midsection. She withdrew the knife, raising it high, a primal scream tearing from her. At the exact moment that her blade connected with the meaty flesh of her opponent's upper arm, the pistol fired.

Agonizing pain shot through her, but her knife had done its work. Abigail's sleeve was torn, blood gushing forth from the rent fabric. Her pistol clattered to the floor. Daisy dove for it, knife still in hand.

Sebastian sat at the desk in his study. The flickering gas lamps illuminated the letters he'd only just begun to read. All of them had been penned in Daisy's neat hand, forwarded from his various estates. Dozens and dozens of them. She must have written until her fingers ached.

How had he ever doubted her? Each fresh line he read was like a booted kick to the stomach. How deeply he had wronged her. By the morning's light, he couldn't blame her for telling him to go to the devil the night before. He was everything she'd accused him of and more. Worse. He had married her in lies, cleaved her to him in deception borne of his own inability to resist her, had left her without word or explanation in the name of duty, and had returned believing her in the wrong.

When the only person who had ever been in the wrong was Sebastian Fairmont. Eighth Duke of Trent, First Marquis of Selfish Arsehole. Daisy had always been true and good and undeserving of the situations in which she'd found herself. She'd been used, and everyone had taken advantage of her. First, her father, abusing her and using her as a lure for suitors who would better himself and increase his wealth, then her would-be suitors, and the League by ruining her, forcing her into a falsehood of a marriage. But finally, there had been Sebastian. He'd not only taken advantage of her every weakness, he had stormed past her defenses. She'd told him that she loved him.

And what had he done, coward that he was? He'd disappeared from her life.

As he flipped through her letters, he could sense her mood shifting. Her epistles began with hesitation and hope. As time went on, she began to enumerate all the things she knew would enrage him. Here, in black ink and paper, was all the proof anyone could require. Yes, these letters proved to him that Daisy had only ever been honest with him.

When he reached the final series of letters, he felt as if the wind had been knocked from him.

*I write you with unexpected news. I am expecting your child. Though you've amply demonstrated your lack of sentiment for myself, I cannot help but hope you may be somewhat less reticent in regards to an innocent.*

The letter dropped from his fingers, wafting to his desk without even a whisper of sound. A child. A babe. Daisy carried their babe. And she hadn't told him. No, instead, she had demanded an annulment.

Dear God, had he been too rough with her last night? How could he have failed to realize what the small changes in her frame implied? He had noted the slight curve in her belly, the generosity in her breasts. But he had enjoyed it, never once imagining how life-altering, how beautiful and wonderful and fucking altogether glorious it all was.

A sudden knock sounded at his door, startling him.

He didn't want to be wrenched from this moment of unadulterated celebration. This moment of realizing that his wife carried their babe within her body. His carelessness, his stupid bloody recklessness, had in the end, turned out to be his saving grace.

His child. Daisy's child. Would it be a girl with golden ringlets and an infallible sense of bravery? Or a towheaded boy with moss-green eyes and a penchant for daring? His heart beat with a wild, uncontrollable rhythm. He felt complete for the first time. Replete. Not a part of him missing.

A babe. How bloody amazing. The notion awed him.

The knock sounded again, this time more forceful than the last.

No more avoidance. Give the devil his due.

"Enter," he called.

But it wasn't his butler Giles who opened the portal as he'd fancied it would be, and stepped over the threshold as he'd anticipated. It was Griffin. And he wasn't alone.

Sebastian stood, mouth going dry, gut tightening. His blood felt as if it leached from his body as he took in the four men flanking his best friend. Home Office brawn, it would appear, though none of their faces were familiar to him.

Surely they hadn't come for Daisy. Carlisle had told him to see to her himself. He thought he had time, for fuck's sake. Time to align all the information into a proper picture. Time to go to Carlisle with undeniable proof of Daisy's innocence so that the Home Office could exonerate her once and for all.

"What the hell is this, Griffin?" he rasped, every last bit of the exultation seeping from his body. He could not lose her, would not lose her now.

"Where is Her Grace?" Griffin asked in lieu of answering. His forbidding expression was one of a man going into battle.

"She is abed in her chamber." He strode forward. "Goddamn it, Griffin. Why are you here?"

"She's in danger, Bast. One of our double operatives contacted me. We haven't a moment to waste." His friend's tone was calm, but his eyes told a different story.

If a man as hardened as Griffin was worried, the danger was real. Everything inside him turned to ice. Daisy was in danger. Their babe was in danger. Christ. His hands were shaking. But there was no time to linger. They needed to act, to get to Daisy, protect her.

"We'll walk upstairs while you tell me what the hell is going on," he demanded of his friend and brother in arms.

Shoulder to shoulder, they strode from the study, the four grim-faced men following in their wake. "Her lady's maid is a Fenian," Griffin said in low tones. "She is connected to Vanreid."

Damn it. Sebastian scarcely recalled the lady's maid, who had turned up at his household after Daisy's departure from her father's home. "You're certain?"

Griffin nodded as they ascended the staircase, taking the steps two at a time. "She was the anonymous source feeding false information about Daisy to the Home Office."

An anonymous source had been supplying information about Daisy. Damning and incorrect information. Why hadn't that occurred to him? Of course. It all made perfect, bloody sense. And he had allowed the woman to enter his household, to remain close to Daisy. Close enough to strike.

A muffled scream sounded just then, followed by the report of a pistol. The air rushed from him. The scream had been Daisy's.

*No. No. No.*

Sebastian broke into a run.

His heart pumping faster than it ever had, he took the stairs three at a time, racing down the hall. Dimly, he was aware of the pounding feet of Griffin and his men following in his wake. But he didn't care. The earth could have opened upon itself and swallowed everyone but Daisy and himself, and he wouldn't have given a goddamn.

Griffin appeared at his side, running to keep pace. "Damn it, Bast, let me go in first. I'm armed."

Fuck. That was how much he loved that woman. For her, he would have run headlong into enemy fire without a weapon and without a second thought. For Daisy's sake, it would be far better to allow an armed man into the chamber first. No one had a deadlier aim than Griffin.

He pointed to Daisy's chamber door as they ran. "That one."

Griffin held up a hand as they approached the door, withdrawing his pistol. With a swift kick of his booted foot, the door splintered open. He strode forward, gun drawn and aimed, prepared to do battle.

Sebastian wasn't far behind as Griffin stopped in his tracks. "Your Grace?"

Daisy stood, looking like nothing so much as an avenging goddess of war, his bloodied knife in one hand and a pistol in the other. Her unbound hair cascaded wildly down her back, and she was clad in nothing more than a dressing gown that gaped badly at the top and bottom. But it wasn't the robe that drew his attention. Rather, it was the damaged right sleeve and flesh beneath, torn open by the undeniable trajectory of a bullet. Daisy's hand that clutched the pistol was drenched in dark, crimson blood that dripped onto the floor, soaking into the carpets.

Jesus Christ.

He raced forward, registering the slumped figure of another woman on the floor, also in a pool of blood. "Daisy," he cried. "You've been shot."

"She was trying to force me to go with her," Daisy said in an oddly toneless voice. Her skin was pale, far too pale. The perfect white of fresh cream. She was going to swoon, he realized. The blood loss and shock combined would be enough to lay low even the most seasoned soldier. "Oh, God. My father is waiting in a carriage below. Sebastian, you must arrest him."

His heart wrenched, and he was prouder than he'd ever been. His brave warrior. She hadn't needed rescuing. She had bloody well rescued herself. Two of her majesty's fiercest spies and a handful of Home Office brawn had not been able to accomplish what one tiny, fierce American duchess had.

Griffin kept his gun trained on the woman moaning on the floor. "Arrest her," he ordered one of his men.

Sebastian didn't waste a moment. He went to Daisy, gathered her in his arms, hauled her to him as tightly as he could. "Buttercup." He pressed his face into her hair, inhaling deeply of her luscious, sweet scent. She was alive, and gratitude hit him with such ferocity that he trembled beneath its weight. If he had lost her... Christ, he couldn't even bear to think it.

But she needed a doctor. The wound on her arm bled heavily. Her blood was warm and sticky, oozing onto him. "We need a doctor," he called out tightly. "Quickly!"

"My father." Daisy slumped in his arms. Her head lolled back, her eyes taking on the glazed, pinned look of one who had just witnessed a great trauma. He'd seen that look enough times to know it. "See that he's arrested, Sebastian. Stop him from hurting anyone else. Please."

He looked to Griffin, who gave him a grim nod before leading the remaining three men from the chamber. Vanreid wouldn't come out the victor. He was outmanned and outgunned.

"Hush, love," he told Daisy. "Stay with me, now. Griffin will arrest your father. You're safe. It's over."

She blinked at him owlishly. "Is it?" Her words were sluggish, slurred. "It is really over?"

He wondered for a grim moment whether she referred to her father's plots or their union. But before he could ask her, she fainted dead away.

# chapter twenty-seven

*2ⁿᵈ June, 1881*

*Darling Daisy,*

*I hope that this note finds you well. Please convey my thanks to the Duchess of Leeds for granting you the hospitality you requested. Your doctor promises me you will mend and that our babe was unharmed, and I am heartily glad, as I cannot fathom a life without the both of you in it.*

*Bravo, buttercup. The newspapers are ablaze with talk of The Daring Duchess. The Home Office assures me that your name is cleared and there remains no shadow of doubt concerning your integrity, bravery, and courage. You were—and are—magnificent.*

*I am unutterably sorry for everything—deceiving you, doubting you, hurting you. I hope you will find it within you to forgive me some day, though I know I'm not deserving of your clemency. Regardless, I'm inordinately proud of my fierce, beautiful, Daring Duchess.*

*Though I must say a hundred pounds on ice sculptures was rather extortionate.*

*Yours,*
*Sebastian*

*P.S. I've begun inquiries into your sister's whereabouts. I won't stop looking until she is found.*

Daisy finished reading the note and allowed it to flutter to her lap. It would seem that her letters had at last found their way into Sebastian's hands. And he had read them. Not only that, but he was searching for Bridget on her behalf. Her foolish heart quickened in her chest.

"Well?" Georgiana demanded, holding a white cat to her bosom as she seated herself at Daisy's bedside. "What has he to say for himself?"

She swallowed, tamping down the unsettled emotions Sebastian's words had brought back to teeming life within her. A week had passed since her world had been torn asunder. Abigail and her father had been arrested, along with a string of other plotters in London and a host of other cities. Still, both Padraig McGuire and Bridget remained unaccounted for, and Daisy could only hope that wherever she was and whatever she had done, her sister hadn't mired herself too deep within the dangerous Fenian organization.

Daisy herself was healing fine. Thankfully, the bullet had only passed cleanly through her shoulder. Daisy had lost a fair amount of blood, but the doctor had been able to stitch her up, and thus far, she remained free of infection. The babe continued to grow, blissfully unaware throughout it all. She'd chosen to recover at Georgiana's home rather than staying with Sebastian, and he had honored her request by keeping his distance. She hadn't seen him since the awful day Abigail had attempted to take her hostage.

She'd spent the last week lolling about in a spare guest chamber, eating pastries and feeling sorry for herself. In the furor of the moment, she had left Hugo behind with Sebastian, which meant she'd been settling for the company of Georgiana's menagerie—which had grown to include a family of mice, a parrot, and a frightfully inquisitive lizard—

whilst she recovered.

"Daisy?" Her friend's gentle voice reminded her that she'd asked her a question.

Ah, yes. Sebastian's bittersweet note. "He says that the newspapers are calling me The Daring Duchess."

Georgiana laughed. "He is correct on that score, anyway. You're being hailed as a veritable goddess. Your bravery will be the stuff of legends."

"There was no bravery, only necessity." She paused, frowning. "Do you mean to say the people who once flayed me alive are now touting my praises?"

"You helped to catch some of the Fenian menace." Georgiana winked, giving the cat a thorough scratch behind her ears. "Lady Philomena Whiskers likes that, doesn't she?"

Daisy chuckled in spite of her unsettled emotions, and then she grimaced when her body's movement pulled at the stitches in her shoulder. "What a ridiculous name for a cat."

"For some cats, perhaps, but not for this one," Georgiana said with a grin and raised brows. "She's descended from feline royalty. Just look at her delicate paws and her sweet, heart-shaped nose. She's destined to marry a marquis, at the least. No second sons for her."

The woman was as ridiculous as the names she gave her animal friends. "But inquiring minds do long to know— how does she get along with the mouse family?"

"The Lilliputians, you mean?" Georgiana winked. "Ludlow has been seeing to their care. Lady Philomena Whiskers doesn't prefer their company. Rather, she would *prefer* their company, but only if they were obliging enough to be her dinner, and we cannot have that."

The mere notion of Georgiana's odd, mountain of a butler caring for a family of mice was just too much. Daisy collapsed into a fit of giggles. "No. You jest."

The Duchess of Leeds raised an imperious brow. "I assure you, I would never joke about such a thing. You'd have to see it to believe it. But Ludlow does have a heart beating beneath that rigid, scarred hide of his. I swear."

How refreshing to indulge in laughter. For a brief moment, it distracted her from thoughts of Sebastian. But in the next breath, the pain was there, beating in her heart, for Lilliputians reminded her of the gift he'd once given her.

*A favorite for a favorite.*

She would never stop loving him. But she needed time, time to find herself. Everything she'd known had been torn asunder, and so many of the people closest to her—Sebastian included—had deceived her. This time of healing was for her body, her mind, and her heart.

Or at least, that was her most fervent hope.

*5ᵗʰ June, 1881*

*Dearest Daisy,*

*I have resigned my position, effective immediately. The only position I wish to occupy is that of your husband. When and if you are ready, I await you here. Also, if it is friendship you require, may I offer my services? Given that I'm no longer a covert operative, I fear that gutting the Earl of Bolton may land me in Newgate.*

*Yours,*
*Sebastian*

She hadn't answered the first two letters he'd sent her.

Sebastian sat at the desk in his study, and it was still intricately carved and polished smooth. It surface remained organized with the meticulous precision he preferred. Everything was the same. For the familiarity of it, nothing might have changed. His secretary had stacked his most recent correspondence in three neat piles in the upper right quadrant. The lower held his pen. The left held the letters

Daisy had sent him, all opened, all read at least half a dozen times.

Her words were windows to her.

He could read them and so easily know what she'd experienced as she'd written them. And so, while all the small pieces of his life ostensibly remained the same, everything had changed.

He had changed.

Griffin had railed against him, begged him not to retire from the League. And he had anyway. His years of service were done. The life he wanted was a life with Daisy. He wanted her back. He wanted their babe. He wanted love and laughter and happiness well into the next bloody century. He wanted to fill Thornsby Hall with children and love and contentment. He would even bring the mongrel.

Hugo, as he was called, wandered about the study, offering a judicious sniff here and there. He'd been sitting by the door for the last half hour, staring Sebastian down, until he'd given up on that game and begun to wander.

He watched the dog sniff, prance to the center of the carpet. "Oh, bloody hell, Hugo. No!"

And raise his leg.

"Damn it."

Some time and some cleanup efforts later, Sebastian set pen to paper to write Daisy another letter. She had asked for time and space, and he had honored her wishes. But damn it, he was still going to fight for her. And if he had anything to say about it, he was going to win her.

*7ᵗʰ June, 1881*

*Buttercup,*

*The Axminster is quite lovely, but I'm afraid your beast has besmirched it on no less than three occasions. All aforementioned outrages occurred in my study. I do think he loathes me. Furthermore,*

*eight shillings a yard seems a trifle profligate as I'm reasonably certain
the going rate is six.*

*Your beast and I both miss you profoundly.*

*Yours,*
*Sebastian*

Daisy pressed a hand to her mouth as she read Sebastian's latest letter, suppressing her unexpected mirth.

"What's so humorous? Do tell." Today, Georgiana held a midnight-black kitten in her arms. He was purring loudly, snoozing so soundly that his tiny mouth had fallen open.

"Hugo is marking his territory on the new Axminster." She grinned.

"Serves him right, doesn't it, Kitty Quixote?" Georgiana gave him a chin scratch, but he kept purring and snoozing just the same.

It was Daisy's turn to raise a brow. "I'm not sure which is more egregious, Lady Philomena Whiskers or Kitty Quixote."

"I can't be sure." Her friend's tone was musing, thoughtful. "One could say we're all tilting at windmills at one point or another, no? Perhaps the only thing that's egregious is the crime of taking ourselves too seriously. What do you think, Daisy dear?"

A smile equal parts sad and reserved curved Georgiana's lips. The scandal she'd wrought with Daisy hadn't roused her husband. He hadn't charged back to England from New York, determined to fight for her heart. He had continued to ignore her. Georgiana was a strong woman, but even Daisy could see that the duke's indifference hurt her.

"I think I'm growing more confused by the day," she admitted.

*11ᵗʰ June, 1881*

*Dearest Buttercup,*

*You were right about my scars. They aren't from a fire when I was a lad. An anarchist set fire to a merchant's building in Cheapside during one of my missions, and I was fortunate to escape with only burns on my arms and hands. The anarchist didn't prove nearly as lucky.*

*Additionally, I applaud your replacement of the portrait of the Third Duke of Trent, Lord Privy Seal. His wig alone was enough to make a man bilious.*

*Ever yours,*
*Sebastian*

He paced the confines of the library, Hugo trotting at his heels. The room smelled of leather and paper and oiled wood. Familiar, comforting. Books were organized by subject now. He'd discovered that in his peripatetic journey. Down one row of books, up another. Daisy had made sense of each title, organizing every bound volume to her liking. Not a spine was out of place.

He stalked the library again and again, taking in all the books waiting for her. Hundreds. Millions of words. So many stories, worlds, characters. All hers for the taking. Those books taunted him, because they waited for her return the same way that he did.

Each day, he wrote her, hoping it would be the day she could forgive him and return home. Each day, he was met with her silence. Not even a one-word response. Keeping his distance from her as she recovered had almost been his undoing, but he had wanted to observe her wishes above all else, even above his concern for her. Her father had robbed her of the power of choice for her entire life. She'd been through so much upheaval—learning that her father and her lady's maid had been engaged in an affair, and that they'd been plotting together against her, that they'd framed her—he couldn't begin to imagine.

He didn't wish to add more stress and worry to her life. But she couldn't remain encamped with the odd Duchess of Leeds forever. He wanted his wife back. He wanted a life with her.

He stilled, his eyes settling on one spine above all.

*Gulliver's Travels.*

He wondered if she'd read it.

Hugo nudged his leg, making a needy canine sound and drawing his attention away. He lowered to his haunches, scratching the dog's soft head. Warm, brown eyes stared into his.

"We need her back, don't we, boy?"

Hugo licked his face, and that was the only answer he required.

*15ᵗʰ June, 1881*

*My love,*

*Your doctor tells me you are fully healed and the babe continues to flourish. I am, and will ever be, awed by your strength.*

*I intend to leave for my estate, Thornsby Hall, in the morning. I'm overseeing improvements upon the library and several other rooms. Your beast will accompany me, though he would be wise to cease his alarming proclivity for carpet annihilation. I trust you are in good hands with Her Grace. Should you need to reach me, send word there.*

*After much pondering, I've postulated a theory that a one thirty-second Your Grace would consist of the opening of one's mouth as if to form the sound of a "y" and nothing more. I've attempted it in a glass on several occasions, and I'm reasonably certain I am correct. You are welcome to debate the matter.*

*Yours as ever,*
*Sebastian*

~~*P.S. I love you.*~~
    *P.S. I love you as I love the sun on my face, the breath in my lungs, the green grass of spring, a faultless summer sky. I love you so much that I ache with it.*

Daisy finished reading Sebastian's latest note.

Her heart was so full that it hurt.

"Daisy," Georgiana said.

She looked up, eyes blurred by tears. Her friend held a small spaniel in her arms, just a wee pup. "What is his name?" she asked, because it was the only thing she could say without turning into a waterfall.

Her delicate condition was making her maudlin. But then, so was Sebastian.

"Puppenstein," her friend answered, her tone serious.

"I love him," Daisy blurted. "I cannot stop loving him, no matter how hard I try. He makes me laugh and he makes me cry, and he makes me want to wake up every morning with him and go to bed each night at his side."

Georgiana blinked in exaggerated fashion. "Puppenstein? I had no idea you cared for him so much. He's yours if you'd like."

"No." She shook her head, smiling like a fool. "Sebastian Fairmont, Eighth Duke of Trent."

Georgiana patted her hand. "Then go to him."

## chapter twenty-eight

DAISY FOUND HIM IN THE LIBRARY WITH HUGO.
They were seated on an overstuffed leather chair, Hugo curled up against Sebastian's thigh, a book opened in his lap. Her lack of grace in entrance—thrusting the door open with so much force that it rattled off the wall of shelving behind it—had his head snapping up. Their gazes clashed and held.

She was out of breath from racing to him, but it hadn't seemed she could reach him quickly enough once the decision had been made. The sight of his handsome face filled her with homecoming.

He stood, his expression fettered. "Daisy."

Hugo barked and leapt down to bound across the chamber and leap upon her skirts. She sank to her knees, receiving the dog's greeting of unadulterated canine delight, never taking her gaze from Sebastian. He remained still on the opposite side of the library, dressed to perfection in black trousers, a white shirt, and a black brocade waistcoat, no jacket. There was something delicious about him in shirtsleeves.

307

"Sebastian," she greeted him at last, standing once more.

"Have you come for your beast, then?" His voice was guarded, quiet.

"No."

"No?"

She moved toward him, drawn by the magnetism he exuded, by the necessity of being near him once again. How had she kept her distance for so long? It seemed unfathomable to her now as she stopped before him, tilting her head back to consider his rugged beauty.

"No," she said again. "I've come to debate your theory."

He quirked a brow, managing to somehow look autocratic and lovable all at once. "My theory?"

She smiled. "A one thirty-second Your Grace. I feel confident that it's only the act of opening one's mouth, not even the forming of a 'y.' One thirty-second is quite a small fraction, as you know."

His sensual mouth curved with an answering grin. "It's very small indeed. You do have a valid argument." He took her ungloved hands in his then, tangling their fingers together. "How are you and the babe, buttercup?"

"We're both well. Better now." She studied his beloved face. "And you?"

"It depends on the nature of your visit," he said softly, squeezing her fingers.

"You said you were leaving in the morning."

"I am." He drew her closer, her skirts crushing against his trousers. "I've been overseeing improvements at my country seat from afar for too long. The time has come for me to devote my attention to the people and places who matter most to me."

"You didn't have to give up spying for me." She withdrew her hands from his so that she could touch him, skim her palm over the whiskers stubbling his jaw. "I understand you were doing your duty."

He pressed a kiss to her palm. "I gave it up for all of us." His other hand went to her abdomen, flattening over the slight curve hidden beneath her corset. "I want to build a new life with you and the babe and at least half a dozen more if I'm lucky. I want Thornsby Hall to ring with laughter and love. Say you'll come with me, my Daring Duchess. Tell me you want that life as much as I do."

"Oh, my darling," she said tenderly. Her heart could not possibly contain any more love than it did in this moment, standing in the library he'd made hers, as he spoke of their future and looked upon her as if she were an angel come to walk among men. As if she were the most precious and beloved person to him. "Of course I will come with you. I'll go with you to Thornsby Hall or the other side of the world if you but ask. I love you exactly as you love me. As I love the sun on my face, the breath in my lungs, the green grass of spring, a faultless summer sky. I love you so much that I ache with it."

She repeated his words back to him, weighty words, wonderful words. Words so powerful they made her knees weak. Her chest felt light. Her heart felt whole. This was where she belonged. He was hers, and she was his, and that mattered far more than duty or countries or distance or time.

"Do you forgive me, my love?" His eyes searched hers. "Can you forgive me for deceiving you and for doubting you?"

"Of course, my love. You were doing what the oath you'd sworn required you to do." It had taken her some time and soul searching to realize that, but when she had, her decision had come easily. He had done his duty to the Crown, had been trapped by his loyalty and honor. Yet in spite of everything, he loved her, and she loved him. Love was enough to heal any wound. "No more talk of the past now. There is only the future for us, and I cannot wait to step into it with you."

With a growl, he pulled her into his arms, his mouth descending on hers in a fierce claiming. Her hand slid into his thick, soft hair to cup the base of his skull, and she kissed him back with all the love and need burning within her. She opened to his tongue, and he tasted of brandy and Sebastian and decadence. Nothing had ever tasted better. Nothing had ever felt more right.

He tore his lips from hers, dragging them down her neck, nipping and kissing as he went. "I love you." Another kiss. "I love you." A silken glide of his tongue on her flesh. "I love you." A nip of his teeth. "Christ, how I love you."

Sebastian lifted her then and carried her to the overstuffed chair before sinking into it and pulling her onto his lap. Her skirts crushed around them, but she didn't care as her mouth found his. They kissed and kissed and kissed until Hugo attempted to leap onto the chair alongside them.

Sebastian broke the kiss, his head falling back against the chair. "Control your beast, Duchess."

She traced the bow of his upper lip, her finger lingering in the perfect groove of his philtrum. "Which beast?"

"Well-deserved," he acknowledged, kissing her digit. "The furred one, madam."

She gave Hugo a gentle nudge. "Shoo, Hugo. Your papa and I need to get reacquainted, and we don't require your assistance."

With a whine of protest, Hugo jumped to the Axminster.

"I'm not that mongrel's papa," he grumbled.

Daisy trailed her finger lower, over the hard line of his jaw before burying her face in the tempting expanse of his neck and kissing him there. "Is that why you were cuddling him when I first entered?"

"I don't cuddle."

His voice was a deep, delicious rumble against her lips, and he smelled so wonderful that she couldn't resist flicking her tongue over his skin. She hummed her delight as she kissed his Adam's apple next.

He groaned. "Daisy, love?"

She began working on the buttons of his shirt, removing them from their moorings as she pressed kisses down each newly revealed swath of his chest. Feeling wicked, she rocked against him, bringing his rigid length in contact with the part of her that ached the most. Ah, yes, that was heaven. She rolled her hips again, seeking more.

"Damn it, buttercup," he groused, "I want you so much I'm going to explode, but your infernal beast is watching."

She burst into laughter. "You had better take me to bed then, my love, and be quick about it. The Daring Duchess is ready to conquer her devilish duke."

He scooped her up in his arms and rose in one swift motion, a smoldering smile curving his beautiful mouth. His lone dimple reappeared. "She already has, buttercup."

She kissed him then because she couldn't resist, her fingers continuing to work on his buttons. "Then perhaps it's your turn to conquer her."

Their mouths met again, and when their lips at last parted, the Duke of Trent carried his Daring Duchess to her chamber, and he thoroughly took his turn.

*Dear Reader,*

Thank you for reading *Her Reformed Rake*! I hope you enjoyed this third installment in the Wicked Husbands series. Sebastian and Daisy's story was a true labor of love for me. Their happily ever after was hard fought, hard won, and well-deserved.

I'm delighted to announce that a brand new spin-off series, featuring the League and its assorted cast of characters, will be coming soon! If you'd like to keep up to date with my latest releases and series news, sign up for my newsletter at:

http://www.scarsco.com/contact_scarlett

As always, please consider leaving an honest review of *Her Reformed Rake*. Reviews are greatly appreciated!

If you'd like a preview of Book Four in the Wicked Husbands series featuring the eccentric Georgiana, Duchess of Leeds, and her sinfully handsome, wayward husband Kit, do read on.

Until next time,

*Scarlett*

# *Her Deceptive Duke*

## Wicked Husbands Book Four

Georgiana, Duchess of Leeds, hasn't seen her husband since he left her on their wedding day for an extended hunting expedition and never returned. But she isn't the sort to wait around pining for an arrogant oaf who can't bother to recall he has a wife, no matter how sinfully handsome he may be.

She finds all the fulfillment she requires in caring for the stray cats and dogs of London's streets. Until, that is, the duke returns, and she uncovers the truth about where he's been…

Kit, Duke of Leeds never wanted to be duke. He was perfectly content with his life as one of Her Majesty's most dedicated spies until his brother's unexpected demise left him forced to marry an American heiress to save the family estate from ruin. The day he married her, he left for a secret assignment in America, with no intention of returning.

Seriously wounded and his cover ruined, Kit's forced back to London where he finds a townhouse running amuck with creatures and a wife who can't bear the sight of him.

With husband and wife beneath the same roof at last, their marriage of convenience sparks into a passion that's as undeniable as it is unexpected. But is desire enough to bring two wary hearts together? And once Kit's wounds are healed, will Georgiana's love be enough to make him stay?

# chapter one

*London, June 1881*

SIX MONTHS AFTER HE'D LEFT LONDON, brimming with the thrill of a new mission, Kit Hargrove, the Duke of Leeds, returned in ignominy. He didn't return to legions of admirers or effusive headlines in *The Times* or the gratitude of Her Majesty. He didn't return a hero; quite the opposite, as his arrival on England's shores had been shrouded in secrecy. And he certainly didn't return to the loving arms of his abandoned wife, who likely never gave a damn if she ever saw him again.

He returned alone save for the company of the servants he'd employed for the dubious task of assisting him on his journey. He returned, uncertain if he would ever be able to regain the proper use of his left leg again. Unable to walk himself to the front door of his palatial London townhome without assistance.

He returned and knocked on the bloody door of his own home as if he were a visitor.

And a behemoth bearing an ominous glare and an ugly

scar on his cheek opened the portal. "Her Grace is not at home," he announced grimly, and then slammed the portal closed.

Devil take it.

Kit gritted his teeth. He was weak, he was weary, and he was currently at the last place he wished to be, undertaking the most demeaning task his mind could fathom. He leaned on his cane, exhaling as a fresh onslaught of pain speared him. Of all days that he could be denied entry to *his own home*, this was not the goddamn day he would've chosen.

He rapped on the door again.

The rude, mountain of a man masquerading as a butler reappeared, scowling. "Told you. Her Grace isn't at home. Sod off."

Kit was prepared this time. He caught the door's slam with his opened palm even though it nearly cost him his balance and what remained of his pride. He steadied himself and glared at the bastard barring him entrance.

"Do you know who I am?" he demanded.

"Do I care?" The insolent bastard returned. "No."

"You'll care when I sack you," he growled. "I'm the Duke of Leeds. Your employer. Now grant me entrance at once."

The mountain's eyes narrowed. "We aren't expecting the duke. He's abroad."

"Behold. He has returned," Kit deadpanned.

The blighter remained unconvinced. "How do I know you're who you say you are?"

"Shall I summon the bloody queen?"

"Ludlow," came a lilting alto voice with an accent that wasn't quite proper. "I need your assistance with Lady Philomena Whiskers. I think she's about to give birth to a litter of kittens."

Surely that sweet voice didn't belong to *her*. And she was talking to the varmint who blocked the doorway to his home as if he were a lord.

From behind the mountain, Kit caught the swirl of navy

silk, a glimpse of chestnut braid, a smooth brow, one wide, green eye. Oh, bloody hell. It was her, alright. He may not recognize her voice, but he would never forget those eyes. Green and gold with flecks of cinnamon, and fringed with decadent lashes.

"Your Grace?" came her hesitant voice.

It would seem that she, on the other hand, didn't quite recognize him.

How lowering.

"Madam," he bit out. "I've traveled an ocean. I'm injured and tired and severely lacking in the sort of patience and understanding one would require in a circumstance such as this."

"Do step aside, Ludlow," she ordered the mountain.

The mountain complied with great reluctance and another scowl. And there she stood in his place. She was lovelier than he remembered. Her hair was plaited in a basket weave and worn high atop her head. Her gown was navy silk with bottle-green underskirts, lace and ribbon adorning a bodice that couldn't help but draw attention to her narrow waist and generous bosom. Even in his weakened state, he felt an unexpected, odd flare of awareness as he took her in.

"Your Grace," she said at last, her too-wide pink lips pressed into a severe frown. "You look ill."

Well, hell. He'd been standing about, thinking how remarkably fine she looked while she'd been taking in his gaunt frame, pale skin, and cane. He was a wreck and he knew it. He leaned heavily on the cane now. "I've been injured. Will you grant me entrance, or am I to stand in the street like a bloody tradesman?"

She blinked, color blooming in her cheeks. "Did you suffer a *hunting* injury, Your Grace?"

Clever minx. He gave her his haughtiest stare. "Yes."

His wife took a step back, allowing the door to open fully. "Come in, then. I suppose I cannot deny you entrance."

With the aid of his servants, he stepped over the threshold. But the effort of walking to the door, combined with the length of time he'd been forced to wait at the door and the crippling pain searing him had made him even weaker. He swayed, losing his balance, humiliation stinging him simultaneously.

How had he ended up here, in this moment, standing before the wife he'd never wanted like a bloody invalid, a strange butler presiding over his disgrace?

Her gaze raked the length of him, going wider still. "Oh dear heavens. His Grace is bleeding. Ludlow, have my chambers prepared for him, if you please."

He glanced down to see that his wound had indeed begun to weep once more, soaking through his trousers. Damn it. "Prepare *my* chambers," he commanded the insolent mountain, gainsaying her.

"I'm afraid that won't be possible," his duchess said without a hint of remorse.

What the bloody hell?

"There's no longer a bed in your chamber," she explained. "It's the main dog chamber now. Even if there were still a bed, I doubt you'd wish to convalesce there."

"The dog chamber," he repeated, wondering if he'd lost his mind along with the blood that had seeped from his body.

"Yes. It will have to be my chamber, I'm afraid, or nothing at all." She turned to give the butler a look that was far too intimate for his liking. "There's no helping it. You'll have to move Lady Philomena Whiskers somewhere else for the birthing."

Dogs and cats and a mountain of a butler who was too familiar with his wife. And he no longer had a bed. Of course, this was precisely the homecoming he should have expected.

317

*Her Deceptive Duke* is coming soon! Sign up for Scarlett's newsletter at http://www.scarsco.com/contact_scarlett for the latest news, exclusive excerpts, giveaways, and more.

## Before you go...

If you enjoy steamy Regency and Victorian romance, don't miss the Heart's Temptation series. Read on for an excerpt of Book One, *A Mad Passion*.

*A lost love...*

Seven years ago, the Marquis of Thornton broke Cleo's heart, and she hasn't forgotten or forgiven him. But when she finds him standing before her at a country house party, as devastatingly handsome as ever, old temptations prove difficult to resist. One stolen kiss is all it takes.

*A proper gentleman...*

Thornton buried his past and his feelings for Cleo long ago. He's worked diligently to become a respected politician with a reputation above reproach. The only trouble in his otherwise perfect life is that he can't resist the maddening beauty he never stopped wanting, no matter how devastating the cost.

*A mad passion...*

Cleo is hopelessly trapped in a loveless marriage, and Thornton is on the cusp of making an advantageous match to further his political ambitions. The more time they spend in each other's arms, the more they court scandal and ruin. Theirs is a love that was never meant to be. Or is it?

# chapter one

*"A beautiful woman risking
everything for a mad passion."*
— *Oscar Wilde*

*Wilton House, September 1880*

CLEO, COUNTESS SCARBROUGH, decided there had never been a more ideal moment to feign illness. The very last thing she wanted to do was traipse through wet grass at a country house party while her dress improver threatened to crush her. Not to mention the disagreeable prospect of being forced to endure the man before her. What had her hostess been thinking to pair them together? Did she not know of their history? A treasure hunt indeed.

Seven years and the Marquis of Thornton hadn't changed a whit, damn him. Tall and commanding, he was arrogance personified standing amidst the other glittering lords and ladies. Oh, perhaps his shoulders had broadened and she noted fine lines 'round his intelligent gray eyes. But not even a kiss of silver strands earned from his demanding career in politics marred the glorious black hair. It was most disappointing. After all, there had been whispers following the Prime Minister's successful Midlothian Campaign that a worn-out Thornton would retire from politics and his unofficial position as Gladstone's personal aid altogether. But as far as she could discern, the man staring down upon her was the same insufferably handsome man who had betrayed her. Was it so much to ask that he'd at least become plump about the middle?

Truly. A treasure hunt? Gads and to think this was the most anticipated house party of the year. "I'm afraid I must retire to my chamber," she announced to him. "I have a megrim."

Just as she began to breathe easier, Thornton ruined her reprieve. His sullen mouth quirked into a disengaged smile. "I'll escort you."

"You needn't trouble yourself." She hadn't meant for him to play the role of gentleman. She just wanted to be rid of him.

Thornton's face was an impenetrable mask. "It's no trouble."

"Indeed." Dismay sank through her like a stone. There was no way to extricate herself without being quite obvious he still set her at sixes and sevens. "Lead the way."

He offered his arm and she took it, aware that in her eagerness to escape him, she had just entrapped herself more fully. Instead of staying in the safe, boring company of the other revelers, she was leaving them at her back. Perhaps a treasure hunt would not have been so terrible a fate.

An uncomfortable silence fell between them, with Cleo aware the young man who had dizzied her with stolen kisses had aged into a cool, imperturbable stranger. For all the passion he showed now, she could have been a buttered parsnip on his plate.

She told herself she didn't give a straw for him, that walking a short distance just this once would have no effect on her. Even if he did smell somehow delectable and not at all as some gentlemen did of tobacco and horse. No. His was a masculine, alluring scent of sandalwood and spice. And his arm beneath her hand felt as strongly corded with muscle as it looked under his coat.

"You have changed little, Lady Scarbrough," Thornton offered at last when they were well away from the others, en route to Wilton House's imposing façade. "Lovely as ever."

"You are remarkably civil, my lord," she returned, not patient enough for a meaningless, pleasant exchange. She didn't wish to cry friends with him. There was too much between them.

His jaw stiffened and she knew she'd finally irked him. "Did you think to find me otherwise?"

"Our last parting was an ugly one." Perverse, perhaps, but she wanted to remind him, couldn't bridle her tongue. She longed to grab handfuls of his fine coat and shake him. What right did he have to appear so smug, so handsome? To be so self-assured, refined, magnetic?

"I had forgotten." Thornton's tone, like the sky above them, remained light, nonchalant.

"Forgotten?" The nerve of the man! He had acted the part of lovelorn suitor well enough back then.

"It was, what, all of ten years past, no?"

"Seven," she corrected before she could think better of it.

He smiled down at her as if he were a kindly uncle regarding a pitiable orphaned niece. "Remarkable memory, Lady Scarbrough."

"One would think your memory too would recall such an occasion, even given your advanced age."

"How so?" He sounded bored, deliberately overlooking her jibe at his age which was, if she were honest, only thirty to her five and twenty. "We never would have suited." His gray eyes melted into hers, his grim mouth tipping upward in what would have been a grin on any other man. Thornton didn't grin. He smoldered.

Drat her stays. Too tight, too tight. She couldn't catch a breath. Did he mean to be cruel? Cleo knew a great deal about not suiting. She and Scarbrough had been at it nearly since the first night they'd spent as man and wife. He had crushed her, hurt her, grunted over her and gone to his mistress.

"Of course we wouldn't suit," she agreed. Still, inwardly she had to admit there had been many nights in her early marriage where she had lain awake, listening for Scarbrough's footfalls, wondering if she hadn't chosen a Sisyphean fate.

They entered Wilton House and began the lengthy tromp to its Tudor revival styled wing where many of the guests had been situated. Thornton placed a warm hand over hers. He gazed down at her with a solemn expression, some of the arrogance gone from his features. "I had not realized you would be in attendance, Lady Scarbrough."

"Nor I you." She was uncertain of what, if any, portent hid in his words. Was he suggesting he was not as immune as he pretended? She wished he had not insisted upon escorting her.

As they drew near the main hall, a great commotion arose. Previously invisible servants sprang forth, bustling with activity. A new guest had arrived and Cleo recognized the strident voice calling out orders. Thornton's hand stiffened over hers and his strides increased. She swore she overheard him mumble something like 'not yet, damn it', but couldn't be sure. To test him, she stopped. Her heavy skirts swished front then back, pulling her so she swayed into him.

Cleo cast him a sidelong glance. "My lord, I do believe your mother is about to grace us with her rarified presence."

He growled, losing some of his polish like a candlestick too long overlooked by the rag. "Nonsense. We mustn't tarry. You've the headache." He punctuated his words with a sharp, insolent yank on her arm to get her moving.

She beamed. "I find it begins to dissipate."

The dowager Marchioness of Thornton had a certain reputation. She was a lioness with an iron spine, an undeterred sense of her own importance and enough consequence to cut anyone she liked. Cleo knew the dowager despised her. She wouldn't dare linger to incur her wrath were it not so painfully obvious the good woman's own son was desperate to avoid her. And deuce it, she wanted to see Thornton squirm.

"Truly, I would not importune you by forcing you to wait in the hall amidst the chill air," he said, quite stuffy now, no longer bothering to tug her but pulling her down the hall as if he were a mule and she his plow.

The shrill voice of her ladyship could be heard admonishing the staff for their posture. Thornton's pace increased, directing them into the wrong wing. She was about to protest when the dowager called after him. It seemed the saint still feared his mother.

"Goddamn." Without a moment of hesitation, he opened the nearest door, stepped inside and pulled her through with him.

Cleo let out a disgruntled 'oof' as she sank into the confines of whatever chamber Thornton had chosen as their hiding place. The door clicked closed and darkness descended in the cramped quarters.

"Thornton," trilled the marchioness, her voice growing closer.

"Your—" Cleo began speaking, but Thornton's hand over her mouth muffled the remainder of her words. She inhaled, startled by the solid presence of his large body so close behind her. Her bustle crushed against him.

"Hush, please. I haven't the patience for my mother today."

He meant to avoid the dragon for the entire day? Did he really think it possible? She shifted, discomfited by his nearness. Goodness, the little room was stifling. Her stays pinched her again. Did he need to smell so divine?

"Argnnnthhwt," she replied.

She needed air. The cramped quarters dizzied her. Certainly it wasn't the proximity of her person to Thornton that played mayhem with her senses. Absolutely not. The ridiculous man simply had to take his hand from her mouth. Why, he was nearly cutting off her air. She could scarcely breathe.

Thornton didn't seem likely to oblige her, so she resorted to tactics learned from growing up with a handful of sisters who were each more than a handful themselves. She decided not to play fair and licked his palm. It was a mistake, a terrible one and not just because it was unladylike but because he tasted salty and sweet. He tasted rather like something she might want to nibble. So she did the unpardonable. She licked him again.

"Christ." To her mingled relief and disappointment, he removed his hand. "Say a word and I'll throttle you."

Footsteps sounded in the hall just beyond the closed door. If Cleo had been tempted to end their ruse before, her sudden reaction to Thornton rattled her too much to do so now. She kept mum.

"Perhaps you are mistaken?" Thornton's sister, Lady Bella ventured, sounding meek.

"Don't be an idiot, Bella," the dowager snapped. "I know my own son when I see him. All your novels are making you addle-pated. How many times must I implore you to assert yourself at more improving endeavors like needlepoint? Women should not be burdened by knowledge. Our constitutions are too delicate."

Cleo couldn't quite stifle a snicker. The situation had all the elements of a comedy. All that yet remained was for the dowager to yank open the door so Cleo and Thornton would come tumbling out.

"You smell of lavender," he muttered in her ear, an accusation.

So what if she did? It was a lovely, heady scent blended specifically for her. Lavender and rose geranium, to be precise. "Hold your breath," she retorted, "if you find it so objectionable."

"I don't."

"Then what is the problem, Thornton?"

"I find it delicious."

*Delicious.* It was a word of possibility, of improbability, improper and yet somehow…seductive. Enticing. Yes, dear heaven, the man enticed her. She leaned into his solid presence, her neck seeking. Even better, her neck's sensitive skin found his hungry mouth.

He tasted her, licking her skin, nipping in gentle bites, trying, it would seem, to consume her like a fine dessert. His hands anchored her waist. Thornton pulled her back against him, all semblance of hauteur gone. Her dress improver cut viciously into her sides.

She didn't care. She forgot about his mother. Their quarrel and complicated past flitted from her mind. Cleo reached behind her with her right arm and sank her fingers into his hair. He stilled, then tore his lips from her neck. Neither of them moved. Their breaths blended. Thornton's hands splayed over her bodice, possessive and firm.

"This is very likely a mistake," he murmured.

"Very likely so," she agreed and then pressed her mouth to his.

He kissed her as she hadn't been kissed in years. Strike that. He kissed her as she hadn't been kissed in her lifetime, deep and hard and consuming. He kissed her like he wanted to claim her, mark her. And she kissed him back with all the passion she hadn't realized she possessed. Dear heavens, this was not the political saint who took her mouth with such force but the sinner she'd once known. Had she thought him cold?

Thornton twisted her until her back slammed against the door with a thud. His tongue swept into her mouth. Her hands gripped his strong shoulders, pulling him closer. An answering ache blossomed within her. Somehow, he found his way under her skirts, grasping her left leg at the knee and hooking it around his lean hip. Deliberate fingers trailed up her thigh beneath three layers of fabric, finding bare skin. He skimmed over lacy drawers, dipping inside to tease her.

When he sank two fingers inside her, she gasped, yanking back into the door again. It rattled. Voices murmured from far away in the hall. "Thornton," she whispered. "We should stop."

He dropped a hot kiss on her neck, then another. "Absolutely. This is folly."

Then he belied his words by shifting her so her body pressed against his instead of the door. She no longer cared why they should stop. Her good intentions dissipated. Her bodice suddenly seemed less snug and she realized he had undone a few buttons. Heavens. The icy man of moments ago bore no resemblance to the man setting her body aflame. Scarbrough had never touched her this way, had never made her feel giddy and tingly, as if she might fly up into the clouds.

Scarbrough. Just the thought of her husband stiffened her spine. Hadn't she always sworn to herself she would not be like him? Here she was, nearly making love in who knew what manner of chamber with Thornton, a man she didn't even find pleasant. The man, to be specific, who had betrayed and abandoned her. How could she be so wanton and foolish to forget what he'd done for a few moments of pleasure?

She pushed him away, breathing heavy, heart heavy. "We must stop."

"Why must we?" He caressed her arms, wanting to seduce her again.

"My husband."

"I don't hear him outside the door."

"Nor do I, but I am not a society wife even if my conduct with you suggests otherwise. I do not make love with men in closets at country house parties. I don't fall to his level."

"Madam, your husband is a louse. You could not fall to his level were you to roll in the hay with every groom in our hostess' stable and then run naked through the drawing room."

She stiffened. "What do you know of him?"

"Plenty."

"I doubt you do." The inescapable urge to defend her wastrel, blackguard husband rose within her. How dare Thornton be so arrogant, so condescending when he himself had committed the same sins against her? And had he not just been on the verge of making love to a married woman in a darkened room? He was no better.

He sighed. "Scarbrough's got scads of women on the wrong side of the Park in St. John's Wood. It's common knowledge."

Of course it was, but that didn't make it any easier to hear. Especially not coming from Thornton, the man she'd jilted in favor of Scarbrough. "I'm aware Scarbrough is indiscreet, but that has little bearing on you and me in this moment. This moment should never have happened."

"We are once again in agreement, Cleo." His voice regained some of its arrogance. "However, it did happen."

Her name on his lips startled her, but she didn't bother taking him to task for it. After the intimacies she had just allowed, it would be hypocritical. She wished she could see him. The darkness became unbearable.

"How could you so easily forget your own sins? You had your pretty little actress all the while you claimed to love me."

He said nothing. Silence extended between them. It was obstinate of her, but she wanted him to deny it. Thornton did not.

"Aren't there orphans about somewhere you should be saving?" She lashed out, then regretted her angry words. That was badly done of her. But this, being in Thornton's arms after what he'd done…it went against the grain.

"I think you should go," she added.

"I would if I could fight my way past your bloody skirts. There's no help for it. Either you go first or we go together."

"We can't go together! Your insufferable mother may be

lurking out there somewhere."

"Then you must go first."

"I shall precede you," she informed him.

"I already suggested as much. Twice, if you had but listened." He sounded peeved.

The urge to stamp her foot hit her with fierce persistence. "You are a vexing man."

"And you, my love, are a shrew unless your mouth is otherwise occupied."

She gasped. "How dare you?"

"Oh, I dare lots of things. Some of them, you may even like." His voice had gone sinful and dark.

The dreadful man. She drew herself up in full countess armor. "I'm leaving now."

Then he ruined her consequence by saying, "Lovely. Though you might want to fasten up your bodice before you go. I should think it terribly difficult to convince my mother we were talking about the weather when your finer bits are on display."

Her finer bits? It was the outside of enough. She slapped his arm. "Has the Prime Minister any idea what a coarse scoundrel you are? None of my...person would be on display if you hadn't pulled me into the room and accosted me."

"You were well pleased for a woman being accosted," he pointed out, smug.

She hated him again, which was really for the best. He was too much of a temptation, too delicious, to borrow his word, and she was ever a fool for him. "You're insufferable."

"So I've been told."

Cleo gave him her back and attempted to fasten her buttons. Drat. She pulled. She held her breath. She tugged her bodice's stiff fabric again. The buttons wouldn't meet their moorings. "Did you undo my lacings?" she demanded, realization dawning on her.

"Perhaps." Thornton's voice had gone wistful. Sheepish,

almost.

Good heavens. How did he know his way around a woman's undergarments so well he could get her undone and partially unlaced all while kissing her passionately? Beneath his haughty exterior still lay a womanizer's heart.

There was no help for it now. She couldn't tight-lace herself. "I require some assistance," she mumbled.

"What was that?"

Cleo gritted her teeth. "I can't lace myself."

"Would a 'please' be in order?"

"You're the one who did the damage. It seems reasonable that you should repair it."

"Perhaps I can slip past your voluminous skirts after all," he mused.

"Please help me," she blurted.

"Turn around," he ordered.

Cleo spun, reluctant to face him again. She could barely see him in the murkiness, a tall, imposing figure. His hands slipped inside her bodice, expertly finding the lacings he had loosened.

"Breathe in," he told her.

She did and he pulled tightly, cinching her waist to a painful wasp silhouette once more. "Thank you. I can manage the buttons."

He spun her about and brushed aside her fingers. "I'll get them." She swore she heard a smile in his voice. "After all, it only seems reasonable I repair the damage I've done."

"Fine then." His breath fanned her lips and she could feel his intense gaze on her. She tilted her head to the side to ease her disquiet at his nearness. Was it just her imagination, or did his fingers linger at the buttons nearest her bosom?

"There you are." Thornton fastened the last one, brushing the hollow of her throat as he did so.

She closed her eyes and willed away the desire that assaulted her. This man was not for her. He ran the backs of his fingers along her neck, stopping when he cupped her jaw.

"Thank you," she whispered again.

"You're most welcome," he said, voice low.

The magnetism between them was inexorable, just as it had been before. Despite the intervening years, despite all, she still recalled the way he had made her feel—weightless and enchanted, as though she had happened upon Shakespeare's moonlit forest in *A Midsummer Night's Dream*.

His thumb brushed over her bottom lip. "If you don't go, I'll undo all the repairing I've just done."

She knew he warned himself as much as he warned her. Sadness pulsed between them, a mutual acknowledgment their lives could have turned up differently. So many unspoken words, so much confusion lingered.

"I must go," she said unnecessarily. She was reluctant to leave him and that was the plain truth of it. "I find my megrim has returned."

With that, she left, returning to the hall, to sunlight streaming in cathedral windows. More importantly, she hoped, she returned to sanity.

*A Mad Passion* is available now. Get your copy today.

**Other books by Scarlett Scott**

## HISTORICAL ROMANCE

### Heart's Temptation

A Mad Passion (Book One)
Rebel Love (Book Two)
Reckless Need (Book Three)
Sweet Scandal (Book Four)
Restless Rake (Book Five)
Darling Duke (Book Six) (Coming Soon)

### Wicked Husbands

Her Errant Earl (Book One)
Her Lovestruck Lord (Book Two)
Her Reformed Rake (Book Three)
Her Deceptive Duke (Book Four) (Coming Soon)

## CONTEMPORARY ROMANCE

### Love's Second Chance

Reprieve (Book One)
Perfect Persuasion (Book Two)
Win My Love (Book Three)

### Coastal Heat

Loved Up (Book One)

# about the author

Award-winning author Scarlett Scott writes contemporary and historical romance with heat, heart, and happily ever afters. Since publishing her first book in 2010, she has become a wife, mother to adorable identical twins and one TV-loving dog, and a killer karaoke singer. Well, maybe not the last part, but that's what she'd like to think.

A self-professed literary junkie and nerd, she loves reading anything but especially romance novels, poetry, and Middle English verse. When she's not reading, writing, wrangling toddlers, or camping, you can catch up with her on her website www.scarsco.com. Hearing from readers never fails to make her day.

Scarlett's complete book list and information about upcoming releases can be found on her website.

Follow Scarlett on social media:

www.instagram.com/scarlettscottauthor
www.twitter.com/scarscoromance
www.pinterest.com/scarlettscott
www.facebook.com/AuthorScarlettScott

Made in the USA
Monee, IL
29 June 2022